THE ALDAR DOMINION

I0745884

THE ALDAR DOMINION

DOMINION RISING BOOK ONE

KATHERINE BOGLE

PATCHWORK-PRESS

Patchwork-Press
Copyright © 2017 by Katherine Bogle
http://katherinebogle.com

Cover Design by *Katzilla Designs*
Interior Design by *We Got You Covered Book Design*

First Edition — 2017

No part of this publication may be reproduced in any form, or by any means, electronic or mechanical, including photocopying, recording, or any information browsing, storage, or retrieval system, without permission in writing from Katherine Bogle.

For Bill and Peggy, my two favorite sci-fi fans.

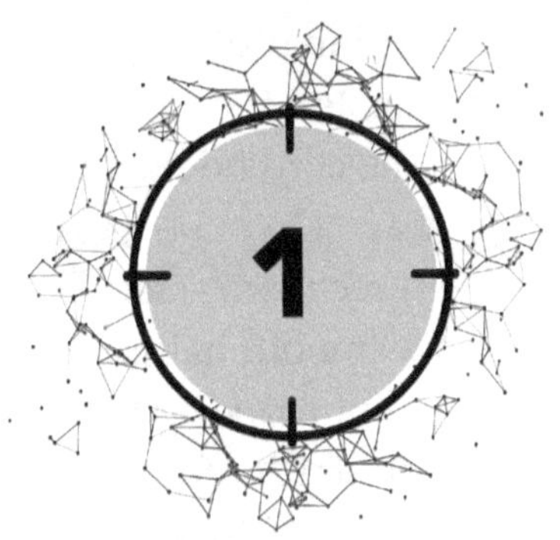

DANGLING FROM THE OPEN HOVERCRAFT door, Selene searched the desert wasteland surrounding the New Manhattan laboratory fifty-feet below. It was late, well past midnight. They had spent the last few days staking out the low security facility on the edge of the city. Its five stories were shrouded by the surrounding barren hills, and small security bots swept the yard. The low thrum of the hover propellers broke the silence of the night, beating in time with her heart.

At the front of the cockpit sat the captain of their small smuggling operation, Rikkard Gunnar. "Stick to the plan," he snapped.

Taking stock of the dark roof one last time, Selene spun in her harness, grabbing onto the bar above the door to pull herself back inside. Meeting her partner's all-too-knowing gaze, she couldn't help but grin.

"Don't I always?"

Rikkard rolled his eyes, swiping a hand through his short dark hair as he turned to the control panel at the head of the hovercraft. He clicked through the ship's navigation system until the craft began to lower. He'd have to hide their ship in the mountains behind the lab while she was inside or risk being seen by security.

"Twenty minutes should do it." Turning from her captain to the open void below, wind whipped at her black and green wig. Not the most conventional of disguises, but neither was her skin-tight suit. She adjusted the straps around her hips and thighs before tugging on the cord hooked above her.

Rikkard turned in his seat. "Don't be reckless."

"When have I *ever* been reckless?" Selene shot him a wicked grin as the craft came to a smooth halt in midair. He was right, of course. After three years of working together, he knew better than anyone she had a reputation for improvising. But before he could answer, she gave him a thumbs up and jumped from the ship. The wind snatched his retort, and Selene swallowed a laugh. She'd have to ask him later what he was so worried about.

The wind's current tore at her body like waves in a hurricane. Selene loved the feeling almost as much as the danger of throwing herself from twenty feet up. A spike of adrenaline rushed through her veins until her harness yanked up. She slowed and landed soundlessly. Brushing her bangs from her eyes, Selene unhooked her harness. She gave it a tug, and it disappeared into the clear night sky as she trotted across the roof.

The roof was barren, a simple sheet of concrete broken only by air ducts and a rooftop exit. With her long legs, it only took Selene a few strides to reach the smooth grate of the air filtration system. Pulling a small blowtorch from her utility belt, she extended its two halves, twisting them into place. She made quick work of it; the grate tilting away from the duct once the torch sparks dissipated. Selene gently laid it on the ground. Returning her torch to her belt, she slipped into the confined space of the air duct.

Cold steel pressed in on all sides. It bit through her suit and froze her bare, sweaty hands. *Breathe*, she told herself, shimmying army-style through the metal tube. Selene squeezed her eyes shut. Forcing the pressing walls from her mind, she visualized the lengths of duct she needed to stay quiet in, and which portions she could rush through as fast as the confined space would allow without alerting after-hours security.

Memorizing maps had always come easy to her.

She moved on. Steel squeezed against her shoulders with every turn, forcing her to pause and take a breath.

Her uncanny internal clock told her three minutes had passed when Selene unscrewed another grate and dropped into a dimly lit room filled with computers. The soft thrum of sleeping fans filled the room; they'd been on standby for some time. Her heart beat faster. An excited grin pulled at her lips.

During the planning stage of their mission, Selene and Rikkard had mapped out the security cameras, which is why a ceiling-high bookcase covered her descent from the duct. The single security camera blinked its red gaze at her only exit from the office. Selene peeked from her hiding spot, holding her breath.

It didn't move.

Lowering herself onto her belly, Selene crawled between desks until she reached the private office at the back of the room. Before rising from the cold tile, she glanced at the corner sentinel. Its smooth gray plastic remained pointed at the exit, unmoving. Selene smiled and raised her hand to the square control panel beside the door. Quickly hacking the keypad, she slipped into the private room.

On the map this room was so small she'd nearly mistaken it for a closet, but instead it was a tiny supervisor's office. Closing the door with a soft click, Selene rose and pushed the office chair from her path. She stood before the desk, flicking her fingers across the computer screen to illuminate it. Once the soft glow lit the room, she tilted the screen up. The computer prompted for a passcode.

"Hm." She cocked an eyebrow at the thin monitor.

Tapping her fingers across the transparent keyboard, she typed in a line of code that usually broke through most security systems. Each key illuminated at her touch, but once she hit enter, an error message popped up in red.

"*Of course.*" Selene gritted her teeth. As much as she wanted to, she wouldn't be able to crack the password herself—she was coming up on the five-minute mark, so she skipped right to her golden ticket. Pulling a small plastic screen from her sleeve pocket, she tapped in her own passcode. Her phone had helped her out of many sticky situations. Opening the small compartment in the bottom, Selene extracted a hard drive the size of a fingernail with a long thin black cord attached. She inserted the drive into the sleek silver monitor's access port.

Twenty seconds later, a black box popped up on the screen, green type scrolling rapidly until the error disappeared and she had full access to the lab's internal network.

Victory.

Grabbing the discarded chair, Selene pulled it into place and took a seat. Her fingers flew across the keyboard as waves of data scrolled down the screen. Rows and rows of jumbled letters and numbers passed by before a single word caught her eye—*experiments*. She paused, her heart sinking into her stomach. Her fingers became fists and she narrowed her eyes at the word.

"Gotcha."

Selene unclenched her claws and went back to work. Images, videos and work logs popped up in boxes of their own. Gorillas, chimpanzees and orangutans—just a few of the species the Dominion *loved* to experiment on. When a map of the complex replaced the bloody images of their tortured subjects, Selene scanned each floor until she found the live tests lab. Her heart clenched.

"I'm coming for you," she murmured, silently praying the apes were still alive.

With her soon-to-be cargo found, Selene accessed the lab's security network. Her screen filled with video screens, different angles of each room and corridor. She flicked through them until she found the three men working security. Two on the main floor. One on the second.

She froze every camera in the building before double-checking her route to the first floor, just in case the map she'd memorized had been out of date. Shutting down the computer, Selene extracted the hard drive linked to her phone and returned it to her utility belt.

She smirked as she stood and left the room. The corner camera didn't blink at her when she weaved through the desks, nor did it budge when she left the room and found the hall.

Selene was on the top floor, with four more below. Her targets were on the first, along with her extraction point. Glancing at the watch pinned to her suit's wrist, she had nearly half her allotted time to rejoin her boss and get away with their cargo before the half-hour system check.

Entering the stairwell, Selene leapt several stairs at a time descending to the main floor—the one certain to be most heavily guarded. Private security teams who ran labs like these generally assumed infiltrators would come from the ground, not the sky.

Selene slowed before she exited onto the main level. Pulling the map to mind again, she stepped into the hall on her right. The experiments were held at the west side of the building, not far from her extraction point in the loading bay. She had exactly six hallways to get through if she wanted to avoid the main security office, but only three if she skipped right by them.

Glancing at her watch, Selene knew what her captain would say. *Don't risk it.* While part of her understood the wisdom of being careful, the reckless side of her jumped at the opportunity to test herself.

She opted for the dangerous route.

Her heart pounded and her palms sweat. Her right hand found the gun at her hip. The assurance of cold metal made her smile.

Peeking around another corner, Selene double-checked the corridor for security personnel. Clear. Slipping out, she started down the brightly lit hallway, which led to the main path several strides away. Stepping into the next hall, a black clad man stood with his back to her not fifteen feet away.

She froze.

With his hand raised to his ear, and a soft buzz through the silence, he spoke to another guard through a comset. Selene crept forward silently. Sweat beading on her forehead, she slowed at each intersecting hallway to check for other guards. Clear.

"Cas, I think there's something up with the cameras." The device crackled slightly and a terse voice answered.

"There can't be anything wrong with them. I just checked."

"I swear, there's something—"

"I know you're new, but everything is fine," Cas's somewhat distorted voice answered. "I'll be back down in two. Go take a booster or something. Nothing happens in these labs. No one gives a shit about some modified apes."

Nostrils flaring, Selene bit back a growl. Her fingers danced around the holster at her hip as she drew close enough to make out a small jagged scar at the base of the guard's neck. The curves of the white stretch of skin had to be from the claw of an animal.

She resisted a scoff. Working in a place like this, he deserved it.

"You're right." The man sighed, shifting toward the main security office. "I'll wait with Grey."

Selene ducked into a nearby hall, plastering herself to the wall while the man joined another guard in the main office, equipped with a wall of monitors. Her heart raced as she glanced around the corner. The second guard sat with a steaming cup of something, facing the security screens. He acknowledged his companion with a nod and a snort of agreement. They sat, their backs to the glass window overlooking the small office. She waited a full minute for him to greet his co-worker and sit down. Once they started talking about the coming election in New Manhattan, Selene leapt from her hiding spot and sprinted down the hall.

Before she reached the glass window, she dropped to her hip, sliding under the open window. Her suit squeaked against the tile—she winced—then leapt to her feet and ducked into a small alcove. Heart pounding, she glanced back out and waited.

The two in the office didn't stir.

Selene took on the rest of the corridor in a few bounds. She listened for the swoosh of a door opening, the squeak of a boot; anything that would indicate she was being followed. Only thing was her pulse thudding in her ears.

Another hall later, Selene found the live tests lab. Her phone did quick work of the passcode before she swept inside, keeping her back to the now shut door.

A blue glow emanated from a line of x-rays displayed on several dark light panels at the far end of the long, dim lab. At least twenty workstations sat in rows, steel tables lined up beside thin computer monitors.

Selene pushed away from the door, stepping closer to the cages lining the back wall. The stench of blood and decay assaulted her nostrils. One hand flew to cover her mouth, while the other grabbed the nearest table. Her head swam. She steadied herself against the cool metal. She cursed the Dominion for the way they tore these creatures apart—all to test boosters and their effects.

Taking a few deep breaths, Selene took stock of the animals she was here to save. Four primates—a baby gorilla and three chimpanzees—blinked back at her. It wasn't as many as she had been expecting. Swallowing the lump in her throat, Selene avoided the workstations littered with carelessly discarded surgical knives still wet with blood.

Pushing tables aside to create an open space, Selene produced two small black squares from her back pocket, their thick plastic smooth between her fingers. Pressing her thumb into the small indent on each, she tossed them into the open space she'd created. Both unfolded into four by four-foot hover plates. Their sleek black surfaces floated several inches above the ground.

Taking the gun from her left hip, she pointed it at the young gorilla. The tranq dart hissed through the hair, hitting him square in the chest. He barely had time for a soft whine before slumping against the bars of his cage. Once he was out, Selene shot the rest. It only took a few seconds for the animals to collapse into unconsciousness, and by that time she was already loading the small gorilla onto the first hover plate.

Gently tugging the gorilla from his cage, she braced her feet apart, lifting from her legs. Particles of grit stuck to her fingertips, his coarse fur greasy from lack of care. Bracing him in her arms, she set him on the first of the hover plates, which dipped under the added weight.

One by one she removed the others from their cages. Setting

the chimpanzees inside their new enclosure, the plate righted itself, hovering a few inches above the white tiled floor. Once they were set, she took the controller from her pocket and clicked a small blue button. A glowing white force field popped up on each side of the plates, connecting at the top to form an enclosure. She clicked another button and the cages followed her to the door. She peered out; all was silent and still. A pungent whiff of cologne brought the hairs along the back of her neck to full attention. Nasty.

Sliding the door the rest of the way open, Selene led the devices further down the hall. She glanced at her watch. She was gaining on her twenty-minute timeline, and if she didn't hurry, the half-hour system check would catch her. Arriving at the loading bay, she brought the hover plates to a halt and peered around the corner, through a wide-open doorway.

Straight into the face of a black-clad guard, not two feet from her.

The man's eyes widened—Selene slammed her foot into his chest. Air exploded from his lungs. She pushed him inside the loading bay and over a railing. His back hit the concrete below with a heavy thud.

Selene swung over the railing after him as he climbed to his feet and reached for the sleek white laser gun at his hip. She drove her heel into his stomach. He doubled over—she slammed her elbow into the back of his head. He collapsed.

Selene bent to check for a pulse. It was steady, but he'd be unconscious long enough for her to escape.

Punching a button on her remote, Selene made her way across the large room to the row of loading bay doors, the hover plates following her. She eyed the line of switches next to the cargo lift—which door would Rikkard be parked closest to?

The furthest to the left would be closest to the rest of the building—an unlikely choice. That left the middle or the right. Shrugging, Selene picked the switch furthest to the right, and flung it.

An alarm pierced the quiet.

Her jaw dropped—this building was *not* supposed to be rigged with alarms. Cursing whatever god she'd clearly angered, she grabbed the door's handle.

"Come on…" The door rolled slowly along the ancient pulley system and into the ceiling. It squeaked against the rusted chains.

Yanking upward with all of her might, the wheels screeched.

Glancing under the door, Selene spied Rikkard in the cargo bay of the hovercraft, waving for her to hurry. She tossed him the remote, and she ducked back inside, shoving the door open further. The hover plates rushed under the gap and into the cargo bay of their ship.

"Hey!"

Selene glanced back as the red beam of a laser shot past her head, burning a hole through the bay door. Her heart leapt.

Five guards clad in black and wielding laser pistols charged through the loading bay entrance. While one stooped to help their fallen comrade, another pointed the barrel of his gun at her. She strained to hear the whine of his weapon over the alarm. Selene ducked under the rising door and leapt the small gap to the hovercraft entrance. Another shot sizzled on the cargo deck, inches from her feet before she ducked behind a large crate.

Rikkard returned fire, blazing shots of red flying through the lab's loading bay. The security guards leapt for cover behind a large shipping container.

"Time to go." She caught Rikkard's disapproving gaze.

He nodded and holstered his pistol as he rushed for the cockpit. Selene approached their new animal companions, keeping low to the floor and pulling her gun from its holster. Flicking off the safety, the gun charged.

"Anytime, Rik," she whispered, peeking from behind her crate.

The soft thrum of propellers hummed louder, and the ship lifted higher. A guard darted from his cover and raised his gun, but Selene was quicker: she squeezed off a shot, aiming for the arm holding the gun.

She was *not* going to see these animals get shot after all they'd been through.

The guard fell back, clutching his shoulder. The hovercraft lifted from the sand covered earth, arching above the roof of the complex. When she was sure they were out of range, Selene checked the knots on the enclosures; they were tight enough to hold. Though the apes were stirring, they weren't out of trouble yet. The lab's personal security team was sure to follow.

Picking her way through the cargo hold, wind whipped at her wig and body, threatening to send her sailing into oblivion. Keeping hold of the safety bar along the wall, Selene found the large red button to close the rear doors.

With the ship pulling higher in the sky, the bright burn of the city came into view above the barren hills guarding the laboratory. Sleek white buildings towered into the clouds, their windows reflecting the night sky. The whole city glowed with fevered nightlife. Its beauty caught her off guard, much like it always did. Selene wasn't one to gawk, but the alien city was hardly a common beauty. A piece of her yearned to be part of it, while the rest of her shied away from the moral ambiguity of the growing populace.

Movement outside the closing cargo doors pulled her from her reverie. Blinking in confusion, Selene stood and holstered her pistol. Beyond the small crack remaining of the outside world, two Class Three speeders flew in pursuit.

"Class Three? Really?" Selene sighed. Sleek metal with huge glass windows and laser turrets mounted on the hulls, pointed her way. For such a minimum-security facility, she wouldn't think they'd send such heavily armored speeders after them.

Her pulse quickened, pounding in her ears. Making her way through the ship, Selene joined Rikkard in the cockpit.

"What took you so long?" he asked in an irritable monotone.

"Just checking on things," Selene lied. She turned to peer at the scanners depicting their surrounding area. Two small blips followed behind their larger ship. "We have two Class Three speeders coming in fast," she added, as two blips became three and then four. "Or more."

Rikkard glanced at the screen. "Hold on tight."

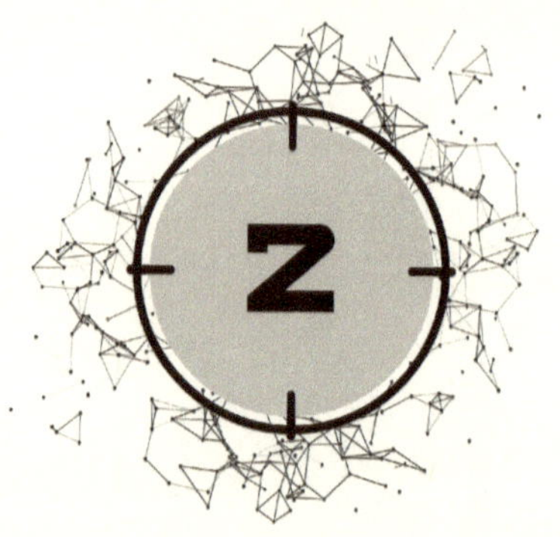

THE SUDDEN JERK OF THE ship nearly ripped Selene off her feet. She tried not to hiss and spit in fury at Rikkard for his reckless driving, while simultaneously holding on for dear life. Skyscrapers blurred past the ship windows, the hovercraft's wings grazing the sleek white surface of one building. Shattered glass dropped below as their undercarriage clipped a fifty story-high window. Spinning between overpasses, Selene gripped the captain's chair tightly; grinding her teeth as the momentum threatened to throw her into the back.

"Would you sit down?" Rikkard droned.

"As soon as you stop flying like a lunatic!" Selene snapped.

The craft flattened out.

"Sit." He pointed at her co-pilots chair. Though she'd normally be inclined to argue, she was more afraid he'd twirl around in the sky again.

Selene slid into her seat, buckling in before giving Rikkard a displeased glare; one he hardly raised an eyebrow at. Checking the monitors, Selene used her fingers to manipulate the images, zooming in and bringing up a detailed look of their pursuit. For such a small facility, they were getting a lot of blowback.

Four unmanned Class One speeders joined the fray, shooting across her screen with alarming speed. A few city patrol cruisers lifted from the streets below, joining the growing armada.

"There are way more speeders following us than there should be," she said, hoping Rikkard might have an inkling as to what was going on.

"You shouldn't have triggered the alarms," he said. "They knew you were there. I guess they figured they had a chance of catching you."

"I didn't know there *were* alarms. Nothing came up in their database," Selene argued. "And there was nothing about them in the lab specs."

"If you hadn't recklessly leaped into the mission, I would have had time to tell you."

Selene blinked at him with widened eyes. This was one of those rare moments she knew he was right. Not that she'd ever admit it.

Ignoring him, Selene manipulated the image of each speeder on her three-dimensional screen, pushing them away one by one with her fingers as she assessed their artillery. Most of the speeders had simple front mounted turrets, while the city patrol and the Class Threes had more advanced gun systems.

She had to do something.

"I'm getting up. Keep us steady." Selene unstrapped herself and crossed the cockpit to the hovercraft's door.

"What are you—" Rikkard cut himself off. His gaze bore into her back as she pulled the Gatling gun from the wall. "Understood."

Clipping her safety belt onto the railing above the door, Selene attached her heavy weapon to the tripod on the floor. She yanked the Gatling gun up, bringing it level with her hips. Pulling the crank back, she signaled for Rikkard to open the side door. It swung free. Wind yanked at her entire body and blinded her with her own hair. Her heart dropped into her stomach. Selene was thankful for the safety belt keeping her from falling to her death.

Skyscrapers rushed past on either side of the hovercraft. Selene scanned the night sky until she caught sight of her targets. The closest ships were small and sleek with a curved windshield. A small red flicker inside the tinted glass told her someone piloted these speeders from afar. Two more Class Ones flew close by at breakneck speed, catching up quickly now that they'd leveled out. Selene would have to blow them out of the sky before they attacked.

"This is gonna hurt." She smiled, aiming her large multi-cylinder weapon.

A speeder darted around the side of the ship, and she fired as the crimson flicker turned its red gaze on her.

The Gatling gun lurched, grinding loudly and spitting red from its multiple barrels, spinning rapidly. Selene dragged it back and forth across the sky, her heart beating against her ribcage as she followed the first speeder's attempt to dodge her attack. Its efforts were futile—Selene was the best shot on her team. The speeder's glass front shattered. Its plastic interior shriveled and melted under the laser's heat.

The rest went down in a blaze of fire.

It careened into a nearby building, bouncing off its side before tumbling onto the dark street below. If Selene could hear over the wind in her ears, she was sure there would have been an explosion.

"One down!" she called back to Rikkard, whether he could hear her or not.

She pulled back on the crank and the used clip dropped free. Selene shoved another inside. She locked it in and scanned the city for her next target. Taking aim, Selene followed a Class One speeder until a muffled shot rang out.

A blast of red missed their hovercraft by several feet.

The enemy had decided to fight back. Selene hoped they had bad aim. Another appeared beneath the hovercraft, gliding upward. Selene shot out its undercarriage. The speeder crumpled, exploding against the roof of an office building.

White titans with neon signs sped by. An image of the upcoming presidential campaign flashed across it: a man with slick black hair, amber eyes and a lop-sided grin. Hatred bubbled within her, but she didn't have a moment to wonder why.

A large armored Class Five pulled from behind a skyscraper. Sleek metal sides, dark windows, propellers attached to each side, and dual machine guns mounted below its center command module. This one had to be military grade, with a full team and heavy artillery—one only used by the Aldar Dominion faction of the government.

"What the hell is that doing here?" Her pounding heart tightened.

Smacking the panel on the side of the door, she twisted the knob to turn up the charge on her gun.

"I'd probably start taking evasive maneuvers to avoid this one!" Selene braced herself, her knuckles white as she turned her gun's aim on their new military pursuit. Laser shots spurted from her barrels, bathing the dark night in red.

"Hold on!" Rikkard shouted.

His warning barely gave Selene time to cut off her attack and grab the bar beside the open door. Her body lurched and her whole world spun in a loop, her feet dangling dangerously close to the open door. She would have been dumped outside if weren't for her white-knuckled grip.

City lights spun past and Selene reached for her weapon, trying to straighten it out. Her fingers brushed steel, but they were flying too wildly and her fingers slipped away.

The blur of the Dominion ship careened after them at full speed. A red glow appeared in the barrels of the front guns as they charged.

"Drop. Now!" she yelled.

The ship fell. The laser blast shot directly overhead, scarcely missing the roof of the hovercraft. The blast tore through the darkened windows of a skyscraper. Rikkard made a hard left, twisting between buildings. Fire rained down. A jolt from the ship threw her against the Gatling gun. She wrapped her forearm around the safety handle, squeezing her eyes shut. The screams of their primate cargo joined the screech of metal, telling her it was a tight fit. They leveled out and Selene righted herself. Heart pounding in her ears, she slammed the gun's power control again, cranking it to maximum.

"Go big or go home." Taking aim as they pulled out from behind a glass titan, Selene gritted her teeth.

Their pursuit came into full view, a dark metal shadow amongst the dazzling white of the city. Her entire body shook with the blast as she fired. She locked her elbows, holding the beam steady. The red scorch of the gun ripped through the front hull of the ship, tearing open the command module. A large plume of smoke rose from the Dominion machine's head. It fell, wheezing as it dropped from the sky. Selene took her fingers off the triggers.

Victory was theirs.

"Got it," she called to Rikkard.

"We're almost in the clear," he said. "Sit down."

"A little gratitude would be nice." Selene wiped the sweat from her brow and pulled her gun inside before slamming the side door shut. As she unhooked herself from above, a rumble shook the ship. "What was that?" Selene looked at Rikkard, who simply glanced back without a word.

"Why are they so heavily armed?" she continued, "and for that matter, why the hell are there so many? That was a low-security, low risk operation. There shouldn't be this much blowback."

Rikkard grunted in agreement while she hoisted her Gatling gun back onto the wall. She had clipped it into place as another boom echoed through the hull.

"Shit," Rikkard hissed. The ship shook again and they made a quick turn. "Sit *down*."

Selene rolled her eyes as an even louder boom echoed. It shook her entire body for a good five seconds before another hit. She jerked forward and back again, her breath flying from her lungs. Alarms blared through the cockpit. Her feet flew out from under her, throwing her back.

Her spine slammed into the rear wall before her head did. She blacked out.

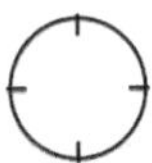

Selene opened her eyes to a mess of blue and black. It blurred through her vision as she pulled it into focus. What was this? What was happening? She blinked slowly. Where was she? The memories didn't come, but her sight eventually did. Selene focused on the bright light above. Below it, shadowed faces hovered in masks.

Something tickled at the back of her mind. Something she should remember.

Gloved hands reached down and she tried to push them away. Her body didn't move. Her body was submerged in some sort of jelly like substance. Cold, slick, and solid. It made her movements painfully slow. Her heart leapt. She tried to combat these mysterious people, who moved toward her with scalpels and other medical instruments. She opened her mouth to scream.

Liquid poured in instead.

Trying to cough and splutter, Selene used every ounce of her strength to thrash away, but the jelly liquid kept pouring in. It pushed down her throat and into her lungs, cold and slimy. Was this what drowning felt like? She couldn't breathe, yet blackness didn't take her back. Selene screamed into the gel, rage fueling her muscles. She tried to rip her arms outward, upward, downward, but it was all futile.

A swift cut on her right leg forced her to concentrate. A needle pierced her other. She tried to lean up, to see what they were doing, but all she could do was wrestle with her own mind and body as the glass of the vat pulled away in a circle to let metal hands with sharp instruments through.

Selene glanced around for some kind of drain to work towards, *anything* that she could use to empty this vat. Glass walls surrounded her, a few cords streamed somewhere into the tank, and there was a tube on her left, but nothing she could reach.

More cuts, more needles, more liquid down her throat. Frustration clawed at her insides like the knives biting at her skin. She wanted to leap out and hurt them.

Gritting her teeth, she tried to thrash again. Her muscles were drained, weak from the effort. She screamed again, but the sound was lost.

Whatever was happening, Selene had no control over it. The only thing she could do was succumb—to watch and wait. She had nearly convinced herself capable of such a feat when a needle pierced her back. This one wasn't like the others. It was thick and painful. It pushed into her spine. When she tried to shout for help this time, it wasn't out of fear or frustration; it was out of blinding pain.

The needle went in deeper and deeper until black spots clouded her vision. She thought she might faint. She prayed she would. But she didn't, and then it was sucking the marrow from her bones. Selene tried to pull at the darkness, tried to call it into her mind. The more she tried, the more awake she became—the more aware of what was happening.

She hoped the nightmare would end. She tried to see a light ahead where she could escape, but when the pain finally stopped, it left her aching.

She closed her eyes, trying to awaken from her terror.

"Selene!" Rikkard shook her and finally she awoke with a start.

Images of liquid filled tubs, needles and scalpels flooded her mind. She gasped in air like she was drowning. Her hands found the person in front of her now that she could finally move. Her fingers gripped smooth fabric, and she tightened her fists around it. Her heart sped.

Had that been real?

Slowly, her breathing evened out. It was just a dream, she told herself. It had to be. Sighing, Selene repeated that to herself several times before her shoulders relaxed.

Though she told herself it was only a dream, Selene could never be sure. Before three years ago, Selene didn't remember a single detail of her life: not her childhood, her first pet, her school or her parents—nothing. One day she just woke up, scared and alone. She'd climbed into the first hiding place she could find, which happened to be aboard Rikkard's ship. It was how they met.

What had happened to her before those three years?

When her tightened muscles finally loosened, the images pulled from her mind, and her head ached.

"Ow." Selene winced and reached for her skull. Feeling along the back of it, her fingers pulled away bloody.

"Are you okay?" Rikkard asked.

Selene looked up at him. His cold blue eyes met hers. She was still holding his jacket in one hand. Her cheeks flushed and she released it. What the hell had come over her? The memory, or dream had faded, but her stomach continued to turn.

"Yeah. I think so." She cleared her throat.

"Good." He nodded and stood, reaching for the small medical kit on a nearby ledge. He handed it to her. "Get yourself patched up so we can get out of here."

Selene couldn't help but roll her eyes. "Your concern over my wellbeing is touching as always, Rik."

Rikkard silently glided back to his captain's chair. While he went to work on the ship, Selene opened the red box and dug through its hastily packed contents. After several moments she found a small palm sized wand with a silver button on top. Pulling the wig from her head, her sun-kissed brown waves tumbled over her shoulders. Doing the best she could while holding her hair back Selene aimed the spray.

The aerosol stung her scalp, cold nanites digging into her skull like needles. Nanobots buried themselves in her flesh before the mending process began. Though they were generally quick, it still left her lightheaded. Her world swam for a few seconds, tipping sideways. She closed her eyes and leaned her head against the metal wall. The small devices could only fix flesh wounds, nothing internal. She'd be left with one hell of a headache.

"So how did we get out of there?" Selene asked to distract herself while the nanobots did their job.

"The same way we always do," he replied.

"A combination of your crazy flying and my insane gunning

skills?" Selene glanced at the front of the ship. Would she catch one of Rikkard's rare smiles?

"Outmaneuvered them." He shrugged and she sighed, somewhat disappointed. She should know better than to try and make small talk with the boss. Shaking her head once the tingling finally dissipated from her scalp, Selene stood and returned the medical box to its designated shelf.

"Ready to go?" Rikkard asked.

"Let's head out." She took a seat in her co-pilots chair, tactfully ignoring Rikkard's glances until he took off.

There was still work to be done.

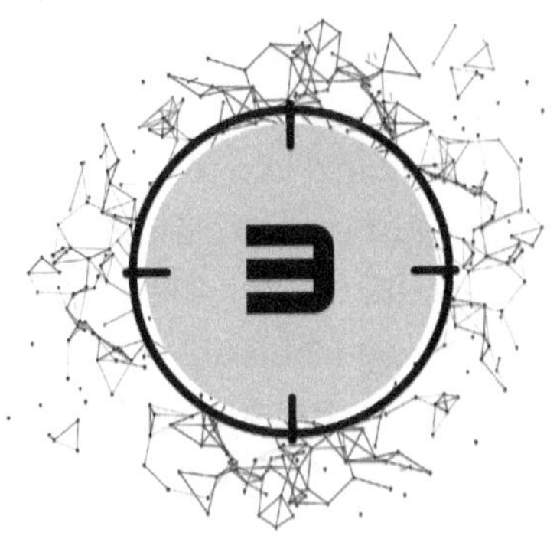

RIKKARD STEERED THEIR SHIP TO a reserve far from any city. When a small town finally flickered over the sand dunes on the horizon, its wooden tops and glints of metal could only mean they'd found what they were looking for. What used to be a zoo hundreds of years ago was now one of the only wildlife reserves left in the world and the only one that paid. Some of the few remaining natural born humans ran it, trying to save and collect any species they could.

As the only humanitarians still in existence, they were some of Selene's favorite people.

When the propellers hummed to a stop and their ship finally landed in the desert, it was a welcome relief. Being in the sky for hours wasn't a big deal for Selene, but the air pressure inside the cabin had turned the dull pain of the concussion into a sledgehammer drumming inside her skull.

Heading to the cargo bay, Selene passed by her new animal friends. They gazed at her unblinking, tilting their heads and making soft sounds at one another. From the lack of metal protruding from their skin, they were among the few lucky to be unmodified.

The Dominion had a bad habit of playing God.

She hit the release on the bay door. It creaked and stuttered from its damaged position. Selene cooed quietly to the apes, which stared back at her with wide eyes. While the gorilla looked on in curiosity, the chimpanzees darted around their small enclosure, tumbling over one another. Selene took her remote from her pocket, and hit the control for them to follow. As she reached the half-open bay door, the sun crested the horizon. Warm light lit the sand dunes for miles, turning the sea of sand to a sea of fire.

"I'll meet you back at the cargo ship."

Selene glanced back. She hadn't heard Rikkard come up behind her. His blue eyes turned to cold ice and his tan skin glowed in the morning sun. Her cheeks heated and she stifled a cough.

"Where are you going?" She raised a questioning eyebrow.

He fixed her with his this-is-need-to-know-information look. It was a lot like his usual glare, but with a quirked eyebrow and narrowed gaze. "I'll see you back at base."

"Is the transport speeder still here?" If he would abandon her in the middle of nowhere, she'd need something to get her over the hundreds of miles back to their floating headquarters. While Rikkard did whatever it is leader's do, she needed to pick up Kong, a friend they'd left to help out the reserve last time she was by. Selene wanted to be sure he could return with her.

"Yes." He turned and disappeared into the craft.

"Ever the chatty one." Selene stepped out onto the sand, sinking slightly as she walked. It warmed her toes, even through her heat-regulated suit. She moved far enough from the hovercraft that the two hover plates followed, the door to the cargo bay closing behind her. Keeping her back to the ship, the propellers kicked up sand, dusting her in thin grains.

The craft lifted and flew out over the desert. It headed east, back the way they'd come. *Where are you going?* she wondered, as the hovercraft became a black dot on the horizon.

Sighing, Selene gave up and made her way to the front entrance of the reserve. The remains of a sign welcomed passersby to the zoo, though most of the letters had long since fallen, leaving only a Z and a single O. Most of the former metal barred cages and enclosures had been stripped away, replaced with sleek steel and plastic bubbles open to the sky. Not a lot had survived the solar flares that ravaged the earth over three centuries ago; leaving Selene confused as to how any piece of such a simple attraction remained standing.

A loud ape-like hoot shattered the silence.

The primates trailing behind her ceased their chatter and Selene stopped beside a leopard enclosure, just in time for Kong to tackle her. Her breath fled her lungs as she rolled across the ground in the safety of Kong's hairy gorilla arms. He hooted and hollered in delight, while Selene lost herself in laughter. When Kong finally stopped rolling, she patted his arms and righted her hair. She winced as her headache returned.

"Kong, it's nice to see you too." She smiled and gently pried his thick fingers from her waist. The metal surrounding his right eye glinted in the sun, and the rest of her primate friends hollered.

Selene hushed her small charges and Kong set her down, though he had a playful look in his eyes like he might tackle her again. The young gorilla was the newest addition to their team. On one of their first missions, Selene and Rikkard had rescued him and brought him to the reserve where he stayed for a brief time. Not even a day passed before he escaped. The zoo caretaker, Aida, had been sure he was trying to get back to them, his two saviors, whom he'd bonded with in the short time they'd been together.

For weeks, Kong repeatedly disappeared from the reserve, and time after time Aida called them to go after him. Each time they'd find him and he would be overjoyed, clutching Selene tightly in his gorilla hug. Eventually they decided it would be easier to keep Kong around, even if he helped out at the reserve every now and then.

Selene had been completely smitten with their big friend ever since.

"Are you ready to go home?" she asked.

Kong nodded vigorously and signed back to her. *Yes. Kong misses home.*

In Kong's first few weeks with the smugglers he had learned

sign language to communicate with his surrogate parents. He caught on quickly, understanding them clearly when they spoke, but his modifications didn't go so far as speech.

"Let's find Aida and drop off our new pals. Then we can go." Selene grinned. Kong did too and beat his fists against his chest like he'd seen in the movies before bounding off in the direction of the main building where Aida and her team were sure to be.

"Selene!"

Past the few enclosures on the main path, a familiar woman jogged toward her.

"Aida." Selene smiled. She joined the elderly woman between the enclosures of a modified cheetah with a half metal skull and mechanical leg, and a pit of alligators. It snarled at them for waking him up, agitating the pit of sleeping lizards on her other side.

"Who do we have here?" Aida's eyes lit up.

Selene chuckled and introduced Aida to their latest rescues. Though Aida was a tough old girl, she melted in adoration over the young gorilla. She had a feeling Aida was remembering when Kong had first come to her.

"They are just darling." Aida sighed wistfully.

"I didn't think I'd see anyone here until at least nine." Selene gave her a teasing wink.

"We're all up." Hands on her hips, her eyes returned to Selene's. Aida's lips twisted in a rueful smile. "Aaron is missing. That's the third member of our community gone in under a month." She shook her head, and ran a hand through her silver strands. "I don't know what's going on, but it's got everyone on edge."

"That's awful." Her voice rose an octave. Selene reached forward to pat the woman gently on the shoulder. She vaguely remembered Aaron from her visits. He was a nice boy with a big goofy grin. "Who else is missing?"

"Gemma and Paulette. They went to town for a few supplies two weeks ago and never returned." Aida stared at the sand drowning her feet. Selene didn't know these ladies, but the pain on Aida's face struck a cord.

"Is there anything we can do?"

Aida shrugged. "I don't think so dear, just keep your eye out. Abductions of *nats* are becoming much more common these days."

If natural humans were disappearing, that had to mean something. With so few left, they were a close-knit group and hardly lost track of one another. But who would want to hurt or kidnap *nats*?

"Has anyone new been on the reserve?" Selene asked.

"Not in months." Aida turned the trio back toward the main building. The sun peeked behind it, illuminating the dark wood roof. "They all go missing in the Outskirts, so for now we're safe here. I don't know what I'd do if this place was found. I don't think the Dominion would be too happy with our liberation agenda." This brought a wicked grin to the old woman's face. A rebel at heart, Aida was always out to avoid *the man*.

"I'm sure they'd be more concerned about you skipping out on taxes." Selene grinned, and Aida laughed. Kong hooted behind them and trotted to their side. Several men and women roamed the flat expanse, tools in hand. Aida raised a hand in greeting as she passed, then halted mid-step and turned to Selene.

"We are grateful to you and your crew for helping us," Aida said, "and I've got to say, I love when you bring them in good shape. Every time one comes in awful condition, I know those clone people are to blame. It's inhuman what they've done to themselves. Maybe they live forever, sure, but that doesn't excuse having no *soul*."

Selene nodded. She didn't necessarily agree with the old woman's clones-are-evil stance, but she'd heard Aida's rants before and knew it was best to stay quiet and move on.

Cloning oneself was commonplace. After the Aldar Dominion virtually saved the world when solar flares nearly wiped out humanity, diseases like cancer had grown at such an alarming rate that by the end of it there were only a billion people left on Earth. When the aliens introduced cloning as an alternative to a disease-ridden life and death, humans jumped on the idea.

With the beaten and bloody creatures Selene had seen over the years, it was getting harder and harder to argue with Aida's opinions and continue to support cloning. Three centuries since it started, and the empathy of the world had seriously deteriorated. As people recycled their bodies and moved their minds to a different vessel time and time again, they didn't seem to notice the type of civilization they were becoming.

"You know, not all clone people are awful," Selene said.

"Oh dear, no I know. You and your friends are angels by comparison." Aida hurried to correct herself. Selene wasn't offended, and tried to smile to assure her friend. "I don't know what we'd do without you. We haven't the resources to send out teams of our own."

"Well, as Rik would say, we need the money." Selene shrugged.

"Oh listen here, I know you're not in it for the reward."

"You're right, I'm not. Can't say the same for the boss man." They both laughed.

"What is that *thing* doing here?" A man approached quickly from the main building, blonde hair, blood-shot blue eyes, and fists clenched.

"*Thing*?" Selene's eyebrows shot up and her fists tightened.

"You heard me," he growled, jabbing a finger into her sternum. Before he could pull back, Selene grabbed his wrist, twisting him around so hard he fell to his knees with his back to her and his arm drawn taught between them. He yowled in pain, his head pitching forward.

He didn't try to pull away.

"Julian." Aida sighed, shaking her head. She didn't move to help the man, only gave him a pitying look. "This is *Selene*. She isn't one of them. You know that."

"I know a *clone* when I see one," he choked out. Selene twisted his wrist again in one quick motion. He gritted his teeth to cut off a gasp.

"Selene," Aida urged.

"All right."

Releasing him, she stepped away. Julian pitched forward

into the sand before scampering a few feet away. His blue gaze snapped between Aida and Selene.

"Racist prick," Selene muttered, hands on her hips.

"Go easy on him." Aida met her green eyes with her own cloudy gaze. "It's his son that's missing."

"Oh." Selene glanced at the man, who stood and dusted the sand from his clothes with angry swipes, muttering under his breath. Her stomach twisted.

"Julian," Selene said. The man glanced back, his long hair tousled. "Aaron is your son?"

Julian glanced over his shoulder at the few co-workers who'd stopped to witness the exchange. He straightened his brown vest, a layer of dust tumbling to the ground.

Nodding, he took a tentative step over. "Yes."

"How long has he been gone?"

"A few days now."

Selene bit her lip. She couldn't help it. If Aaron had been missing that long, he wasn't out partying like the other natural kids. Still, she wasn't going to tell that to a distressed parent.

"Do you have a picture of him?" Selene asked. "I'll keep an eye out in town."

"Really?" Julian's eyes lit with hope. He stepped closer, pulling a wallet from his back pocket. He produced a dusty photo with torn edges and held it out to her.

Selene took it. The boy in the photo couldn't be more than thirteen. His hair was dirty blonde like his father's—the same blue eyes and tan freckled skin too. She recognized his grin stretching from ear to ear. He sat on top of a brown and white dappled horse, arms wrapped around its neck. He was too young to be missing.

Clearing her throat, she met Julian's gaze, handing back the photo.

"He's a bit older now, but still has the same smile." Julian's eyes clouded over, glazing with tears. His hands shook when he placed the photo back in his pocket.

"I'll keep my eye out," she said. Julian met her eyes and

nodded in understanding. He said a quick goodbye and took off toward a row of sheds where several overall-clad workers spoke in hushed tones.

"I hope you find him." Aida's lips pressed into a thin smile.

"I hope so too."

Now that Julian was gone, his co-workers slowly dispersed. They whispered as they went, glancing back at the clone girl who didn't belong. Selene shifted awkwardly on the sand.

"I think it'd be best if you get going dear."

"I think so too."

Selene said her goodbyes and whistled for Kong, handing the remote for her rescues over to Aida. Taking the device with a nod and a smile, the old woman stepped away as the happy-go-lucky gorilla jogged across the sand, a toothy simian grin spread across his face.

Following Kong to the westernmost point of the reserve, near the buildings where Aida and her comrades were housed, she waved to the few workers she was familiar with. No one stopped to say hello. They were all wary. If so many natural born humans were missing, they had a right to be unnerved by her.

As she reached the speeder and loaded Kong into the back, she glanced back at Aida's people. Suspicious eyes darted toward her and her ship. She sighed and climbed onboard, hoping all the while Aaron and the other missing people would show up, and their distress would be for nothing.

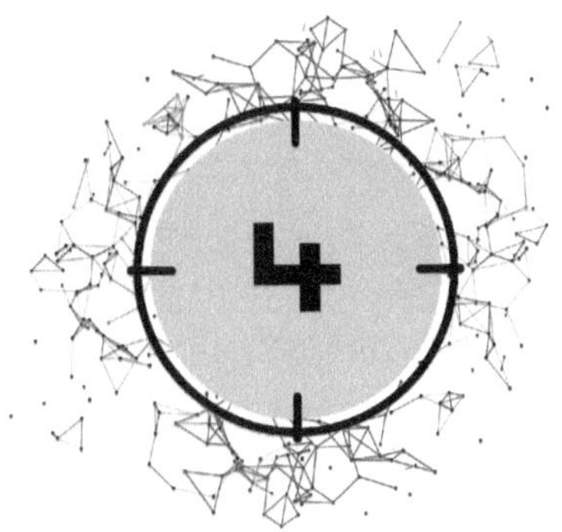

HIGH ABOVE THE SAND DUNES, the smugglers' home base rose like an ugly metal behemoth in an otherwise beautiful blue sky. Late afternoon sun crested the colossus as she arced around the side of the ship, hovering where the dark steel was smoothest. The gray monster quaked, a pair of doors sliding free to accept her speeder. Selene glided in; docking beside a sleek hovercraft with its rear doors bent inward.

Black scorched the sides of the craft they'd been using that morning. Selene raised an eyebrow at the large metal bird, surprised to see Rikkard home so soon.

She hopped from the cockpit, sliding the door shut before releasing Kong. She signed for him to go check in with their resident chef and muscle, Darius, if he was hungry. Kong didn't sign back before leaping from the small cargo hold. He ran from the bay like his butt was on fire.

Selene laughed and her stomach rumbled. She might be a little hungry as well.

Weaving through the crate-laden cargo hold, she followed Kong through the intricate maze of steel corridors to the dining hall.

Once upon a time, the cargo ship had belonged to a much larger crew than their small group of seven. The ship could sleep a couple hundred people comfortably, and feed them in the great dining halls and kitchens. She'd always wondered how Rikkard obtained it as their headquarters, but he'd never deigned to explain it.

A loud bang pulled her from her reverie. Her right hand flew for her pistol. She glued her back to the wall, shoulders pressing against cold steel. Her heart leapt into her throat.

Glancing left and right, only bleak gray halls stared back at her. Shouting rose in the distance.

Rikkard.

Ripping her gun from its holster, she ran the length of the hall. Her boots slapped against the metal grated floor, racing in time with her heart. She skidded to a stop at a four-way intersection. The shouts grew louder. Right.

Selene dove into the adjacent hall, following the voices. They grew louder and louder until she was nearly upon them. Was this a foreign invasion or just her crew?

She rounded another corner. Selene dug her heels in, nearly running headlong into a woman with nearly translucent skin and vivid violet hair. She pulled back just in time, holstering her weapon.

"Holy hell, you scared me Sarah!" Selene took a few calming breaths, hand held to her heart. An embarrassed flush spread through her cheeks.

Blinking back at her with wide alien eyes, Sarah's face lit in a toothy grin. Sarah was their resident physician, veterinarian, and a former part of the Dominion. She also happened to be Selene's best friend, and the wife of second-in-command, Kayl.

"I scared *you*?" Sarah laughed. "Where are you running to?"

"I heard shouting."

"So you ran in guns blazing?" Sarah's large purple eyes twinkled with amusement and the intricate pattern of silver designs on her high cheeks and sunken temples swirled.

"Well you never know!" It was useless to explain. The moment she'd run into Sarah, she was doomed to the kitchen. Even though Sarah's black clad, pierced and tattooed self gave her the appearance of a criminal not to be reckoned with, she was the mother hen of the smugglers.

"Did you just get back?"

"A few minutes ago. I already sent Kong along to see Darius."

"And you weren't going to follow? Have you even eaten today?" Selene shook her head at Sarah's aghast expression. "I swear Selene, you would die of starvation if you didn't have me around!" Sarah linked her slim arm with Selene's and forced her back toward the dining hall. Though lithe like a dancer, Sarah's strength overpowered Selene. There was no arguing with Sarah when her well-being was involved.

"I'd be fine. Clones don't need to eat very much."

"Be that as it may, you still need to eat at least once every twenty-four hours." Sarah steered her through hall after hall until they arrived at a large dusty blue room adorned with stainless steel circular tables, each with eight white backed chairs surrounding them.

Rem, their resident tech wiz, waved from the only occupied table.

"Sit with Rem while I go get something from the kitchen."

"Yes, mom." Selene rolled her eyes, but she knew Sarah simply cared about her. They exchanged amused smiles before Sarah took off into the back and Selene weaved through the tables to join Rem.

"Selene, hello!" Rem looked up from a pile of papers scrawled with new weapons designs and grinned beneath his mop of white hair. "How was the trip?"

"Great." She smiled as L3, Rem's small boxy robot companion with minor artificial intelligence, peeked from behind Rem's head. Perched on his shoulder, its black eyes blinked back at her. "Everyone is safe and sound. How are you and L3 doing?" L3 beeped to acknowledge her presence before tucking itself behind the seventeen-year-olds' neck. Instead of an affectionate name, Rem had very practically called his robot L3, as he was the third and finally successful model.

"Fabulous!" He grinned again, flashing his teeth. "Rikkard has me working on new undetectable laser rifles for you guys. I'm making my own adjustments too of course." Still beaming, Rem wiggled his eyebrows.

Selene laughed. "That must *really* excite you."

"Oh it does!"

"I can tell! What are these new guns for?" she asked.

"No sweet clue!"

"You're not curious at all?" It was Selene's turn to raise her brows.

"Not really." He shrugged.

"You're just in it for the tech aren't you?"

"You bet your sweet ass he is!" The growl of a deep voice across the room drew Selene and Rem's attention. Darius and Sarah emerged from the kitchen's swinging doors, holding a tray half the size of his wide chest. Tattoos circled his arms and his thick muscles bulged under the weight of this smorgasbord. He strode across the room with a toothy grin.

Ignoring the comment, Selene turned back to Rem. "Did we invite him to this conversation?"

Rem shook his head.

"Down kitty." Darius grinned. His clean-shaven skull flashed under the bright fluorescent light as he plopped down on Rem's other side, placing the large spread before them. Purple pasta, green rice, and golden breaded sandwiches with small tentacles sticking between the slices of bread were only a few of the dishes served. The rainbow of delicacies made her mouth water and her stomach growl. Darius may be all brawn, but he was a wizard in the kitchen.

Rem gaped. "Are you trying to turn us into overstuffed hippos?"

"I think they're hoping we'll choke on it all, Rem." Selene stared at the pastas, curries, sandwiches and soups, mouth agape.

Sarah swatted her, and they all grinned at one another. "We're trying to give you *selection*. You two know nothing about the culinary arts!"

Selene and Rem exchanged a look. Rem shrugged. "At least

they're not trying to feed us that alien seafood crap again."

Sarah gasped. "That is a delicacy where I'm from!"

They all burst into laughter until a dark shadow strode in. Rikkard, clad in his usual long black coat and emotionless expression, joined them. Selene quirked an eyebrow. Who had he been arguing with? Only Rikkard's second-in-command, Kayl, was missing. Those two got into it now and then, but there usually wasn't any shouting involved.

"Hey." Rikkard sat across from her, his gaze lingering on a plate of sandwiches.

The mood quickly shifted to stoic silence.

Sarah and Rem grabbed plates and spooned food onto them, while Rikkard leaned back and hoisted his boots on the table, cleaning one of his knives with a rag.

While the rest awkwardly avoided eye contact with the boss, Selene tried to get his attention. "So where is Kayl?" she asked, trying to be discreet in her curiosity.

Rikkard's blue gaze flickered up to hers for only a moment before he resumed playing with his knife. "Why don't you ask his wife?" His tone remained flat. Annoyed.

Selene was confident in deducing it *had* been Kayl he was fighting with.

"I'm asking *you*." Selene crossed her arms and set her jaw. Unlike the others, she wouldn't let Rikkard push her around.

Rikkard held her gaze with surprising intensity as he removed his boots from the table. He leaned forward and plunged the tip of his knife into the smooth, tough metal of the table.

She winced.

"He's going on a run for *good* intel this time." The threatening gesture should make her back off, but Selene saw it for what it was. He was trying to get her to shut up.

Selene arched an eyebrow. They'd found what they were looking for and escaped in one piece. "What wasn't good about it?"

Rikkard made a hand motion to brush her off before he leaned back. He sheathed his dagger. "How were today's profits?"

She froze.

He must have already known—he did *not* look happy.

On the return trip Selene checked in to see how much Aida had credited to them for the four rescues. It was just under their usual pay, which wasn't much. Rikkard just wanted to bully her into saying it. It was a waste of time if the animals weren't paying.

"They were fine." Selene shrugged. She needed to think of a good excuse to go back to the conversation about Kayl.

"Four hundred is what you call fine?" Rikkard glowered.

"It's fine for now." Selene had to resist rolling her eyes. "It's not like we're hurting for supplies."

"And how would you know that?"

"You've got Rem working on a new project. If we were hurting, you wouldn't have assigned him any new tasks." Rikkard gave her a level look, one that would tell the others to leave it alone. She of course ignored it. "And why are you not answering my questions about Kayl for another matter? Were you two—"

"*Selene*. It's none of your business."

"Fine."

Rikkard was settling into one of his *moods*. She exchanged a look with Sarah who tried not to smile too widely. Sarah always said they'd make a perfect couple. Selene couldn't see it.

Though she was still curious about Kayl, and why Rikkard was unwilling to talk about it, she let it go and ate in silence. Eventually the others resumed some sort of normal conversation, staying clear of sensitive topics while trying to keep the mood light. Selene blocked it all out and ate until her head ached enough that sleep called to her. She said her goodbyes, her goodnights, and left the large room, hoping sleep would make a bit more sense than her waking hours.

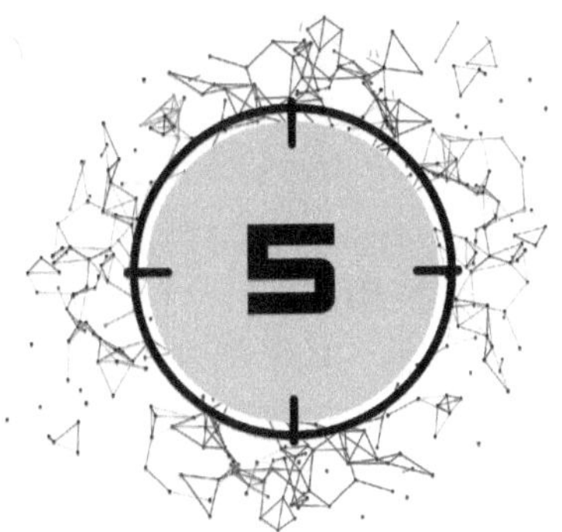

SELENE OPENED HER EYES TO a blur of blue and black. Something about this was familiar. But why? Blinking to clear the haze from her eyes, she slowly focused.

A blinding light flashed on overhead.

She winced. The movement didn't yield any result. Her limbs were stuck. The beat of her heart hammered inside her head. It was the only sound. She tried to shimmy her hips and wiggle her shoulders. Nothing.

She was encased.

Cold pressed against her skin, slimy and wet. Realization dawned on her when she tried to take a breath.

Blue liquid poured into her throat and nostrils, suffocating her. Frustration and panic flooded her, and she thrashed, her movements stilled by the gel.

Three people in masks loomed over her prison. She would have started in surprise if she could move. She tried to will them to get her out of here. She tried to look into each of their eyes, even if she could hardly see them through the blur of gel.

No matter how much she willed it, they didn't let her go.

Instead, they thrust needles and knives through the gel, piercing her hips, spine, and shoulders. At one point she swore they had invaded every part of her. Just when she thought it was over, two needles came from above, directly over each eye.

Her scream was lost on the gel.

More than ever Selene tried to get away. Her heart raced as she tried to push, pull, kick, and punch. She hardly moved an inch. Tears seeped from her eyes. She glanced left and right—anywhere but up.

When the thick points finally pierced her pupils she lost consciousness, only to wake up with the liquid pouring from the vat. The side came free and dumped her onto the cold metal floor. Her breath fogged the cool air and her whole body trembled.

Finally able to move, Selene gazed around the lab, expecting the mask clad people to jump out. No one did, and somehow she wasn't blind. Tears welled in her eyes as cold air bit at her naked body.

Finally, she was free.

Selene awoke, gasping and reaching for safety. Sweat coated her skin, and she shook uncontrollably. Images of cold dark liquid and glass vats splashed across her mind. No matter how hard she tried, she couldn't push them away. She could see herself suffocating in the blue gel, her body stuck inside. It was cold, so cold. Her body trembled and she rolled out of bed. Her knees struck the cold tile and she fell to her side. She sucked in a breath. Pricks of pain flashed across her skin like the needles that pierced her again and again and again. Then her eyes.

Why in Aldar's name would they go for her eyes?

Nausea soured her stomach and welled inside her throat. She stumbled to her feet so fast her knees scraped the ceramic flooring. She rushed to a nearby switch on the wall. Her fist slammed against the plastic. A small commode shot from the wall, just in time for her to vomit inside.

When her body was empty, and her strength gave way, she slid to the cold floor. Curling in on herself, Selene willed the images away.

She just wanted them all to go away.

Once the shivers ceased and she regained some sense of self, Selene pushed everything to the back of her mind. She had to concentrate on the here and now—the feel of the cold floor, the sweat caked-hair against her skin, anything but the wretched thoughts crowding her consciousness.

"What the hell is wrong with you?" Selene couldn't picture a past in which she had to deal with these things. Until she'd hit her head on the back of the ship she'd been over it, happy not to remember and content in her new life. These images were calling to mind things she didn't want to know, and she loathed them for it.

Sighing, Selene rose from the floor. She showered, dressed and was heading to the dining hall when she realized the sun had barely risen.

Certain no one would be around when she entered, Selene was surprised to find the dining hall occupied. Huddled close together, Sarah and Kayl sat at their usual center table, ignoring their breakfast while they held hands. The only other alien in the group, Kayl was as startling to look at as Sarah. With dark skin, navy blue eyes and thick dark green hair, they complemented each other nicely. Though she would most certainly call Sarah's inhuman form beautiful, she wasn't sure if she would say the same for Kayl. While his wife's sparkling eyes could light up a room, Kayl's were somewhat bulbous and buggy, even as he made lovey eyes at Sarah.

They smiled, and Sarah leaned forward, her free hand brushing against Kayl's hair as she whispered. Selene stayed frozen in the doorway, a grin working its way up her cheeks.

Sarah and Kayl had both been children of foreign delegates. While Sarah was studying medicine, betrothed to another, Kayl taught her dance lessons for her coming nuptials. When the two unexpectedly fell in love, they ran as far away as possible—all the way to New Manhattan.

Selene couldn't help but envy their perfect love.

Sarah leaned back and giggled at whatever Kayl had said. Her purple gaze flashed up and she caught Selene staring. Her smile didn't falter, and she quickly waved Selene over.

"Good morning, lovely," Sarah said.

"Morning all." Selene stepped forward warily, waiting until Kayl turned and his dark blue eyes met hers. His smile fell and the sparkle of delight in his eyes faded to shadow.

Selene sat beside her best friend. Her mind tore away from her dreams and settled on the scene she'd heard yesterday. She wanted to launch right into questions about the fight with Rikkard, but with the irritated look on his face, she chose not to.

"What's going on?" she asked.

"Nothing much." Sarah wrapped her thin fingers around Kayl's wrist, her thumb trailing up and down the black markings swirling around his forearm.

"It's a bit early for you isn't it?" Kayl turned his annoyed gaze on her.

Selene sighed. She had never gotten along with the man. She always thought it was something to do with the changes on the ship when she joined. Suddenly the smuggling operative had gone from dangerous high profile heists, to freeing endangered species. Still, why wouldn't he be happier with his wife around? She shook her head. Kayl had always been a sourpuss and she tried not to take it too personally.

"It is," she said. "Couldn't sleep." She didn't feel like elaborating, not with the lingering sense of fear from her dreams littering her mind. She didn't need to explain herself to Kayl anyway.

"Is everything okay?" Sarah asked. Though the aliens had no eyebrows, her forehead wrinkled from each side. "Rikkard failed to mention until you went to bed that you got hurt yesterday."

"That little bump?" Selene let out a humorless little laugh. "Considering it's Rik, I'm surprised he mentioned it at all."

"He has a soft spot for you." Sarah grinned.

Selene and Kayl both rolled their eyes. "Not this again."

"What? You know it's true."

"So Kayl…" Selene turned to the tall man, in hopes of moving this conversation in a more productive direction. "Do we have any leads? Intel? Something to do? At this point I'm damn near ready to do dishes if the washer is broken again."

Normally her poor attempt at a joke would diffuse the tension in the room. But this time, Kayl only sighed and flicked his fingers at the small screen lying on the table in front of him. It lit up, casting a soft blue glow on his angular features. He scrolled through until finally settling on a listing.

"There's something about Bengal tigers being used for gambling in Bakura." Kayl shrugged. "That's pretty much all we have at the moment. Slow month."

"I'll take it!" Selene said without hesitation. They all knew Bakura well enough, and even a simple mission was better than sitting around doing nothing.

Kayl slammed his fist on the table. It rattled loudly, and startled them both. "I haven't even explained the possible complications, and you just jump right into it. You're too rash and you're going to get someone killed."

Selene blanched. She'd thought he'd be pleased she was taking some of the grunt work instead of sitting around letting someone else take care of it.

"Kayl!" Sarah snapped, violet eyes kindling to purple fire.

Now that Selene could gather her bearings, she chimed in. "I've never gotten someone hurt on my missions. I don't know what the hell your problem is, but if there are complications, I'm all ears."

"My problem is you don't *think*, you just act impulsively and you *will* get someone hurt if it doesn't stop!"

"Why are you yelling at me? If you're having issues with someone else you know I'm not going to let you take it out on me, Kayl," Selene growled. "I just want to take the job, rescue those damn tigers and get on with whatever is next. I may be reckless, but at least I get the right intel and get the goddamn job done."

Kayl's face started to twist in rage, veins bulging on his dark face, when that dark shadow waltzed in again.

"Take the job." Rikkard took a seat beside her and narrowed his eyes at Kayl. "We can't afford to be picky." Tension built in the room so quickly she thought they might suffocate. It was one thing for her to argue with Kayl or Rikkard, but to have the boss and second-in-command fighting was like having the team's parents gearing up for divorce.

"This has nothing to do with—" Kayl began but Rikkard's increasingly intense glare silenced him. "Fine," Kayl hissed, turning his rage back on Selene. "Take the damn job." He rose and stalked from the room. On an average day, Sarah might follow, but instead she stared after her husband in silence, her purple lips set in a stern line.

It only took a few seconds for the silence to be disturbed, and not in the way Selene had expected.

Charging into the dining hall, hooting and hollering, came Kong, a pair of dark blue denim pants between his teeth. He leapt over tables and chairs before dissolving into a fit of laughter near the other side of the room.

Darius burst through the kitchen doors next, in the buff aside from his boxers. His face twisted in irritation so great a vein popped up on his bare head. Kong was going to get it this time.

"Kong!" Darius bellowed as he ran after the amused beast. He spit and swore across the hall as Kong dodged aside, leaping to grab the rafters. Kong dropped the pants onto one of his feet so he could dangle it above Darius's head.

"Give me the pants!" Darius jumped and grabbed for the denim. Each time his fingers came within inches, Kong lifted them out of reach and started to hoot and laugh again.

Before Selene and Sarah choked on their laughter, Rikkard stood and held up a hand towards Kong, who immediately froze.

"Kong," he said in a serious tone. "Give them back."

Kong made a few whining noises, trying to decide whether Rikkard's wrath was worth the fun he was having.

"*Kong*," Rikkard repeated.

Sighing heavily, Kong dropped from the ceiling and grumpily returned his prize to Darius. His gaze roamed the room and met Selene's; he looked like a misbehaving teen. Selene smiled and inclined her arm to him, motioning to the poor gorilla. Kong skulked over, avoiding Rikkard's gaze as he slouched beside Selene, leaning into her one arm embrace. She rubbed his hairy neck gently and whispered assurance, all while everyone attempted unsuccessfully to hide their amusement from Rikkard.

"What is everyone sitting around for?" Rikkard raised an eyebrow before motioning outward. "We have tigers to save!"

Selene smiled. He never had been one to let everyone sit around and take a day off. They had that in common.

"Someone will have to wake Rem," Sarah said.

Rikkard nodded and flipped on the earpiece he often wore. "Rem," he said. There must have been some sleepy shuffling involved on the other end because it took a moment before Rikkard continued. "Take us to Bakura. We have a new mission." He paused. "Yes, you heard right." Another pause. "No, you cannot get drunk." Rikkard's expression said that a lot more options for fun things Rem could do in Bakura were being suggested. "You'll have to stay with Kong while we're there." Pause. "No, you may not gamble. Rem just set course for Bakura." Rikkard hung up the line.

"Looking for a fun night out is he?" Selene grinned. She had fond memories of their last adventure in Bakura as well. The group had spent all day getting drunk at the bar, and proceeded to harass the Bakura residents for half the night.

"Indeed." Rikkard turned to them with his signature why-are-you-all-not-moving glare.

"What's the plan, boss? Who's in?" Selene asked.

"I am!" Sarah jumped up.

Rikkard glanced at her briefly before shaking his head. They all knew Kayl wouldn't approve. Whatever trouble Rikkard had been stirring up with his second-in-command, he wasn't about to create more of it.

"I'm in." Darius joined the group—with pants this time.

"You know, I probably don't even need any help." Selene arched a brow at Rikkard. "It sounds simple enough."

"I see Kayl's point now," Rikkard said. Selene flushed. "Selene, Darius, you're with me on this one."

"With *you*?" Selene snapped.

"Yes. Is that a problem?"

"I suppose not."

"Then everyone suit up. We should be at Bakura within the hour."

WHEN RIKKARD TOLD HIS CREW to suit up, he meant it—especially in Bakura's case. The old navy ship had been abandoned for hundreds of years in the desert sand until a few shady black market dealers got their hands on it. Now converted, Bakura was the region's epicenter for criminal activity. Slave trade, gambling rings, illegal exports—you name it, Bakura had it.

Bakura was not for the faint of heart.

Selene tightened her sheaths of knives around each bicep. Along with her throwing knives, she had her usual laser pistols on each hip, a long knife in her right boot, and a smaller dagger on her left thigh. She touched her shoulder. The empty space on her back was a reminder Rem had her rifle in the shop.

Making sure her weapons were charged and ready, Selene zipped up the remainder of her one-piece black suit and tucked her long wavy hair into a bun before fixing her half black and half green wig to her head. She was ready.

Returning to the mess hall, Selene joined the rest of the crew. They all wore similar attire, mostly black with knives and guns out in the open. There was no need to hide their weaponry in a criminal-infested hang out.

"Everyone ready?" Rikkard gazed at each of them. They

all nodded. "Good. Selene, Darius, as you know, you're with me. Kayl, Sarah and Rem, enjoy Bakura but *do not* leave Kong unsupervised." He fixed them with his *serious* look before continuing. "Otherwise don't get yourselves in trouble, and stay away from the west side of the ship." This sparked some raised eyebrows, but Rikkard ignored them. "Selene, we're going to head through Radley's bar to the elevator. There's a boxing ring in the basement where we should find your cats. Darius, you know what to do."

Darius nodded.

"A boxing ring?" Selene asked.

"Yes, I believe they have the tigers fight each other, and the audience places their bets on which will win."

Her stomach dropped.

She didn't like the sound of this already. She had a bad feeling these tigers would not be in as good of shape as the apes they'd saved yesterday.

"We want to make sure this is *good* intel this time, so we'll work our way in with that in mind," Rikkard continued.

At the clear jab, Kayl glared at the captain before he stormed off. Selene wasn't the only one who shifted awkwardly. She tried not to think of him like a teenager not getting his way. Whatever was going on between Rikkard and his second, they clearly weren't over it.

"So we *are* allowed to go trade in the market right?" Rem piped up, his little robot friend beeping by his ear.

"I do have some medical supplies to gather," Sarah added.

"And I need some parts for your new weapons." Rem wiggled his eyebrows excitedly.

"Like I said—" Rikkard eyed them both. "—as long as you take care of Kong, do whatever you want." Rem nearly bounced up and down with joy while Sarah radiated appreciation. "We should be landing momentarily."

Rem nodded and checked the small phone like device of his. The phone was much more complicated than that, but Selene had been ranted at enough times to call it otherwise.

"And we're here!" he called. They couldn't hear the propellers slow from this deep in the ship, so they had to assume Rem was telling the truth.

Exiting through the maze of halls and out the cargo bay, Rikkard made Rem and Sarah swear one last time that they'd check on Kong in an hour before they took off. Once the three of them were left standing on the platform, Selene let her gaze wander to the navy ship.

Bakura towered fifty stories high, and at least three times that in length. Though the old guns and cannons had been stripped off long ago, the bones of the ship remained. Even rusted and covered in sand it was still a magnificent sight to behold. She couldn't imagine how daunting it must have looked at sea a few centuries ago.

Rikkard stopped before leaving the cargo bay doors. Darius paused a few paces ahead. He turned to her, giving her a once over before settling his gaze on her green eyes. Selene pushed back the flush that rose to her cheeks.

"Stay close," Rikkard said. "You know women can be used as currency in Bakura."

Selene scoffed and rolled her eyes, resting a hand on her pistol. It charged as she raised an eyebrow at Rikkard. "Please, I'd like to see them try." Rikkard and Darius exchanged smirks before entering the long-beached naval vessel.

Rikkard took the lead, Selene and Darius trailing after him. The grimy halls of the ship were familiar, and inspired her inner perfectionist. It had been decades since these halls saw a mop.

Twenty paces ahead a pickpocket slipped a wallet from a man's pocket, while his female accomplice dazzled the grungy man with her smile and hefty bosom. The young pickpocket glanced their way. One look at their plethora of guns and knives, and his smirk dropped. Selene was reminded of the last time a man tried to steal from one of their crew. He didn't get away with his fingers.

Walking through the general market, Selene scanned the rows of makeshift metal stands and shelves, filled with assorted weapons, poisons, foreign delicacies and other black market materials. Bright fluorescent lights swung from the ceiling, and dust cascaded down on the catwalk as someone stomped by overhead. Selene wrinkled her nose and wiped her shoulders clean.

Taking a back exit from the market, Rikkard led them westward toward the bars, miniature casino, and brothel.

Several establishments kept the ship going, with a few shadier businesses like the slave trade and illegal booster distribution in the basement. Selene went out of her way to avoid the businessmen involved in those ventures.

They had just reached Radley's when she looked back to find Darius no longer followed. There weren't many places he could have disappeared to, but she had to assume this was part of Rikkard's plan—one he had failed to fill her in on, most likely as punishment for always leaping into things. She had to trust the captain wouldn't get her killed.

Glancing back at Rikkard, she went to point out Darius's absence. Only Rikkard strode across the bar. Instead of trying to blend in like he usually did, he pushed across the grungy bar floor, past a few curious onlookers and stopped close to a man shadowed in the back. While Selene trailed behind more slowly, she tried to get a good look at the cloaked figure. The darkness surrounding him masked his features all too well.

The bar's patrons leered as she stepped inside. The stomach curdling scent of vomit, booze and body odor crawled up her nostrils. She wrinkled her nose.

Most of the customers wore tattered leather and had thick beards. The dim light did little to hide the large guns strapped to their person. Stepping around a group of men with long swords, a large man at the bar with oily black hair and a dirt-covered face winked at her. Her skin crawled and she resisted the urge to shiver. Skirting the bar, she checked on Rikkard. She hoped he wasn't causing trouble before they had a chance to complete their mission.

Rikkard handed the man several credits from beneath his jacket and the cloaked figure disappeared out the back hall. What the hell was he doing? Rikkard started to turn when a rough hand cupped her ass. Heat blossomed in her chest.

Selene spun, grabbing the pervert's wrist and twisting it behind his back. The sharp crack of his bone breaking told her he got the message. The man yowled and struggled. He was several inches taller than her and much bulkier, but she held him with ease.

"You need to learn to *respect* a lady," she hissed. "Touch my ass again, and I'll do much worse than break your wrist."

"Okay, okay," the man gasped through pained breaths. "I'm sorry, let me go."

"And you won't do it again?"

"I won't! I swear it!"

Selene released him. Ignoring the snickers at the surrounding tables as she placed her boot on his behind, she kicked him head first into a nearby table. He crashed into it and toppled onto the wood floor. A few people laughed. She turned and caught Rikkard's gaze. His eyebrow raised, she swore his lips twitched into a smile. This was probably the most amused she had ever seen him. Selene had to resist grinning. As quickly as his smile appeared, it was gone and he turned on his heels, motioning for her to follow.

Rikkard led the way into the back hall. He turned down a long dark corridor with flickering lights and peeling gray wallpaper. They turned a few corners and stopped at an elevator door, rusted to hell and creaking as it ascended. It dinged as it came to a halt, the doors opening to reveal what was once a red upholstered interior. Several men stepped out with two scantily-clad women in tow. They staggered and laughed, brushing past Selene and Rikkard, whiskey heavy on their breath. They didn't give the pair a second glance.

Rikkard stepped into the elevator, but Selene paused, giving it a once over. It groaned under Rikkard's weight.

"Is that thing even safe?" Her stomach churned.

"Since when are you worried about safety?"

"Since now when you asked me to step into that death trap."

"Get in."

"Fine."

Selene stepped inside, and Rikkard punched in some sort of code. The doors closed and they began their descent in silence. While they waited, her nerves prickled. Though she'd had a few fun experiences in Bakura, she wouldn't call it her favorite place in the world. Now here she was descending into its bowels where Aldar knows what awaited them.

Rikkard maintained his usual calm demeanor. She took a deep breath and tried to emulate him and not raise her hand to her gun. She liked to be prepared, but she doubted jumping out with her pistol raised would get her anywhere but a trip to the morgue.

When the doors finally opened, the roar of a hundred voices echoed through the large chamber, crowded with observers. Her eyes went wide. How hadn't they heard the noise from above? The stench of alcohol, animal feces and vomit reached its way up her nostrils and wouldn't let go. She clamped her lips shut.

"You couldn't have warned me to bring something to plug my nose?" she said, a hand flying to her mouth. She held back her gag.

"I didn't know," was all Rikkard said. He stood gazing at her a moment, an odd look in his eyes before he took her hand and led her through the crowd. His touch sent a spark from her fingers to her toes, even if she couldn't feel the heat of his skin through her leather gloves. Her breath caught in her throat and she stared at the back of Rikkard's head while he tugged her forward.

Stunned, Selene let herself be led. The crowd parted to let them through. She mentally slapped herself, repeating again and again that it meant nothing. She could hear Sarah's snickers now. She groaned internally.

Rikkard led her to a set of stairs where he released her hand and motioned her up. Her heart sank to her toes and she tried not to miss the warmth of his hand. They reached the top after a couple bounds, and Selene gawked at the open space below.

This room was *much* bigger than she had expected.

With a full boxing ring in the center, shielded by a metal cage, rows of bleachers rose around the main event on every side. On each sidewall a viewing booth protruded from the concrete, thick bulletproof glass shielding more people leering downward at the travesty below.

Two blood soaked Bengal tigers circled each other in the center ring. They snapped and snarled, ears back, and tails flicking. Their muscles flexed under their dirt-laden fur. Selene gasped as they lunged at one another, batting each other with their claws. One was missing an eye and the other limped from a grievously wounded hind leg. Both were emaciated beyond belief.

Selene moved to rush down the stairs, her hand flying to her gun. Her heart broke as she watched these once beautiful beasts tear each other apart. Rikkard must have anticipated this reaction, because he'd already grabbed her arm before she could step away.

"We have to help them." She turned her gaze on him. Desperation welled inside her chest as she stood locked in Rikkard's surprisingly empathetic blue gaze.

"We will," he said. "But there's a plan, and we need to stick to it."

Selene nodded, trying to rein in her emotions. Her heart swelled, and her fists clenched. Anger stole her breath and pulled her gaze back to the tigers. Removing her hand from her gun, she took a deep, calming breath. *Chill*, she commanded.

"We've done the recon. The intel is good," she said. "Let's put the rest of the plan into action."

"Not yet."

"Not yet?" Selene shot him an irritated look.

"Just wait."

"For what?"

"For this."

Rikkard pulled her into a crouch, body and arms shielding her. A large explosion rocked the arena, silencing the crowd. A *crack* echoed through the chamber. Selene glanced under her protective barrier. People ducked all around. Dust layered the room in a gray haze. Bits of plaster and cement fell from the ceiling in clumps.

Once the dust settled and no further gunfire or explosions rang, Rikkard slowly released her. They both stood, Selene blinking in surprise at the gaping hole in one of the viewing booths.

"Oh," she said. "That is a good plan."

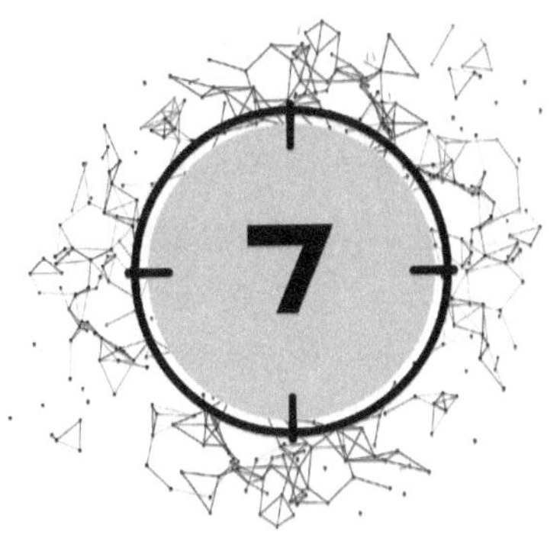

SMOKE WAFTED THROUGH THE ARENA, sending spectators racing for the exit. A cacophony of boots pounded up the steps and elbows jabbed Selene from all sides. A few shrill screams rang out, but most simply ran. The dark smoke settled, revealing a plastic strewn floor and agitated tigers. They no longer circled each other, but instead snarled, ears flat against their heads, hackles raised. As a few of the remaining criminals moved forward to check out the rubble, a limp body careened through the blast hole in the viewing booth.

It thudded on the bleachers below, twisting as it rolled down the last few tiers before slamming against the cement floor. Selene peered over the crowd to get a better look. The man lay lifeless, clad in black Dominion garb. She cursed as another body came flying through, Darius stepping into full view of the spectators' box, or what was left of it. With a laser pistol in one hand and smoke canisters in the other, he winked at Selene and Rikkard. The remaining crowd looked on in curiosity until he tossed the canisters into the open arena.

Lasers fired somewhere in the distance. Darius looked behind him and dove out of sight. The crowd scrambled through the growing smoke, heading for the exits. There had been a lot more to this plan than Selene first realized. She shot Rikkard an irritated glare—this was not the time to get back at her for leaping into things too quickly yesterday.

"Take this," Rikkard said, handing her a small circle of black plastic.

A smoke mask. Placing it against her upper jaw, she pushed her finger into the small indent on the device. A black mask wrapped around her jaw, shielding her mouth and nose from the smoke. It was thin and layered with mesh, allowing her to breathe easily. Selene nodded to Rikkard, who wore the same mask. He moved aside as a few ladies in heels pushed past. Once they were clear of the jostling crowd, he led Selene down onto the next platform. He pulled a gun from his coat and aimed it at the two snarling tigers.

"Wait, Rik—"

One shot, then two shots rang through the room. The noise caught her off guard and she stared in shock as the tigers collapsed onto their sides. An image of two desert coyotes mangled and bloody flashed before her eyes—two creatures Rikkard had taken down in the past when he thought they were beyond saving. Before she could scream at Rikkard, or ask him what the hell he thought he was doing, he grabbed her wrist and pulled her through the thinning crowd. Bodies slammed against her in their desperate attempt to escape. Elbows collided with her side and back over and over. If the Dominion was in Bakura, where criminals paid to keep them away, things were about to become chaotic, and here they were running headlong into the battlefield.

When they finally pushed their way to the main floor, Rikkard released her wrist and sped to the console beside the stage. Selene ducked under the rising bars, checking the pulse of both immobile creatures. A tranquilizer dart was embedded in each of their necks.

"Thank Aldar." She sighed in relief before rising to her feet. From the console Rikkard raised the cage bars, which folded neatly into the ceiling. Once they were gone, he joined her on stage. "I thought you killed them."

Rikkard considered this. "It would have put them out of their misery."

"But you didn't."

"No."

"Good." Selene pulled two thick black plastic squares from her pocket. Tossing them to the side, they quickly unfolded into five-by-five foot hover plates. Together they heaved the first tiger from the floor and onto the hover plate, careful not to touch its wounded shoulder, a deep gash running between thinning hairs.

Blood stuck to her gloves, the fur coarse and brittle. Scars ran back and forth on both, wide and white, too thick to allow the fur to grow back. Whoever had owned these tigers before Bakura hadn't taken good care of them. Selene frowned while loading them onto the black surface, her heart thudding in time with the boots clamoring up the bleachers. They had to get these two to the reserve as quickly as possible if they were to recover properly. Nothing could heal their mental wounds, but hopefully they'd come to trust Aida and her group in time. She couldn't help but think how horrible it would feel to be caged against your will and hurt like this.

An image of the vat in her dreams came to mind. She went cold and tiny pinpricks like needles washed over her skin.

Selene paused mid-lift, staring at the bloodied fur of the second tiger. Her gut twisted. Something told her these dreams were more than nightmares. Somehow she knew they were real. They stuck with her too long to be anything else.

"Selene," Rikkard snapped.

Selene glanced up. Everything was muffled, like the sound had been stolen from the room. Rikkard's lips moved slowly behind his mask. He was saying her name, but she could barely hear it. She didn't know what was happening, but she concentrated on his face, on his eyes—those blue eyes that could pierce her soul.

Taking a breath and shaking her head, sound returned. Selene finished heaving the beast onto the hover plate. The cold washing her skin vanished. Stepping back, she pulled the controller from her pocket and hit the button to raise the safety field around the enclosures.

"Where is your head?" Rikkard asked. She wouldn't actually expect him to look concerned for her, but the look of irritation wasn't helping.

"Forget it," she hissed. "Let's get out of here before we have more soldiers on our hands."

Rikkard nodded, and bounded back over to the console. He keyed in a few commands and the floor began to lower. Rikkard joined her back on the platform.

"The loading bay is below," he explained.

"Convenient." Selene turned the controller in her hands a few times, anticipation clawing at her gut. She was used to being in charge of her own missions and wasn't sure if she liked having the captain boss her around. In most cases she would have already planned out exactly what she was doing and where she was going, but instead she had to follow Rikkard's lead and trust he wasn't leading them into a firefight. Not that she hadn't landed herself in one of those recently.

Once the platform lowered enough for her to see below, she peeked out. The large open hangar was filled with hovercrafts and speeders of all shapes and sizes—none of which were any of theirs. Selene got the distinct impression they would have a hard time getting out of here.

"Hey! There they are!"

Three Dominion soldiers rushed from a back stairwell fifty-feet away. However well Darius's distraction had worked, it hadn't accounted for these guys.

"Looks like it's time to go." Selene pulled her pistols from her belt. Rikkard put a hand over hers and sparks shot up her arm at the touch.

"Go find a ship. Pick the fastest you can find, and get our cargo loaded," he said.

Selene knew the look she gave him was twisted in confusion. She was the gunner. Her aim was far superior to his, and she could have these men off their tail in seconds. Instead, he wanted her to scurry on ahead. She shook her head. This was not the time to question Rikkard's sanity—that would come later.

"All right." Selene holstered one of her pistols and took out her remote. The platform descended painfully slow, creaking as it lowered. She waited for as long as she could, bouncing back and forth on her heels, her eyes darting between the coming Dominion soldiers and the cement floor. With six feet to go, she pushed the button for the hover plates to follow.

"Good luck," Selene said. Rikkard nodded and she leapt from the platform, ducking into a roll to escape injury. The plates zipped after her, catching up easily as she jumped to her feet, already sprinting. Her long legs carried her across the concrete floor and between the rows of ships separated by yellow-painted steel pillars.

From above she'd gotten a decent look at the lay of the land. The ships were set into rows, seemingly arranged by size. Selene let her feet carry her to the furthest aisle. There she was bound to find a cargo speeder.

Keeping her head low and her pistol ready, she weaved through the aisles. Shots rang through the hangar. Energy guns charged and laser fire flashed, sending streaks of blue and red light dancing across the wide-open space. She bit her lip and hoped Rikkard was faring well.

After a full view of the row, there was only one real option—a Dominion cruiser. Sighing in exasperation, Selene stopped at the back cargo door, flipping open the emergency control panel beside the cargo hatch. She took her phone from her pocket and ripped the control panel out of the ship. Dozens of colored wires lay against the metal hull. She pawed through, separating the wires and linking a hard drive attached to her phone's cord. Her system booted. She hoped Rem's device could hack alien technology.

The whine of charging lasers and subsequent fire echoed closer. Selene tapped her fingers impatiently against her thigh as her screen lit, code dancing across it in white and green.

How was Rikkard doing? She hadn't heard his shout, but had

he been hit? An explosion deep inside Bakura rocked the hangar. Dust rained down from the ceiling. Her heart leapt.

"Come on!" Selene slapped the cargo door.

More laser fire, more shouts—but none were Rikkard's.

The type flying across her screen flashed green and a click from the cargo door told her she was in. Relief washed through her. Grinning from ear to ear, Selene stepped back to allow the cargo door to lower. She whistled for Rikkard, hoping he heard and knew she was ready. While her phone could hack most security systems, it would be useless against the control system. Rikkard, however, could hack a control system in thirty seconds flat.

The cargo door hit the cement with a soft bang. She stepped onto its slick surface, looking back down the aisle of ships. Where the hell was Rikkard? She paced the door, shots still firing through the hangar. If they were firing he was alive. But if he didn't get here soon, she'd need another plan.

"Rikkard, you're killing me here." Sweat trickled down her forehead.

She was about to call it when Rikkard rounded the corner, running full tilt, his black pistols glinting in the afternoon light that streamed through the hangar's open hatch. Two soldiers skidded after him, one slipping onto his side while the other charged after Rik. Selene stepped from the ship, pulling out her second pistol and taking aim at the soldiers in pursuit of her boss.

The first shot caught one guy in the leg, and the second hit the other in the side as he scrambled off the ground. Minor enough injuries. A third guard appeared, firing, his shots scorching the ground at Rikkard's feet as he ran. He still had ten yards to go. Selene dodged into the hull as a shot blasted the side of the ship, inches from her face. She leaned out and returned fire.

Rikkard gained the cargo door, panting, the closest pursuing guard three ship lengths away and gaining. "Here." She tossed him the controller for the two hover plates. "Get them inside."

Rikkard complied without question—rare for her boss. The hover plates zipped inside and Rikkard's boots slammed against the metal ramp as he dove further into the ship.

Another shot fired from the Dominion soldiers, narrowly missing her head. Selene ducked behind the cargo wall, charging her guns for a heavier shot.

"Let's go, Rik!" she shouted. The thrum of the propellers and the rising of the ship was his answer.

Grinning, Selene jumped up and fired a few more shots at the advancing soldiers. She raced to the other side of the cargo door, looking for the control panel. Darting between crates, she found it, and slammed her fist against the close command. The door began to rise as the soldiers came into view, but it was too late; they were already in the air. Giving the soldiers below a big grin and a wink, Selene disappeared back into the cruiser, making sure the tigers were secured to the floor before joining Rikkard in the cockpit.

"That was quick." Selene took a seat in the co-pilot's chair.

Rikkard grunted in acknowledgement as he steered the cruiser clear of the bay doors, using an unfamiliar control panel that curved around the inside nose of the ship. Bright afternoon light flooded the small room as they passed the hangar doors.

"Rem is going to have a run for his money when he sees how good at hacking you're getting." Again Rikkard didn't respond, only pulled the mask from his face and discarded it somewhere behind him. Selene shot him a glance before peeling off her own mask. Breathing freely, she sat back, checking the satellite view of their surroundings.

Not a hundred feet from their rear a small platoon of manned Class One speeders flew from the open mouth of the hangar.

"Damn it, no wonder you're so quiet." Selene buckled herself in. She didn't want any more head injuries. "Can you outrun them?"

"I'm not sure."

"Well that's comforting." Selene pulled up the ship roster and checked through their weapons specs. She froze. Foreign lettering accompanied the weapon controls. "Of course we'd pick the transport ship with alien fire power. What am I supposed to do with this?" Selene motioned at the screen full of unfamiliar characters.

"We?" He raised an eyebrow.

"Okay, *I* picked the ship, but you said to choose the fastest, and this was our only option." Selene flicked away the ship roster and pulling up the three-dimensional satellite image of their ship and its pursuers. She zoomed in on the Dominion speeders. "Whoa." She paused, and then zoomed in on the others.

"What?" He glanced at her screen.

"Heavy artillery." She glanced back at him. "These guys were ready. This may be a transport cruiser, but it has some pretty good backup."

"How many?"

"About a dozen."

"Shit."

"I know, right?" Selene double-checked her findings before shutting the image down. Red flashed on Rikkard's control panel—incoming fire. He pulled the ship higher, banking left and right to dodge their shots. "What were these guys doing in Bakura anyway?"

Rikkard shrugged.

She cocked an eyebrow, hoping he didn't notice the sweat trickling down her nose. "You're not curious? They're Dominion soldiers in *Bakura*. This wasn't a raid on crime if they have a transport ship with them."

Rikkard didn't even glance her way; his eyes were glued to the radar scans in front of him. "I don't think we can out-fly them."

"You're serious?"

Just as he was about to confirm that indeed they were doomed, an explosion rocked the ship. Alarms screeched throughout the hull, warning them of a breach. Selene held fast to the dashboard, leaning forward to peer out the window. They were spiraling out of control, diving from the sky. Debris-strewn sand rushed up far quicker than she liked.

"Rik, do something!"

"Hold on!" he shouted.

The sand came up fast, and Selene hoped their new cargo was okay. The hover plate enclosures should keep them safe, but she wasn't sure how bad the damage would be. Glancing back through the curved front windows, Selene's eyes widened as several pod-like shapes flew from the back of their cruiser. She had hardly a second to wonder why. Their ship crashed head first into the desert.

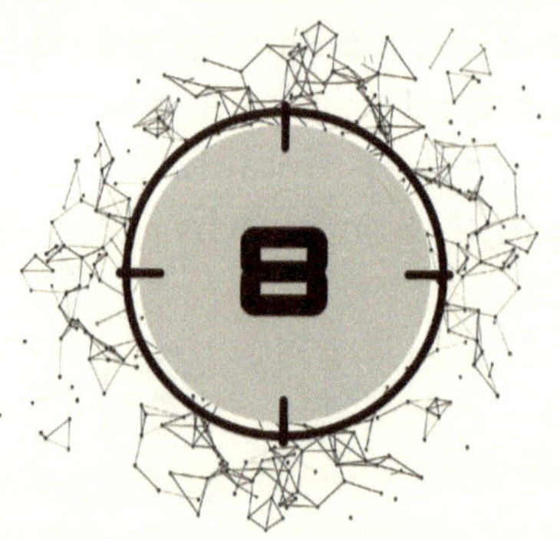

SELENE RETURNED TO CONSCIOUSNESS, DIZZY but alive. When the world came swirling back, it took her a moment to remember what had happened. She vaguely remembered the crash, not the impact, but just before. The sand came up at them, pods flying from a breach in the cargo bay, and the speeders on their radar. Once she had the memories, the pounding in her head pushed forward. Groaning, Selene opened her eyes. The blue lights zipping through the cockpit had winked out—they'd lost power. The rest of the hull seemed mostly fine.

Unbuckling herself, Selene slid out of her seat. She grabbed the dashboard, balancing between the uneven floor and the curved dash. They had crashed at a slant. Great. Selene turned to check on Rikkard. Her heart fluttered in temporary panic. A large gash tore up the side of his face, receding into his hairline. Blood dripped to his chin. Something must have come loose in the crash.

"Rikkard." Selene reached forward and shook one of his shoulders. Her heart leapt into her throat. She'd kill him again if he was dead. "Rikkard, are you dead?" When he didn't answer, she shook harder. The pounding in her ears intensified. "Rik! Come on, don't die on me."

Rikkard groaned much louder than she had when she'd

returned to consciousness. Relief flooded her body, though, from the looks of the blood welling against his collarbone, his headache was going to be a long one.

"Good, you're alive," she said, unable to hold back her smile. "Now get up."

If Rikkard had the energy to glare at her, he didn't bother. Unbuckling himself, he fell forward, pinning her under his weight. Hard muscle pressed against her curves.

"Okay, come on now." She sighed, doing her best to hold him up until he steadied himself. "First time I've ever seen you beaten up, boss. It's a good look on you." This time he did glare. His look of disapproval only reassured her he'd be fine, but she tried not to push him in his delicate state. "Are you good to climb out of here?"

Rikkard nodded before taking a look around the hull. She had a feeling he was looking for what the hell had struck him in the face. "No internal damage."

Selene nodded, concentrating on keeping him upright. "I'm sure the soldiers we stole it from will be happy to hear it." She flushed, all too aware of how close they were. If it weren't for his status as captain, she might spend more time thinking about the solid muscle beneath her fingers. "We should get out of here."

"Agreed." He stepped toward the door, hardly making it two feet before he started sliding to the ground. Rikkard held the captain's chair for support, his head in his other hand.

"Well you're clearly not okay." Selene made her way up the small slope and peeked down the hall. No enemies in sight. "This is the only way out." She turned back and held out her hand for Rikkard. She was pleasantly surprised when he took it. She hadn't been sure if he'd be too proud to accept her aid.

Wrapping his arm around her shoulders, she held him up with one arm and pulled out one of her pistols with the other. If there was a platoon of Dominion soldiers out there, she wasn't about to go down without a fight.

When they reached the rear door, she glanced at her partner, making sure he wasn't about to pass out. He seemed alert enough, his eyes roving and searching for danger, but she untangled herself anyway.

"Wait here," she said.

"Selene—"

She pulled her other gun from her belt, cutting off his protest. The loud charge filled the dry silence. "No time for that. Wait here while I check things out."

Without waiting for an answer, Selene opened the door and slipped inside, letting the door swish closed before she snuck down the short hall and into the cargo hold. The entire back half of the bay had been ripped away, leaving a hole where the doors used to be. Sand spilled through the opening and scorch marks climbed the walls where a fire had whipped up in the blast. Sand appeared to have drowned the flames. Most of the crates had been overturned before or sometime during the crash, their contents strewn across the cargo floor and out onto the sand. Machine guns, assault rifles, and every type of laser gun imaginable littered the hold. Behind the ship lay at least a dozen black metal pods, all eight feet in length.

What were they doing here? She quirked an eyebrow. Rikkard had some explaining to do.

Selene stopped to check on their tiger friends who continued to sleep soundly, held secure by the g-force correction of the hover plates.

A distant explosion pulled her attention from the animals. Forgoing stealth, Selene raced the length of the remaining cargo bay and peered outside. Eight speeders flew through the cloudless blue sky in attack formation. Her heart skipped. But they weren't dive bombing Selene and Rikkard. Instead, they fought a losing battle with a sleek metal colossus, curved on both ends. The abnormally well-equipped salvage ship blasted the Dominion speeders from the sky.

Huge cannons fired from the front and sides of the enormous scrap ship, at least forty-feet in length, the boom breaking the quiet of the desert. Selene blinked in confusion as speeder after speeder crashed in a blaze of fire. She couldn't guess why this salvage ship would be helping them, so instead she returned inside the ship.

"You'll never believe what's going on out there," she called as she opened the door. Rikkard straightened to attention and focused on her with visible effort. Selene had a feeling she'd caught him sleeping standing up. That couldn't be good. "Come on."

Hoisting his arm around her shoulders again, Selene supported the majority of his weight. Rikkard held onto her as much as she held him, his warm, hard body pressing into her side as she walked. Keeping her gun at the ready, Selene led Rikkard outside onto the sand in time to see another two Dominion speeders blown from the sky. Their metal parts scattered over the sand in a hail of steel and plastic. The few remaining speeders retreated in the direction they'd come, leaving Selene and Rikkard staring up at the large ship, which nearly blocked out the sky.

The salvage ship didn't land, simply hovered fifteen feet above the ground. A long set of stairs unfolded from a side port. A large force of forty or so men and women in tattered clothes exited the steel behemoth.

Selene bit her lip, wishing she had tried to escape instead of gawking. "Let me do the talking." Though she used her joking tone of voice, nerves prickled inside her. She didn't like the look of the group coming towards them. They reminded her of the Bakura criminals—grimy, torn clothes, dirt-caked skin and tangled messes of hair. Resisting the urge to crinkle her nose as they surrounded them, Selene stayed standing tall, her pistol charged and ready.

"Pirates," Rikkard hissed under his breath.

Selene caught his eye. He was serious.

If these were pirates, that meant only one thing—trouble.

As soon as the lot finished encircling them, the charge of laser pistols littered the quiet. More than twenty barrels pointed their way. Selene tried her best to ignore them. They were only grunts trying to intimidate for their master.

A tall man approached through the parting crowd, with dark

skin and long black dreads laced with beads, metals, and bits of green feathers. He was well built, and dressed to show it off, his gray muscle shirt dipping to his ribs. Though the man appeared to be in his late thirties—more than a decade older than her clone—he was quite handsome. It occurred to her that he *chose* to appear this way. He was a clone, which was evident from his poreless skin, and could make the choice to appear however he pleased, just like the rest of them.

"What do we have here?" the man growled, flashing his white teeth in a large grin. One hand rested on his belt and the other clutched a black laser pistol. "A couple of smuggling *rats*?" The group around them chuckled. "You shouldn't steal shit you can't keep your hands on, *pretty*." His amber gaze regarded her with interest.

Selene resisted the urge to point her gun at him. Her snappy attitude on the other hand, would not be contained. "If you think we're the rats, you should really take a look around. You run with *a lot* of them."

"Spunky." The man grinned. "I like my ladies feisty."

"Of course you do," she said, her tone flat.

"Why don't you be a good girl and hand me that gun of yours? Wouldn't want you getting hurt now would we?" He extended a hand, his fingers covered in silver and gold rings.

"What on earth makes you think I'm a good girl?" Selene flicked her power output higher and the energy charged loudly.

The pirate captain's grin dropped as each of his men pressed their guns forward.

"Now, now, let's play nice." He motioned for everyone to lower their weapons. Selene glanced at Rikkard, surprised he wasn't chiming in. He glared straight ahead. Once the pirates lowered their weapons, Selene holstered hers. "The name is Captain Erock. I'm a very generous man, young lady, so why don't we make a deal?"

"What kind of deal?" she asked. Rikkard squeezed her shoulder. Selene dutifully ignored him.

"You have something we want. A lot of *expensive* somethings."

Erock grinned. "In exchange for your lives, I'll take them off your hands. You don't have a ship to bring them home anyway, now do you?" Selene narrowed her eyes.

"Doesn't sound like much of a deal to me. You get all the money."

The man tilted his head back and laughed. "Of course we do! We're the pirates!" Erock settled his gaze back on her, his pupils slit like a cat's. Selene raised an eyebrow. An interesting aesthetic mod. She tried not to shift uncomfortably when he stepped closer, his breath hot between them. "We take those pods and make millions. *You* can keep your lives. We won't kill you and take what we want. I'll even throw in a speeder to get you two out of the desert. How does that sound?"

"You want the Dominion after you *that* badly?"

"I welcome the challenge."

Rikkard squeezed tighter. Selene shot him an irritated glance. His cold eyes bored into hers, telling her not to make the deal. It struck her then that Rikkard had known about the cloning pods. He didn't want to give them up. The Dominion had been there for Aldar knows what reason, but somehow Rikkard knew about it, and staged the tiger operation to cover his tracks. Was he even going to tell their crew about the millions he would have made?

Gritting her teeth, Selene looked back at Erock. She wasn't about to get killed over pods Rikkard had lied about and nearly gotten them killed over.

"Deal," she said. "With one condition."

"Unless that condition is a night in bed with yours truly, then I'll have to decline." Erock looked her up in down in a way she'd normally shoot someone for. "I don't think you're in any position to add conditions, *pretty*."

Selene bit her tongue against a comeback. Instead she raised her chin and looked him sternly in the eye. "There are two Bengal tigers in that cargo bay. They are currently unharmed, aside from the injuries they sustained prior to our care. My only condition is that you load them up and take them to a veterinary specialist. That's all. If they ask you for any cash, let them know they can ask Selene next time I'm in."

"*Selene*, eh?" Erock purred out her name. She winced. Her fingers twitched toward her gun. "I'll agree to your condition since you gave me your name." Selene started to sigh in relief when he continued, "Now I'll be able to find you again."

Eyes wide, Selene fought back the flush rising to her cheeks. He laughed.

"Not creepy at all," she muttered.

The rest of his crew joined in, even as Erock motioned them all to work. The crowd slowly dispersed, some heading toward the pods, while others returned to the ship. While they were gone, Selene checked on Rikkard, who sagged in defeat, barely holding on to consciousness.

When she looked back up, Captain Erock held his hands out to display the Class One speeder in front of him. It was modified with no roof, only a screen to block out the sand. In this style two could fit on its back, though it would be a tight squeeze with her *and* Rikkard. She'd only ever seen one similar in junkyards— remnants of past centuries.

"*This* is the speeder?" Selene asked.

"I personally improved upon this one." He wiggled his eyebrows at her.

Selene didn't bother concealing her eye roll. The man stepped forward and offered to shake her hand. She did very briefly before helping Rikkard onto the speeder.

"I also got one of my men to bring this down," Erock said.

The captain produced a small injector and plunged it into Rikkard's thigh before Selene could stop him. "This booster should keep him awake for the return trip home. Wouldn't want your man falling from the sky." Erock grinned.

"*Thanks*," Selene snapped.

Rikkard blinked to life, holding tightly to the seat in front of him. Whatever Erock had given him had done the trick. Good. She had a bone to pick with him. Selene swung her leg over the seat. The machine felt awkward in her hands, even more so than most. She had to lean forward to reach the steering, which protruded from both sides of the control panel. At least the rest of the dash was familiar.

"You okay back there?" She glanced back at Rikkard, who was pushed up against her back. This speeder was not meant for two.

"I'll be seeing you around *Selene*." Erock gave her a wink and his signature grin. Selene had a feeling he had helped them simply to do just that—see her again.

Revving the engine, Selene flipped on a pair of goggles hanging from the dash. She handed a second pair to Rikkard.

"I hope not!" She pushed the engine hard for takeoff. Rikkard grabbed her waist, fingers locking against her sides, most likely fearing for dear life and still in shock from whatever adrenaline booster Erock had given him. Erock's laugh drowned in the wind as they climbed higher.

She took a moment to get used to the controls of the speeder. She adjusted her handholds, brushing sand and dust from the control panel. She keyed in autopilot and set their destination for Bakura. The Dominion soldiers should be long gone by now, giving them easy access to their crew's ship, but on the off chance they weren't, they'd have to case the place for a while.

Clear of the pirate ship and its occupants, Selene turned to have a look at her boss. Eyebrows scrunched together, lips turned in a frown, Rikkard looked utterly sour. It reminded her she had questions for him.

"What the hell were those pods?" She narrowed her eyes at him, "and why did we have them?"

Staring back at her with cold blue eyes, Rikkard shrugged.

"Did you set this all up?" She paused. "Rikkard, did you know those Dominion soldiers would be there? Did you know I'd pick their ship?" He didn't answer, but he didn't deny it either. "What the hell were you thinking? Those were clone pods weren't they? Didn't you figure they'd have a small armada guarding them? Did you stop to think what a horrible idea this was? We could have *died* in that crash."

Rikkard gazed away. "How the hell do you think we make our money? It's not by saving your *damn* animals."

His words sent a knife through her heart. "So you think I'm an idiot? That I'd never find out? Do the others even know?"

Again, he shrugged.

"This has been going on the whole time hasn't it? Every creep you meet in a back room is really there to trade with you isn't he? You just don't bring the protos, or pods, or whatever else you're slinging, so you don't get caught. That's lovely. Real nice, Rik."

Rikkard met her gaze levelly. She had to restrain herself from throwing him off the speeder. "What do you want me to say? That it isn't true?" He raised a condescending eyebrow.

He had used her. That was the only explanation. He used her to get those pods and Aldar only knew what else. He'd been her mentor since the day they met, and it was all for show. Selene couldn't trust him, not anymore.

"You're such an ass," she hissed, turning in her seat. Grabbing hold of the controls, she pushed them ahead at full speed. Selene didn't want to spend one more second with someone who could so easily lie to her.

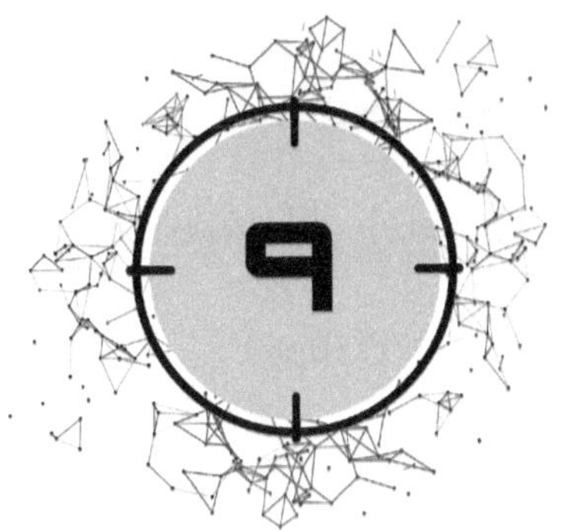

"WHERE THE HELL DID THEY go?" Selene gazed around the spot where their huge cargo ship used to be. They'd landed in Bakura after carefully staking it out for half an hour. When it was clear the Dominion was gone, their awkward silence ended on the deck of the naval ship.

"*Rem,*" Rikkard growled, not bothering to hide his irritation. Flicking on his comset, Rikkard radioed their resident tech expert. "Rem, where is the ship?"

Selene could imagine the conversation on the other end, the confusion, the whispers, and the excuses.

When he was done, Rikkard continued, "Get back here now and you'll see what I mean." He paused. "Yes, gather the others as well." Pause. "Is Kayl with you? No he would not go off with the ship. Rem, get everyone here *now.*" Hanging up the line, Rikkard shoved the comset back in his pocket.

Normally, Selene might approach him, ask him what the deal was, but right now she didn't care. Her chest tightened every time she looked at Rikkard, betrayal souring her stomach. More than ever she wanted to punch the man, if not beat the hell out of him. It was hard to believe he could lie to their entire crew about something he had been doing for years. When she originally joined and they made the switch from smuggling protos to animals, he'd seemed fine with it. It had given everyone purpose.

Sighing, Selene folded her arms across her chest, avoiding his gaze and staring at the empty spot where their ship used to be. It only took a few minutes for the others to arrive, and when they did, they all gawked.

"Where did it go?" Sarah blinked wide-eyed at the empty space.

"How do you lose a ship that big?" Darius looked at Rem. "That's almost impressive."

"It wasn't *me!*" Rem cried, throwing his hands in the air.

"Then who was it?" Darius asked.

"Did you check on Kong?" Rikkard's icy stare settled on Rem. The white haired boy blanched and stared back guiltily. "Find out where the ship is," he commanded. "We'll go find something to get us there."

"Rikkard! What happened to your head?" Sarah gasped, that motherly instinct coming out in a flash. She closed the distance between them and began investigating the wound, fingers pulling away his blood caked hair.

"I'm fine," he said.

"He really isn't," Selene said. "I'll get us a ship. You take care of him."

"Will do." Sarah nodded and Selene took off deeper into Bakura.

When Selene returned twenty minutes later, she'd purchased the only ship available for a half decent price. Most of the hangar was empty after the afternoon's events, leaving them few options. A bunch of criminals weren't about to stick around when the Dominion had come to ruin the party.

Docking the old hovercraft, Selene put it on autopilot before lowering the rear door for the crew to pile in. The craft was around the same size as the one she'd taken on her last mission to the New Manhattan labs. It was a decent size, with a small kitchen and a few bunks to rest in. It had the necessary supplies for their next trip, so Selene had to hope no one would put up too much of a fuss, even though it wouldn't be the fastest. Coming out to greet the others, she could already hear their sarcastic complaints before they uttered a word.

"*This* is the ship you acquired?" Rikkard asked. Instead of being slumped against Sarah, he stood tall—Sarah must have given him something.

"Yep, deal with it boss," Selene said, not ready to deal with his crap when she was already mad at him. "It's all that's left."

Rikkard grumpily climbed aboard, followed by the others, including Kayl. Where he had come from, she couldn't be sure, and didn't bother asking. He was always off doing Rikkard's bidding. Selene closed the rear door and joined the crew in the cockpit.

"So where did Kong take the ship?" she asked.

Rem sighed loudly and brought up a three dimensional map from his phone. He had it jacked into the system console, giving him a much further range than the small device could pull up on its own. Rem motioned to their position in Bakura, then flipped across the screen until they landed many, many miles away, close to the New Manhattan Outskirts.

"It'll take hours to fly there in this thing," Rem groaned.

"You should have thought about that before leaving Kong *alone* on our ship," Rikkard snapped.

"Down boy," Selene said. "Just get us there Rem. Preferably before Kong gets himself into trouble."

"As for you…" Sarah narrowed her eyes at Rikkard, tilting her pointed chin up. "Now that we have supplies, I need to fix that head wound and you need to get some rest." Darius and Rem poorly held back their grins of amusement while Sarah bossed around the captain, leading him into the kitchen. "Kayl bring my medical kit!" Kayl sighed and followed.

"We should take their lead. Let's get some rest," Selene said. "Who knows what shenanigans Kong has gotten himself into."

Rem and Darius nodded in agreement.

"Set course for the Outskirts, it's going to be a long trip."

Selene awoke not long into the night. She held her pillow in a death grip, and may or may not have stabbed it a few times with her knives. Judging from the carnage, she guessed she had. She blinked in confusion through the dim light. Feathers tickled her nose. Covering her nose so she wouldn't sneeze, she pushed away the tattered remains and crawled out of her cramped bunk.

Crossing the room as quietly as she could, she pulled on her boots and slipped into the hall, gently closing the door behind her. Leaning her back against it, she closed her eyes. What had she been dreaming about that was so traumatizing she'd stab the hell out of an innocent pillow? Selene shook her head. She had to be losing her mind.

"Why are you up?"

Selene started, her right hand flying to the gun at her hip. In the captain's chair, staring at her with a raised eyebrow was Rikkard. He had a small bandage on his cheek and circles under his eyes. Apparently no one was getting any rest tonight.

"Couldn't sleep." She shrugged. Without anywhere else to go, Selene trudged the length of the short hall, seating herself in the co-pilot's chair. She checked a few radars and their three dimensional surroundings before shutting them down and sighing. Leaning back in her chair, she looked beyond the helm of their ship into the dark night sky. Stars flickered above, winking at her in their endless mischief.

After a few minutes of silence, Selene's gaze slid from the view and back to Rikkard, who stared lost in thought, at the control board in front of him. His fingers tapped absently on his thigh. His angular jaw, curve of his nose, and the depth of his cheekbones were highlighted by the cold moonlight. She'd been staring longer than she should have when his blue eyes found hers. While she'd been taking in his view, she'd suddenly remembered why she was angry with him. Tearing her gaze from his, she faced the sky again. At least the stars couldn't lie to her.

"What is it?" he asked.

"Nothing." She promptly folded her arms. She didn't mean to sound like a child, but after a moment she realized that's how she must be coming off. Her chest burned with both irritation and embarrassment. "Just thinking."

Rikkard didn't need to ask any questions; instead he prompted her with an eyebrow.

She paused. Selene didn't know how to put her thoughts into words without sounding overly naive. "You've been doing the protos, or pods or whatever behind my back this entire time haven't you?" She kept her voice even. She didn't want to yell at him, or punch him (as much). She wanted answers.

"Yes." He hesitated, but at least he admitted it this time.

"You make a lot off of them don't you?"

Rikkard shrugged.

"That's where our money all comes from isn't it? The money we make off the animals barely makes a dent." She didn't need to ask the question, she knew it was true. It had to be. What they made off her creature compassion was hardly anything in comparison to what he'd make off of even one pod. It would make enough to keep them going for years, if not retire. "So what, do you just pocket all the extra money?"

"It goes back into the ship mostly."

"Why do you bother with the animals then?" She sighed. She felt at a loss in this conversation. There was so much she had yet to think of.

Rikkard didn't answer at first, only looked at her long and hard. He was trying to tell her something in that gaze. After a long minute, when he realized she wasn't going to get it, he sighed loudly and pushed a hand through his thick dark hair.

"I do it for you."

"You what?" Her jaw dropped. "Why?"

He leveled her another irritated look. "Because it's what you want. The protos make us money, but you give us a purpose."

"Oh." That was the most profound thing she could think to say. Selene had never thought of it like that. Even though it was just as dangerous to smuggle protos and pods, she couldn't really blame him for it if he was doing it to keep the crew going. It took her a minute for the realization to come to her, but if Rikkard was doing this all for her, it could only mean one thing.

Did the boss actually care about her?

"You should go back to bed."

Selene slowly nodded, a bit stunned. Her mind swirled with possibilities. She stood without a word and made her way back to the bunks. Once she settled in, she clutched her defeated pillow to her chest and stared at the ceiling. Full thoughts refused to form, so she closed her eyes. Eventually she found sleep.

When Selene awoke the next morning, she was happy to find she'd slept through the night without any startling dreams. Even in the unfamiliar bunk, she felt rested and alive. It had taken the entire evening and through the night until dawn to find their cargo ship. Unfortunately, when they did finally stumble upon it, half the ship was buried by sand dunes.

"Really?" Rem sighed, tapping his fingers on the control dash. They were the only two awake to observe the mess. She wasn't sure when, but eventually Rikkard had gone to bed as well.

"Really," Selene concurred. "How long do you think it'll take to dig that out?"

"A long time."

"I thought as much."

"Should we wake everyone?"

"Probably. We'll have to check for Kong inside."

"I'll get them." Rem rose and stretched, cracking his neck and fingers before proceeding down the hall. He hastily slammed open the door to the bunks before shouting for everyone to rise. Loud grumbling ensued followed by a smack.

"Hey!" Rem squeaked. "That was so unnecessary!"

"As was waking me up," Darius groaned.

"The boss lady told me to!"

"Boss lady?" Rikkard asked.

"We found the ship," Rem explained.

"Already?" Sarah yawned. "What time is it?"

"Early." Kayl grumbled something Selene couldn't hear.

"Up and at 'em!" Selene shouted. "You'll all want to see this."

When the crew finally assembled in the cockpit, each of them took turns glaring at the sunken ship before puzzled looks took over. Of course there was first the aggravation of knowing how much work it'd be to *unbury* the ship. Then there was the confusion of how Kong managed this in the first place.

"That gorilla is baffling sometimes." Rem tapped in a few commands to lower the ship. They began their descent, landing gently in the sand.

"Shouldn't have left him alone that long," Selene said.

"I told you so." Sarah smiled.

"I know, I know. Give me an earful later. Let's make sure Kong is still on board before we play the blame Rem game."

Rem stood, and led them all from the ship. Warm sand encased Selene's feet, and the brilliant light of morning became even more agonizing. Trudging through the desert, they worked their way to the base of the cargo ship.

"How are we supposed to reach that door?" Sarah pointed upward. Ten feet above their heads was the rear access port. If they couldn't get to it, they'd be digging through sand until they found another.

"Perseverance." Selene grinned.

"You have a plan?" Rem asked.

"'Course I do." Selene took Darius' arm and positioned him under the door before she gracefully scrambled onto his shoulders.

"You're a lot heavier than you look," Darius grunted, but supported her legs so she wouldn't fall.

"It's all the guns!" Selene flushed, glaring down at him.

"Nice ass though." Darius grinned up at her.

Selene reached up, probing the hot metal door until it realized she was there and swooshed open. "Got it!" She hooked her arms over the ledge and pulled herself up. She didn't bother with the graceful climb she'd done before, and instead used Darius's head as a stepping ladder. He grumbled, but probably knew he deserved it. Once she was in, it was a simple task to get some rope from a storage locker and throw it down.

Ten minutes later and they were all inside.

It only took them another twenty to figure out Kong was

nowhere to be found.

"Figures that ape would skip out after he realized how much trouble he'd be in." Kayl paced the room.

"You really should blame Rem for this one, dear," Sarah said, a flash of amusement in her eyes. Kayl stopped beside her, sighed and rested a hand on his wife's shoulder. Sarah smiled and leaned her head against his arm.

"We are playing the blame Rem game!" he groaned. "I knew it!"

"Let's calm down and get a plan together." Rikkard motioned for them all to sit. They convened in the dining hall, conveniently the center most point of the ship. "Now, let's think. Where could Kong have gone?"

They all paused in thought. There wasn't much around but desert.

"Maybe he wandered into town," Sarah suggested.

"Isn't there a *nat* town a few miles from here?" Rem asked.

"There is." Kayl confirmed with a swift nod of his pointed chin.

"He may have headed that way then," Rikkard said. "We'll form two teams. One to excavate the ship, the other to go after Kong." His gaze hesitantly slid towards Selene, who shrugged and nodded. "Selene, Sarah and I will go in town to search. The rest of you, have fun."

Selene glanced at Rikkard, wondering if he was making a joke. When no one laughed, she shrugged it off and stood, happy to be free of the grunt work. While the others groaned in unrealistic agony, Selene waved them off and joined her two partners. It made sense that Kong would head into town to find something to do. If he wasn't having fun somewhere, he generally moved onto the next best thing. The only issue heading into this particular town was that it was a *nat* town—a town made up of natural humans, some of the only ones left. They weren't generally a friendly bunch, as Julian had reminded her at the reserve. She doubted they'd be happy to find two clones and an alien walking into their midst.

"Is this a *nat* only town?" she asked.

Rikkard pulled up some data on his phone before answering. "No. I believe it used to be, but it looks like they have a booster store now." He leaned over to show both women the photo.

Typically, when the Aldar Dominion wanted to modernize a town, they started with a booster store, giving the area new commerce and a reason for clones to visit. The booster store was made completely from glass, large on the bottom with a spire leading to an observation deck above. There were gardens and other pretty things up there, but what really caught her attention was its height. The highest point had to be at least five stories up. From there they'd be able to see the entire surrounding area—including their missing gorilla.

"That's where we'll go," she said.

"The store?" Rikkard raised an eyebrow until he caught her meaning. "Good plan."

"We'll have to blend in with the townsfolk," Sarah added, clapping her hands together. She loved a change of pace and a chance to dress up. This wasn't the first time Selene and Sarah infiltrated a Dominion operation. "If there are Dominion soldiers guarding the store, they'll pick up on anyone who stands out."

"And no energy weapons." Selene leaned back in her seat. The last thing she wanted was to start another shootout. But on the other hand, she also needed to get up there and see where Kong had gone.

"I have a few old school guns locked away. You can use those," Rikkard said.

Selene was getting the distinct impression he was trying to suck up. Narrowing her eyes in suspicion, Selene accepted anyway. She wasn't about to go into a Dominion run building without firepower.

"We should pick up some vehicles in town as well." They both looked at Sarah, who smiled from ear to ear. Her protruding cheekbones flushed lilac. "If we want to blend in, we can't be driving in Class Twos." She winked.

They both agreed.

"Let's get ready and meet at the hangar in ten," Rikkard said.

"You got it." Selene and Sarah nodded.

Riding into town on an old-fashioned jeep, Selene was reminded of how long it had been since their civilization had taken a turn. Instead of fossil fuel, most of their transportation ran on wind and solar power. Some utilized alien technology like city patrol crafts and Aldar weaponry, but most used simple clean energy. This jeep on the other hand, was stuck in the Stone Age. It bumped along over the sand covered road, wheezing in the heat.

Rikkard sat beside her, eyebrows scrunched in irritation. He didn't like the car any more than she did. While they took the jeep, Sarah decided on an old model speeder fit for one. It reminded her faintly of the one Captain Erock had given her.

While the boss drove, Selene took in the landscape and the heat. Where she was usually clothed in a temperature regulated suit, today she couldn't stand out quite so much. Stuck in a pair of denim shorts, a thin plaid cotton vest and a white tank top, Selene felt like an eyesore now more than ever. Even with her natural hair down, thrashing in the wind, and black shades to hide her foreign, vivid green eyes, Selene felt like a beacon of irregularity. She couldn't imagine any Dominion soldiers wouldn't see through the disguise. Even if there were clones around, there probably weren't many the soldiers didn't recognize in a town like this one. Her insides churned.

"When we arrive, you should head in with Sarah alone."

Though her gaze had been riveted on the landscape, Rikkard's voice brought her back to the present. He glanced at her twice to make sure she'd heard.

"What about you?" Selene couldn't help her suspicion. If Rikkard could lie to her for three years, who's to say he couldn't take off on them now?

"I'll wait outside," he said.

"Why?"

Rikkard shot her a look. He didn't like to be questioned. "I'll stick out. You and Sarah could pass as tourists."

Selene took a moment to think this over. Her gaze roamed his bare forearms, taking in his thick muscles and tattoo-ridden biceps. Between her, Sarah, and Rikkard, she had to admit Rikkard would stick out the most. He looked like a criminal, dressed in black, a gun hanging from his belt.

"Fine," she agreed.

They lapsed into silence, Selene watching the downtrodden buildings pass them by, while Rikkard watched the bumpy road ahead.

When the booster store finally came into view, Selene was racked with sweat and nerves.

"How do people live like this?" she groaned, mostly to herself.

"Like what?" Rikkard glanced over.

"In this heat."

Selene looked over in time to see an amused smile flick across Rikkard's face. It was there and gone so quickly she couldn't be sure if it had been a trick of the light. She didn't have time to dwell on it. They pulled to a stop in the busy booster store parking lot.

Several similar vehicles sat on the black asphalt. Natural-born teenagers milled in and out of the store. As expected, two Dominion soldiers stood with energy rifles at the entrance. Selene took a steadying breath. Here goes nothing.

Trying to appear casual, Selene dismounted the jeep, giving a little wave goodbye to Rikkard, who remained completely straight-faced. She smiled.

When Selene turned back around, Sarah waved from across the lot. She jogged to meet her by the main entrance, sweat slicking her back in the blistering heat. They linked arms, and Sarah took the lead.

"Can you believe this unyielding heat?" Sarah groaned, plastering on a fake smile. Selene emulated her best friend, smiling and laughing.

"It's *unbearable!*" Selene agreed. Her gut somersaulted as they approached the alien guards. Their bulbous eyes were covered by black shades, and sweat stood out on their pale skin.

"I can't believe you talked me into leaving the city today," Sarah continued. "Worst decision *ever!*"

Selene held her breath, while Sarah flashed a dazzling smile at the soldiers. The guards nodded, but beyond that paid them no attention as they passed. Air whooshed from her lungs as they slipped inside. Glorious air conditioning assaulted her skin.

"Wonderful," Selene moaned, smiling as they continued past two tall glass slabs, presumably energy detectors. Sarah pulled her through and into the main part of the store.

From the outside, the booster store appeared to be made of glass and mirrors. From the inside, a plethora of colors, tables, games, shelves, and people, littered the store. Humans of all shapes and sizes roamed, including clones and a few aliens. Selene heaved a sigh of relief after spotting them. Even Sarah visibly relaxed, a real grin replacing her fake one. They exchanged smiles and played the part of tourists. Though there were plenty of booster stores in the cities, city-folk still liked to head into the Outskirts to see what life in the desert was all about.

Outside the booster store, the Outskirts were nothing like the new-age establishment. Impoverished, an old town half-submerged in waves of sand, the Outskirts were the slums of New Manhattan. The booster store was a way of forgetting all that, drawing young *nats* into the clone-fold. Selene shook her head.

They wandered around for quite some time, chatting with one another and a few other tourists at a rainbow counter with free samples. Each booster could temporarily change the color of one's skin. The small pills glittered blue, red and purple. Two of the tourists, both teenage girls, tossed back a capsule. Within seconds their skin changed from dark brown to iridescent blue. They both shrieked in delight. Selene and Sarah laughed, and said their goodbyes before picking a booster at random. It was time to get the job done.

Both ladies proceeded to the checkout. After paying with her credits, Selene led the way to the back stairs. They'd only be allowed to take them inside, so Selene swallowed back a small black capsule with bits of green glitter. Selene had never found boosters effective, and chose a night vision booster.

The drugs were mostly used by *nats*, and clones. Aliens were generally unaffected by them, while the others enjoyed them as cheap temporary boosts, instead of having to pay for the entire upgrade on their next clone, which if they modded like most, would have to be replaced after half a decade. Boosters could produce anything from enhanced strength, to rainbow skin. They were used in all sorts of capacities, from the mundane to the criminal. Most of the stores had safe places for civilians to hang out if they were so inclined. Though rare, it was a good area to be in case an allergic reaction occurred.

"Let's head upstairs," Selene said.

"I don't think we've been under scrutiny," she agreed. "Let's go."

Leading the way, Selene took them to the elevator. The large glass case was stationed in the far wall, allowing a three sixty view of the store and the wasteland outside.

Several floors later, they emerged into the sun once more. A warm breeze ruffled her hair and slicked her skin with sweat. Selene sighed. The air-conditioning couldn't last forever.

Half a dozen couples sat around the platform, some eating lunch from a small stand beside the elevator, while others tested their newfound abilities. Two more Dominion guards stood watch, rifles held lazily in their arms. They gazed around the deck periodically, but mostly kept to themselves. It had clearly been a long time since they saw any action.

"We've got to be able to see Kong from here," Sarah gasped, leaning over the railing, their only safeguard against a long drop.

"Definitely." Selene stepped up beside her. The debris covered wasteland fell away in every direction. Heat rose from the sand and blurred the horizon.

"You know I always thought it was cute how you and Rikkard adopted Kong." Sarah nudged her elbow, winked and flashed a knowing smile. Selene narrowed her eyes at the woman. She didn't like where this was going. "What happened between you two on your last mission? You seemed a bit icier than usual to our dear old captain."

"Honestly, he's been lying to us this whole time about a lot, and I found out the hard way." Her fingers wrapped around the cold metal safety railing, her knuckles white.

"You found out about the protos didn't you?" Sarah smiled sheepishly.

"Protos?" Selene blinked at her.

"It's hard keeping those things from your wife," she explained. Kayl had been around since day one, so Selene had to assume he'd been in on it since before she dropped into their lives. What had the smugglers been like before she arrived? Had Kayl been happier without her around? "Fight or not though, passion makes for a good couple!"

"Wipe that wicked grin off your face." Selene glared.

"So you're telling me you've never thought about it?"

"Well..." Selene paused, heart thumping loudly in her ears. She twisted her lip between her teeth, while Sarah gazed at her expectantly. "I suppose I have. It's just hard to picture Rikkard caring about anyone but himself." The previous night's conversation came to mind. He claimed he was doing the protos, gambling with his life and his money, for her. Even though she'd always seen Rikkard as a frosty grump of a man, he did care about someone. Maybe even her. Her heart raced.

"True." Sarah leaned her cheek against her hand. "But you never know. He does treat you a bit better than everyone else. I'd say that's caring... for Rikkard at least."

Selene shrugged. "Maybe. We'd never have something like you and Kayl, though." The couple had always been so close, always at each other's side, backing the other up. It was *so* clear that they loved one another. Selene couldn't fathom a relationship like that with Rikkard.

Sarah laughed. "Every relationship has its own rhythm."

"You're right." Selene smiled and stepped further onto the platform, ready to move on from this conversation. She'd have plenty of time to gossip with Sarah later.

From the top of the tower the desert fell away for miles. The small town circled them—houses, bars, and shops—the usual things. Sand dunes rose as far as the eye could see. New Manhattan was a faint shadow on the horizon. The city was elegant in white, stunning in the morning sun. Everything was clear from here: blue skies, and not a cloud in sight. Selene smiled, until she finally caught sight of that troublesome ape.

"There." She pointed to the east. Kong wrestled with a large black dog behind a small grocery shop. "Looks like he's making friends."

"That silly boy will never learn." Sarah laughed and motioned Selene back to the elevator. Selene followed.

They stepped inside the glass box, Sarah hitting the key for the only other available floor—ground. The doors slid toward one another. Inches apart, a gloved hand whipped out, holding the door open. Selene started and two Dominion soldiers peeked inside.

One held a comset to his mouth. "We've got them."

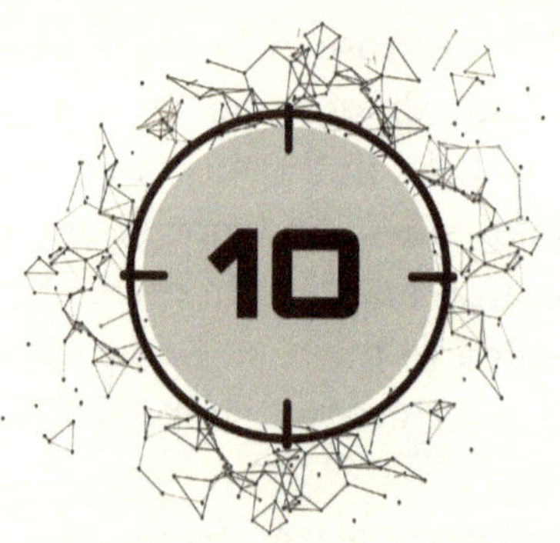

REACTING ON INSTINCT, SELENE SLAMMED her boot-clad foot into the guard's face. He fell back, blood gushing from his nose. The doors closed tightly before he could recover. Selene took a deep breath as her heart sped. Shit. Why now?

Taking out the old fashioned gun tucked in the band of her shorts, she checked the clip. Full. Good. She clipped off the safety. Both women glued themselves to the sides of the elevator as it began its lazy descent. Sarah met her eyes, her forehead creased with worry.

"As soon as that door opens, there will be a long counter on our left." Selene shifted to watch the door intently. Sweat built on her brow and goose bumps ran rampant over her arms. "I'll cover you while you get behind it."

"Understood." Sarah nodded. They both kept their guns at the ready.

There could only be two reasons why the Dominion wanted them—either they caught Rikkard and figured out who he'd arrived with, or they realized that Selene and Sarah were packing heat. What other option was there?

The elevator slowed to a halt, level with the main floor. The doors dinged open. Selene peeked into the open. Several aliens clad in black Dominion uniforms held white laser rifles pointed their way. Selene swallowed.

It was now or never.

Selene squeezed the trigger. The loud bang of the gunshot rang in her ears. Several civilians screamed, eyes wild with panic as they leapt for the exit. Terror caught like wildfire. She shot again. More screams rose with each empty shell that hit the ground.

Sarah rushed for the counter, bent low, while Selene provided cover fire. A sea of bodies pushed from the large room in every direction, a distracting flurry of colors. Sarah reached the counter, ducking behind before leaning out. The beautiful alien woman squeezed off a shot.

It was her turn.

Selene leapt from the elevator, taking two soldiers in the shoulder with her bullets before sliding in beside Sarah.

There were a dozen guards on the floor with at least two busy evacuating civilians. She'd taken down two already, so that left them with eight. The rest had their energy weapons trained on their hiding place. If they weren't quick, they'd get a limb blasted off, or worse.

"Did you see any other exits?" Selene leaned around the corner of the counter to lay some suppressive fire. The soldier she aimed at ducked behind a metal pillar, her bullet grazing his protruding arm. Blue blood spattered the tile. Selene didn't want these soldiers getting any closer.

"One on the far side," Sarah said, her gaze wandering around the room briefly before settling back on Selene. Sweat beaded on her forehead. "I don't think we can make it. Our best bet is the front entrance."

"Of course it is. Just our luck."

The shrill charge of an energy rifle ushered her back. A hot blast flashed millimeters from her nose. Her heart leapt into her throat. Too close. Sliding away from the right side of the counter, Selene motioned for Sarah to move along it. Sarah nodded and ducked until she reached the end. Once she was at the other end, Sarah signed her plan, the same way Kong used to communicate.

Two at the door. Civilians almost evacuated. We need to go now.

Selene nodded in understanding and rushed to join her. Her heart pounded loudly in her ears. Once they were together, Selene leapt out and took aim at the soldiers. Sarah joined her, firing off shot after shot. They took two in the gut and one in the chest before ducking behind a large shelf of boosters.

"These guys must not have seen any action in some time." Selene flashed an adrenaline filled grinned at her comrade. Her heart beat wildly.

"Their aim is terrible," Sarah agreed.

Glancing up at the shelf concealing them, an idea sparked. "If we can lure them in front of this, we should be able to push it onto the closest two and make a run for the door." Selene checked her ammo. She only had a few bullets left. "I've got an extra clip. It should be enough."

"All right." Sarah positioned herself to the right side of the shelving unit.

When they were both in position, they fired at the remaining Dominion soldiers. Energy shots went off, burning holes in the wall, as well as their shelf shield. Melting plastic filled the air with a pungent odor. Selene wrinkled her nose. The soldiers closed in, stepping within range of their protection. Selene signaled for Sarah to join her. They pushed the shelf on top of the two men.

It clattered to the floor, burying the guards in merchandise. Boosters spilled across the floor. With the shelf gone they were completely exposed. Selene took aim as Sarah weaved around the gaming area. Jumping over the teller counters, Selene dodged a blast that singed her hair. Sarah joined her behind the counter, taking in deep breaths. Sweat coated her pale skin.

"That was close." Sarah nervously flicked her hair from her shoulders, twitching and glancing at every noise. Sarah wasn't a soldier. She shouldn't be involved in this.

Selene bit her lip. It was her fault she was here. She shouldn't have let her come. "We're going to be okay," Selene said. "Maybe not such a straight shot to the door after all, but we've got this."

Sarah simply nodded while Selene glanced at the remaining

ten feet to their left. There was a single shelf cover, and a low counter to duck behind. But the soldiers had to know what they were planning by now.

"Come out with your hands up and no harm will come to you," one of Dominion soldiers called.

Rolling her eyes, Selene slid to the edge of the counter, peeking out. Five energy rifles remained poised in their direction. "Put down the guns and maybe we'll consider it!" Selene pulled the used clip from her gun before snapping in another.

"We will not negotiate with criminals," another soldier yelled.

"You're the one who opened a line of communication here!" Selene chambered a bullet. "I thought we were just shooting at each other, but this is kind of a nice break."

Sarah smiled. Even in a tough spot, Selene couldn't help her humor. It hadn't saved her life yet, but there was a first time for everything.

"I will repeat, come out with your hands up, and your weapons down. If you do, no harm will come to you."

"Now you're getting repetitive," Selene said. "Why don't you nice boys just let us waltz out of here? We haven't done anything wrong."

"You killed one of our men!" one shouted.

"You shot at us." Her gut clenched. She hadn't meant to. Her new clip ready, she nodded to Sarah, who joined her at the corner. "Really, I think we all know whose fault this was. But if you guys take your portion of the blame, I will accept that maybe we did maim a few of your guys. Even if it *was* self-defense."

"*Self-defense?*"

Selene leapt out and shot the shouting soldier. Blood burst from his shoulder. She'd try not to kill any more men today— even if they *were* trying to kill her. A few more bounds with her long legs and she was out the door, Sarah on her tail.

Rikkard pulled up in front of her.

"Get in," he said.

Selene obeyed, while Sarah dove the last few feet to her speeder. Rikkard slammed the gear into first, dust spitting up under their tires as he hit the gas.

"What did you do?" Rikkard snapped once they were free of the parking lot.

"Why would you think I did something?"

"Because I know you."

"This time something tipped them off. I'm not sure what." Selene glanced at Rikkard, who narrowed his eyes in concentration, glancing between the road and the rearview mirror. Sweat dripped down his temple.

"Someone's after us," he said.

Selene craned her neck to look behind them. Sure enough, thirty feet back were two black jeeps decked out in solar panels. Just as she spotted them, Rikkard turned quickly. Holding onto the seat, Selene whipped around. Another black sedan leapt from a sand dune, landing right in their path. The sleek black metal winked under the harsh afternoon light.

"I don't think we killed enough Dominion soldiers to warrant this," she said.

"Something else is going on." Rikkard spun the wheel, making a hard left. Something in the way he kept glancing at her, panic in his eyes, made her think he had an inkling of what was going on. If only he'd share this information.

The black jeeps gained quickly on the clear road.

"Warn me before you turn." She didn't have time to question Rikkard.

Standing, Selene turned in her seat. She braced herself against the car and took aim at their pursuit. She shot two bullets into the front tires before realizing they had to be made out of something besides rubber. Shit. Two men smirked behind the windshield. She narrowed her eyes and shot through the glass. The windshield shattered and the driver slumped. The first jeep flew off the road, horn blaring.

"One down," she whispered before taking aim at the second.

"Turning!" Rikkard called.

The warning barely gave her enough time to grip the arm supports before he made a wide right turn. Gravity threatened to dump her onto the sand, but she held on.

Irritation blossomed in her chest. Instead of glaring down at Rikkard once they straightened out, she took down the second jeep, shooting the driver through the windshield. It crashed into a small shop, shattering the poorly constructed wood entrance. Selene turned and sat down.

"Where's the third?" she asked. Rikkard shrugged. "He's got to be around here—"

The third vehicle skidded to a stop in front of them. Rikkard slammed the brakes. Her eyes went wide as they skidded in a circle. She held onto the dash, praying they didn't go into a barrel roll. The jeep came to a halt with the passenger side facing this new threat. Selene eyed the man in the driver's window. He grinned so wide she thought his face might break. Was he enjoying this? Her blood boiled. This was no game.

Raising her gun, Selene shot.

The glass shattered, and the man took the bullet in the face. His cheek imploded around the wound, his head snapping back, but no blood filled the injury.

Selene and Rikkard stared in shock and horror as the man faced them again, his grin remaining as the wound healed itself and the bullet popped back out.

"Drive!" Selene snapped, shooting erratically several times before Rikkard put the jeep in gear and took off over the sand dunes. "What the hell was that?" she asked, her voice high and clouded with fear. The Dominion had a lot of technology they didn't fully understand, but last she heard they hadn't developed synthetic skin that could literally take a bullet.

"I don't know," he said. "But I have to get back on the road. We're not making any progress on sand with this thing." Rikkard hit the dash.

"Head right. We should hit the main drag again."

Rikkard nodded and turned.

The black vehicle reappeared a few yards in front of them as they hit the main road. The trunk popped open. Selene braced herself. A grappling hook shot from the shadows. They both ducked on instinct, but the hook only dug its claws into the hood of their vehicle. Their car began to slow.

"What the…" Rikkard trailed off, violently spinning the steering wheel. "It's charged." He motioned to the hook. "It's messing with the power steering."

Selene nodded. Cold washed her skin. What did he want her to do? They needed to get the hook off, but she couldn't exactly crawl onto the hood and pry it off if it was charged with electricity.

Rikkard gave her a meaningful look.

"I'll do my best." She sighed. Selene stood and aimed her gun at the hook. She shot off three bullets before one of the claws came free. The two others refused to budge. "I'm out." She dropped the empty clip into the back of the jeep. "What do you have?" Rikkard handed her a laser pistol. "Perfect." Selene fired at the claws a dozen times. Nothing. The high-powered laser didn't even phase it. "What is that thing made of?"

"You have to get it off."

Selene met his eyes.

"If you don't, we're done for."

"No way, we can—"

He cut her off. "We can *nothing*, Selene. That pistol is all we have."

"That pistol isn't all we have." She paused. Her mind raced. "Call Rem."

"I can't."

An exasperated growl passed her lips unbidden. "Why not?"

"I forgot my comset."

"You forgot your fucking comset." Anger flared to life inside her chest so quickly, she fought for breath. She punched the dash with all of her strength. She couldn't believe this. "What are they after, Rik?"

"I don't know." She could see the lie in his eyes.

"Tell me!" She grabbed his wrist. Instead of wrenching away, he met her terrified gaze.

"*I don't know,*" he said slowly. Selene had never seen her boss scared before, and refused to believe he was now. She released his heated skin and steeled her resolve.

"If I die, it's on your hands."

Climbing over the windshield, Selene held tightly to the pistol in one hand and the windshield in the other. The jeep shook beneath her, and her sweaty palms fought for proper grip. Black asphalt rushed by beneath their wheels. Selene aimed the laser pistol at the claws and shot several times at close range. Nothing. The more time she wasted, the slower they drove. The black vehicle ahead did most of the work, dragging them along the sand-covered road. She had only one option. Raising her foot, she kicked the hook twice before getting the shock of her life.

"Selene!" Rikkard gasped.

Electricity coursed through her body, pain exploding inside every inch of her. Her body tensed, her trigger finger shooting off without her willing it. She tried to turn her head to make sure she hadn't hit Rikkard. The shot must have just missed him, though still startled him, because then they were turning hard. Her hand ripped from her hold on the windshield and she sailed through the air. Blue sky spun above, fluffy white clouds, and then sand—lots of sand. Somewhere the jeep rolled and crashed.

Then she hit ground. If she had been in less pain from the shock, she might have felt the burning hot sand beneath her. Instead she closed her eyes and willed the spasms to stop.

When they finally slowed, she opened her eyes again. The sun blinded her. Taking in a few deep breaths, she squinted into the sky. It was hard to believe she had survived that.

"Rikkard!" Her throat tightened. Selene stopped to listen before trying again. When no answer came, she tried to move. Her body wouldn't respond. Cursing, she tried calling for Rikkard again. Muffled footsteps approached.

A wave of relief passed through her, relaxing her muscles. She tried to turn her head to see him, but her head felt heavy. She sucked in air to call again when a dark figure stepped up beside her. His black shadow loomed with the light of the sun at his back. Whoever this was, he was not her boss.

"Rikkard!" she screamed as he leaned down. She caught his manic grin. Selene didn't have time to call the captain's name again before her world descended into darkness.

92

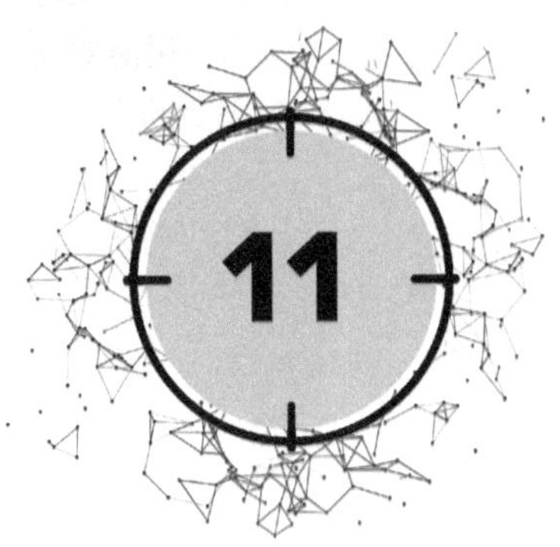

SELENE AWOKE TO A FAMILIAR blur of blue and black. At first she felt like she was floating. Somewhere in the back of her mind, she had to wonder if this was a dream or a nightmare. She quickly pushed the thought away. The floating was somehow comforting, and she closed her eyes and enjoyed the feeling.

Was she dead because of Rikkard's stupidity? Or was this some sort of limbo between sleep and the conscious world?

When Rikkard came to mind, she remembered screaming his name. Why? Why had she been calling for him? Where was the boss man? Was he okay? Why did she think he might *not* be okay?

Where was she?

Her eyes flew open. A blue blur clouded her vision until a bright light flashed on above. She winced. This was familiar, too much so. Wait. Her heart skipped a beat. The dreams.

Cold gel crawled against her skin, holding her limbs immobile, and gagging her screams. *No.* Not again.

There was no escape. There was never any escape.

Selene squinted up into the bright light. This wasn't death—death wouldn't be so unkind.

Her lungs ached. She needed to breathe. But if she did, she knew what would happen. She held on until her chest burned and her body grew hot. When black began to crowd her vision, she finally inhaled. The gel poured into her mouth, numbing her throat until her lungs were full. She couldn't breathe. She couldn't move. She was stuck in this brightly-lighted hell, naked and immobile.

Frustration racked her. Angry tears flooded her eyes, mingling with the gel. Selene gathered all of her strength to thrash toward the surface. Her fingers moved painfully slow, the gel somehow heavy and light at the same time. She made it a few inches. It inspired her to push harder. She thrashed, kicked and punched. When several minutes past and her energy was spent, she had only risen half a dozen inches.

Trying to scream again, Selene choked on the liquid. She couldn't fathom how she was still awake. Her lungs burned and contracted, but a tingling sensation welled in her chest. Somehow the gel was delivering oxygen to her body, because she had yet to pass out.

Calm yourself. She needed to hold on to rationality.

This was just a dream. She had had them before. She was stuck in this case, but she would be free. She'd wake up. Selene shut her eyes and tried to will herself awake. She clawed at the darkness behind her eyelids, trying to come thrashing to wakefulness, or sit straight up. Nothing happened.

When she opened her eyes again, several faces loomed overhead. Dark bulbous alien eyes scanned her naked form, expressions hidden by white masks.

Starting in surprise, she tried to shift away. She was quickly reminded that there was no moving in this vat. She glared upward.

Their mouths moved behind thin paper and Selene tried to decipher what they were saying. Vague mumbles permeated the goop, but nothing concrete. After nearly ten minutes, a faint click echoed through the vat. She tried to turn her head, willing herself to move and see what it was. Her head wouldn't budge. The searing pain of a needle pierced her thigh.

Unlike in her dreams, Selene felt the pull of her blood draining from her veins. When it stopped, another entered her other thigh from a circular hole in the top of the vat. Warmth spread through her veins, and she calmed. She instantly disliked it. She wanted to hold on to her anger. It would get her through. They couldn't keep her in this thing forever. The second she was free, she'd grab the nearest weapon and fight.

The sudden pressure against her lower back told her another needle pushed forward. It pierced her skin and dug its way into her spine. Selene gasped. She pushed desperately for the surface, but the needle dug deeper. Selene gritted her teeth. *Bear it*, she commanded. Fire blossomed behind her bosom.

She'd kill them all for putting her through this.

Jamming her eyes shut, she tried to think of anything but the pain. She pictured herself moving through the gel, smashing a fist through the lid of her prison. She'd grab the nearest doctor by the shirt and smash their face into the tub. Once the first was dispatched, she'd leap out, grab whatever medical instrument she could and slice their throats.

She held onto this vision for what felt like hours.

When the needle finally left her spine, several more pierced the rest of her body. *Stop*, she begged the nightmare. The image of leaping free of her prison was all that kept her sane.

The doctors above soon disappeared and the blazing white light winked out. The needles left her body and she could finally relax. Darkness embraced her like an old friend. Selene closed her eyes.

Wake up, she commanded. *Wake* up.

Another click sounded in the vat. Selene held back a groan. Every muscle in her body tensed, waiting for whatever was next. The gel gently pulled at her skin while slipping from her flesh. No more torture? The liquid slowly drained from her prison. Then, all at once the side of the vat opened and spilled her onto the metal grated floor.

Her shoulder slammed against a cold metal grate. She gasped as the rest of the vats contents washed over her like a cold bath, pinning her to the floor while she coughed and sputtered, vomiting the liquid from her lungs.

Selene savored each trembling breath. Sweet air passed down her throat several times before she registered the cold licking her wet body. She wrapped her arms around herself and curled into a ball, trying to still her shivering.

"It's just a dream," she whispered, forehead resting against the smooth metal below. She took another deep breath. "It's only a dream." But she didn't wake.

Rubbing her arms, Selene sat up and eyed her glass prison. It was far less menacing from the outside—or at least the tub was. All around it were tables of instruments. A spiderlike contraption hovered above, needles and scalpels for hands at the end of long metal arms. Tubes ran through the arms of each needle, ready to inject or take what they wanted.

She shivered again, and stood. "Just a dream. Just wake up."

Selene turned from her own personal hell to take in the barren lab. Her eyes landed on two figures. Her eyes widened and she covered herself with her hands. What the hell were they doing staring at her?

"Welcome back, Selene," the man said. He was quite tall, handsome and no more than thirty. His black hair was shaved on both sides, the rest pushed back like a twentieth-century mobster. She raised an eyebrow. His piercing amber gaze roamed her naked body, pausing too long on her hands. He was somehow familiar. But where had she seen his face before?

More importantly, how was she going to protect herself from him? Her thoughts trickled back to the scalpels hanging from the spider device. If she could pry one free she could use it as a weapon.

"It's nice to finally meet you, sister."

The second figure was a girl of maybe eighteen. She was stunning with sleek pale ginger hair and freckles. The look in her green eyes told Selene little sanity lay behind them. Confusion twisted her foggy mind. Not only did she not have a sister (that she knew of), but this woman looked nothing like her—with the exception of her green eyes.

"What's going on?" she asked tentatively. Although exposed and vulnerable, her curiosity was piqued. If these dreams really were memories, maybe she could figure out something helpful by getting them talking. "I haven't seen you before."

The two exchanged amused looks.

"We have met, even if you don't remember." The man smirked, his lips pulling high on one side of his face. "Ivy, on the other hand, is a new addition to the Dominion family."

"Dominion?" Selene echoed. That was right. Before blacking out she'd been chased by Dominion soldiers. Dread welled inside her stomach. If these two were part of the Dominion, that could only mean she had herself in one hell of a mess.

"Of course," he continued. "But where are my manners. I should introduce myself." He stepped forward, and offered her his hand. She didn't take it. "My name is Pate. We go way back. I believe we've known each other for five or six years now."

"Pate." Where had she heard that name before?

"Oh, and this is *not* a dream, my dear. You are very much awake." Pate grinned. "It has been too long since I gazed upon your beautiful face." He reached to touch her chin.

Selene slapped his hand away. "Don't touch me!" Her racing heart filled the hollow silence left by her slap. "I don't know you, or this place, or that girl. Whoever you knew, I'm not her." Dread boiled her insides, turning her stomach.

Pate raised a hand, fury lighting his face. For a moment she thought he might slap her back. Instead, he took a breath and composed himself. Righting his perfectly tailored suit, Pate took a step back. "Whether you think so or not, doesn't matter. You are the original Icarus, and you will rejoin your family and do the duty you were created for. Hit me again, and there will be consequences."

"Bite me." Selene narrowed her eyes.

Pate smirked and shook his head before turning back to Ivy, who frowned profusely. "I don't think she understands yet, little Ivy."

"I don't think so either," Ivy purred, voice smooth like honeyed wine.

"There is nothing to understand. If I'm not asleep, I demand you free me from whatever the hell this place is!" Selene backed towards the vat. She needed a scalpel as soon as possible. She had to protect herself.

"Icarus don't make demands." Ivy giggled, and rolled her eyes.

"What the hell is an Icarus?" These people were just frustrating her now. If she wasn't asleep and this was real, she wanted information and then she wanted the hell out. She had to get back to her crew and see if everyone was all right. Taking another step back, her butt hit the cold glass of the vat. "And where is Rikkard?"

"You won't be seeing that piece of smuggling trash ever again." Pate rolled his eyes. "You're part of the *Icarus Elite*. It's what we made you. You've been genetically modified to contain an alien host. The process is fairly hard on the human body, so not many survive. You're the only one to live through the procedure. Ivy is from the second generation; Icarus version two we call her. Ivy for short. The version two models weren't quite as intricate as the first, thus they'll remain part of the original *Elite*… even if they don't serve their original purpose."

"You're insane." Selene stared in horrified confusion. She couldn't be an experiment. She was a clone. From her perfect skin, to her unbelievably green eyes—it was the only thing that made sense. Everyone was either a clone or an alien in the twenty-fourth century.

"I assure you, I'm not." Pate smiled. "You were one of the few *nats* that tried to live the city life before I found you. What a foolish idea. You didn't think anyone would notice. A natural human among clones. It really was silly."

"You're lying." Selene's fingers twitched toward a nearby tray. "That's impossible."

"Think about it. Think about my face. It's familiar for more than one reason. I knew you before all of this, before you were changed, before you escaped. I'm the only one who holds the key to who you are, Selene."

"I don't need to know who I *was*. Clearly that's all you know." While he was distracted with his little speech, Selene glanced at the scalpel claw hanging from the spider's web. When he took the time to look back at Ivy, she leapt, ripping it from the robot. In the same instant, a flash of movement came from across the room.

A fist slammed against her gut. Air exploded from her lungs before an elbow crashed into the side of her face. She collapsed to the floor. Her abs sung in pain but her fingers tightened around the knife.

It was now or never.

A foot smashed her wrist. The crack of bones was audible above her labored breathing. She gasped. She had no choice but to release it. It clanged against the metal floor, falling uselessly through the grate. Her heart raced.

Pulling her up by her hair, Ivy yanked Selene to her feet before throwing her into a tray of medical equipment. She soared over it and into another, its contents crashing to the ground. Selene hit the linoleum, holding her hip painfully where she'd slammed it off the cart. Before she could climb to her feet, Ivy was on her. Several more hits to the face, and Selene couldn't take anymore. She was out like a light—again.

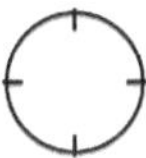

"I'm going to live in New Manhattan."

Seventeen-year-old Selene sat with her parents around their tattered kitchen table. She wanted a new life, away from the slums of the Outskirts. She was tired of the crime, the pirates, and most of all, the sheer boringness of the life she had grown up in. Selene wanted to see the cities, and the technology that came with them. She wanted to meet a clone, or an alien who wasn't a Dominion soldier. She wanted a life like her family before her never had.

"Of course you're not." Her mother rolled her eyes. A brown

eyed, brown haired beauty, she was where Selene had inherited her looks. She had also contributed to Selene's attitude. "Don't be ridiculous. Any city is unfit for a natural."

"Where did you get this idea?" Her father leaned forward. Dark haired with blazing blue eyes, he radiated his typical fatherly disappointment. "It was from that girl down the street wasn't it? She's a terrible example. You shouldn't be hanging around with her."

"I've saved up enough money for a cheap hotel while I find a job. I'm going." Selene crossed her arms and stared at them. She was stubborn, a trait passed down from both her parents.

"How do you expect to live amongst those people? The Dominion has never been kind to anyone against their ideals," her mother snapped.

"Who says I'm against their ideals?"

"You want to be a clone then?" her father gasped. "You want to live forever, moving from body to body until your mind rots and every piece of empathy you have disappears?"

Selene sighed. Her father raved constantly about all the Dominion's misdeeds, but Selene had yet to see it for herself. She stood, the legs of her scrap metal chair scraping against the dingy linoleum. "No, father, but I want to find out for myself if any of that is even true. Neither of you have been to a city. How do you know that's what they're really like? The only thing you know is what merchants tell you. You only know what the damn criminals in this town spout, most likely to keep us all here and keep us buying."

Both of her parents stared at her in silence.

"I'm going to New Manhattan. Whether you like it or not."

Later that week, Selene left for the city. She packed a small bag, and bought a scanner jammer. The device, if attached to her wrist at all times, would block any Dominion scans from seeing her as a natural human. Their machines would tell them she was one hundred percent clone, leaving them with no doubt she was employable. It cost nearly half her credits, but it was a necessity for any *nat*.

Selene wasn't one for tear filled goodbyes, so she took her leave early in the morning. Sneaking out of the one-bedroom rundown bungalow was easy. Fleeing the Outskirts even more so. The Outskirts were an easy place to live. Many of the citizens acted as if they were caged there, but there was no physical force or being keeping them in their old ways. The only prison present was the one in their minds.

Hitching a ride on the first citybound hovercraft she could find, Selene left the only world she had ever known, and entered an alien plain.

New Manhattan was beautiful. With its tall white buildings, new age architecture and as many glass panels as there were stars in the sky, the city was everything she had dreamed of and more. The technology was like nothing she'd ever seen. The cars, trucks, hovercrafts and speeders were sleek and elegant. Everything was clean, with small white disks running this way and that across their surface, scrubbing away the dirt. Nothing like the sandy streets of the Outskirts. Sky trains soared overhead, running on invisible rails high above the streets. Hardly any vehicles ran on a mundane road anymore; most of them flew or hovered.

Not only was the city alien, but so were the people. Everyone was beautiful and different in their own way. The fashion was clean, with harsh lines, much like the buildings that surrounded them. Skin ranged in color from violet to red, orange to green, blue to pink. A rainbow could be represented on a single street. Aliens. Clones. Each was more unique than the last. With smiling faces, they passed her by, occasionally giving her a curious look or a polite hello.

Suddenly nothing of the evil Dominion her parents loathed made sense. How could a place so incredible really be evil?

For several days, Selene lived at a cheap motel in the old part of town next to what was once the docks. She couldn't imagine the ocean that once spread from its harbors, water as far as the eye could see. Her meager savings from her old job as a dishwasher were enough to pay for a small room. But instead of finding a new employer, Selene took in the beauty of the city. She went to clubs, parks, government buildings, public pools, and everything in between. It wasn't until three days had come and gone that Selene remembered her goal to find somewhere to work. She fabricated a resume and looked for employment.

She soon realized that it wasn't so easy to get a job without a permanent residence, proof of identity or reliable references. Her lack of education stunned most.

A few more days passed and Selene was sitting in a nearby restaurant with a cup of tea as her only meal. Her funds were running dangerously low. Though the beauty of the city had initially intoxicated her, she now realized her mistake. Without the aid of her family, she had hardly met anyone, let alone landed work.

"Not having anything to eat today, dear?"

Selene looked up to meet the wondering eyes of the restaurant owner. He was one of the oldest clones she had seen yet. Somehow his presence soothed her, as if he was the only real person in this city.

"Not today, Drew." She smiled.

"Coming down with something?"

This would have seemed like a normal thing to ask if clones didn't get sick. Then again, she wasn't one. Selene composed her startled expression and shook her head.

"Of course not," she said.

Drew gave her a look along with his raised eyebrow. She always had a feeling he knew more than he let on. "It's not busy, why don't I whip you up something on the house."

"I couldn't—"

"I insist." Before she could argue, he sidled off to the kitchen.

When Drew returned, he planted a large plate of noodles with a purple sauce and something pink as a garnish, in front of her. Selene stared in utter confusion and horror, until Drew laughed and explained it wasn't a trick. So Selene ate, and Drew talked. He told her about his life, and how he came to own his shop. He even let slip that he had once lived in the Outskirts nearby, but had since chosen to join the legion of clones littering the city. Selene couldn't help but confide in him, and together they launched into a long conversation about her hometown.

Drew hired her to waitress in his small retro restaurant. She had never been so grateful for a single person in her whole life. Drew became like a father to her. Over several weeks Selene made more friends, and found a small apartment, beginning her new life in New Manhattan. That is until one day when three handsome clone boys entered the restaurant.

"Have a seat anywhere you'd like!" she called from the hostess booth. Pulling three menus from the shelf, she tapped each clean, plastic screen to wake them up before handing them to her new customers. "What can I get you guys to drink?" she asked, tablet poised and ready to take down her notes.

Now that Selene had a better look at the boys, she realized they'd be more readily described as men. In their mid-twenties, they were all equally handsome, with their perfect clone faces and hair. She had begun to grow accustomed to the beauty of clones a couple weeks ago. Their pretty smiles and dazzling eyes no longer pulled butterflies from her stomach.

"What would you guys like?" she repeated. One of the guys grinned at the others. His lips quirked up on one side, and he looked her over in a way she pretended not to see.

"Ginger booster juice for me," one said.

"Red beer for me," the other said.

Selene blinked at them. "I'm sorry, we don't sell beer or booster juice here." In fact most restaurants didn't, especially small diners. Alcohol was restricted by the Dominion, and booster juice was reserved for booster stores, clubs and bars.

"What a shame," the first said.

"Come on, you've got to have *something* good back there," another said.

"Wouldn't you double check for us?" The last grinned.

Sighing, Selene put the tablet under her arm and poised a hand on her hip. She wasn't a pushover, and wasn't about to let these three weasel anything out of her. "I'm sorry, but it's against regulations."

"What a poor sport."

"What do you even have then?"

"Gentlemen, she's just doing her job." The first winked. "Let the pretty lady be a good girl for her boss."

Something about the way he spoke made her skin crawl. Selene shifted awkwardly and pulled her tablet back out. "If you're not ready to order, I can come back in a few minutes."

"Are you on the menu?" The first grabbed her wrist and pulled her off her feet. Startled, Selene landed in his lap where he caressed her back with one hand. Face flushed, Selene slapped the man hard across the face before leaping up.

"Excuse me," she said, dashing off into the back. Laughs rang behind her from two of them, but not the third. Peeking from the safety of the kitchen, she found the one who'd grabbed her with a frown on his face.

Selene sighed and stayed back there for almost fifteen minutes before the cook shooed her out. She suddenly wished her boss was around. If he had been, he'd scare them off. She knew he had weapons hidden in his office, just in case.

Selene returned to the group, determined to get them fed and out of there as soon as possible. "Are you ready to order *now*?"

They did, each of them listing off something or another. The entire time they joked and poked at each other, but mostly left her alone. To her relief, the first didn't try anything again—at least not this time.

For the next few weeks, these men became regulars. Sometimes the dark haired, amber eyed one who had grabbed her would come by himself. He'd hit on her, try to touch her, but she'd grown wary of him and always dodged his advances. As the days went on, he became more and more brazen until Drew had to intervene, telling them not to return until they learned some manners. Selene was thankful not to see them for an entire week. She'd nearly forgotten about their existence, until one morning on her way to work.

Selene rushed across the street, the diner still a block away.

She hadn't been late yet and wasn't about to start now. Dodging around New Manhattan citizens, cleaner bots, and hovercars, Selene arrived just across the street from the restaurant.

It was at this point she smelled it—smoke.

Rushing toward the front doors, Selene burst inside. Fire blazed out of the kitchen, licking the floor and ceiling. A cough burst from her chest as she inhaled. Covering her mouth with her sleeve, she gazed wildly around the diner.

"Is anyone in here?" she called. Pausing to listen, Selene inched her way inside. Drew was opening today. He'd never let something happen to his diner. "Drew? Are you here?"

A moan sounded from inside the kitchen. Her heart leapt double time. She ran to the back of the restaurant and tried the kitchen door. She hissed in pain. The metal handle burned her hand. She pulled back.

"Drew! I'm going to get help!" Not waiting for a response, Selene lunged across the restaurant and out the front doors. "*Help*!" she called. "There's a fire! Someone is stuck inside!"

Several people stopped and muttered to one another. One pulled out a small plastic phone and called for the fire brigade while Selene raced to the back entrance to the kitchen. Locked. Hissing in frustration she ran back to the front where smoke billowed through the open doors.

Selene waited impatiently for the arrival of the fire brigade, pacing the length of the street. By the time they arrived, and she was ushered aside, the blaze had nearly enveloped the front of the diner. She didn't know how someone could survive that. Holding onto hope, Selene watched the flames die down, the firefighters putting out the fire slowly but surely. Once the fire was gone, they went inside.

They moved through the diner and back into the kitchen. Selene held her breath, hoping her friend had survived.

"There's a body back here," a man called from inside.

Selene's heart sank, and her legs gave way. She sat down hard on the sidewalk.

"There are signs of an accelerant," said another.

Selene buried her face in her hands. How could this have happened? She'd just seen Drew yesterday, and what was worse, he was alive when she'd arrived, but she'd been too much of a coward to fight the blaze to save him.

Selene cried until a hand rested on her shoulder. When she looked up, wiping her eyes, two Dominion soldiers towered over her. They asked her questions she couldn't answer, about who she was and her employment with Drew. She did her best to cooperate until another man, clad in black walked over. Dark hair and piercing eyes. Selene recognized his face.

"I believe there's someone who has some information for you," he said, motioning to a girl that stood several feet away. Selene recognized her as one of her regulars. The two soldiers split up, one staying with Selene, while the other took the woman's statement.

When several minutes had passed and the soldier started to look back at his comrade, dread welled in her stomach. Words drifted to her ears; *natural, set the fire, the owner knew, turn her in, killed him, cover up.*

Selene stared in stunned confusion until the two men returned and hoisted her up by her elbows. They took her kicking and screaming from the scene, charging her with arson and first-degree murder. Selene tried to reason with them, but they wouldn't hear it, not when the tall handsome man confirmed the woman's story.

"He's lying!" Selene hissed, trying to pull from their grasps as they directed her towards a hovercar several feet away.

"You have real nerve to suggest Governor Pate would lie about such a thing," one of the soldiers snapped.

"Governor?" she echoed.

Confused, Selene let them place her in their vehicle. As they pulled away, Selene caught the gaze of the man that did this to her. She watched his lips quirk into a lopsided smirk. He winked at her before the hovercar turned a corner and he disappeared from sight.

He had set the fire. She knew it. What was worse, he'd convinced someone to lie about her, and corroborate his ludicrous story. But the real cherry on top was that he was in government. The people of New Manhattan had voted this man in. He had power, and he was using it to ruin her.

Selene closed her eyes. He'd killed her first clone friend, one of the few good people in this world and for what? She didn't know. But she wanted revenge—she would find him when she was free, and she would kill him.

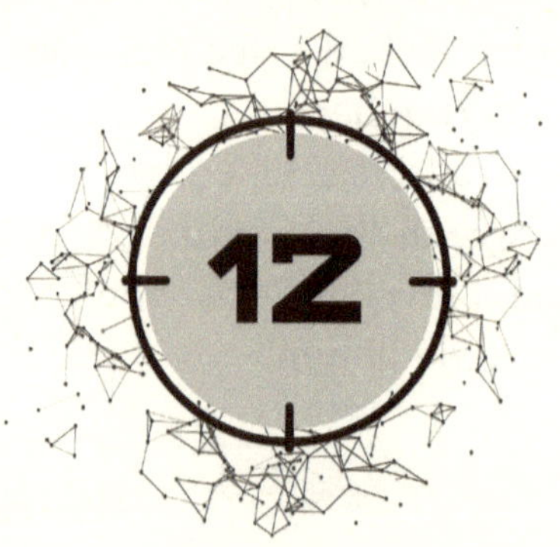

PATE HAD RUINED HER LIFE. He was right. She knew him. In fact, she loathed him.

When Selene awoke the morning after Ivy knocked her unconscious, her blood boiled. She finally remembered who she was. She *was* a natural. She'd had a life before Pate came along. She had parents, maybe even siblings. It hadn't been the best life living in the Outskirts but when she'd come to the city, she had truly enjoyed it. Until *he* ruined it, for whatever selfish reason he had.

Clenching her fists, Selene stared at the white ceiling above. Before she could escape this place, she had something she needed to do. She had to kill Pate.

It was several hours before someone came for her, and when they did, she did not go gently.

Kicking and screaming, Selene used her entire body of combat knowledge, to fight through the first three men to grab her.

Her foot slammed against their wrists, knocking their tasers away before she knocked them unconscious. Each fell to the floor in a heap with bloodied noses and bruised cheeks. They were seriously underestimating her if they thought three men could contain her.

Selene stepped into the hall. Fluorescent light seared her eyes.

She squinted, rubbing her eyelids. Selene glanced left, then right. No visible way out, only long white corridors. Though she wanted to find out what was really going on here, every nerve in her body told her to run. Choosing at random, Selene jogged the length of the corridor, her heart racing as she paused briefly at a three-way intersection. She chose left, taking the hallway in moments.

"Come on," she hissed. She needed to find a way out.

She pushed herself harder and faster, her bare feet slapping the cold linoleum until she rounded a bend. She skidded to a halt. Half a dozen armed soldiers barred her way. Her heart skipped a beat. Selene stared them down. Where she was clad in a white hospital gown, they were in black Dominion gear, covered head to toe in armor. There was no getting through them.

Selene glanced down the intersecting passageway to her left, and right, taking in her options. Neither direction had a flashing red exit sign. She stepped to her right.

The hum of a taser bullet shot through the air, slamming into her chest like a sledgehammer. She jerked back, the subsequent charge ripping through her body, sending her whole body writhing on the floor.

Collapsing into spasms, Selene held her eyes shut and waited it out. When they finally stopped, rough hands yanked her from the floor and propelled her down the next hall.

"Pushy much?" she hissed, half out of breath. Her whole body quivered with exhaustion.

The guards ignored her, and formed a circle to keep her in. Damn. She could fight off a few, but a dozen would be a challenge. Selene used what little energy she had to glare at them.

They marched down the plain white halls until paint gave way to glass walls. Labs passed on the right side of the hall, researchers or scientists clad in white lab coats inside. Metal tables held animals that had been torn apart.

Her heart sank into her stomach.

So this is what the Dominion was doing with them? Experimenting to make whatever the hell Icarus were.

Her heart rammed faster as they pulled her past the labs and back into regular white halls filled with sleek silver doors.

It felt like they walked for hours, but it was probably only a few minutes before the two soldiers holding her up dumped her through an open doorway. The door swooshed closed behind her and locked with a click. Selene jerked back to her feet and checked the door, but there was no lock for her to pick—not that she had anything to pick a lock with. She sighed.

The room was stark white with a simple bench in the center and a row of clean white lockers at the back. A row of windows faced her from the opposite wall, with another locked door to its side. At the far end an equally bland bathroom stood through an open door. Selene had a bad feeling about this place.

She took her time going through every locker, and inspecting every nook and cranny. There were no weapons, nothing not bolted to the floor—nothing to help her escape.

Selene showered quickly before putting on the only pair of clothes left for her: a simple set of tight gray pants, white undergarments and a plain white tank top. Pulling them on, Selene couldn't help but miss her black suit and laser guns. She felt naked and vulnerable without her protective layers and utility belt.

She had hardly dressed when a loud ding sounded from the ceiling. Selene started. The door beside the row of windows slid open, disappearing inside the wall. Curious but wary, she peeked through. Only a long featureless gray hallway greeted her.

"Lovely," she said.

What fresh hell awaited her this time?

With nowhere left to go, Selene entered the hall. The door slid shut behind her, its lock clicking. Her heart sank to her toes. That couldn't be good. Trying not to worry about the ominous feeling welling inside her, she trudged down the hall. At the end was another door. It slid open and shut tightly behind her. Selene emerged on a platform.

A large room with a domed ceiling. Huh. Silently wishing the ceiling were a skylight instead of paneled with fluorescent light strips, Selene glanced around the wide space.

She stilled as her eyes landed on an obstacle course. Long metal platforms ran parallel to each other. Several hurdles were visible, with bars in between, a rock wall on another and churning water below. Large axes swung too and fro several feet from a patch of burning coals. She winced. Shit.

A spectators' booth was set into the far wall at her left, several dark shadows moving behind the tinted glass. Opposite her platform was another, with a familiar orange haired beauty lounging against the railing. Ivy waved, an amused smile playing on her lips.

What on earth was this all for? If she really was one of these experiments, she could only assume this room was to test her. But why in Aldar's name was Ivy here if she was the one being tested?

It dawned on her that maybe they would pit them against each other. But what would happen if they refused? Fists tightened at her sides, Selene stepped away from the rails. No way. She wasn't doing this.

"Are you ready to play *Selene*?" Ivy shouted. She drew out the second *e* in her name like a child might. Selene's skin crawled.

Leaning against the wall, Selene crossed her arms. She wasn't going anywhere, and she was *definitely* not playing Ivy's game.

"Come *on*, sourpuss! If you don't play, they'll get angry!" When Selene refused to respond, Ivy continued, "Or maybe you're a masochist. You liked the vat didn't you? All the needles, the gel… You liked being suffocated." Ivy laughed, long and hard.

Selene closed her eyes and tuned her out.

"If you don't do what they say, they'll put you back in there. Over and over, they will! All you have to do is be good and play with me to avoid it."

Somewhere between the crazy talk and the mention of the vat, Selene started to listen. She couldn't help it. Memories of that place boiled to the surface and that familiar dread settled in her stomach. She did *not* want to go back there.

"Who are *they*?" Selene called back after a long hesitation.

"The Dominion, the lab people, our keepers—whatever you want to call them. *They* are in charge."

Selene didn't like the sound of that. "What do I do?"

"Listen to what they say and do what they tell you."

Selene was about to ask for clarification when a loud ding filled the chamber. An overly pleasant and somewhat robotic female voice came over a speaker system.

"Please descend to the training field," it said.

Selene looked across to Ivy, who pointed below. Sighing, Selene descended the stairs to her right. When she reached the ground floor, the voice started up again.

"Please take your positions at the obstacle course," it said.

Though Selene couldn't see Ivy for direction, she had gotten a good look at the training field. Pacing the length of the room to what she had to guess was the beginning of the course; Selene found the starting line painted white on the concrete floor. Ivy met her there.

"Take your positions on the platform," the voice said.

Selene stepped up onto a square metal platform. Ivy did the same, smiling and waving again before dropping into a ready stance. Selene took a deep breath and mimicked her, checking out the obstacles ahead. A long stretch of metal with spikes was her first obstacle. She'd have to be careful, or the rest of the course would be covered in blood. A set of ropes, slopes and steps to climb towered ahead. Over a mound of hardened earth, she could only dread what came next.

You can do this.

Selene tried to get her head in the game. All she had to do was run this course. She'd follow along and do what they said and wait for her moment. What she would do with that moment, she wasn't sure. If she could get answers, she would. But more than anything she wanted freedom. She didn't need to know who or what she was—she just needed out.

Stretching her arms and legs; she waited for the speaker to count down.

"Begin in, five, four, three, two, one, go!"

Lunging forward, Selene danced across the intervals of spikes, watching her footing carefully until she was across. Leaping a short wall, Selene was surprised to find hot coals on the other side. She grabbed the dangling bars above, her heart beating in her ears. The heat below stung her toes, and steam fogged the air, making her hands slick with sweat.

She swung across as quick as she could. Selene glanced at Ivy, who already climbed the wall on the other side. Damn she was fast.

Gripping the bars tighter, Selene pushed faster, reaching the straight rock wall on the other side. Using thin handholds, Selene hoisted herself up. Sweat slipped down her temples, keeping her all too aware of the burning hot rocks below. Her slick palms curled around an inset in the wall. She reached for the next, a foot above her head. Her fingers grazed the smooth rock, but her other hand slipped. Selene gasped, her feet teetering off balance. Her shoes scraped against the wall as she slid down, her fingers grasping wildly at anything within reach.

Her heart pounded against her ribcage. Inches from the hot coals, her fingers dug in, wrapping around a handhold. Selene breathed heavily, glancing down at the steam rising from below. Too close. She gulped the lump in her throat and resumed her climb.

When she finally made it to the top, she swung onto another metal platform. A large medieval guillotine crashed up and down in its wooden arms, blade slicing through the floor six feet away. Selene clenched her fists and ran at it. Her timing had to be perfect or she'd be cut in two. The large blade rose and fell, rose and fell. The metal platform beneath her shoes quivered. Her feet beat against the metal floor. Just as the blade began to rise, she leapt.

She scarcely made it through before the blade dropped with a loud *clang*.

A giant axe swung from her left. Selene dropped, pinning herself to the cold metal floor. When the axe swung to the other side she jumped up, thanking Aldar for her quick reflexes. Another blade swooshed by, the air pushing against her. She sprinted from its path, lunging through two more axes before she slammed into the next wall. Her breaths came in quick succession and sweat drenched her back.

Selene scrambled to the top. A long rope swung from the ceiling on the other side. Between this platform and the next was a pool of churning water. Bubbles rose violently as something grey and scaly flashed under the surface. She did *not* want to know what was down there.

Hoisting herself high on the rope, Selene swung to the other side. Rope burned her palms. Gritting her teeth, she reached with her toes for the edge. Her sneaker nearly slipped, sending her heart racing. Swinging her other foot out, she caught it. Selene pulled herself to safety, not letting the rope go until she was grounded.

A laugh from ahead startled her. Selene looked up to see Ivy smirking over her shoulder. The woman winked before diving over another wall. Selene narrowed her eyes, irritation flashing through her chest. She wasn't about to let this child beat her.

Selene dove off her perch and into the next set of obstacles. Large planks of wood, at least her height and width spun in rapid succession. They created a maze on a narrow metal platform. Below, a sheet of spikes awaited her. Wind pulled at her hair as she approached. The wooden sheets rotated in alternating directions with barely enough space for her to shift through. Selene took them at a running start. Following their movements, Selene wedged herself between two, placed within feet of each other. Harsh wind nearly forced her off balance. She teetered on her heels, pushing through the first two. A third plank clipped her shoulder, sending her spinning to the floor. Another clipped her foot with a hard smack. Selene winced and retracted her limbs before climbing to her feet. Once she was steady, she steered through the rest, pushing all of her concentration into avoiding the spinning planks.

When she finally reached the other side, Ivy had stopped

ahead on a metal platform identical to the starting one. The ginger-woman inspected her nails without a lick of sweat on her pale skin.

Selene worked her way through the last row of spikes before catching her breath on the finishing platform.

"Is that all you have, Icarus?" Ivy laughed. "You're pathetic."

"Winner; Icarus version two point zero," the voice came from above. "Please proceed to the starting platform." Ivy immediately jumped down and circled the course while Selene stared back in confusion.

"You've got to be kidding me." She panted. "How many times are we going to do this?"

"Please proceed to the starting platform." The voice above was her only response.

Grumbling under her breath, Selene reluctantly obeyed.

Over and over they pushed Selene to run the course. While Ivy continued to soar through it and win time after time, Selene fell further and further behind. Even with the course becoming familiar, Selene took her time in order to survive. She wasn't about to lose her head or a limb over a silly competition.

It had been over half a dozen times through when Selene finally collapsed on the finishing platform. The cool metal was a welcomed relief. Ivy rolled her eyes, placing her hands on her hips, her gaze wandering the room as if this was nothing.

"Winner; Icarus version two point zero. The score is eight to zero. Please proceed to the starting platform."

Selene groaned and lay still with her face in her hands. She wasn't sure she could do another one. Her whole body ached. Her feet were sore from the hot coals and small cuts she'd sustained. Her muscles kept cramping and her lungs were tired of being overworked. How could they expect her to go on?

"Please proceed to the starting platform."

Ignoring the voice, Selene took even breaths. Again and again the voice repeated for her to get going. After its tenth attempt it changed its tune.

"Proceed to the starting platform *now* or face the consequences."

"I *can't*," Selene hissed between her fingers.

"Proceed to the starting platform now."

"Shut the hell up." Selene looked up at the ceiling. "I'm not going again."

"Proceed to the starting platform now or face the consequences."

When Selene refused to move after the voice commanded a third time, a door opened in the otherwise seamless white walls. In came the six guards who had subdued her and brought her here. Selene stood, her legs nearly buckling beneath her. She was too slow.

The black clad men grabbed her arms, yanking her from the platform. They dragged her through hall after hall until she entered a familiar lab.

"*NO!*" Selene cried, finally pulling back. If she weren't so drained, she would have fought. She would have taken down at least two of them before they got her in that thing. But she was tired and weak. The men easily hoisted her inside the vat and shoved the lid closed. Her fists pounded against the glass and she screamed at them to let her out. They disappeared from sight, leaving her to scream her tired lungs out alone.

From a hose in the wall, gel gushed forth.

"You can't do this!" she yelled, trying to use her body to block the flow of liquid.

In it came, sloshing from several other entry points. Panic surged through her. Using her feet and hands, she tried to block the holes oozing blue. It slipped between her fingers and toes, cold and slimy to the touch. It pooled beneath her, slowly rising. Selene shivered and jammed her palms against the two entrances on her right. Her foot slipped and in it poured. Selene floundered, trying to block the flow, but it was too late. The liquid rose faster, pulling her body in. When it finally encased her and she could no longer breathe, Selene gasped for air. The liquid filled her lungs, and hardened to keep her immobile.

Selene grasped at anything she could to stop the pain and the panic. Again they stuck her with needles; again they cut away and injected her with things. She thoughtlessly grabbed towards anything she could, trying to numb herself to it all.

She thought of her crew, her friends, and of Rikkard. She held his face in her mind, the small smiles she'd nearly missed, and the irritated raise of his brow. If she had any regrets in this vat, it was of him. Even though he'd betrayed her trust, she still felt something for him. What it was, she couldn't be sure, but she wanted to find out if there was more between them than missions and small moments.

Selene didn't know how long it went on. Hours maybe, or hellish weeks. Finally, the jabs stopped. They spilled her from the tank. She was stripped naked and blasted with water so frigid it bit at her skin. The pressure of the hose threw her against the wall. When she was finally clean, they took her back to the small five by five-foot room she'd woken in. She'd hardly crawled into the small bed before her mind and body had had enough. With thoughts of a man she may never see again swirling through her head, she fell asleep.

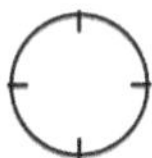

In the coming week Selene was forced to run that course again and again. When she couldn't do it anymore, they dumped her in the vat, and then sent her to her room. Only thoughts of what she'd left behind kept her going. In the morning she'd be forced to start all over again.

Though she improved, it still wasn't good enough. They ran her longer, harder, faster. She still couldn't keep up with Ivy, but at least Ivy was starting to break a sweat.

When ten days had passed, Selene ran the course like she'd done it for years. She flew across the spikes, swung like an ape over the hot coals and leapt through the rest of the course like she'd been made for this. She didn't even have to think about it anymore, only ran with a blank mind and a dull ache in her chest, letting her body do the work.

On the eleventh day Selene stopped on the finish line, an empty platform to her left.

"Winner; Icarus version one point zero."

Ivy screamed from the platform of spikes leading to the finishing square. Her fists shook at her sides. Selene smiled weakly. *Finally.*

No message followed to return to the starting platform. She was allowed to retire in peace. No vat, no blast of ice cold water, no desperately clinging to the images of her friends to keep her sane, no running the track until her feet bled.

Selene collapsed in bed early, wide-awake with only one thought in her mind—escape. She had to get out of this place. She *would* get out or die trying.

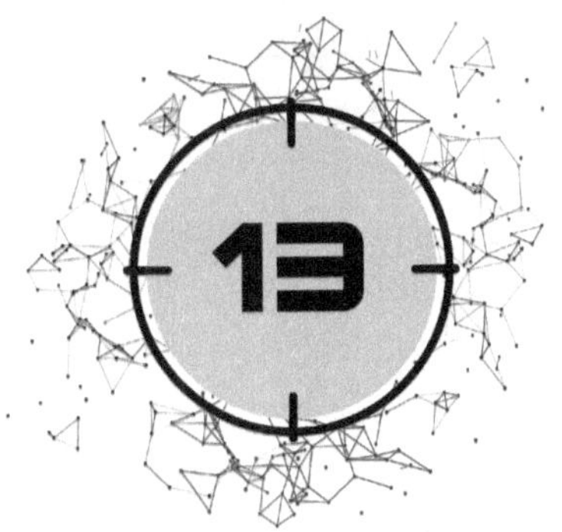

WHEN SELENE'S DOOR WHISKED OPEN for dinner, she was ready. Leaping from her position against the wall, Selene slammed her heel into the man's hands. A tray clattered to the floor as she swung around, smashing her foot against his chest. He flew into the wall on the other side of the hallway. She froze.

It wasn't a random soldier bringing her food this time—it was Pate.

Selene leapt at him with a snarl on her lips. She hadn't seen him since the day she arrived in this hell. Heat coursed through her veins. Forgetting her plan to escape, vengeance clawed at her heart and pushed her to attack him.

Her fist collided with his jaw. She spun, jabbing his ribs with her elbow. Gloved hands wrapped around her biceps and pulled her off. Throwing her elbow backward, she caught the soldier in the nose. Blood spurted from his nostrils. Selene spun with one leg extended, dropping the six-foot man to the floor.

Turning from the soldier, Selene pushed Pate against the wall. Air exploded from his lungs and her hands wrapped around his throat. She squeezed, his stubble biting at her fingers. Pate stared at her with wide eyes, his face red as he tried to inhale. His short nails clawed at her hands, but she only pressed harder. He struck out with his knee. Selene dodged the blow, digging her nails into his pale skin.

His pulse weakened beneath her fingers. A malicious smile pulled at her lips. This was it. Her revenge.

Strong hands ripped her away, and tossed her across the hall. *No!*

She stumbled back and a soldier pinned her to the opposite wall. Snarling at him to release her, Selene bucked and pulled one arm free, only to have another soldier deliver a swift jab to her abdomen. Air spilled from her lungs and she gasped loudly, doubling over. While he had the upper hand, the soldier spun her around. Hand in her hair; he thrust her face against the wall, twisting one arm painfully behind her back.

"Be still," he growled.

Selene narrowed her eyes and tried to rip her arms free. He punched her spleen. Pain burst through her side and she went limp.

When her body relaxed, the man cuffed her hands and turned her back around. While he fumbled with the plastic cuffs, she glared across the hall at the disheveled Pate. His dark hair fell forward and he met her eyes with rage in his own. A bruise formed on his cheek. Red hand marks stood out on his pale throat.

"You little brat—" He advanced on her.

Selene spat in his face. "You ruined my fucking life!" Anger seeped from her every pore. "All because of what? Because I didn't *like* you? Because I wouldn't go *out* with you? Because I wouldn't let you fondle me in front of your friends? You sick pig."

Pate pushed the guard aside and grabbed her hair, slamming her head against the wall. Stars danced before her eyes. Keeping her pinned, his lips brushed her ear. One hand squeezed her throat.

"You need to learn some manners." His hot breath brushed her neck, sending a shiver down her spine.

Selene tried to turn away, but he gripped her hair tighter. Knives of pain shot through her scalp. She bit down on her lip to keep from crying out.

"I'll show you what a *sick pig* could do to you, just you wait. You'll be begging for me to stop."

"You wish—"

Pate pulled her neck back and slammed her head into the wall. "Manners." He released her.

Head spinning, Selene leaned against the wall. If it weren't for the black clouding her vision, Selene would have lunged after him again. Before she could, the guards un-cuffed her and shoved her back inside her cubby of a room. The door locked with a click.

Selene leapt at the door and pounded her fists against it. Anger boiled her insides.

"I will fucking *kill you* Pate! Just you wait and fucking see."

Her only answer was the retreat of footsteps. Selene turned and slid to the floor. She would attempt to escape again and again until he was dead and she was free. Clenching her fists, Selene looked at the barren white ceiling. She had to escape. There was no other way.

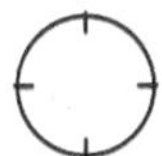

The next morning, Selene woke to sirens blaring through the Dominion complex. She started from her sheets, the sound ripping her from unconsciousness. Shielding her ears and cornering herself in the room, she gritted her teeth against the pain exploding in her skull.

What the hell was going on?

Selene waited it out for a good five minutes, but the alarms kept blaring and no one came for her. She moved to the door. She had to be ready in case someone came in. The door whisked into the wall. Selene stared in confusion at an empty hall.

Peering around the corner, Selene checked both ends of the corridor. Nothing. Blood spattered the white walls and pale linoleum floor. Her heart beat faster. Could this be her chance?

Selene fled in the opposite direction of the blood. She had yet to get the lay of the land in this place, but she knew the training field was the other way. Heading down several hallways, Selene skidded to a halt. Two black clad figures turned a corner twenty-feet away. Selene darted into a side corridor, and turned into another hall, running smack dab into a dead end.

"*Shit*." She turned back around.

"I think she went this way," the low voice of a man echoed through the hall.

"Damn it." Selene darted to the end of the hall, hiding around the corner so that she could surprise whoever rounded it. And surprise them, she did.

Leaping on the first man as he rounded the corner, Selene tripped him face first onto the floor and rammed her heel into the second, launching him back into the third. The familiar charge of a laser pistol made her turn and boot the fourth, knocking his gun away. He lunged. They fell to the floor in a heap, rolling over one another in a tangle of limbs, in an attempt to get to the gun first.

"Whoa, hold up!" one of the others called, yanking his mask off to reveal the round-cheeked, freckled face of a natural. With his large-pored complexion, that's what he had to be. Clones were never so imperfect. "That's her, that's the girl we're here for."

Both Selene and the man she struggled with froze.

"Me?" Selene blinked in confusion.

"You're Selene?" the man she grappled with asked.

"Yeah," she said. "Who are you?"

"The Alliance," he said. "We're here to rescue you."

Her eyes went wide. She never thought she'd hear those words.

"Well it's about damn time someone did." Selene untangled herself. Standing, she reached down to help the man beside her to his feet. "But who is the Alliance and why in Aldar's name are you here to save *me*?"

They all smiled as they pulled the masks from their faces, exchanging looks with one another. Each held a perfectly imperfect face, some with freckles, and others with scars and wrinkles. She had never been so happy to see a natural face in her life.

"We're the rebellion," another answered—the one she'd taken out first.

"On second thought, I don't care who you are, as long as you're here to get me out," she said. "Let's get the hell out of here."

The four of them nodded and led the way through hall after hall. They tangoed with a few Dominion soldiers, taking them down in a flurry of hits, kicks and laser fire. It wasn't long before they entered a large hangar. They trotted toward a Class Four speeder at the other end.

Selene glanced at the people around her, her suspicion growing. If they were here to save her, how had four of them gotten into this facility? There had to be hundreds of soldiers here, and she had yet to find a single exit in her few botched escape attempts.

"Wait." She stopped, and so did they. Curious gazes landed on her. She cursed herself, wishing she had kept her mouth shut until they were out of here. Even if they turned on her, she could have gotten free out in the open. "How did you get in here?" she hesitated. "How do I know you're really who you say you are?"

Their curious gazes turned amused. Two of them exchanged wicked grins, and then four rifles pointed at her. *Shit.*

"It took you long enough," one laughed.

Selene took a step back. "What do you mean?"

"You *really* thought we were here to save you?" another chuckled. "It's hilarious. You're really that naive."

"What the *hell* is going on?"

"Everything you do here is a test." The first rolled his eyes like it was obvious. "I can't believe you honestly haven't figured that out yet. Did you really think you could take us out so easily?"

"I take everyone out pretty easily." Selene shrugged.

The one she'd taken down first swung the butt of his rifle at her. This was her chance. Selene dodged and jumped back out of reach. Her fingers danced against the open air. She needed a weapon. She took a moment to calculate the likelihood of her getting one of those rifles.

The odds weren't good.

"Cocky bitch," he growled.

"Considering I got the jump on you without even trying, you should know better than your friends here." Selene motioned to the others. She had to keep them distracted so she could make her move.

He lunged at her again. Selene whipped in a roundhouse kick, catching the man in the jaw. His rifle clattered across the floor as he stumbled and fell. Selene leapt for the weapon but another stepped in her path. Blazing green eyes stopped her.

Now she understood.

Why would naturals help the Dominion? Heat blossomed in her chest. They weren't simply naturals—they were part of the Icarus Elite. Like Ivy, they were enhanced versions of real people. Their humanity had initially caught her off guard, but she wouldn't let them fool her again.

"Icarus." Selene jumped back.

She lost her chance. With his rifle back in hand, the four of them stared her down. Each of them held a devious smile.

"*Finally*, she gets it."

"She'll get it all right." The first stepped forward. "It's back to the vat for you."

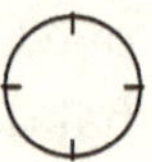

A few weeks later, Selene collapsed in bed. Every inch of her ached; from her muscles, to her skin, and bones. She groaned, her fingers curling around the edges of her thin, rock hard pillow. She squeezed her eyes shut against the bright overhead light, and buried her face. Time and time again the Dominion put her through drills, obstacles, courses, mazes, and escape scenarios, all to test her abilities. She couldn't trust anyone trying to help her escape. All it got her was time in the vat and more visits from Pate.

Her fingers dug in deeper, clawing at the scratchy white fabric. *Pate.* He was behind this—all of it. She took a deep breath, rolling onto her back and releasing her hold on the pillow.

How long had she been here? How were the smugglers faring? Was Rikkard okay? She swallowed the lump in her throat. She hoped he'd survived the crash. She hoped Sarah had found Kong and brought him home.

What *was* everyone up to without her around? She hoped they kept finding animals to save, and had let Aida know she might not be coming back to help those tigers. If Rikkard was alive, she wished he would give up on smuggling protos, and dedicate himself to something nobler—though she doubted very much he would.

Some part of her wondered if Rikkard really did care for her, and what that meant if he did. She tried not to reflect too much on the last words he'd said to her, or that night searching for their cargo ship. She couldn't be sure if his words meant anything when his actions spoke otherwise.

Selene laid her arms over her eyes, blocking out the white light behind her eyelids. She wished someone would save her.

Why is no one rescuing me? Drawing her hands over her eyes and down her face, she knew the answer to that. They thought she was dead.

Her mind continued to swirl until her door swished open and in waltzed Pate. She no longer bothered sitting up at his presence. Selene took her small rebellions where she could. At least irking Pate hadn't gotten her time in the vat—*yet*.

"Good morning." He placed a tray on the small bedside table.

Selene kept her eyes closed. Her senses were sharp enough to know he stood exactly two feet from her cot. She didn't need to open her eyes and further acknowledge his annoying presence.

"I know you're awake." He leaned against the adjacent wall. "You've really become quite dour lately. What happened to my little spitfire?"

Her eyes flashed open and she glared at him. He meant the adjective to bother her, and it did. He wanted to see a spitfire? She was more than tempted to show him one. But if these weeks had taught her anything, it's that Pate's game was to get under her skin. She wasn't about to let that happen, no matter how much she wanted to choke the life out of him.

"There are those pretty green eyes." His lips quirked to one side, his signature lopsided smirk. "Why don't you eat something? You have a *long* day ahead of you."

Selene sat up, stretching her back and cracking her neck. She took one look at the perfectly adjusted breakfast on her plate and her skin crawled. He had touched this food, prepared it, and carried it to her. She wouldn't eat anything brought to her by this man.

"What's the matter?" he asked. "Not hungry?"

"No." She stood and brushed past him to wash her face and pull back her hair.

"Don't be a brat."

Selene ignored him.

"Not interested in conversing today?"

Silence.

"Fine. Let's go then." Pate led her into the hall, his movements stiff, and his cheek twitching. Her small platoon of Dominion soldiers waited dutifully to escort her. At least they no longer dragged her along the floor.

When Selene stepped out onto her personal dome platform, her gaze met Ivy's across the room. She ignored the enthusiastic wave and waited for the room to tell her what to do.

"Please proceed to the maze," it said.

Selene quirked an eyebrow at the unseen voice then glanced at Ivy, who's expression mirrored hers. Mild confusion, but also interest. Sighing, she followed Ivy's lead and descended to the arena floor.

"Please proceed to the maze," the voice repeated.

Skirting the obstacle course, Selene inspected the gray outer walls of the maze. She'd seen it from above. The maze was three times the size of the obstacle courses, with areas ranging in height and danger. Though it was hard to see from her side of the dome, she had a feeling Ivy knew it well. She'd be at a disadvantage once again.

Selene took deep breaths and approached her entrance. Her heart raced all the same as she tried unsuccessfully to tame her anxiety. By the time she stopped, her palms were sweaty, and nerves soured her stomach.

"Please step up to the starting line."

Selene glanced down. A white line appeared on the cement floor. Stepping up to it, Selene stretched out her muscles and waited for the voice to continue.

After several moments of silence, she gazed at the ceiling. The crackle of speakers blasted through the room. She winced. It cleared a moment later and the voice of a man came over the intercom.

"Good morning my Icarus stars," Pate purred over the speakers. She gritted her teeth and clenched her fists. "You both must be wondering what we're doing today. Ivy you've seen the maze before, but to give you each a fair chance, we're going to mix things up a little." Selene did *not* like the sound of that. "But don't let me ruin the surprise. When the buzzer sounds, you will enter the maze. When you find one another, you will fight. Simple as that. Keep an eye out though, we have a few surprises hidden for you."

The crackle of the speakers died and Selene stared at the white line ahead of her sneakers. Pate wanted them to fight—no doubt to prove who was better in close quarters. Selene bit her lip. Surprises were all she needed. But fighting Ivy had to be the priority. If she couldn't best her, she'd be sentenced to more time in the vat. Her whole body trembled at the thought of that cold blue liquid on her skin.

Selene shook her head. She had to focus.

"Enter the maze in three, two, one, go!"

Selene stepped over the white line. The maze wall slid up to block her exit. With a sigh, Selene glanced back and forth at her two options. Right would take her along the back wall while straight would take her deeper. Selene chose straight and took off into the maze. She didn't have time to stand around. If these surprises could help her, she wanted to find them quickly, before

Ivy had a chance to launch an attack.

Sprinting around corner after corner, Selene searched row by row for whatever Pate's awful surprise could be. She kept her breathing even, and her heart steady. She didn't want to be worn out when she came face to face with her enemy. Taking another sharp turn, Selene came to an abrupt halt. The walls of her prison had become mirrors.

"What kind of sick joke is this?" Selene looked back the way she'd come. Her own reflection met her eyes, repeated endlessly at odd angles. "Lovely."

Selene proceeded with caution, watching her haunted expression, taking in her tired eyes and bedraggled appearance reflected all around her. Vainly, she wondered when she'd get to wear something more flattering again, or maybe even a splash of makeup. Sighing to herself, she tried to think of the last time she'd cared about either of those things.

"There you are."

The charge of an energy gun broke the silence. Selene barely had a second to react. Diving down the nearest passage, she took off running. Ivy's feet pounded after her, her reflections following close behind. When Selene turned another corner, the floor sloped upward. She careened up it. Her long legs were to her advantage as Ivy fell behind; clambering to follow while Selene turned another corner. She emerged on a platform. A dead end. But from here she could see a portion of the uncovered maze.

"Damn it," she spat. Should she turn back and try another way, or jump into the maze below?

"Can't outrun me forever, Icarus!" Ivy's sing song voice floated from nearby.

It was too late to turn back. Selene looked back into the maze. Three rows over two plastic sword hilts glanced from another raised platform. She only had a second to memorize the way there.

Ivy rounded the corner and let out a gleeful little squeak. Her blazing green eyes and sleek ginger hair appeared in the mirrors all around. The whine of the energy gun charging sent Selene diving off the platform.

Selene landed in a roll, sparing her ankles the impact. She jumped into a run, ducking corners and staying low.

"Right, right, left, right..." she mumbled, keeping the maze in mind as she turned again and again, constantly misled by her own reflection. "Right, right, left, right."

Selene skidded to a stop. A grin spread over her face. She raced the last few feet and grabbed the forearm length black hilts from their hook. Diving around the next corner, she crouched and untied them.

"What the hell?" She blinked in confusion, inspecting the black plastic. It was layered with indents and grooves. Pressing her fingers wherever she thought there might be a button, she tried to find a way to use them.

"*Seleeeeene,*" Ivy sang.

Goosebumps came to life on her arms. Ivy was far too close for her liking. Picking up her hilts, Selene ran as quietly as she could, all the while trying to play with her potential weapons.

A few turns later she came to an open area with platforms, stairs and slopes heading in all different directions. This had to be the center of the maze. She heaved a sigh of relief, thankful it wasn't completely covered in mirrors.

"Come out, come out, wherever you are!"

Selene ducked behind a set of stairs. Her reflection disappeared around her. "Come on you stupid things!" Frustration drove her to smash one of them into the wall. A beam flared to life from the top of the hilt. Her heart leapt and she dropped it. The light winked out.

A sword?

She picked it up again, and prodded along the bottom of the hilt. There was a button. Pressing it in, a blade came to life. A blue glow lit her face in soft cold light. The sword was thin and long, bright but usable. Clicking to life her second blade, Selene realized what the blades were—twin short-bladed laser katanas.

"You've got to be kidding me. Swords?" She glanced from

blade to blade. "She gets a laser pistol and I get these? Real fair."

"Found you!"

Selene jumped from her hiding spot. Ivy leapt at her, kicking one of the hilts from her hand. It clattered across the ground, light disappearing. While Ivy reigned her foot back in, Selene swung her leg out, reflexes moving faster than she was used to. With one sweep, she sent Ivy's shocked little face to the floor. Instead of diving for another blow, Selene lunged across the ground to pick up her second weapon.

The red beam of Ivy's gun flew at the dome ceiling as her back hit the floor, blackening the light panels upon impact. Before her foe had fully recovered, Selene leapt the steps two at a time and plastered her body behind a wall for safety. Her breaths came quickly, adrenaline working through her veins.

"You got me that time Icarus!" Ivy laughed. Selene had no idea which direction her voice came from. That wasn't good.

Working her way calmly down the long hall, she peered down each joining path. Nothing but a confusing array of her own sweat-covered face.

Selene slid to the next corner and peeked around. A charge whined loudly. Selene barely had a second to pull her face back. The laser blasted the mirror behind her, searing the surface black.

"So this game is to the death I see." Selene gulped, tightening her grip around both blades. It was now or never. She couldn't play cat and mouse with Ivy for much longer. Her patience was wearing thin. Waiting with her back to the wall, Selene hoped her reflections would confuse Ivy when she went to round the corner. She didn't have much time to think on her feet. Her heart pounded against her ribcage.

Ivy peeked around the corner.

Instead of flaying her with a laser katana, Selene slammed her foot into Ivy's gut. Her kick wasn't square, and hardly took Ivy off balance. Ivy skidded into the mirror at her back. Selene pressed her advantage and lunged, swords at the ready. But Ivy was quick, and ducked just in time.

While Ivy rolled back to her feet, Selene slashed again and

again. With the flashing of light, the mirrors, and sensory overload, Ivy went on the defensive, blocking with her arms. It wasn't long before Ivy's dodges stopped and angry green eyes met Selene's. Ivy leapt back from Selene's blade and fired, taking back control of the situation. Selene reflexively brought her blade up, and to her surprise, her sword absorbed the shot.

"Huh."

Ivy stared wide-eyed at Selene's sword. Taking Ivy's shock as an opening, Selene chopped at Ivy's gun. Ivy pulled her weapon back, but Selene's blade sliced a clean line across the back of her hand.

Ivy's face contorted in anger and she gasped. Selene spun, ramming her foot into Ivy's chest. The gun flew from her grasp and Ivy collided with the mirror behind her. It shattered, creating wings on either side of Ivy's body. Before she had time to peel herself from the broken wall, Selene was on her, holding the katanas in an X against her neck. If she moved any closer, Ivy would lose her head.

"It's over Ivy," she panted. Selene couldn't help but grin. Finally, she'd bested this girl at something other than obstacles.

"It's never over, you moron," Ivy hissed. "We're both trapped here, and you're just making it worse."

"You're trapped here?"

Before Ivy could respond, a buzzer went off overhead.

"Winner, Icarus version one point zero."

Selene stepped back, dropping her swords. They both winked out before clattering to the floor. Her gaze never left Ivy's.

"If you're so sick of my being here, why don't you do something about it?" Not waiting for Ivy to answer, she turned and left. She had no more time to waste on Ivy's games.

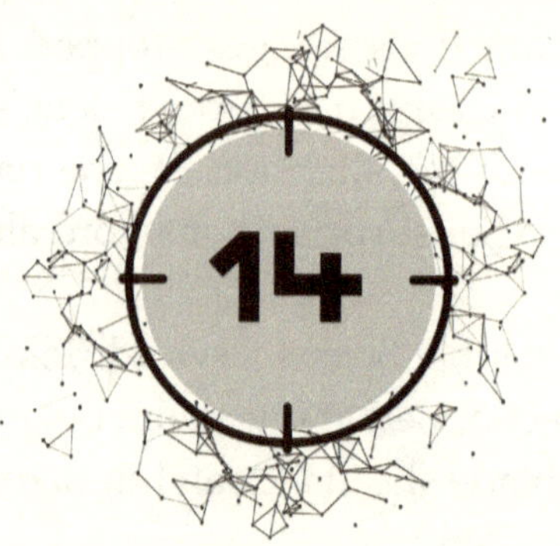

THE CONSTANT HUM OF ELECTRICITY drummed in the back of Selene's mind. It remained there, irrelevant until the sound ceased.

The overhead lights flickered. Once. Twice. Her world turned black.

"What now?" Selene sat up on her bed. It creaked beneath her.

The buzz returned, softer this time. With it came a soft blue glow. There were no alarms, no sirens or wails in the distance, only the soft buzz of silence.

Selene stood and her door swooshed open. *Another trick,* she thought. Her eyebrow quirked up, and her face twisted in irritation. They'd done these drills so many times now it was hard to tell what they wanted her to do. Sometimes she started in the arena, others during transport.

The few times they'd started their fake escape routines from her room, she'd gone, and each time got time in the vat.

Though freedom called to her like the distant buzz of technology, she still hesitated. Did she want more pain? Did she want to keep suffering? The answer was simple. She didn't. But more than anything, Selene wanted to get the hell out.

Stepping from her room and into the dim hall, she glanced left and right. Not a soul. Not a sound. Only the steady thump of her heart broke the quiet. Choosing left instead of right, Selene walked calmly. There was no need to rush to her fate. She might as well see if she could map out more of the complex in her mind.

Several halls later, she paused mid step.

Tap. Tap.

Her brows cinched. *What was that?* She twisted in every direction, stuck at a four-way intersection. Where had the noise come from? She waited.

Tap. Tap.

There it was again. Her heart leapt. Selene picked a direction and jogged, turning her head left and right, holding her breath while she listened.

Tap. Tap.

Selene stopped. Her skin cooled, goosebumps rising to the surface. The door to the lab—the one with the vat—waited for her.

She sucked in a sharp breath and backed away. "No, no, no." Selene shook her head. Cold slithered across her skin and her breath fled her lungs.

Tap. Tap.

The door whisked open. No one stood inside. The lights were dim like the rest, and inside the *tap tap* grew louder. It was coming from inside the vat.

Selene swallowed the lump in her throat and took a few deep breaths. There was no one inside to force her inside the vat. No one could hurt her. Her fingers danced at her thighs. She wished she had a gun.

Drawing every ounce of courage she had, she stepped inside. With the lights dimmed, she took a moment to get the lay of the land. Her hip bumped a cart, sending metal instruments clattering to the floor.

"*Shit,*" she hissed.

Tap. Tap. Tap.

The tapping grew louder, increased in its urgency. Selene reached the glass case to find the vat half full, and a small boy inside. Her heart leapt into her throat. Desperate blue eyes met hers. She lunged forward, grabbing at the glass lid.

"I'll get you out!" Her sweaty fingers slipped on the glass surface.

The boy only nodded, letting his hand rest. She groped for a latch to free him. Cold metal brushed her fingertips. There. She threw the top open and reached inside.

Her whole being protested as cool gel slipped around her hands. It hadn't yet completely solidified, but it still felt heavy. Wrapping her fingers around his biceps, she pulled the small blond teenager from his cage. He couldn't be taller than five feet, with gangly limbs and tan skin. He breathed heavily, his eyes wide with fright.

When he was finally clear, she set him on the floor. He shook violently. Selene grabbed a lab coat from the wall, wrapping it around his trembling limbs.

"You're free now." She pushed his thick hair from his face. Something about him was familiar. It had been so long since she'd been outside these walls, she didn't know if it was from the life she remembered or her past. "What's your name?"

He met her gaze with tear-filled eyes. "A-Aaron."

Why was that name familiar? Selene smiled while she racked her brain. "Aaron. I'm Selene."

"Hi." His gaze darted around the lab.

Then she remembered. "Aaron! You're Julian's son." It had been so long ago that Julian had confronted her in the wildlife reserve and shown her a picture of his missing son. She'd nearly forgotten she'd promised his father to keep an eye out for him— and here he was in her own personal hell. Her heart dropped to her stomach.

Aaron nodded. "You know my dad?"

"I do. He's been looking for you."

Tears spilled down his face. "I don't know how long I've been here. I want to go home."

Selene nodded. Her heart broke for this poor child. "I'll get you to him." Though the Dominion had put her through escape attempts again, and again, this was the time she had to do it. She had to get out of here, not just for herself, but for Aaron. "We've got to go. Can you walk?"

"I think so." Aaron wiped his tears on his sleeve. Selene stepped back, holding his wrists and gently pulled him to his feet. He wobbled, but stood straight. He was small for a teenager and thin as a pole.

"Let's go."

Selene led Aaron to the door and peered down the dim blue cast hall. Her heart and mind raced. What would happen if she couldn't get them out? Would they turn Aaron into one of the other Icarus? She shook her head. There was no time to dwell on that now.

Not a sound echoed through the empty corridors. She motioned for him to keep quiet, silently wishing he knew sign language like most of her team. Picking a direction, Selene took off at a leisurely jog, making sure Aaron could keep up before moving faster. Though he'd been unsteady at first, he moved with purpose now, determination filling his blue-green gaze.

This is what the Dominion was doing. They stole naturals from their homes, the Outskirts and the *nat* towns surrounding the cities. They took them and they experimented on them, trying to make them into Icarus—whatever that meant.

Fury flooded her chest. How dare they? This was a *child* for God's sake.

Keeping one eye on Aaron, and one on their path, she urged him along. They had to get out of here, and fast.

A siren cut through the hall. The blue glow turned red.

"*Shit.*" Selene stopped.

Aaron did the same. "What now?"

Her mind raced. She had no idea how to escape this place, but she had to try. She looked back and forth for a way out. She saw none. Biting her lip, she turned left. "This way!"

Aaron didn't hesitate in following.

They travelled quickly, turning time and time again until boot-clad footsteps sounded in the distance. Selene didn't stop, not until more came from up ahead. *Damn.* She skidded to a halt.

She slammed her fist against the control panel to her right. A door swooshed open.

"Get inside and hide," she said.

Aaron nodded and rushed in.

Selene paused for a moment longer before joining him. The door shut behind her. Inside the room was nearly pitch black. She could hardly see a thing, let alone Aaron.

"Where are you?" she whispered.

No voice answered.

"Aaron?"

The lights came on. White flared from every direction. Selene cried out, knives of pain shooting through her eyes and into her skull. She shielded her face, waiting a few moments before she opened them again. When she did, the room was entirely white. Several sets of fluorescent lights lit the small space. The room was devoid of furnishing.

Selene turned from the corner to find Aaron. A Dominion soldier stood behind him, holding Aaron's throat in one hand and a gun to his forehead in the other.

"Aaron!" Her heart raced. "Let him go!"

Fear shot through her bones. Her fingers closed into fists and she broke into a sweat. A black mask obscured the soldier's face, just like the rest of him. Aaron stared at her with wide eyes, tears welling in their depths. His lips quivered in a whimper.

"Put him down!" Her voice shook. The soldier did nothing, said nothing, and didn't move. His finger rested against the trigger. "What do you want? You can take me back. Just release him. He's too young for this." Panic bubbled inside. She had to get Aaron out of this, had to get them *both* out.

How fast could she get across this room and disarm the soldier? It would only take three bounds and an elbow to the man's shielded face. Her fists clenched. She could do it, but not before he shot Aaron.

"Please, let him go." Selene stepped forward.

The soldier's finger twitched on the trigger. That's all it took. The shot was deafening in the hollow space. Her ears rang, drawing all other sounds from the world. Blood splattered the white room, and Aaron's eyes lost their light. The soldier dropped him unceremoniously. Aaron's eyes stared at nothing while a pool of blood expanded around his halo of blonde hair.

Selene couldn't think, couldn't feel. Cold replaced her panic. She gaped, and then screamed. What had he done? *Why* had he done it?

She rushed forward, catching the soldier by surprise.

Selene slammed her fist into his gut, and spun reflexively to dodge his return blow. Her elbow smashed into his head. He crumpled, much less gracefully than Aaron had. She tore the gun from his grasp and shot him through the head. Her ears rang. With a non-laser pistol there was no sealed wound, no lack of spray. With a bullet, everything was messy. The white of the room and her clothes became flecked with red. She didn't think.

The swoosh of the door caught her attention through the haze and ringing in her ears. She spun, her arm outstretched and shot. Once. Twice. Three times.

Three soldiers fell, dyeing the room further with their blood.

When the next came, she emptied her clip. No one else tried to enter.

Selene dropped the gun. She hardly heard it hit the ground. What had they done? What had these monsters done? This was too far. This was a young life. This was an innocent.

She stared at Aaron's lifeless body, and dropped to her knees in his blood. She bent over, hands clutching her hair and she screamed. She screamed and screamed until boots beat the floor outside and a taser bullet took her out. Selene fell to the floor in spasms. She didn't let go of Aaron's lifeless face in front of her. She clung to the image of him. She clung to it until she blacked out.

Alarms blared to life so suddenly they pulled her from the darkness of sleep. Her whole body quivered, the shrill sound pushing into her skull. Selene groaned and covered her ears while backing into the wall behind her bed. She opened her eyes to find something was different about her room. It took her a moment to notice, but as the alarm continued its wail, she had a moment to wake up and take in her surroundings. Though her room was still stark white, it was bigger, with a large bathroom off the adjacent wall and a small desk in the corner.

"What the..." Selene shimmied off the bed, hands cupped around her ears. As she approached the desk, her door swung open.

Something in her came to life. Selene leapt at the man stepping into her prison. She bashed his face into the floor once before he reared an elbow into her chest.

Air exploded from her lungs.

Selene sat back hard on the floor. The man turned to face her, nose bloody and black hair disheveled from where she'd grabbed it. He growled something at her, but she couldn't make out his words over the alarms and the pounding in her ears.

Reflexively, she kicked his feet out from under him. The man fell, his head slamming off the corner of the desk. Her eyes widened as his body went limp. Blood gathered around his head. His eyes stared unseeing back at her.

She hadn't meant to kill him, only stop him long enough to flee.

Gunshots in the hall brought her back to reality.

The urge to flee overcame all of her senses. She had to escape. *Run.* Selene leapt to her feet and sprinted from the room. She had to get out of here, had to move, had to find a way out while she could. Entering the brightly lit hall, it was different too. Instead of being pristinely white, it was dingy yellow with a brown border at the top.

Selene pushed on, adrenaline rushing through her veins, lending speed to her feet. She rounded corner after corner, the alarm above never stopping. She had no idea where she was going, but she had to get out.

Fresh air brushed her limbs. Her heart leapt.

Heading in her hopeful direction of safety, she stopped dead as a black clad figure stepped through an open doorway, laser rifle at his shoulder. Selene ducked back into the safety of the clear hallway. He hadn't seen her.

She waited a few heartbeats, and then peered back around the corner. At the far end of the hall the wall was blown out. An open cargo bay with metal walls and flooring was filled on either side with storage crates. Beyond were the wings and propellers of a docked hovercraft. Outside the metal machine was the night sky.

Selene ran, ignoring the potential danger. She leapt through the hole in the wall and onto the cargo bay lift. Her feet carried her into the ship, her heart pounding in her ears.

A sudden screech ripped through the hall. She spun to face it.

"Wake up damn it!"

Selene awoke with a start, a soldier shaking her shoulders. She blinked in confusion, her memory clinging to her conscious mind. Where was she? Selene sat up. She was back in her small white room, no desk or pool of blood in sight.

"Finally," the man grumbled. "Get up and get moving."

Alarms rang overhead. So it hadn't just been in her dreams. The wail wasn't as loud in reality—it was distant and hollow, not ear splittingly shrill. Selene shook herself, trying to rid the haze clinging to her brain before she obeyed. Pulling her shoes on, she followed the man into the hall. An armed escort awaited her.

"Of course." She sighed.

They circled her quickly, as per the routine. At least they didn't throw cuffs on her this time. They were either too busy to think of it, or something big was going down, something they were in a hurry for. Cold metal stabbed between her shoulder blades, shoving her forward. Selene shot the masked soldier a glare.

The black faceless look he gave her brought her back before her dream, before the alarm—Aaron. Her heart seized.

The man pushed again, forcing her to follow in line with the others. With blood still fresh in her mind, Selene had a hard time concentrating on where she was being led. White hallways blurred into yellow. Her mind conjured images of her old room, the halls and that hovercraft she'd escaped to. Each image was dashed with blood—spray on the walls, the floor, across her white clothes. Her eyes stung.

"Selene!"

Selene stopped in her tracks, skin crawling at the sound of his voice.

"The truck is waiting for her." Though Pate spoke to one of her guards, his predatory gaze didn't leave hers. Cold fire blazed in her chest and her nostrils flared. She hoped he saw how much she hated him and what he'd done, not just to her, but to all the naturals brought here. "Bring her to the garage."

"Yes sir." The man nodded and motioned them down another hall.

Pate stayed with them, irritatingly close. Her skin itched, inches from his black coat. Heat radiated from his skin. She was unable to ignore his presence.

"How can you live with yourself?"

Pate glanced at her, his smug look dropping for a moment. "I don't know what you're talking about."

She glared. "You let them kill that boy. He couldn't have been older than fifteen. You're a fucking *monster*." Tears welled in her eyes.

His jaw set, and he looked forward. Pate ignored her, walking the length of the hall with his brows furrowed.

When silence reigned for more than five minutes, curiosity got the better of her. "What's going on?"

Pate smirked, returning her sidelong look. He was all too pleased that she decided to converse with him. "Nothing to worry about, kitten." He grinned. "We'll get you to safety."

Selene bristled at the pet name and barely resisted baring her teeth. More than ever she wanted to leap at him, claws at the ready. If he wanted a kitten, she'd show him a tiger.

"Is someone attacking?" She had to get *something* out of him.

"Why in Aldar's name would you think that?"

"I don't know… the alarms were kind of a giveaway."

Pate smiled and ignored her glares and questions. Usually it was very much the other way around.

Several halls and stairwells later they emerged in a dark garage littered with armored vehicles and land speeders. Groups of soldiers trotted throughout the long room, loading naturals dressed in white into trucks. How many were there?

They barked out orders, jabbing them with laser rifles. Pate took hold of her bicep, his fingers hot against her skin. She recoiled, but he only yanked her forward, leading her across the room to a large black van with its back doors wide open. Inside, chains were hooked to its floor, cuffs sitting on the seat waiting for her. Her heart sank.

"Lovely." What else had she expected? What could she really do? She couldn't fight her way past the dozens of guards in the garage. And what would be the point anyway? Aaron's face flashed in her mind, his blonde curls soaked in blood. She shook her head. She wasn't getting out of here until the Aldar Dominion got what they wanted, or she was dead.

"I'll see you soon." Pate passed her off to the soldier in charge. He let his fingers linger on her arm a little longer than necessary before pulling away.

The soldier pushed her inside. Two of her guards clambered in after her. They sat on the bench opposite to her, leaning forward to cuff her hands. The cold metal bit her wrists. She pulled up, chains rattling. She couldn't move her arms more than a few inches. It was clever of them to keep her arms down, but they hadn't accounted for how fast she was with her feet.

Leaning her head back against the wall, Selene ignored Pate's little wave goodbye before he took off. She concentrated on her surroundings.

Two guards were nothing to her. But could she get the keys *and* take them out in time to escape? The doors of her prison slammed shut and a loud bar slid into place.

Did she want to escape? Was it really worth it? Her eyebrows furrowed. Was there a point in escaping? Her friends were obviously fine without her, or they'd have figured out a way to rescue her by now.

The van jostled beneath her, the engine revving.

"Did you see the new campaign ads in the holofeed last night?"

Once en route, Selene's guards relaxed, pulling their masks off and chatting about what they saw on the news yesterday. While they lounged across from her, occasionally giving her curious glances, Selene worked on her cuffs, wiggling her hands. She had nothing better to do. Her wrists may be small, but her cuffs were tight. She'd have to dislocate her thumbs to get them off. But there was no way to do that with these bozos watching. Sighing in defeat, Selene tuned into her guards' conversation.

"It's been awhile since I've seen the Eaton base." The scruffy redhead guard grinned like a fool, alien eyes bulging, stripes lining his yellow skin and flat nose.

The other shrugged. "I was there last year, it's nothing special." Beige skin and blue hair, he was handsome for his age.

"Really? I heard you see a lot more action out there."

"If action's what you're expecting, you're going to be sorely disappointed, kid."

"Come on old man, don't you miss the war? It's a lot more interesting than dragging pretty girls around." War?

His comrade rolled his eyes while the redhead's eyes darted toward her.

"Your chatter is interesting and all, but what is the Eaton base and why are we going there?" Selene interrupted. She meant for her words to bite with their usual sarcasm, but her tone sounded flat, even to her.

Two sets of eyes locked on her. The older of the two raised a tattooed eyebrow while the younger grinned, ready to fill her in. He probably would have if his lieutenant didn't cut him a sideways glare.

"Oh sure, you're all chatty until the prisoner wants to talk." Selene rolled her eyes half-heartedly.

"We don't consort with prisoners," the older of the two huffed.

Just her luck.

Bumping along the desert road, Selene watched the night sky

through the driver's viewport. She wished she knew the stars well—at least then maybe she'd have a clue where they were headed. She leaned back against cold steel and shut her eyes. She wasn't getting out of here anytime soon.

It was nearly dawn when the driver made a small gasping sound. Selene's guards looked forward in concern while Selene twisted her wrists, gripping her thumb, ready to yank it out of place.

A high-pitched sizzle approached from outside. She froze and stared at the viewport with wide eyes. *Shit.*

"There's something—" the driver was cut off.

A loud roar rocked the silent night before an impact sent them flying tail-over-head. Selene yelped and held fast to her chains, trying to keep herself in her seat. Everything became chaos in the back as they rolled. The men's laser pistols, combat knives and spare energy rounds bounced around the hollow space, smacking her in the head, face and chest numerous times.

All she could do was hold on as another roll sent Selene's head bashing into the wall not once but twice. Blackness dipped in and out as her consciousness came and went. The dim light flickered above, body parts flying in her wake. She mindlessly grabbed at any weapon that flew by, but she never could reach any. Boots clobbered her body again and again, an elbow to the gut was nothing compared to the body that nearly crushed her hands.

When the rolling finally stopped, Selene lay in a mess of limbs, her wrists aching. Blood poured from her nose. Copper blossomed on her tongue. She'd be a mess of bruises by morning.

Groaning, she tried to pull out from under the mangled body of one guard. Her head swam and her whole body ached like it had gone through the worst beating of its life. Tires screeched, followed by gravel spattering the back of the van. She pulled one leg from under the redhead. Murmured voices drifted from outside. Doors opened and slammed shut. Boots ran through the dirt, and then were silenced by the sand.

What now?

"Over here!" someone called.

Fear tightened her chest. She froze. Selene knew this game well. For weeks the Alliance pretended to rescue her, and when she figured it out they put her in the vat. Again and again they'd done it, until they killed Aaron. The boy's soft features and blond hair came to mind, lying on the floor in a pool of his own blood. She couldn't take it anymore. Shaking her head, Selene pulled at her chains. They rattled against the floor turned ceiling. Her head was foggy and sore, as were her wrists. They were rubbed raw, blood trickling down to her elbows.

"Not again." She feebly pulled on her restraints. Half hanging from the ceiling, tears welled in her eyes. She couldn't take that dark place again. It was so cold and painful.

What had she done to deserve this hell?

The doors wrenched open and light poured in. Selene struggled to pull her other leg out from under her guards. With her hands cuffed, she couldn't protect herself. She squinted into the light. It pierced her skull like knives.

"Stay back!" She pulled on the cuffs again. Her wrists ached with each yank.

"Selene?" one of the shadows asked. She couldn't be sure which. Headlights blinded her, turning her supposed rescuers into silhouettes. The shadows came closer.

"I said, stay *back*!"

The men paused, but only for a moment to pull the doors wide. They scraped along the rocky terrain before slamming off the back of the vehicle. Two figures came in, pulling the bodies out with them. Once they were gone, another approached. Selene grabbed her chains, pulling herself up and bracing her upper body as she kicked out, nailing him in the face.

The man fell back, illuminating black military fatigues and a young face with a broken nose.

"We're here to rescue you!" another shadow snapped. Selene ignored them, and kicked at anyone who came near her. Her sore muscles protested, but she heaved herself up.

"I'm *not* going back into that damn vat!" she hissed. "Leave me here until Pate has had enough and I can go. I'm not letting you damn Icarus fool me one more time."

"Icarus?" one echoed, peering in through the open doors.

"We're not with the Dominion." Another sighed. "This isn't a trick, I promise."

Selene shook her head and kicked at him. He caught her foot. Selene kicked with the other. He grabbed it too.

"I'm not going anywhere!" Though struggling now seemed futile, she squirmed anyway, even as the two others restrained her, and her cuffs were removed. She wriggled in their grasp, trying to gain purchase with her elbows, knees, anything she could use to get away.

"Would you be still?" the tallest of the trio snapped. He was the one holding both of her legs, locking her knees together so she could only kick out uselessly with her feet.

"Holy Aldar, she is strong," the one holding her left arm grumbled. His voice was deep, irritated and amused all at once.

"They've had her in training for weeks I'm sure, of course she's strong," her leg keeper snapped back.

"I think we need to knock her out, Sav. There's no way we'll get her all the way to HQ like this." The man to her right gritted his teeth, pinning her arm behind her, holding onto her shoulder to lock her into place while simultaneously carrying her with the others.

"You will *not* knock me out!" Selene bucked hard, and the man at her legs, the one she assumed was Sav almost lost his grip.

"Definitely going to have to." Sav grunted as he reigned her unruly legs back into his grasp.

"Wait—" She was abruptly cut off by a hit to the head.

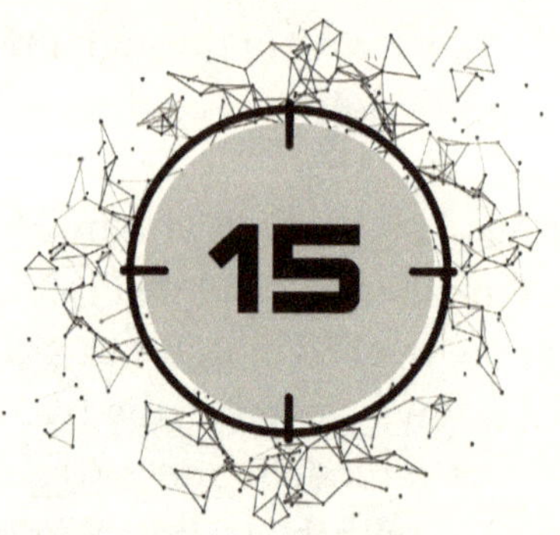

15

SELENE CAME SLOWLY TO CONSCIOUSNESS instead of all at once. Her brain felt fried, dragging her down again and again into the blackness of sleep. When she finally opened her eyes, it wasn't because the fog had disappeared, but because her last waking moments returned to her.

She blinked in confusion up at the white ceiling. What the hell had happened?

"Not in a vat," she said. Selene paused to mull this over. "Good start."

She sat up and glanced around. The room was eerily similar to the one with the Dominion, but this one had down filled pillows instead of the flat hard piece of fabric she was used to. More suspicious than ever were the soft sounds of chatter outside her door.

"Curious."

A mirror caught her reflection across the room. She stood. She hadn't seen her own face since her fight with Ivy in the maze. Her nose wasn't bloody, her head wasn't bruised and even her hair remained mostly untangled. Whoever had taken her at least cleaned her up. She even had on a new pair of white slacks and a pale yellow tank top. The only evidence of her previous night's adventure were the bandages wrapping her wrists. They ached,

146

still raw.

More interested than worried, Selene stepped away from her reflection and up to the door. It whooshed open.

"Hm."

Stepping into a white hall, the linoleum chilled her bare feet. The overhead lights were glaringly bright, the walls white with a few abstract paintings hung up. This wasn't the Dominion she'd come to know. She followed the chatter. Could she be dreaming?

Her stomach turned. This had to be another Dominion trick. They were full of those lately. When she finally emerged at the end of the hall, she was sure of it.

A large group of people stood in a rectangular room, clustering in small groups or alone. They seemed to be waiting for something. Selene scanned the crowd and froze. While most were clones, a few large-pored naturals stood among them. Icarus? The hair on the back of her neck stood at attention. Each of them could betray her. Selene stepped away from the naturals.

Dressed in identical yellow shirts and white pants, each person stared ahead with the same glazed expression. A large seamless monitor with flickering lights and a large question mark in the center faced the crowd.

A young boy with shaking hands stepped up to the board. He pressed his palm to the screen, and the question mark disappeared. Question after question popped up, flashing by faster than she could read at this distance. The boy answered each one with a flick of his fingers. When he finished a large red circle appeared at the center. He sighed and stepped to the side. A door swooshed open and he stepped through it.

An exit. Selene's heart leapt double time. She slipped through the crowd of bodies until the door closed. It didn't reopen. Where would she go anyway? If she didn't go through with whatever new trick this was, she would end up getting more time in the vat—or worse, she'd get someone killed again. Her heart sank.

Selene fell in line with the others, taking a deep breath as she waited.

It took several minutes for the others to go through. Several men, women and children answered each question dutifully before leaving the room. Each person got the same red circle at the end.

Then it was Selene's turn. Stepping up to the screen, she placed her palm on it. The question mark disappeared, leaving Selene with her first question. Where did she come from? It gave her options: New Manhattan, the Outskirts, Old Washington, and so forth. Grimacing, she did her best to come up with an accurate answer, since in truth she had no idea. After the first question she hardly thought about the rest. She answered the first few yes or no questions, followed by a few multiple choices. Most of them revolved around her status as a natural human, her descent, which she knew little of, as well as her economic status, aptitude, emotional balance and even her stance on animal experimentation.

When the last question disappeared and another didn't flick into place she blinked in confusion. Was that it? She waited for the next question or the red circle, but nothing appeared. No one moved, and the monotonous chatter in the background ceased.

"What now?" Selene asked, to no one in particular.

No one answered. The screen flashed green and then retracted into a slat in the floor, leaving her staring into a vat of blue liquid. She gasped.

"No!" Selene cried, eyes widening and heart pounding. She backed away from the vat. "Not again! *Please* not again!"

Two guards she hadn't realized were in the crowd came from behind.

"No!" Selene ran for the exit.

Someone from the crowd caught her, and she spun, elbowing him in the groin. He doubled over. Another reached for her arm. She slammed her fist into his gut. Pulling away from their rough grasp, she ran down the hall she'd come from, her legs pumping with renewed energy. Whatever this was, she had to get away.

She hadn't even gotten past the first door before she was tackled to the ground.

Air rushed from her lungs in a gasp. Panic bubbled inside as she clawed at the floor. She had to get away. She couldn't go back. Not again.

"You must come with us," the man grabbing her waist bellowed. He pulled her across the linoleum. Her shirt rolled up and her skin burned against the floor. She gasped in air, her fingertips slipping across the clean tile. *Not again, not again.* A second man grabbed her arms. They heaved her up and dragged her back, kicking and screaming.

Her heart rose into her throat as she stared down at the pool of blue. It was brighter than she was used to, more aqua than indigo. Swallowing the lump in her throat, Selene hardly had a moment to take a breath before she was thrown forward.

Falling headlong into the blue, she squeezed her eyes shut and held her breath for as long as she could. The liquid pulled her in, squeezing her ribs before solidifying and keeping her still. She lasted two full minutes before she couldn't take it anymore. She took a breath. Liquid poured down her nostrils and throat, suffocating her. She coughed and spat, tried to push it out, but nothing helped remove the liquid from her lungs.

After several long minutes passed. Tears stung her eyes. She focused less on breathing, having become accustomed to drowning, and concentrated on the strange soothing warmth of the liquid. The sensation of floating was calming, the heat like the arms of a lover. Her worries quickly drifted, and with it her suspicion.

By the time hands gripped her arms and pulled her out she was nearly euphoric. Part of her was miffed that her previous vat experiences hadn't been like this, while the other half of her was grateful to breathe again. Once she'd rid her lungs of the liquid, she started to regain some of her wits. Her state of ecstasy faded as gentle hands washed her face of the remaining gel.

"What the hell was that?" she murmured, half dazed.

"Nothing like the vat you're used to," a pleasant female voice whispered back.

Selene opened her eyes to take in a beautiful pale blue face with blazing red curls and dark blue eyes. Her first thought was this alien woman was part of the Dominion. Her second was that someone with such a soothing voice couldn't have anything to do with them. But if that was the case, what was going on?

Keeping silent, Selene let the woman wring her hair out and help her stand. Her body wasn't sore anymore, but light as a feather. One look at herself and she realized the bandages on her wrists were gone, and the skin beneath had been healed.

"Where am I?" she asked.

The woman only smiled, her dimpled cheeks glowing pink. The pastel color was a surprise; she'd never seen an alien blush before. She didn't answer, and Selene didn't pressure her to. Instead, she watched the alien woman with curious eyes.

After almost ten minutes out of the blue gel, her senses fully returned. She stepped away from the woman, who only smiled and nodded before motioning her to the door. They were in some sort of bathing room, with a steamy pool nearby and showers lining another wall. The woman led her out, and the door closed behind them. Her skin chilled.

Her clothes had literally evaporated. She no longer wore anything but a thin film of pale blue gel that hardened to her body from the neck down. It left her not completely exposed, but not exactly covered. She shifted her limbs, expecting the substance to crack like wax. It didn't, and remained pliable as she twisted her wrists.

"Will clothes be provided?"

"Soon." Her hostess laughed, guiding her through a long hall slanting downward.

Selene followed. The alien woman led her to the end of the hall, into a large room filled with people and gym equipment.

"So you've brought me to a gym. Interesting choice."

Again, the woman laughed and motioned her forward. Selene obliged, stepping inside. When she looked back, her escort had disappeared.

"Wonderful." Selene faced the room. So now she was pretty much naked, in a room full of strangers, in unfamiliar territory. If this wasn't the Dominion they sure had strange rules about hospitality. Hope stirred in her chest.

A tall black-skinned man with swirling tattoos and blazing green eyes sauntered across the room. He grinned, stopped a few feet away. Something about him was familiar. She stepped back, her guard up. Having a pretty little alien woman guide her around unfamiliar territory was one thing, but this guy had the look of a soldier.

"You made it," he said.

Selene cocked an eyebrow. Her previous curiosity quickly dissolved into blind suspicion. *It's a trick. It has to be a trick.*

"Where the hell am I?" she snapped.

His smile grew. Selene narrowed her eyes, instinctively reaching to her right hip. She was disappointed to find no laser pistol. Part of her missed being able to whip one out to get answers, even if she *should* learn less violent methods of interrogation.

"You're safe now," he began.

Her gaze flicked around the mirror-walled room, meeting many sets of curious eyes. Her presence had garnered some attention.

"That doesn't answer my question." Her fingers itched for a weapon while her legs tensed to run. She couldn't help it, something about him made her want to kick him. She recognized his voice, but couldn't place it.

"You're with the Alliance now—"

"I've heard that one before, and all I got were Icarus with a blood lust. How the hell do I know you're not one of them?"

His smile turned pitying, and Selene bristled. She wasn't anyone's little charity case, and even if they were who they said they were, she hadn't a clue who the Alliance was or what they could possibly want with her. She needed answers, before she started hurting people. If this was all a trick, who was she really hurting? The Dominion.

"You don't," the man said. "I'm sure nothing at this point can convince you otherwise, but we're not the bad guys. We aren't the Aldar Dominion. We're the rebels, the ones who saved your sorry ass *by the way*."

She froze. Now she could place his voice. In the van after the crash. His name was Sav, and he was the one who gave the order to knock her out. Selene whipped a fist at him.

Sav dodged. She spun for a roundhouse kick. Like the previous night, he caught her foot. She yanked back, spinning into a sweep. His eyes widened as he fell to the floor. But he never hit, only braced himself and flipped back to his feet.

Selene didn't give him a moment to rest. She went at him with her fists, elbows, knees and feet, lunging after him with hit after hit. No one stepped in to stop her—no one tried to save Sav from her attack. And Sav never lost that stupid grin.

She finally took a moment to breathe, and it was his turn to lunge at her. Pushing forward, he shot a fist at her head. She ducked and swept her leg for his ankles. He leapt over her leg and came down on her, pinning her to the floor. Selene kneed him in the gut, rolling over him to gain the upper hand. Fist raised, she went in for a punch when he erupted in laughter.

Stunned into silence, Selene froze mid swing. Was this guy laughing at her? She was literally about to punch his jaw so hard he'd have a bruise tomorrow, and he was laughing?

"You're amazing," he said when he'd finally calmed down. "It's been awhile since I've fought another Icarus."

Selene blinked in confusion. "Another?"

"Yes." Sav smirked at her. "You thought I was born with these pretty boy eyes?" His eyes blazed like emeralds. Just like hers.

Selene shook her head. She'd thought he was a clone.

"I'm like you, or at least, somewhat. Version three point one, how about yourself?"

Selene stared at him a few moments longer, looking for signs of deceit. He could be one of them—one of the Icarus to torture her inside the Dominion lab. But what if he wasn't? What if he was telling the truth? Though she'd always hoped her friends would save her, maybe this Alliance really did exist.

Stepping from his chest, Selene stood and offered a hand to pull him up. She didn't know if he was lying or not, but she was willing to find out. He accepted her hand, coming to his feet with an expectant look on his face.

"One point zero," she said.

"The original." His eyes widened.

"So I've heard." She shrugged.

"No wonder you put up such a fight last night. You still don't remember everything do you?" Selene cocked an eyebrow. It was a rhetorical question. "Of course you don't. When I got ahold of some Dominion files it said the originals had their memories altered, some even erased."

"You were there?"

"Not at the same lab. I'm from down south. The Alliance rescued me two years ago."

"The Alliance, huh?" She'd been hearing a lot about this mystery organization. So far all she knew for sure was that they were against the Dominion, or were some sort of rebel force. If they were powerful enough to rescue her from her enemies, maybe they were worth knowing.

Sav grinned. "How about you let me introduce you to some friends, and then we'll get you some answers?"

Selene couldn't contain her sigh of relief. Finally, she was going to get somewhere. "As long as this shit all makes sense soon."

"You got it."

SEVERAL DAYS LATER, SELENE MIGHT not have gotten all of her answers, but she was fairly certain Sav was telling the truth. The Alliance was on a mission to save the Icarus not committed to the Dominion—or at least that's what they claimed. They had rescued her from a living hell and she couldn't be more grateful, but part of her revolted against these good people. How could she be sure they were who they said they were? What if they were another Dominion trick? It would be the most elaborate one yet, but she wouldn't put it past them.

Sav promised on day one that she'd meet with the board members—the ones in charge of the Alliance. Before she did it was all about trust. Selene needed to trust them as much as they needed to trust her. But trust wasn't something she gave out freely.

"Good morning."

Smiling faces greeted her as she made her way to the cafeteria. She forced a smile and waved back.

At first she had been frightened by all the kindness they showed her. She went out of her way to avoid it, unable to trust that they wouldn't suddenly turn on her, that this wasn't just another of the Dominion's tests, even if they'd assured her it wasn't. Sav had taught her to relax and open her heart again once he realized what she was doing. After all, a lot of them had been through the same as her, if not worse. At least much of her memory was still lost; most of them retained everything that had happened to them.

"Selene!" Sav called from his usual table.

He sat with his two comrades, the ones who'd been with him the night they rescued her. Whereas Sav was a natural human turned Icarus, one of his friends was an alien and the other a clone. They were an amusing group to sit with. Most of the time they ragged on each other or shared battle stories about other rescues. Sav's two friends had been the ones to rescue him.

Selene sat beside Flik, an alien with flaming red hair, orange skin, black eyes and a toothy grin. He had been the one to knock her out—something she still didn't fully appreciate.

"What going on?" She an eyebrow at their grinning faces.

"It's official, the board is ready to see you," Sav said.

"It's about damn time."

"We've actually never seen them move this fast." Lan, or Lanny as Sav affectionately called him, was a clone, more of a tech guy than a soldier, but still well-muscled. Lanny was fairly laid back, with soot black hair, olive skin and brown eyes. He looked to be about thirty, but as a clone he was most likely older.

"You must be special." Flik shot her a wink.

"Obviously." Selene rolled her eyes. She said it with heavy sarcasm, but she had to agree. If this was a strange occurrence, it was probably her status as Icarus getting her in the door so quickly. Though she enjoyed the trio's company, she was ready to get her answers and get out of here. Selene had disappeared from her crew's life for long enough.

More than a month had gone by, and she couldn't make them wait any longer. For all they knew, she could be dead. They had probably assumed as much when they didn't find her body after the crash. Once with the Dominion, your fate was sealed.

Sav smiled into his toast. "We'll take you after breakfast."

"We?"

"The three of us."

"Why's everyone going?"

"To hear your story."

"What story?"

"The story of how you got the way you are, and are where you are now I suppose." Sav shrugged, and devoured the rest of his breakfast in a single bite.

"What about my answers?" Selene exhaled loudly, fear working its way up in her spine. She shivered, and had to remind herself again that she was safe.

"You'll get them. But they want to hear from you first."

"Typical," she said.

"Don't worry about it, you won't have too big an audience." Flik grinned.

"If you hadn't noticed, I'm not exactly shy."

"We've noticed." Lanny exchanged a look with Sav.

"What's that supposed to mean?"

"You didn't exactly hide your lady bits in the gym the other morning." Flik chuckled.

Flush rushed to her face. "I wasn't exactly given clothes beforehand!"

"Sure, but you didn't have to show off either."

Crossing her arms, Selene fixed her bench mate with a glare. He grinned sheepishly and gave her big, innocent eyes.

"You're awful," she said.

"He really is," Sav agreed.

Once breakfast was finished, the group picked up and left. Sav led the way through the complex, which she had come to know as the Alliance headquarters. They wouldn't tell her exactly where it was, just that it was hidden in the mountains somewhere near Old Washington. She didn't bother pushing the matter: she'd find out soon enough.

Sav stopped several halls later at a large boardroom with screens littering the walls and several businessmen and a woman at the head of a long conference table. Selene had expected more of a crowd from Sav's commentary, but she counted herself lucky to be amongst only three strangers.

"Selene, welcome."

The three board members stood, one a tall alien woman with white hair, silver skin and sky blue eyes, dressed in a lab coat. The other two aliens were dull by comparison, with gray skin, black hair and eyes, dressed in tailored suits.

"Thanks." Selene stepped inside with her posse at her back. She took a seat near the other end of the table, while Sav and his comrades hung back.

"This is Director Tine." Sav nodded in the woman's direction.

"Nice to meet you."

"We've spent a long time waiting to find you," the Director said.

"Uh huh... so catch me up. What's going on with this place?"

"As much as we'd like to pour out the secrets of the rebels to you, we still don't know if we can trust you." The woman's grimace deepening as she spoke, revealing gray lines in her perfect silver skin. "You're a hard person to track down. We can hardly find any history on you, and that leads us to worry. If you're working for the Dominion, we would have no choice but to detain you."

Selene sputtered a protest, fear rushing through her like a wave splashing her with ice water.

Tine raised a hand to stop her. "But from what our intel tells us, this is most likely not the case. We want to use you in our rebellion, Selene. You're what the Dominion wants—without you they're stuck with that pawn of theirs."

Both of the men scoffed and exchanged knowing gazes.

"What pawn?" Selene asked.

"Governor Pate."

Selene bristled at the name.

"He's been working with them for years."

"Yeah I definitely got that." Selene rubbed her clammy palms on her pants.

"What we'd like from you, Selene, is to see you in action. We want proof that you're willing to fight for us," Tine continued.

"Fight for you? I just want to go home."

The Director blinked at her, pausing while murmurs from the boys pulled her attention.

"So you don't want to see the world change?" the woman continued. "You don't want to see a better order? You don't want to see the Dominion punished for taking *nats* and experimenting on them? They've killed hundreds of you."

Selene sank back in her chair. When she put it like that it was hard to argue. She did want to see the world change. She wanted the Dominion to suffer for what they'd done to her. And more than anything she wanted to kill Pate. For Aaron, for the Icarus, and for herself. She wanted to avenge them. She *would* avenge them.

"Maybe we were mistaken about you—"

"No, you weren't. I'll fight for you on one condition." Selene leaned forward.

"And what is that?"

"When the time comes to take Pate out... I pull the trigger."

The corners of the Director's gray lips twitched into a smile— the first to break her stony expression. "It's a deal. But we'll still need to see you in the field."

"Sure." Selene shrugged. "What do you want me to do?"

To prove her worth to the Alliance, they wanted her to go on a mission with Sav and his crew. In order to gain their trust, Selene had to trust they weren't leading her to her death. They weren't permitted to tell her the plan—which sparked another protest. Fortunate for the Director, she wanted answers enough to put her trust in Sav.

Poised in her new full body black suit, laser weapons and sheaths full of knives, Selene was starting to feel like herself again. She stood with Flik and Lanny, gripping a safety bar above their heads. Harnesses wrapped their hips and they double-checked their ammo.

"You cats ready to go?" Sav entered from the cockpit, joining them on the lift. Wind brushed her long hair against her face, the current trying to yank her outside the hovercraft and into oblivion.

"Born ready." Flik flashed his pointed teeth, while Lanny gave a thumbs up.

"What is the plan exactly?" Selene quirked an eyebrow. If the Director wasn't willing to trust her, she hoped Sav would.

The only thing she'd been told about their coming adventure was that it involved guns, scanner jammers and full body projection technology. Lanny had created a tool to alter the perception of others, so they would appear like Dominion soldiers while in the Dominion laboratory instead of two Icarus and a clone. It was in fact how they'd been spying on the Dominion for ages. Selene couldn't fathom this technology, but she'd seen Rem do some pretty crazy things over the years. If Lanny was anything like her favorite little tech geek, she had a feeling these would be of great help to their cause.

"The four of us will lower ourselves to the roof, where we'll dispatch the outer patrol and take their places. Lanny can make quick adjustments to our appearance on the fly so no one will be the wiser." Sav shot his friend a proud glance.

"And then?" she prompted.

"Just you wait and see."

Selene didn't like the sound of that. This had *Rikkard* mission written all over it.

"Ready?" the co-pilot shouted. Before they could answer, the lift opened wide, revealing a dark night and lights on the mountainside lab below. It wasn't exactly well hidden, but then again, the Dominion supposedly had nothing to hide from humanity.

"We jump on three." Sav made sure each of them nodded before counting. Selene tugged on her cord one last time. It held strong. "One, two, three!"

She stepped into the abyss, letting the darkness of night swallow her whole. Wind rushed around Selene on all sides, pressing against her sides and tearing at her hair. Warmth bubbled inside her chest, the thrill of falling prompting a large grin. She held back a hoot of joy, and instead concentrated on the building fast approaching beneath her. Fifteen feet from the roof, their decent began to slow, and then they were landing soundlessly on the sand covered laboratory.

Sav motioned toward the roof access. Selene did a quick assessment of the lab's outer security—two watch towers and black-clad men patrolling on foot—before following.

Lanny kneeled at the entrance and attached a small thumb drive to the keypad. Selene tapped her foot impatiently, keeping in the shadows of the roof access while she scanned the yard. Her heart beat loudly in her chest.

"Got it," Lanny said.

The door swung open and they all rushed inside. Their boots made a racket as they took the stairs two at a time. Selene shot them glares of warning, but they ignored her. The men were much louder than she was used to.

No one spoke a word until they hit the top floor. Selene pressed herself to the wall beside Sav while Lanny unlocked their next door. Instead of flinging it open like he had before, he opened it gently, peeking inside.

If this had been her mission she would have had the maps and the routines of the guards memorized. In comparison to her usual adventures, this seemed like sloppy work. But it wasn't her mission, and she had to remember that. Waiting in the stairwell as instructed, it only took Sav and Flik a little over sixty seconds to slip into the hall and knock the four guards on the floor unconscious. They pulled them back into the stairwell, dumping their unconscious bodies on the floor one by one. Four black-clad aliens stared up at her. Her fingers itched toward her gun.

"What about cameras?" Perspiration turned her hands clammy.

"They won't be a problem." Sav helped Lanny lay the men on their backs.

She hoped he was right, and they'd already taken care of them. If they hadn't, they'd be found out any minute. "Won't these men be missed? Won't someone check—"

"Just let them work." Flik shrugged, giving her a look that said to *drop it*.

Sighing, Selene watched and waited. She didn't like this, not one bit. Goosebumps rose on her arms, the hair standing on end. Once their mission was over she was going to present them an itemized list of things to improve upon.

One by one, Lanny stepped up to each fallen soldier, using a blue light scanner to take in their bodies. When he was done, he handed a chip to Sav, then Flik, then her. Selene followed their lead and attached it to her suit. Though she couldn't see any change in herself, when she looked up again, three Dominion security guards surrounded her. She started, her fingers flying to the pistol at her hip.

Lanny's gaze flicked between her gun and her face. She lowered her hand.

"Okay… that's pretty cool." Her heartbeat slowed. "You've got to teach Rem how to do this."

"Rem?" Lanny cocked a brow as he attached a chip to the collar of his suit.

"My crew's techie."

"You have a techie?" Lanny perked up and a smile spread on his guard's face. It was strange hearing Lanny's voice on this tall rough and tough man. It almost made her laugh out loud, until Sav shot them a stern glare.

"Time to get going," Sav said.

They all nodded. One by one they stripped the unconscious guards of their weapons and hoisted them into a janitorial closet.

They stepped out into the hall, assuming a routine formation: marching in rows of two, Lanny at her left, with Flik and Sav at her front. From her time in the Dominion labs, she remembered the guards marching much like this.

The further they descended into enemy territory, the worse Selene felt. Images flashed through her mind of the Dominion, vats, and Pate, all waiting for her around the next corner. Her stomach soured and she gritted her teeth. How well did she really know these people? How could she believe the Alliance with hardly any details on their existence? Heat rose in her chest. Sav and his friends had done their best to fill her in on what they could, but the Alliance's goals seemed to be on a need to know basis—and she was yet to be in the know.

Down flight after flight they went until they entered the core of the building. On their way, their small platoon had passed three other groups of four soldiers each. They had nodded in greeting, and not said a word. Her heart sped with every encounter.

This facility was much stricter than the ones she was used to entering. Her usual targets were quiet buildings with only half a dozen security guards. Even though it was the middle of the night, the complex was full of security personnel, leaving her with a ball of doubt sitting in her stomach.

When they finally hit the third floor on their downward spiral, they entered a long white hall—and Selene froze. She was back in the Dominion lab. Everything was the same, from the sterile smell to the glaringly bright florescent bulbs. Soldiers marched nearby. Any minute she would be taken to the vat. She'd be submerged and drowned *again*. Her world started to tilt, and she tightened her grip on her rifle. She held it to her chest like a child.

She needed to get away. She had to escape. She wouldn't let them take her, not again.

"I can't breathe." Eyes wide, her heart pounded in her ears. She could feel the gel sliding down her throat, chocking her. She could see the bright lights flick on above, and those needles as they pierced her body.

"What is it?" Lanny nudged her.

She shook her head. Everything came flooding in. Tears sprang to her eyes. She wanted to run, but she was frozen. Blood splashed the white halls. Aaron fell before her, a hole through his temple.

Guard Sav turned from his spot at the head of their team, and put himself fully in her line of sight. The white hall disappeared behind him.

"It's all right Selene, you aren't there." Bright amber eyes locked on hers. His fingers pressed into her shoulder. Distantly she realized those weren't Sav's real eyes, but his voice was familiar.

She leaned into it, trying to cling to something that would return her to her senses. "You're safe. You're with us. You're not going to the vats, or the trials or a dome. You're safe now."

Selene started to shake her head.

"What's going on?" Flik hissed.

"Selene," Sav snapped. His fingers dug into her skin. He held her gaze. "You aren't with the Dominion anymore. You're safe."

Slowly, Selene nodded, clearing her throat and mentally slapping herself. She wasn't in the Dominion. She was safe. She was with her new Alliance friends. They were the rebellion against everything she hated. She repeated that over and over in her mind. As long as she was with them, nothing bad could happen to her.

Breathing deeply, Selene closed her eyes for only a moment. When she opened them again, the hall wasn't familiar at all; in fact it had pale blue walls instead of white. The bulbs were bright above, but they weren't as harsh at the ones in her old hell. She wasn't back there. She was safe.

"I'm sorry," she began, but Sav held up a hand.

"Forget it. I've been there." He shrugged off her apology and motioned for them to continue down the hallway. Lanny gave her a concerned glance before falling back in line.

Selene watched Sav's back. Her heart slowed. How long had he been with the Dominion? How long had he been their prisoner? Lanny and Flik were the ones to save him two years ago, but they hadn't told her how long he'd been with them, or what had happened to him in that place. She'd didn't ask, not now, and wasn't sure if she ever would. She knew what he'd been through. He'd been through hell and back. He was a survivor— just like her.

A few halls later, and the populace of guards became less sparse and more present. She wasn't the only one getting nervous. Lanny nearly twitched out of his disguise every time someone took a second look at their group, while Flik's finger danced on the trigger of his laser rifle. Sav continued their march at a dutiful pace, hell bent on completing their mission. Selene followed his lead and steeled herself, repeating over and over in her mind that she was safely disguised, and no one could see through it.

"We're almost there," Sav whispered after another group went by.

Selene was the only one to nod back. She wasn't even sure the others heard him. Sav held up a hand. They all stopped. He motioned, and his comrades moved like dolls, lining up against the wall. Sav produced a keycard from his pocket and swiped it over a silver keypad. The panel lit up, blue glowing from a rectangle at the top. The door swooshed open.

"Wait here." He gave Lanny and Flik a stern look, and then motioned for her to follow.

She hesitated, peering into the blackness beyond the open door. She could do this. She had to. Taking a deep breath, she joined Sav, wading into the dark depths of the unknown.

Once they were both inside, the door swooshed closed and lights flashed on. She squinted, rubbing her eyes as knives pierced her skull. She looked around.

Long sterile white walls, similar to the pre-trial prep room she had been subjected to. From the bench at the center of the room, to the shower stalls and the lockers etched in the wall, everything was pure as snow. Sav raised his gun and moved around the room, rigid, like a trained soldier. Selene mimicked him, repeating to herself over and over that she was safe. Several doors lined the far wall. She stepped up to the first. It whooshed open.

Sweat dripped down her temples. She peeked into the small five by five-foot cubby with nothing but a cot, a sink and a toilet. Nothing useful. She did the same with two others, bracing herself each time for an enemy to leap out. None did, and then Sav called her over.

"Here!"

Selene exited the room she was inspecting and joined him at the door to another. A young blond girl was curled in the corner with familiar green eyes. She opened her mouth to scream.

Leaping forward instinctively, Selene clasped a hand over her mouth and held her gingerly against the wall. She didn't want to frighten her, but she couldn't have her crying for help either.

"It's all right," Selene whispered. "We're here to rescue you." She glanced at Sav for confirmation. Seeing this little girl, Selene finally understood why they were here.

Sav nodded back grimly.

"If I take my hand off your mouth, I need you to be quiet and listen. We aren't who we seem."

Tears welled in her big eyes.

Selene glanced back at Sav, who sighed and took the small tab from his shirt. His disguise disappeared. The girl gave a startled gasp under Selene's hand. Selene smiled and scooted back, rising from her crouch and pulling her chip off as well. With both of their guard costumes gone, the blonde girl perked up, smiling from ear to ear while tears spilled down her rosy cheeks.

"You're here to save me?" she whispered.

Selene knew that look. She had been here a short enough time that hope was still present. She hadn't lost it all like Selene had.

She envied her that.

"We are." Sav smiled.

Lunging from the bed, the girl wrapped her frail arms around Sav's waist. Selene couldn't help but beam at them both. How could she not with a tiny teenage girl hugging such a huge man?

"We've got to go," Sav urged a few moments later.

"Yes," Selene agreed. "Our comrades are waiting." She paused, her questioning gaze not leaving Sav's face. She had no sweet clue how they would get this girl out of here without interference.

"Take this." Sav placed a small silver circle in the girl's hand. "It'll disguise you like us."

"How?" she asked.

"Honestly, I am not the one to explain it to you." He chuckled. "You can talk to Lanny about it once we get out of here."

She nodded vigorously and clipped it to her shirt. Between one blink and the next, that pretty young blonde went from one person to another. Now a tall dark-skinned man with flat gray eyes and army fatigues, he looked like any of the other Dominion guards. In fact, he was a combination of them. The skin of Sav's, the hair of hers, the eyes of Lanny's and the nose of Flik's. Lanny had simply combined them into one image to make a fifth person. Clever.

"Let's go." Sav nodded, and they both slipped back into their disguises. "Stay between us, you'll avoid suspicion that way."

Blondie nodded and followed Sav out the door. Selene followed suit.

"Finally!" Flik hissed the moment they returned to the hall. Sav's glare silenced any more conversation. He didn't want to risk the mission this late in the game. Selene knew what was in his mind, because it was the same thing in hers. They had their cargo, now they had to get themselves to safety before anyone realized something was amiss. It wouldn't take long, not in a facility like this. She'd be surprised if someone didn't already know something was wrong.

Falling into line, Blondie trailed between the two pairs, glancing nervously at each end of the corridor. Sav and Flik fell in beside each other while Lanny joined her to bring up the rear. Sav set the pace, keeping them all at a purposeful walk. She silently thanked him for it, because every muscle in her body screamed for her to run. Nerves crept through her, slicking her forehead with sweat. She checked the safety on her gun more than once, as well as her ammo. Nothing changed, but the repetitive tasks kept her mind busy.

Into the stairwell and up to the fifth and then sixth floors they went. It all seemed too easy—that is until an alarm tore through the silence.

"Shit." Selene brought her laser rifle to her shoulder and aimed behind them. Lanny mirrored her. She flicked off the safety and kept her finger on the trigger, ready to take down the next soldier to run through the door.

"*No,*" Blondie whispered.

"We weren't fast enough." Flik groaned.

"We're almost back to the roof," Sav snapped. "Stay calm."

"Get us there fast, Sav." Selene shot him a warning glance, her eyes wide. They both knew better than most what evil the Dominion could conjure. She wouldn't let them be recaptured and subjected to that hell again. She'd die before going back.

"You got it." He nodded, unable to hide the worry in his eyes.

Before they had run the length of the hall, soldiers careened out of the nearby elevators. Selene dropped to one knee and shot. The rifle whined and a charge of energy flared from the tip of her gun in a red beam. It blasted the man in the chest. He fell back, a gaping hole where his sternum used to be. Selene didn't blink and shot again and again. It was the Dominion versus them now. They were the bad guys and she would stop at nothing to rid the world of their disease. After four men lay dead on the floor they stopped running from the elevator. At least the remaining were smart enough to keep from sight.

"Go," Selene commanded.

They ran to the next stairwell in the middle of the hall. Selene stepped more slowly, her back to them and her gun trained on the enemy's hiding spot. Sav yanked the door open as she joined them. A black-clad man stuck his head out. Selene shot, a growl rising in her chest. The plaster beside the elevator exploded. Idiot.

They gained the stairwell. The door to the top floor slammed behind them. Selene shot the lock.

Sav ushered them all up the stairs, sending Flik to the head while he joined her at the rear. Their boots pounded the stairs.

"You're a good shot," he panted. No sweat dripped down his disguise but she had a feeling he was pushing himself under that mask. Fear was evident in his voice.

"Thanks." They reached a landing. Selene watched the stairs behind them while the rest burst into the last hall before the roof. Clear. She turned to join the others. As they entered, Flik grabbed her arm and yanked her into an alcove. He wrapped one arm around her waist, pinning them to the wall. Across the hall, Blondie and Lanny huddled behind a pillar, keeping low to the ground. "Well shit."

"You can say that again," Flik grumbled into her hair.

Sav joined them seconds later, keeping his back to the wall. "How many?"

"Too many." Flik nodded down the hall in both directions. "Half a dozen at the back stairs. Another dozen blocking our exit." Her heart pounded in her ears. That many already?

"The ship isn't going to wait much longer," Lanny whispered from across the hall.

"We need to take them out." Selene wiggled away from Flik. "Do we have anything bigger than these rifles?"

Sav began to shake his head when Lanny waved to get their attention. He pointed to a small round grenade in his right hand. Selene and Sav exchanged grins.

"Perfect." She gave Lanny a thumbs up while Sav motioned a plan to the rest of them.

Lanny began to count down from four. Each finger that dropped sent a shot of adrenaline coursing through Selene's veins. Her finger tapped the trigger guard and she forgot all about her time with the Dominion. Instead she concentrated on getting their asses out of here.

Lanny's last finger dropped. He threw the grenade at the back stairwell. They all ducked. Three seconds later, an explosion rocked the floor. Her ears rang and plaster rained down from the ceiling. In the chaos, Selene was the first to leap from their hiding spot. She aimed at the blocked escape. Three men ran towards them. A moment of surprise passed over their faces before she shot them all. Sav leapt in the other direction, shooting the rest at the opposite end of the hall.

Selene advanced with Flik backing her up. Several more soldiers glanced their way. She smiled. Only one got a shot off before they were all dead on the floor. Another pair leapt in their wake as someone hit the floor behind them with a thump. Her first instinct was to turn and help whoever had fallen, or worse, been shot. But her second instinct won out. She raised her rifle, charging it on high before letting two red blasts tear through the remaining soldiers.

"Hey, wake up!" Lanny shouted behind them.

"What happened?" Selene snapped at Flik, keeping her guard up and her aim tight as she slowly made her way to the other end of the hall. She didn't dare look back, not until she was sure every soldier blocking their path was dead.

"Blondie is hit!" Flik's footsteps retreated.

"Damn it." She risked a glance back. A blonde mass of hair draped over Sav's arm. Her disguise was gone. Sav cradled her, cooing gently. Blood dripped down her limp arm. Selene's heart clenched.

"She's dead." Lanny sighed.

"We've got to go." Flik glanced at their only escape.

"She was so young," Sav whispered.

"This isn't the time Sav," Selene snapped back at them, her eyes back on their exit. Her muscles tensed and her heart pounded. The urge to flee had yet to leave her. Kill or be killed. Flee or fight. That was all she could think. If she stopped thinking about battle, and thought about Blondie, or Aaron or the other hundreds of dead Icarus, she would lose herself again.

She couldn't let that happen.

"Give him a second!" Flik growled.

"We need to *go*."

"He needs a minute."

"We don't have a minute!"

When Selene looked back and Sav was still on the floor with Blondie, she steeled herself and lowered her gun. "Watch that end." She gave Flik a stern look as she passed him, ripping the chip from her suit.

For a moment she almost thought he'd argue, but instead he gave a curt nod and raised his gun to his shoulder.

Selene joined the trio kneeling on the floor. She grabbed Sav by the back of the shirt and yanked him to his feet. The blonde girl tumbled onto the once clean tile. Pushing him against the wall, she pinned him with her forearm.

"Selene!" Lanny gasped. "What are you—"

"Sav, snap the hell out of it!" she barked.

He stared over her shoulder at the dead girl.

She grabbed his chin and turned his head to face her. "We need to go *now*. Do you want your friends to end up like her?" Sav's gaze slowly slid to meet hers. The vacant eyes of his guard costume stared back at her. She found the chip on his collar and tore it off, throwing it unceremoniously down the hall. Panic rose inside her chest and turned her stomach. Did her fear show on her face?

Sav shook his head.

"Right, you don't. I know it hurts. So many have died because of them, but you can mourn her later. She's another Icarus lost at war, and she won't be the last."

Releasing him, Selene stepped back and raised her gun again. Sav took a moment to raise his, but when he did he nodded. He was all right, just in shock. Selene nodded back, and took the lead.

"Follow me." She led them to the end of the hall where dead soldiers and blood littered the white floors. Vacant eyes stared at the ceiling. Selene stepped over them as carefully as she could, swallowing the lump in her throat.

She headed for the stairs, her boots beating the metal steps loudly as she ascended. A bright red exit sign had her sighing in relief. She slammed the door open and ran out onto the sand-covered roof, where alarms still blared and floodlights lit the yard. Selene searched the sky for their ride. With the floodlights messing with her night vision, she couldn't make out the black mass hidden among the stars.

"Where is the—"

A thunderous boom drowned her out. Red beams flashed through the sky from a guard tower. Twenty feet away from the lab fell their only way out. Another explosion rumbled when it hit the ground. Fire erupted from the engines, dousing the group in warm light. The remains of their hovercraft crackled and snapped between the flames. They were too late. All of their dawdling had cost them not only a life, but quite possibly four more.

17

"WAS THAT…?" FLIK TRAILED OFF.

"Our way out?" Lanny finished.

"Yep." Sweat dripped down her forehead. It was okay, there had to be another way out. "What's the backup plan?" Only silence greeted her. Her heart dropped to her stomach. "Please tell me there was a goddamn backup plan." Her glare fell on each of them in turn. She did not like the guilty looks they gave her.

Lanny shrugged. "Our missions are our choice. If we don't make it out—"

"Then you die? You're left under the Dominion's control?" she snarled. Anger flooded her veins, burning through her like acid. "Why did none of you tell me this before I agreed to this suicide mission?"

"We've always gotten away with minimal casualties," Lanny said.

"Minimal?" she snapped.

Sav winced at her escalating tone. "We had this lab canvased for weeks. We thought we had everything covered, but—"

"But clearly you weren't prepared enough."

Selene looked away from the trio. Her chest burned. She couldn't believe their naivety. How did they expect to continue

172

these missions with only *minimal* casualties? The Dominion would have seen through their schemes eventually and set them up. Of course she would be caught between them when their luck finally ran out.

Growling in frustration, Selene stepped away from them to look for a way out. There had to be something. There was always a way out of her messes. She didn't have Rikkard and her friends to bail her out this time.

Her gaze darted around the barren roof, the surrounding desert wasteland, the rocky hills behind them, and the two patrol stations at each corner of the grounds. Nothing. If they couldn't take to the sky, their only option was land. But where would they get a vehicle big enough to fit all four of them? Blinking back frustrated tears, Selene looked to the starlit sky.

I was almost home.

She shook her head. Peeling her eyes from the sky, two speeders flew across the sand.

Selene froze. "That's it."

From the outer patrol stations came more soldiers riding hoodless desert speeders, flooding towards the main complex in waves. Several were left carelessly by the entrance in their haste, but with the main gate closed, they'd need something to blow it open.

She had an idea.

"Any more grenades on you, Lanny?" She glanced over her shoulder. Lanny shook his head. She thought not. "Could you make an explosive with the energy reactors in one of those speeders?" She pointed to the bikes below.

A spark of hope lit his eyes. Lanny stepped up beside her and peered over the roof's edge. The bright blue reactors at the speeders core would explode if they weren't contained correctly. If Lanny could time this right, they had a way out. "Yes, I can."

"How long would it take?"

"Only a few seconds. The reactors are unstable once freed from their chamber."

"Good. Because seconds are all we'll have."

Each of the men exchanged a look with each other. At this point her plan was the only one. Whether it got them killed now or later, at least it was something. When each of them nodded, giving her the go ahead, she motioned them all into a circle. "Here's what we're going to do. Sav and Flik, you need to buy us some time with the roof access."

Flik nodded, while Sav gazed at her solemnly.

"Got it?" She quirked an eyebrow at the man. He sighed and nodded. "Okay. While you two give us some time, Lanny and I will grab one of those bikes and rig it to get us out of here. When I give the signal, you both need to join us on the ground. We'll only have seconds to get those speeders and get the hell out of here before someone realizes what's up."

"Let's do this!" Flik pumped a fist in the air.

Selene couldn't help but smile. At least someone believed they were getting out of here alive.

Once Flik and Sav took off to the roof access, Selene led Lanny back to the edge of the roof. Lucky for them, he'd thought to bring a rope. Attaching it to a nearby air vent, Selene tugged to make sure it could hold their weight. When the rope held after her third yank, she tossed it over the edge of the building. It didn't reach all the way to the ground, only to mid second floor. They'd have a bit of a drop, and there'd be no returning once they descended.

"You're sure you can get that speeder to explode?"

"Of course." Lanny gave her an incredulous look.

"Sorry, didn't mean to offend." She grinned.

Despite their current circumstances, she was glad to be in this mess with these three and not some incompetent Alliance lackeys. The only others she'd prefer to these would be her own crew. A pang in her chest reminded her of their loss. She'd see them soon; she just had to get out of here alive.

Taking the rope firmly in her gloved grasp, she slung her gun over her shoulder before making the leap off the roof. Her boots landed quietly on the concrete wall, muffling her movements. Holding on tight, she shimmied down the rope, reminding herself not to look down. Once out of rope, Selene wiggled to the very end of the cord, dangling for a few seconds before dropping. She landed soundlessly behind a hedge, and ducked into the shadows. Taking a calming breath, she tried to still her rabbit heart. She waited for Lanny.

A full minute later, Lanny landed not so gracefully beside her. A jibe came quickly to her lips, but the turning of her stomach zapped her comment before she could make it.

The buzz of speeders and flash of headlights drove across the yard. A small squad of soldiers parked by the cement sidewalk and dashed inside. Selene scanned the front yard of the lab. No one in sight. Motioning for Lanny to follow, she stepped from the bushes and made her way over to the row of hastily abandoned speeders.

"Go for it," she said.

Lanny nodded and went to work.

Keeping her eye on the yard, Selene ducked behind a black speeder, her rifle at her shoulder. Metal scraped quietly as Lanny tinkered with the speeder, disassembling the power cartridge from the outside. A minute later, she jumped when Lanny tapped a finger on her back. She spun to look at him.

"Ready."

Selene nodded, giving her heart a moment to settle before she helped Lanny turn the speeder in the direction of the main gate. Once she was sure it would head in a straight line without fail, she cranked the on switch and flipped on autopilot. Seconds later, it was careening towards the thick metal gate between two watch towers, its soft thrum moving quickly over the sand covered yard.

They didn't have long. Stepping up to the remaining speeders, Selene and Lanny started four of them. They came to life quietly, the glow of their control panels dim against the harsh beams of the floodlights. Once they were prepared, Lanny joined her, melting into the shadows. Selene whistled for their comrades on the roof to join them.

"They've got thirty seconds to get down here before that

blows." Lanny glanced nervously at the roof.

Selene glanced up. "I hope they're not afraid of heights."

One shadow repelled down the wall, and a second glanced over the edge. Her heart sped.

Hurry.

"Almost there," she said. "Get ready."

Lanny mounted his speeder.

A crash sounded from the roof. The remaining shadow looked back. A red beam broke the dark night, ripping through the shadow's shoulder. Selene gasped. Another beam lit the roof's ledge. The figure slung himself over the ledge, clinging to the rope, sliding down slowly past the sixth floor.

Selene raised her rifle and took aim at the roof's lip.

"Get down here this second!" she shouted at them.

When the first soldier appeared over the edge of the roof, she shot him through the skull. The second, she took in the heart. Selene gritted her teeth. They didn't have time for this. They had to *go*.

Sav thumped down beside them, followed by Flik. The redhead bled profusely and shook all over. If they didn't get his wounds healed, and fast, he would bleed out.

"Wrap that," she snapped at Lanny before returning her gaze to the roof. She shot two more soldiers through the head. Their shadows went limp on the stone ledge. "Get him on a speeder."

A loud boom from the other side of the yard nearly drowned her out.

"Shit," she hissed. "We've got to *move!*"

Lanny helped Sav situate Flik on the back of a speeder, tying him on with a seat belt. Sav took the seat in front of him while Lanny hopped back onto his own. Shouts rang out from inside the lab as their speeders kicked up sand.

Selene took a few more shots at the roof before slinging her legs across the back of her own speeder. Her heart pounded in her ears. The dim blue lights of her getaway vehicle turned to blue fire as she revved the engine.

She braced her feet on the speeder before pushing off, flying several yards away. She had to delay them somehow, or they'd be caught in the desert. Selene slowed, angling her speeder toward the lab. The blue fire dulled as she stopped. She raised her rifle to her shoulder and aimed down the sight.

The line of parked speeders sent her heart racing. "Perfect."

Selene shot one of the parked speeders' energy chambers. A blue explosion thundered outside the main entrance to the lab, throwing shrapnel in every direction. Her ears rang as the neighboring speeders exploded as well, tearing through the cement building, plaster crumbling from the hole she'd created. Stone pillars collapsed against the entrance, blocking the Dominion soldiers inside.

Putting her speeder into high gear, Selene pushed it to max speed. Wind whipped her hair and tore at her clothes, but she kept her eyes on the main gate, which now had a black hole through its bottom half, and a crater scorching the surrounding earth. She zipped through after her comrades, and out over the open desert. Shots fired somewhere in the night, leaving streaks of red further and further behind. Shouts echoed over the sand, but on desert speeders, there would be no catching them.

Half an hour later, Sav brought them to a stop in the remnants of an abandoned town. Walls and roofs were torn away, and tumbleweeds bounced by in the late night breeze. She'd never seen a town so destroyed. Once the group was tucked away between the last remaining wall of a supermarket and its somehow still standing garage, Sav motioned them all into the light of the moon.

Selene, Sav and Lanny dismounted their speeders and stepped to the side while Flik moaned in his seat.

"He's not going to make it much longer." Sav glanced back at Flik, his lips twisted into a frown, and his eyes widened with concern.

Her brows cinched together. Selene couldn't imagine the guilt Sav must have felt. Flik was one of the two to save his life from the Dominion. She'd never be able to forgive herself either if Flik died because of her own recklessness.

"We're miles from HQ. That'll take hours on these things." Lanny glared at the speeders like they were at fault.

"Where are we anyway?" Selene asked. There had to be somewhere close by they could take Flik to.

"South of New Manhattan I think. Probably a few miles from the Outskirts." Lanny shrugged.

A thought struck her so fast she grinned like a Cheshire cat.

Sav and Lanny raised their eyebrows at her.

"If you're right, that means Bakura is east of here."

Both men exchanged a look. Clearly they didn't see where she was going with this.

"Isn't that the black market?" Sav asked.

"Yes. But it's also our best bet at getting supplies." But what was really on her mind wasn't medicine. Her crew might very well be there, and if they were, Sarah could fix Flik up in a flash. She'd never seen a woman so fast with a needle or scalpel. Even if Sarah wasn't around, they could surely bribe another doctor.

"I don't know. We've always stayed away from those sorts of—"

"It's our best bet," Selene interrupted Sav, already mounting her speeder. Her heart raced. "I'll lead the way. Stay close, and when we arrive, follow me, and let me do the talking."

With no other option, Lanny and Sav followed, hopping back on their speeders as Selene pulled away, a large grin still glued to her face.

When Bakura's dark shadow appeared over the horizon, Selene thought her heart might leap from her chest. She drove them faster and faster until Bakura wasn't just a smudge, but a behemoth towering above. Its black mass leaned against the sand of what used to be a large dock. It was an eyesore against the otherwise clear desert, but to Selene, it was a beacon of hope. Leading the way to the docks on the eastern side of the ship, Selene slowed their roll, keeping an eye out for what she prayed she would find. Coming around the head of the ship, she found what her heart yearned for.

Her crew's cargo ship was docked in its usual spot, an ugly

metal mass. Part of her had expected some monumental change when she returned, but the unattractive ship still looked as it always had—a hunk of junk that somehow flew.

Selene led them down, taking care to glance back to make sure the others were all right. Flik sagged against Sav's shoulder, and looks of worry met her eager gaze. She quickly peeled the smile from her face and turned around. She had to remember; it was the injury of a friend who had brought her back.

Landing in front of the open cargo doors, Selene hopped off and stilled the engine. She motioned for the trio to follow. Lanny and Sav supported Flik as they lifted him from the back of the speeder. He was out cold. As quick as her heart leapt into her throat, it now plummeted to her stomach. Flik needed Sarah *now*. It was almost too late.

"This is my old crew's ship," she explained as she led them between speeders of every class, crates just as large and piles of Rem's leftover gadgets. "I'm not sure if they're all here or in Bakura, but I know our medic will be able to fix Flik faster than any Alliance doctor."

"I hope you're right," Sav whispered.

"I am."

Leading the group further into her old home, voices drifted through the halls. She couldn't help the grin that spread on her face or the tears that leapt to the surface. Overwhelming relief washed over her. After weeks apart, finally she was going to see the only family she'd ever known.

Selene had hardly stepped into the dining hall when a loud hoot broke the quiet. Kong flew across the room, leaping chairs and tables until he reached her. He pulled her into his arms so fast he knocked the breath from her lungs. Swinging her in a circle, Selene couldn't help the laugh that bubbled from her throat.

"Kong!" Overwhelmed by not only the sudden spinning, but the affection that flooded every inch of her, Selene fought back tears as she wrapped her arms around the gorilla's hairy neck. "It's good to see you too, but I need you to put me down."

Gasps met her ears from across the room. Chairs squealed as they scraped across the floor. When Kong finally set her down, she was left staring at a tearful Sarah, and a shocked crew. Wide eyes and open mouths greeted her. Everyone was there, including Rikkard. It was probably the most emotion she'd ever seen him convey. Something lurched in her heart, and her previously giddy smile turned shy.

"Hey guys." She gave a little wave.

Sarah raced the length of the room, flinging herself into Selene's arms while she stammered over her words, unable to form a solid sentence.

"Sarah, it's good to see you too." Selene squeezed Sarah tightly before reality caught up with her. Sav cleared his throat. Stepping out of Sarah's embrace, Selene motioned to her new Alliance friends. "I'll do intros later, but we have someone who really needs your help." Flik groaned to solidify her statement. At least if he was moaning he was alive.

"Oh my!" Sarah's jaw dropped. Stepping forward, she quickly accessed Flik's injured state, her fingers probing his wounded shoulder. It only took her a moment to usher them through the dining hall. "Hurry, bring him with me. There isn't much time!" Sarah led them toward her office, the clack of her heels echoing in the hollow space. Selene watched them go, silently crossing her fingers, hoping above all else that Flik would be okay.

Rem and Darius came next. Each clamped a hand on one of her shoulders, their huge grins matching Selene's own.

"Back from the dead, eh?" Rem hugged her with one arm, while L3 beeped on his shoulder.

When she let go, her eyes fell on Rikkard and Kayl from across the room. Rikkard's eyes were wide and his mouth agape like he'd seen a ghost, and Kayl's face twisted in horror.

"Good to see that sweet ass of yours again!" Darius growled a laugh, and Selene swatted him before hugging him too. When she released him, Kayl was nowhere to be seen, and Rikkard was still looking at her as if she were an alien creature.

"Good to see you guys too," she said. "Can't get rid of me that easily."

"Apparently not!"

Holding Rikkard's gaze, Selene gave him a small smile and a wave. She quirked a brow. He was acting stranger than normal. At her prompt, her boss finally stood and crossed the room in an instant. Rem and Darius made room as he came right to her, his hands flying to each side of her face. Heat rose to her cheeks so fast, she thought she might pass out. She blinked in wide-eyed confusion at Rikkard, whose face conveyed a thousand emotions at once. She, on the other hand, was stunned into silence.

Slowly, Selene raised her hands and placed them over his. Part of her had always wanted this, while another part of her shied away. His hands were warm beneath her fingers. She'd always been close with the boss, or as close as anyone could be to Rikkard. But she wanted more with him, more emotion, and less sarcastic jabs. She wanted him, and not just as a friend. Her mind flew back to that night he'd explained why he'd lied to her about the protos. He'd done it all for her. How had she not seen this side of him until now? It seemed like eons ago he'd lied to her, and yet here she was, forgiving him without a second thought.

After what seemed like a long time, his lips finally parted. "You're alive." He searched her face.

Before she could utter a word, his lips met hers. Her face flushed, but her surprise ebbed as she melted into his touch. She forgot all about her friends looking on and kissed Rikkard like she'd always imagined being kissed. His hands cupped her cheeks, and she intertwined her fingers with his, oblivious to everything but him.

When he finally pulled away, it was too soon. She watched the passion in his eyes harden into fury—but not fury directed at her. He gave her a quick embrace before taking off into the ship.

Selene turned to give Rem and Darius a confused look. They both shrugged.

Deciding it was best to follow, Selene rushed to catch up with the captain. Her boots beat across the metal floors, only a sparse minute behind. When she got close, a crash sounded. A few thuds came from Kayl's room. The charge of an energy pistol stopped her in her tracks.

"Try it. I *will* kill you," Rikkard snapped.

Rounding the corner quickly, Selene slammed her fist against the control panel beside the door. It whooshed open.

"Stop!" she shouted. "What the hell is going on?"

The room was a mess, a desk overturned and papers lying everywhere. Against the back wall, Rikkard held Kayl by his collar with one hand, his pistol in the other. Kayl held a long serrated knife, his eyes wild. Rikkard glanced back at her and quickly released his second in command. He stepped back, pushing Kayl aside.

Kayl gave Rikkard a glare as he rushed passed her, pushing out into the hall. His loud footsteps echoed down the corridor until he disappeared.

"Rikkard." She tried to grab his attention while assessing this unusual situation. "What are you doing?"

Holstering his gun, Rikkard avoided her gaze, instead choosing to stare after his second. "Kayl told me you were dead. He said he saw your body."

"He did?"

"Yes. If I had known..."

Selene smiled sympathetically. "You would have what? Come looking for me? Scoured the sand-covered earth for clues? None of you had any idea where I was. But why would Kayl lie about it?"

"I don't know." He sighed. "But I'm going to find out."

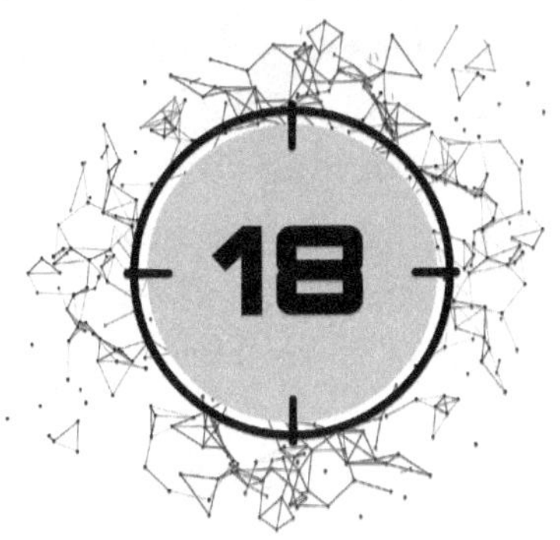

"WOULD YOU LOOK AT ME already?"

Rikkard refused to.

Selene sighed and took his hand, leading him from the messy room. While she had more important things to do than have a heart to heart with Rikkard, she couldn't very well let the silent treatment continue.

Towing her boss past her room and his, she led him to a featureless metal hall with a single access hatch. She swiped her palm over the keypad and the door swung open. Wind gusted inside, brushing back her hair. Selene stepped over the threshold, pulling Rikkard after her. A sleek metal ledge protruded from the side of the cargo ship. She wasn't sure the rest of the crew even knew about it, as it was usually her quiet spot. Releasing Rikkard, she returned to the hatch, securing it with a twist of its metal handle.

Selene turned back around to find Rikkard seated with his legs bent and his face in one hand, fingers gripping his temple. She joined him on the smooth metal still emanating warmth from the day's sun. Glancing at the forty-foot drop below, her heart leapt into her throat. She swallowed and shied back from the edge.

From Bakura she couldn't see New Manhattan, or the

Outskirts, or anything but sand and sun. It was peaceful with only the wind in her hair and gulls cawing in the distance. When a few moments passed in silence, Selene's gaze wandered back to Rikkard, who stared angrily at the horizon.

Selene inched closer and bumped her shoulder against his. She wasn't sure where to begin with this newfound touching thing, but this would be a start. He finally glanced at her.

She started at his glassy stare. Her eyes widened. This was new, even for Rik.

Selene reached up and touched his cheek. Stubble bit her fingertips as she trailed them down his jaw. His lips parted wordlessly. Talking could wait. Selene pressed her lips against his.

Instead of the desperate kiss he had given her before, this one was soft and tender. This one told her he wanted this, that he wanted her. Her heart fluttered as his arms encircled her and held her to his chest. Selene wrapped her arms around him in return, and soon their kiss dissolved into a quiet embrace. He held her tightly, face in her hair. She held him back, her heart pounding in her ears as she desperately tried to push down all the feelings bubbling to the surface.

She'd have to tell the crew what had happened, where she'd been, how she'd gotten there and gotten out. Her stomach soured. She tried to push it all away and stay in the one place she alone occupied with Rikkard. Selene squeezed her eyes shut to stop the forming tears.

When she finally managed, Rikkard stroked her hair. She sighed and leaned up to give him another kiss. Glassy eyes peered down at her. Her breath caught in her throat. He didn't smile, or try to look away again. He only looked at her. Selene wrapped her fingers in his hair and pulled him down to her. She kissed away every negative feeling that boiled within them until the sun was setting and her gut told her it was time to go.

"We should go see the others," she said.

Rikkard's long sigh brushed through her hair, tickling her cheeks.

"I have a lot to tell you all."

"I know," he said.

"We'll figure the rest out later."

Rikkard nodded.

Peeling herself off the ground, Rikkard helped her to her feet before pulling her into his arms. He kissed the top of her head and held her until the sun disappeared behind the sand dunes.

"Let's go."

When Selene and Rikkard returned to the dining hall, everyone but Kayl had gathered there. Sav, Lanny and even Flik mingled with the smugglers as if they'd known each other their whole lives. Though Flik was pale, the orange zapped from his skin, revealing heavy bruises under his eyes, he still grinned that toothy smile, and waggled his eyebrows at Sarah, who gently pushed him away, but secretly kept an eye on him from under her thick lashes.

Selene and Rikkard stepped around the discarded chairs Kong had flung earlier and joined the others at the center table, the largest in the room. They sat together at the head of the metal table. A hush fell around them. Her gaze landed on Flik, who gave her a thumbs up to let her know he was all right. His torso was wrapped in bandages, and his left shoulder was purple, but still his smile warmed his eyes. Selene grinned back; grateful they'd made it in time.

"I have a lot to explain," Selene began. Sarah gave her a reassuring nod from across the table, while the others looked on curiously. Kong returned to lean against her, his weight nearly knocking her off her seat. Still, he was a comforting presence. "So let's get started."

Selene explained how she had been taken, and by whom. Rikkard stiffened every time she mentioned the vat, and the drowning feeling. Sav chimed in with his own experiences, helping her work through the more painful bits. When it became clear to everyone that the Aldar Dominion wasn't just a corporate entity running the alien side of the government, her friends grew still. Though the government faction had helped humans and clones for over three hundred years, it was clear they had a much deadlier agenda.

"The Aldar Dominion isn't just a corporation." Lanny straightened. Unease shadowed his eyes. Selene nodded for him to continue. "Though they used to be a council of alien business men and women, they aren't who they say they are."

Flik cleared his throat. "Our people used to be governed by the Zahkx Alliance. The Aldar Dominion worked with our government, both business and science working in tandem. Centuries ago, when we came to Earth, the original team was supposed to watch over humans and study them."

"They *were* careful not to disrupt us or change the course of our history," Lanny added.

"True." A rueful smile quirked on the alien's face. "But what the original expedition didn't know, was the Aldar on board had different orders."

Selene swallowed the lump in her throat.

"The expedition was further than my species has ever travelled, and once on Earth, they'd have no way of contacting our home planet until they built a beacon. The Aldar knew this and counted on it." Flik's fists clenched atop the table. His dark eyes narrowed as he stared at the table. Selene had never seen the man so serious. "We're fairly certain they killed every one of the Zahkx aboard before they could emerge from cryostasis. This way they could introduce themselves as the Aldar Dominion— the saviors of the human race."

"But why didn't they announce themselves when they first arrived?" Rem asked. His eyebrows cinched.

"We don't have all the Dominion files, but our best guess is they have some kind of plan for Earth," Lanny said.

"That doesn't sound good." Sarah shifted in her seat.

Cold swept through Selene's limbs. "Do you think the Icarus have something to do with their plan?"

Sav exchanged a look with Flik and Lanny. "Absolutely, but nothing we've been able to steal mentions what we're for."

Dread turned her stomach.

Unease filled the eyes of her friends as they continued. In the last few decades, the Alliance had returned with a vengeance, sabotaging all they could, while gathering followers and soldiers to overtake the Dominion government. Somehow the Icarus were involved. The Dominion was creating an army. The Icarus Elite. The Alliance was desperate to stop them.

But in over three hundred years, the Dominion had yet to place an alien mind inside a clone body. The bodies simply deteriorated too fast to function. A natural human on the other hand had much more stable chromosomes, and could be trifled with. The Icarus were born soon after, the Dominion's greatest achievement yet, even if they couldn't quite create a Host for themselves.

"Only one in one hundred humans can survive the procedure to ready the human body and mind for an alien host." Lanny's gaze slid to Selene. He nodded at her. "Selene is the only successful Host in existence. The rest, end up like Sav, stronger than humans, faster than clones, but not quite alien enough."

The group fell silent as the knowledge settled over them. Selene's chest tightened. If she was the only true Icarus, the Dominion would stop at nothing to get her back. She bit her lip. More souls than she'd ever imagined had been lost to these experiments, and for what? To control humans and clones completely and totally for whatever scheme was next? Could that be it? She bit her lip. Something wasn't right.

When Lanny and Sav finished their explanation, Selene steered the conversation back to her time with the Dominion and her escape. She tried to glaze over the rougher details, including the mental torture and death of young Aaron. She stuck mostly to what she'd learned. When she arrived at her rescue, Sav helped her fill in what she didn't know. Everyone grinned when he explained how Selene kept trying to beat them up, even while injured and chained to the ceiling.

Once they were done, Sav added in their plans to overturn the Dominion, something she hadn't heard much of yet.

"We have a plan to expose the Dominion," Sav began, his eyes seeking hers. Selene nodded for him to continue. "If we want the Alliance to have any traction, they need to know what the Dominion is up to. We want to start by showing the world who Pate really is. He's not just a presidential candidate, he's their pawn."

"A damn sick one at that." Her fists tightened on the table.

Rikkard glanced at her, and she reminded herself to cool it. She wasn't there anymore; in fact she was right where she wanted to be—plotting his downfall.

"Exactly." Sav nodded in agreement. "We want to bring him down on election night, and splash his misdeeds across the media. We want to show the world what he's done, then take him. We won't make him a martyr, but we'll kill him if we have to. We won't leave him around to dispute us either."

Selene's eyebrow quirked up. The Director at the Alliance had promised her the shot; she hoped their end of the deal would be kept.

"I'm in," she said. "You know what the Director promised me."

Sav nodded. "Of course. You'll have your shot, and the Alliance will be ready to take over when the Dominion falls."

"Will you all join us?" Selene looked at the others. Though she couldn't care less who was in charge, she did care about the humans and animals the Aldar Dominion destroyed. If the Alliance was going to stop the experiments, she'd join their cause. "I'd feel a lot better having you guys involved."

"Of course we will!" Sarah nearly leapt from her seat. "Right?"

Kayl chose this moment to walk up. Selene wasn't sure when he'd crept into the dining hall and their conversation. With one black eye, and a sour expression, he had the look of a viper. "You're not seriously considering this? We aren't rebels." He sat beside his wife, who settled back in her seat. "Do we really need another reason to get the Dominion after us?"

"This affects every single one of us, Kayl." Selene narrowed her eyes. Seeds of doubt worked their way through the smugglers faces. She gritted her teeth. "How can you be so naïve?"

"I'm being naïve?" he scoffed. "You're the one taken in by this fairytale. You hardly even know these people. Who says the Dominion are the evil ones? Who says it isn't the Alliance who you should be afraid of?"

No. He was wrong.

Selene leapt from her seat, a snarl at her lips. "I know because I was *there*. The Dominion takes humans and experiments on them. I met others, Kayl. I met them and they weren't good anymore. The ones that weren't sucked in by their power were children, and they killed them in their games."

Kayl faltered, taking in her expression. Sarah took his hand. "You're sure it wasn't a trick? You're sure the Dominion are at fault?"

"I've never been more certain of anything," she said.

Kayl nodded solemnly, glancing at his wife who gave him a reassuring nod. The second-in-command had always stood against her, so when he turned back to her with a firm nod, she stared at him with widened eyes.

"Okay," Kayl said. "I'm in."

A smile pulled at the corners of her lips. "Thank you, Kayl."

Kayl only sat beside his wife, who gripped him in a one armed hug.

"Any more complaints?" All eyes settled on Rikkard. Everyone shook their heads. "Good."

Sav didn't even try to hide his grin. It spread fast on his face and he pounded a fist on the table. "All right! That's what I like to hear."

"If we're all in agreement, then I think we should head back to Alliance HQ," Selene said.

They all nodded, especially Sav and his group. They were probably eager to get home and share the good news with their employers.

"Isn't the election in a few days?" Rem asked, fingers tapping nervously across the table.

"Three days." Lanny shrugged.

"That's a little soon." Darius raised an eyebrow.

"Plenty of time to get set up, I'm sure." Selene grinned. "We've done more with less."

"You're damn right." Darius flashed her a toothy smile.

"Then it's settled." Rikkard stood. "Rem, set course for Alliance headquarters. Get one of them to direct you." He motioned to Sav and his friends. Lanny leapt up and together they scurried off. "As for the rest of you, make yourselves useful."

SEVERAL HOURS LATER, THE LARGE cargo ship docked at Alliance headquarters, attaching an access port to one of the long corridors in the loading bay of the facility. They all joined together at the mouth, waiting for the hatch to open. It moved slowly, but with everyone's nerves on edge it was probably a good thing.

The door banged open, and Selene was left staring down the barrel of a gun.

"Hello to you too." Selene raised an eyebrow. Her gaze roamed from the muzzle up to a masked face. Her heart lurched, an image of Aaron being shot through the head by a Dominion soldier in a black mask flashing through her mind.

Sav pushed forward, waving the men down. "They're with me."

Selene cleared her throat. "You should be expecting me." None of her usual bite backed her words.

Their armed escort muttered apologies and lowered their weapons. Half a dozen black-clad soldiers stepped away from the door to let them through.

"The Director is waiting for you." One of the masked men motioned to Sav, who nodded. Lanny joined them, with Flik's arm slung over his shoulder.

"We'll need to escort Flik to medical," Lanny said.

"We'll take him," one of the men droned. Two masked soldiers stepped forward and took on Flik's weight.

"Well ain't this the royal treatment?" Flik grinned, his words slurring together. Sarah had him on some pretty intense painkillers.

"See you soon." Sav gave him a thumbs up, which Flik returned before he was carted away. "Looks like we'll have to detour before we get you guys settled in."

Selene shrugged. "That's fine."

They had only followed Sav a few paces when the surrounding guards stepped in their path. "You can't bring your weapons in here," one said.

While Selene had the chance, she'd taken a few minutes to shower and change into her usual black bodysuit, equipped with rows and rows of throwing knives, daggers, and her usual two pistols.

She raised a brow at the soldier. "We're the good guys. We're not here to shoot you all up."

"Leave your weapons here." He motioned to a long white table at their right. "That goes for all of you."

"Better just do as they say." Sav removed his own pistol from its holster.

"Fine."

Selene unstrapped each row of knives from her biceps, her right thigh, and the long dagger in her boot. She unhooked her holsters from her belt and lay them side by side. Rikkard and the others unloaded a plethora of weapons, from obscure, hidden places in their clothing.

Selene turned back to the guard blocking their path. "We good?"

After a short pause the guard nodded and turned on his heel, leading them deeper into the complex. Selene rolled her eyes and followed alongside Sav, who motioned at the joining hallways.

"The cafeteria is down there. You all *have* to try Chef's famous seafood chowder." Sav grinned.

Selene wrinkled her nose, recalling the last time someone force-fed her alien sea life. She shot a look at a smiling Sarah. "We'll have to see about that."

When they finally reached the same conference room she'd met the Director in previously, the woman was already seated, her sleek white hair pulled back, and her lab coat pristine.

"Welcome back," Tine said. "I see you brought guests."

After quick introductions, they all took a seat. Rikkard hovered alongside Lanny at the back of the room.

"Your mission wasn't a success." Tine directed her statement at both Sav and Selene who sat side by side. Neither of them said a word. "That's unfortunate. On top of that, one of my men was gravely injured. I was hoping for more from you, Selene."

Selene held the arms of her chair so tightly they splintered under her angry claws. "Excuse me? I'm the one who got your men out of there alive."

"Flik is alive right now because of her," Sav snapped.

"Is that so?" The woman inclined her head in Selene's direction.

"Yes." Sav stood. "When I froze up, she got us to the roof. When our escape crashed, she formed a plan and got us the hell out of there. When Flik was shot, she took us to a medic before he bled out."

"What is the reason for your failure then?"

"I..." Sav started and stopped.

"You've been rescuing Icarus for some time, right?" Selene asked. The Director nodded. "The Dominion was bound to catch on eventually. There are only so many takedowns you can do before they're going to fight back."

"You make a good point, Icarus," Tine said. "Well in this case, I will give you the answers to your questions about the Alliance. A document will be delivered to you this evening that should cover everything. If you have any questions, we can arrange a time to speak." Selene nodded. She had already received the majority of her answers from Sav and his crew, but it wouldn't hurt to go over the details. "Now why don't you all get settled? We will meet tomorrow to detail the plan for election night."

Selene rose, and the others did the same. "You'll remember our deal, won't you?"

The Director nodded. "Of course."

The guards led them from the room and back to their weapons. Since the Director had deemed them non-hostile, the Alliance soldiers allowed the smugglers to suit back up. Selene didn't complain, and quickly strapped in her gear, the weight of the pistols on her hips bringing more pleasure than expected. There was nothing like feeling helpless for weeks to make her grateful for being in control.

Once they were set, Selene's Alliance friends led the way to the cafeteria where they ate dinner with their comrades. Sav tried to pressure her into seafood chowder, to which she politely declined. Flik joined them, bandages gone from sight and shoulder fully healed. Sarah was shocked and made him spill every detail of his recovery. While they ate, many Alliance members looked on curiously. She had a feeling they were the latest gossip in a small community. It was obvious they didn't see many outsiders.

Dinner ended and Sav led them to rooms prepared for each of their crew. Kayl, Sarah, Rem, and Darius quickly disappeared for the night. Sav was just leaving her at her room when Rikkard slid in behind her. He shut the door with a soft click.

The room was white, much like every other room in Alliance HQ. It came equipped with its own bathroom, desk, dresser and double bed. All the furniture was made of sleek steel.

"You really glossed over parts of that story didn't you?" Rikkard asked.

Her heart dropped. Selene glanced over her shoulder. Rikkard inspected an abstract painting hung over the bed. She recognized this tactic as a way to avoid showing his emotions. Rikkard had never been interested in art.

Turning back to the desk, Selene unclipped her various weapons and laid them out side by side. She liked to keep her weapons in line, in case the time came where she needed to throw them on fast.

"No one needs to hear the gory details." She unstrapped a row of knives from her left bicep and layed them down neatly.

"So you aren't going to tell me?"

Selene sighed and braced her hands on the desk. The metal chilled her fingers. She leaned into it, trying to keep the heat from rising in her body. She didn't know how to answer Rikkard's questions. She could tell him she hadn't planned to, or ask why would she bother, but she didn't want to keep him from opening up to her. Selene had no idea what they were to each other now, or even if they would be a *we*. She didn't have time to think on it either: there were much more important things at stake in the next few days.

"I don't know." Gnawing her lip, she resumed unclipping her throwing knives.

"Would you?"

A light touch to her back made her flinch. Surprise flickered through her. A moment ago Rikkard had been across the room. Turning to face him, he stepped back. She tried to ignore the disappointed pang in her chest.

"What good would it do?"

He shrugged. "I know it was worse than you say. You're not good at hiding your feelings."

A smile pricked at the corners of her lips. "And you're all too good at it." She kept her tone teasing. She didn't want him thinking she was some injured animal like the ones they always saved. She wasn't someone who needed to be fixed.

Rikkard saw right through her teasing. He leaned against the dresser, crossing his arms. He raised an expectant eyebrow at her.

"I can't talk about this with you." She spun around to face the dresser. Red-hot embarrassment heated her chest and warmed her cheeks. Unstrapping her holsters, she slipped them from her hips and onto the table. Next was her utility belt. She folded it at the end, checking the pockets for something to do—anything to keep from turning around.

"Would you prefer talking it over with someone else?"

"Well, no." She paused with her fumbling. "It's just that, you're.... you." She bit her lip.

Fabulous description, Selene.

"I'm me?"

"Yes."

"You need to explain your criteria."

"You're maddening." She groaned. Anyone else would get she didn't want to talk about it and leave her alone, but not Rikkard. Either he did understand, and didn't care, or he really was that oblivious.

With all of her weapons off, she took the opportunity to throw herself in bed. Burying her face in the pillows, she wrapped her arms around them, resisting the urge to scream. After several moments of silence from Rikkard, she glanced up. He placed his pistols, rifle and daggers beside hers. Each sat in perfect order. Sighing, she re-buried her face. She had a feeling Rikkard was not going to leave her alone until she spilled.

"Fine, I'll talk," she grumbled into the pillow.

"What did you say?"

Raising her head, she looked at Rikkard, who sat tentatively at the edge of the bed, the perfect mask of emotionless indifference.

"I'll talk."

Rikkard nodded, and waited as she sat up and got comfortable. When she launched into the details, she found it wasn't quite as hard as she imagined. The vat came back to her without question, and the feelings of it all quickly poured from her mouth. She explained the drowning feeling, the needles, scalpels, and unceremonious way they always dumped her on the floor. She told him about Ivy, and the trials they put her through. It took her a long time to get through it all, mostly because she had to stop and rein in her emotions.

Fear licked her skin and chilled her bones. She didn't want Rikkard to know how truly afraid she was, not now, not ever.

She told him about Aaron. Her heart broke again at the memories and she avoided his eyes as she detailed the boy's death and how she knew him.

Lastly, she told him about the false escapes, when they tricked her into thinking she was going to be free again and again.

"That's why you attacked Sav and the others when they rescued you," Rikkard said.

Selene nodded, and leaned back against the wall. At some point Rikkard had crawled up beside her, and sat shoulder to shoulder with her. When he didn't say anything else, she leaned her head against his shoulder. She pushed every thought of vats, training fields, and the Dominion from her mind until calm settled inside her. She couldn't keep living in a world where she was just an experiment, or an Icarus. She was an international smuggler, a fact she was quite proud of.

"I wonder how many others went through this," she wondered absently. Rikkard didn't say a word. He just let her think.

Eventually her thinking drove her to drowsy eyes and yawns. She snuggled down under the covers, forgetting how close Rikkard was. The smooth fabric wrapped her limbs, much more comfortable than the scratchy Dominion sheets. Sleep took her into its embrace so quickly she was lost to it before her head hit the pillow.

Dreams of vats, scalpels, and spine piercing needles eventually woke her. From the depths of her nightmares, she came awake with a start, her whole body lurching for a single moment before she went still. Her heart pounded in her ears. Her mouth was dry, and her limbs cold. She took a deep breath and opened her eyes. Darkness greeted her, with only a single pale light streaming under the door. Cold, featureless walls, sparse furnishings and a single door locked her inside. Her pulse sped up and her eyes widened.

Sweat slicked her palms and she gripped the sheet near her face. She was back with the Dominion. She knew it—it had all been a trick. Her eyes burned with tears.

A warm sigh brushed the hair along the nape of her neck, tickling her skin. Selene froze. Slowly, she glanced over her shoulder. Rikkard lay behind her, his arm wrapped around her waist, and nose gently pressed to her upper back.

Selene took a deep breath, her limbs relaxing and tears coming to a halt. She brushed the wet from her face. *Thank Aldar.* She was in Alliance HQ, not the Dominion lab.

Glancing back at Rikkard, a smile pulled at her lips. She gently laid her hand on top of his. For a while, she listened to his steady breathing, wondering how he survived in all of her hair without suffocating. Snuggling closer to Rikkard's warm body, sleep called to her again. Her blurry mind had nearly pulled her under when a soft squeak cut through the silence outside her room.

Her eyes flew wide. The sound had been so faint; she couldn't be sure she really heard it. She held her breath in an attempt to hear better. When nothing reached her ears, she let her breath go, and waited. She wasn't sure what she waited for, but something told her to get up.

Gingerly slipping from Rikkard's arms, she tiptoed across the floor. Stopping where she assumed the desk was, she felt around the cold metal surface until her fingers brushed the hard plastic of her belt buckle. She clipped it on quickly, holstered her pistols, and strapped on a single set of knives. She didn't want to be *too* presumptuous. For all she knew, she'd just heard soldiers making their rounds or the midnight cleaning crew.

Selene slipped on her boots and opened the front door enough to push her slim body through. Sliding it shut, she turned to the white-walled hall. Fluorescent lights glared back at her. She rubbed the sleep from her eyes and sighed. She was just being paranoid. But since she was up, Selene decided to take a little walk.

Taking her time, Selene padded up and down halls, losing herself in the maze of the Alliance. It was strange being up by herself, but the quiet was soothing. There was no one around to bother her about her past, present, or the coming days. There were no worries to be laid upon her or battles to fight. She was alone in her serenity.

Passing by the cafeteria doors, she stopped. Was there a noise in the kitchen? She peeked inside. Nothing.

"What is up with you tonight?" she mumbled. She slipped

inside the dining hall. The lights were dimmed, but she could still make out the clean lines of metal tables and chairs.

Slipping between the furniture, she made her way to the back. The kitchen was a black hole, completely devoid of light. She stepped inside and searched the wall for a light switch, but found none.

"Lovely." She sighed.

The lights came to life.

"Voice activated, huh?"

No response came. Selene moved through the kitchen, her fingertips trailing over cold metal cabinets, counters, and large appliances. It reminded her of the furniture in her room, but smudge proof.

She rummaged through the cabinets until she found a good size glass. The sink was imbedded into the counter below. She filled her cup, shutting the water off when the glass was half full. The quiet swoosh of a kitchen door caught her attention between *plinks* of water dropping into the sink.

"Who's there?" One hand flew to the holster at her hip, while the other set her glass down with a hollow thud. She was grateful to find the cold metal of her laser pistol. Part of her wanted to pull out a gun right away, but the other worried it was just someone with a midnight thirst. When no voice returned, she shifted from foot to foot. The back of her neck tingled; the overwhelming feeling that someone was watching her drove her to the far end of the kitchen, where another door led to the buffet.

Selene withdrew her gun from its holster and flicked off the safety. The high pitch charge broke the silence, a soft blue glow lighting her tawny olive cheeks. Keeping her back to the door, she slowly pushed it open, and slipped through before turning to push it closed.

A hand slammed into the hand holding her pistol. It flew from her grasp and clattered across the floor, sliding under the buffet and across the cafeteria, skittering to a stop beneath a table.

"Whoops, my bad." Selene recognized that voice immediately. Ivy.

A knee flashed out, catching her in the gut. Selene forced her body to unfold from her doubled over state, only a moment before Ivy whipped a knife at her.

Selene leaned away. The knife sailed over her head, taking a few strands of hair with it. She lunged, wrapping her arms around Ivy's waist. They toppled to the ground. Selene landed hard on top of Ivy's chest. Air burst from her lungs. Ivy wrapped her limbs around Selene, rolling Selene onto her back.

Selene battered Ivy with her palms and reached for her knives. Twisting, Selene rolled Ivy onto her back. Ivy wrapped her legs around her hips, holding her inches away from grabbing her knives.

Ivy bit down on Selene's finger, and Selene hissed. "You stupid bitch! Why the hell are you here?"

With one big heave, Ivy pushed Selene over and onto her back. Selene's head slammed against the buffet. Stars circled her line of sight. Ivy only laughed, while Selene desperately reached for her throwing knives, scarce inches remaining between her fingertips and her black daggers. Ivy's cold fingers wrapped around Selene's wrist.

Selene needed an advantage against Ivy. If her time training against this girl had taught her anything, it was that they were equal. Without luck on her side, or a weapon, this was anyone's game.

With Selene's back pressed to the cold linoleum, Ivy rammed her fist into Selene's cheek. Pain exploded through her face, and she winced. Selene blocked her head with her arms as best she could, but Ivy's jabs were relentless, stabbing her ribs and chest again and again.

Gritting her teeth, Selene wiggled her fingers closer to her opposite bicep. Ivy's fingers tightened their grip. *Just a few more inches.* Another jab sent a shock of pain through her abdomen. Air rushed from her lungs as her fingers wrapped around the hilt of a knife.

The knife cut through the air, all of Selene's force thrown with it. It sliced through Ivy's shoulder. Blood sprayed the metal buffet.

Ivy shrieked, and Selene heaved, kicking the girl off before springing to her feet. Ivy came at her with twin daggers whipping in every direction, blood soaking her gray uniform. Selene dodged her blows, pulling her gun from its holster. She flicked the safety off and took aim. Ivy's eyes widened as she leapt to the side, throwing her own dagger. Selene's laser fired as the dagger sunk into her abdomen with a painful *thunk*.

Selene gasped. *Shit*. Pain exploded through her midriff.

"Fucking bitch!" Selene turned her gun on Ivy a second time.

The girl barely dodged her shot. Selene held her wound in one hand and shot with the other. Blood poured between her fingers, slick and wet. A few of her shots singed Ivy's hair and clothes, leaving a foreign stink in the air. Selene fired and fired, driven rabid by the pain.

Ivy leapt like she was dancing, spinning and twirling around her red laser fire, a mocking grin plastered to her smug face. Selene's frustration burned brighter as Ivy worked her way closer, dodging between tables and chairs. Selene pulled the trigger even faster, leaving less time between her shots. Each red shot burst through the air with minimal power until Ivy danced a little too slow, and one of her shots hit home.

A hiss of fury flew from Ivy's lips, her green eyes going cold. Then a smirk grew on her face. A dark black scorch mark frayed the arm of Ivy's gray suit.

Selene had barely grazed her.

Ivy spun in a roundhouse kick, ducking her laser beam, and knocking the gun from Selene's hand.

Selene growled and plowed a knee into Ivy's stomach. Another shock of pain tore through her abdomen. While Ivy was doubled over breathless, Selene threw a dagger. It plunged deep into Ivy's forearm.

Ivy recovered impossibly fast, a howl on her lips, and threw a punch.

Selene blocked Ivy's fist and jabbed her sternum with her elbow. Ivy fell to the floor and rolled, leaving a thin trail of blood in her wake. When Ivy returned to her feet, she had Selene's pistol in one hand.

Her eyes widened. *Damn it.*

The charge of the gun sent Selene to the floor. The blast left a charred hole in the wall at the far end of the lunchroom. Her heart pounded in her ears. She had to get her gun back. Selene found shelter behind a table for only a few seconds before Ivy blew it into shards of metal and plastic. Selene jumped behind another overturned table. The whine of her pistol had her rolling for another. Every bit of movement sent strikes of pain like lightning bolts through her torso. Selene was bleeding fast, and there wasn't a chance she could dodge as artfully as Ivy.

"Why are you doing this?" Selene called from behind an overturned table. Catching her breath while Ivy charged her next shot, Selene winced. Each breath made her shudder.

"Because I was told to." Ivy shot, and missed. Selene rolled behind a water cooler. "If *you* did what you were told, I wouldn't have to kill you."

"Why would the Dominion order you to kill me?"

"You're a liability."

Another shot rang out, bursting the water cooler. Selene slipped on the slick floor and tumbled to the ground. Her blood mingled with the water. Every bit of her ached.

"I know about the Dominion, Ivy," Selene spat as she scrambled for cover. "They wouldn't kill me. I'm all they've got."

Ivy laughed loud and hard, shooting several times while Selene slipped in her own blood. She landed with a hard thud, her entire upper body tensing. She gritted her teeth against the pain, trying to keep one eye on Ivy. She had a good view of the underside of everything, but not a very good view of her adversary.

"Why would they need *you* when they have *me*?" Ivy cackled.

"Because only one of us can do what we were created for." Selene breathed heavily. If what the Alliance had found out was true, Ivy was a soldier, an Icarus Elite. Her gaze slid from the underside of the table and chairs and finally rested on something below—her second pistol. "Only one of us is a *real* Icarus, and it isn't you." Her heart raced and her fingers inched across the wet linoleum. *Yes, this was it!* Her muscles ached as she reached for her gun. "We were created to be slaves to the aliens, just a body for them to possess so they can take over humanity. I won't stand by and allow it."

"What are you talking about?" Ivy snapped. The laser pistol she held was charged, but she had yet to fire.

"You don't know? We were created to be inhabited, like clones. We weren't meant to stay a person." Selene's fingers closed around cold metal. She breathed a sigh of relief. The safety was already off, her gun fully charged for its next shot. Selene pulled it to her body and waited for Ivy's next move.

"You're lying."

"Why would I lie about that?"

"To distract me."

"Why don't you go home and ask your precious makers what you're for? Ask them what your original purpose was. Let me know their answer."

Selene leapt from her hiding spot before Ivy could respond, taking aim in an instant and firing her weapon. The blaze of red streaked across the room. Ivy dodged at the last second, and cried out as it collided with her unwounded shoulder. She was quick, fast enough to avoid the blow to the chest. But with a gaping hole in her shoulder, there wasn't much she could do.

"Why don't you tell me why you're really here?" With the last of her energy, Selene smirked.

Ivy collapsed to her knees, screaming soundlessly as she clutched her wounded shoulder. "I'm here to kill you!" Ivy's shriek echoed through the hollow cafeteria. Green fire stared back at Selene. Orange hair fell from its bun in a halo around Ivy's face, contorted in rage. "You stupid bitch!" Blood flowed between her hands. "I will *kill you* for this!"

"Try it." Selene's finger tapped against the trigger. Her pistol whined as it charged. She wouldn't miss a second time.

With one last scream of rage, Ivy rose to her feet, turned, and ran from the room. She left a trail of blood behind, leading into the hall. Selene stared after her a moment before dropping her aim and collapsing to her side. Her whole abdomen screamed in pain, but still she held it tightly. The ceiling swirled before her eyes. She would not let Ivy be the death of her.

One dagger to the ribs was not enough to kill an Icarus.

WHEN BOOTS FINALLY RUSHED INTO the room, Selene wasn't sure how long it had been. Her ears rang and her head swam. At some point she'd lost her grip on both her pistol and her wound. So much red soaked the floor. How much of that blood was hers?

"Selene!" someone gasped. Hands gripped her arm and gently turned her onto her back. Her gaze met Sav's. "Get help!"

Footsteps rushed from the room. Selene blinked slowly, Sav's emerald green gaze blurring. A quiet buzz rolled over her. Faintly she realized Sav was speaking.

"You're going to be okay. Lanny's getting help." Pressure on her ribs brought stabs of pain through her mental haze. She groaned softly. "Good, if you can still hurt, you're still alive." Sav smiled.

More boots ran through the hall.

"Where is she?" a sharp voice snapped. The doors to the cafeteria slammed open.

Between one blink and the next, Rikkard kneeled beside her. "What the hell happened?" he growled. His temper wasn't directed at her, but at Sav. She had a feeling he had the look of a wild cat, or at least that's what his tone conveyed.

"I thought this was supposed to be a safe place," Rem squeaked nearby.

Her mind drifted. There was something she needed to tell them, something about what had happened. Her fingers twitched on the floor toward the back entrance. She needed to tell them what happened, who had done this to her. She needed to tell them so she could be avenged.

"Ivy," she whispered, a dull ache coming to the forefront of her mind.

"Did she just say something?" Rem asked.

"Selene?" Rikkard leaned in.

She couldn't help but smile at his handsome face. Tan skin over striking features, muffled by dark stubble and piercing blue eyes. He was almost too beautiful to look at.

"Ivy," she repeated.

"Ivy?" Rikkard looked up at Sav. "That Icarus from the Dominion. This was her work." His pretty eyes returned to her. "Where did she go, Selene?"

Selene parted her lips to speak, but that dull ache was becoming one hell of a headache. Her brows cinched together. She twitched her fingers faintly in the direction of the rear door. She flicked her gaze that way and Rikkard understood.

"I'll be right back." Rikkard paused. *Do not die.*

His blue eyes held her green ones. She nodded wordlessly. He stood and walked away. At first she wondered where he was going, but that damn pain in her head stopped her mid thought.

"Rem, Darius, you're with me. Come on." Boots ran to the far end of the room and a door clanged shut.

"Selene!" Sarah flew through the doors, a large bag and Lanny in tow. She dropped with a thud at Selene's side, pushing Sav out of the way. Her fingers wrapped around Selene's biceps. "Selene, what on Earth have you done this time?" She unfurled her hold. Sarah's violet hair hung in loose curls around her shoulders, brushing her skin. Gentle fingers poked and prodded at Selene's body. "Scalpel."

Sav shimmied up beside her again and tore open the bag, handing her a thin knife. Cutting away the cloth around her wound, Sarah gasped.

Her heart lurched. Was Sarah okay? Was *she* okay?

"It's so deep," Sarah said. Was Sarah biting her lip? That's usually something she did when her voice went low like that. "Stay awake!" Sarah snapped.

Selene's eyes flashed back open. She hadn't been aware they were closing.

"I'm going to give her a boost. She's going to pass out soon otherwise." Sarah's tone was all business. Rummaging through her square green bag, Sarah produced a long white cylinder. From its tip shot a needle. Orange liquid swirled inside.

Images of the vat, and its needles flashed to her mind so quickly, it was like adrenaline shot through her veins. Her eyes went wide and her fingers sought her pistol. Her heart beat painfully against her ribs.

"No, no, no," Selene mumbled over and over. She used what little energy she had left to squirm away. Pinpricks washed over her skin and her body went cold.

Sarah's eyes widened and her forehead creased with worry. She turned to Sav.

"The vat. They used a lot of needles," he explained.

Sarah frowned and gazed back down at her friend. Her fingers gently brushed Selene's cheek. "Don't worry Selene, this will be the only one." Sarah set the needle aside. "We need to get this dagger out first and seal the wound. We can inspect for internal damage after we stop the bleeding."

Sav nodded.

"Hold her down."

Something heavy pressed against Selene's shoulders.

"I'll count down from three. Three. Two. One."

Blinding pain coursed through her ribs, causing her to black out.

When she was brought back a moment later, it was with a surge of energy. Selene bolted upright, gasping for air, and clinging to Sarah with one hand. The other found her pistol. Tiny bolts of electricity ran through every vein and muscle in her body. Selene breathed hard and glanced around the dining hall.

"Selene, it's okay. Take a breath." Sarah gently removed Selene's hand from her shirt and squeezed her fingers. "You're okay. I got the dagger out. I just gave you some adrenaline. You need to stay awake so we can get you to the infirmary."

Wordlessly, she nodded.

Sav took her by the elbow and pulled her to her feet. Her entire world spun and took its sweet time righting itself. When it did, she blinked back stars. "Holy shit."

"It's a bit of a shock, huh?" Sarah laughed. It had been a long time since Sarah used adrenaline to keep her alive. Last time hadn't been close to an infirmary either.

"You can say that again."

Together, Sarah and Sav supported her arms, swinging them around each of their shoulders. Her limbs turned to jelly, but they helped her stay standing, and walked alongside her, half dragging her uncooperative legs. Now that the adrenaline was dying out, and she let go of her gun, everything came flooding back.

"Ivy. She was here. She attacked me in the kitchen."

Sav nodded. "We know. Or at least that's what we assumed you meant when you said Ivy."

Selene raised a questioning eyebrow.

"Rikkard and your crew went after her. I doubt they'll find anything though. From the looks of this floor, you've been bleeding out for a while."

Selene nodded, and let them lead her from the blood spattered dining hall. Lanny held open doors and led the way, stopping every few moments to look back. They had just arrived at the infirmary when Selene sighed and tugged at Sav's arm. He looked down at her.

"Ivy didn't know about us," she said.

"What?"

"The Icarus," she clarified. "Ivy didn't know what they want us for, what we're created for. I don't think any of them know."

Sav paused. "That would explain an awful lot." It would. Like how the Icarus worked for the Dominion and tortured her for days on end.

"I want nothing more than to kill that woman, but you should have seen her face when I told her."

"I bet she didn't believe it."

"Not yet, but she will."

"How did she find us anyway?" Again, her gaze met his. Her lips pressed into a hard line. He knew how. "Someone knows our location, don't they?"

"Someone has to," she agreed. "Someone we trust."

Several blurry hours later, Selene had gone through an anesthesia-induced sleep, been woken up in the same blurry state, and tried to listen to others as well as answer their questions. With her head spinning it was all a bit overwhelming, but she powered through. There wasn't much to say, except to describe the fight and tell them which way she'd gone. Other than that, Selene was clueless as to how she found them, as well as how the hell she got inside. From what she'd seen, this place was like a fortress.

A few dead guards later they had their answer to that question.

She couldn't help but feel responsible for their deaths. Ivy had come here for her, and they lost their lives because of it.

"You should be good to go now." A cute, blonde, curvaceous nurse smiled before scurrying off to help another patient.

"Lovely. Is my head going to feel like this all day?"

Sav chuckled. "It'll wear off soon."

Selene really hoped he was right.

The smugglers, as well as the new additions to the family, gathered around her hospital bed. Flik and Darius bonded by both making suggestive comments at her expense, while Lanny and Rem inspected a nearby medical spider, one scarily similar to those used by the Dominion to torture her in the gel.

Sarah sat with her while Kayl stood guard at the door. Rik leaned against the wall nearby. He was back to his usual too-cool-for-this attitude. It didn't bother her like it might have once. All she had to do was think about the way he sounded when he found her dying on the floor. He might not show it, but Rikkard cared.

A soft knock at the door interrupted the group's bonding. An Alliance soldier dressed in black peeked his head in before opening the door fully. Selene got the impression he was making sure everyone was decent.

"Your presence has been requested in the conference room," the soldier said.

Selene looked around at them all. "Everyone's?" He nodded. "It's a good thing that's a big room."

Flik and Darius chuckled to themselves. Sarah smiled and helped Selene up. Much to her chagrin, everyone seemed bent on treating her like an invalid. After her quick surgery and surgical nano repair, she was feeling good as new, though still a bit foggy. If anything, she wanted a shower. There was enough dry blood caked on her skin to last a lifetime.

"Might as well get this over with."

Together they made their way back to the conference room. Kayl bumped her shoulder on their way out. His presence didn't bother her so much as it did Rikkard, who bristled when the man stepped away quickly.

Selene shot him a glare. There was no time for petty rivalries.

They stuffed themselves into the conference room, Selene sitting close to the head of the table alongside Sarah and Sav. The Director was already present, and greeted them with a humorless nod.

Once the room quieted, Tine addressed them. "Thank you for coming. I'm glad to see you are in good health." Selene shrugged. "It has come to our attention that this attack can only mean one thing. There is a spy among us. I won't make speculations as to whom, but this changes our plan considerably." She let the gravity of her words sink in for a moment.

Sarah shifted uneasily beside her. Selene gave her a reassuring nod. They'd get through this, together.

"I'm sure Sav has filled you in on some of our plan already. As of now we are keeping this on a need to know basis. The full plan will only be disclosed to our key players, including you." Her eyes roamed the group. "Everyone else will know his or her duties alone. We cannot risk a breach in security. Our plan revolves around this going off without a hitch. If it doesn't, you could all be put in danger."

"Yeah, yeah. We get it. Do your jobs or you're dead." Selene rolled her eyes. "Just tell us the plan."

The Director sighed and shook her head. "Fine. Selene, you've requested to be the woman behind the shot that kills presidential candidate, Pate?" She nodded. "You'll be on the roof of the Camros building overseeing the entire operation. You may bring someone with you of course. You'll have a sniper rifle, and binoculars. I hear you're a good shot. Don't disappoint me."

"Wouldn't dream of it."

"You will only shoot given our plan to capture Governor Pate fails. Do I make myself clear?" Selene nodded. "Good. As for the rest of you, you'll be briefed in the morning. I can't have any more information leaked before we are in motion." The Director gazed upon her crew with suspicion.

Selene didn't like it one bit. She couldn't imagine who had given their location to the Dominion, but it certainly wasn't one of hers.

"When do we take off?" Sav asked.

"Again, all information will be given at the last possible moment. Be ready."

"Cryptic," Sarah mumbled beside her, bringing a smile to Selene's face. She had to agree with both Sarah and the Director. Having the plan divulged at the last moment would keep from any information getting out. On the other hand, she was sure none of them were the mole.

"We'll be on high security this evening, so I urge you to stay indoors until morning." With a nod of agreement, the Director seemed satisfied and stood. "Until tomorrow."

"Peace." Flik grinned as he saluted the Director.

Ignoring his antics, the Director fled the room.

"So what now?" Rem asked the group, his eyes darting from

Selene, to Rikkard to Sav. She had a feeling he was trying to decide who was in charge here.

"We wait until morning I guess," Sav answered.

"What can we do for fun around here then?" Darius stood and stretched. Telling the smugglers to wait around patiently was not going to fly.

"We're not all about fun here." Lanny gave him a look.

"From the look of Grumpy Face, I figured." Darius hooked a thumb over his shoulder in the direction the Director had disappeared. Selene snorted.

"We could hang out in the ship?" Rem suggested. "I have some new gadgets to pass around."

"Oooh what is it this time Rem?" Sarah grinned and stood.

Once everyone was on board, Selene shot a look at Sav and his crew. It was obvious they weren't sure whether to jump in or shove off.

"You're all welcome to join us." She grinned. "But be warned, Darius will whip out the booze as soon as we're on board, and he doesn't believe in taking it easy."

"Booze?" Lanny blinked.

"How on Earth did you come across any?" Flik beamed. She'd never seen an alien glow before, but Flik was damn near close.

"Isn't alcohol prohibited by the Dominion?" Sav arched an eyebrow.

"Who cares?" Darius grinned and made his way to the door. "Not like anyone's going to find out!"

"We *are* smugglers." Selene stood. "Or did I forget to mention that?" The three Alliance members' heads whipped around to stare at her in shock. "So I did forget to mention that. Silly me."

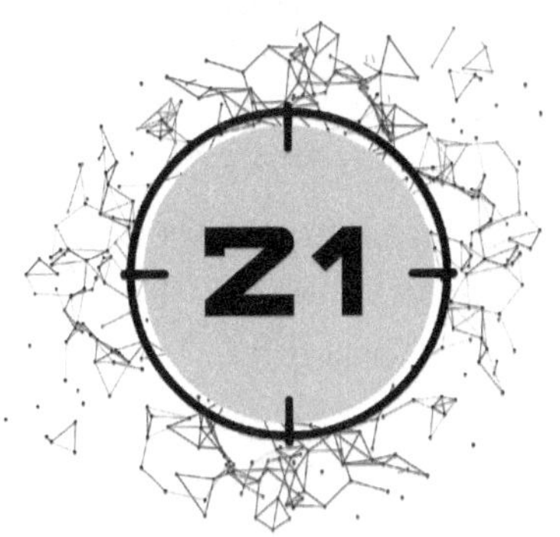

ONCE SELENE AND THE OTHERS had boarded the cargo ship, they gathered in the dining hall. Darius and Flik went to get booze and food in the kitchen, while Lanny and Rem took off to gather the new gadgets Rem had mentioned. Sarah tapped into the room's speaker and flipped through music while Kayl looked on over her shoulder. Together they murmured softly and made lovey eyes at each other.

While the others were busy, Selene took a moment to slip away. A shower called to her, along with some medication for this headache. She'd barely reached her door when Rikkard joined her, sneaking up and slipping into the room behind her. She wasn't sure if this was behavior to discourage, or encourage.

"Following me are you?" She shot him an amused smile.

The door slid shut and Rikkard wordlessly leaned against the wall, an eyebrow quirked at her. Selene sighed and stepped over to her shower, turning the water on hot before she flicked on the overhead fan. She didn't want to steam up the room too badly.

"All right, what are you dying to ask me?" She knew it had to be something, or else Rikkard wouldn't be following her around like a curious puppy.

"I'll be with you on the roof," he said.

Selene shot him a questioning look before she unzipped her

suit. It went from her collarbone to just below her navel. She'd done so before realizing this might be a little sudden with Rik in the room.

She cleared her throat. "Will you now?" Selene tried unsuccessfully to push back the flush rushing to her cheeks. She turned her back to him, and stepped behind the foggy glass of the shower. She stripped the rest of her suit off, dried blood flaking to the floor as she tossed it.

"It isn't negotiable."

Selene rolled her eyes as she stepped under the hot water. Pain burst across her skin. *Hot!* She recoiled and quickly adjusted the temperature. Sighing blissfully, she stepped under fully and submerged her head. The loud beating of water on her skull drowned out all noise. For a moment she could believe she wasn't about to head into war. She could even forget about the last awful month, and the lives she'd taken and those she failed to take.

A knock on the glass interrupted her reverie. She snapped back and stepped from beneath the gush of water, wiping her hair from her face.

"What?" She tapped a few instructions into the shower's control panel.

"You're not arguing with me," Rikkard stated.

She glanced at his shadow hovering on the other side of the glass. Her nakedness brought back her embarrassed flush. "No."

"That's unusual for you."

Selene stilled. "It is, isn't it?"

She hit the button for shampoo. The showerhead dispensed pale yellow foam into her hands. She worked it through her hair, letting herself be overtaken by the blissful warmth and wonderful vanilla. She gave herself several minutes of peace to clean off and get ready for tomorrow's events.

Once the blood was scrubbed from her skin and suds removed from her hair, she shut the water off and rang her hair out with her hands.

Selene peeked out from behind the glass. "Pass me a towel

would you?" She motioned to a drawer insert in the wall.

Rikkard raised a brow but didn't say a word. He found the right cabinet, and clicked the open button. It slid out with a whoosh. Rikkard grabbed the first towel inside and tossed it to her.

"Thanks." Selene caught it and went about drying her hair and body before wrapping herself in its soft, but damp fabric. She stepped out from behind her protective barrier, and gathered a fresh suit and headache medication.

"Why do you want to kill Governor Pate so badly?"

Selene froze. She stood in front of her mirror, hair dripping wet and towel just covering her lady bits. This wasn't exactly the moment she pictured divulging her life story to Rikkard. Before she could answer, she caught his gaze in the mirror. Though she was used to his expressionless glares, questioning eyebrow quirks and unhappy mouth set, she wasn't used to this brief look of concern. It took her more off guard than his question.

Unsure what to say, she started by getting herself set in more appropriate attire. She motioned for him to turn around. He politely complied. Selene stripped her towel off and made quick work of her suit. Once she had it zipped above her breasts, she shook her limbs out. They cooled to her regular body temperature. She had missed her suits.

"I want to kill him because he was the one that ruined my life five years ago."

Rikkard took this moment to glance back. When she gave him the all clear, he turned around and went back to leaning on the wall. She took that as a sign to proceed.

"After I hit my head when we saved those apes awhile back, I started having dreams. Memories. At first I wasn't sure, but now more than ever I am. I finally saw what my life was like before I met you. I wish I could go back to forgetting." She looked away, busying herself with filling a glass of water and gulping back pills. When she was done, she had no other reason to delay. "I was a *nat*. I had parents. I was only a teenager when I packed up and left to see the big city." Selene rolled her eyes at her own foolish self.

"So I left home and went to New Manhattan. I got a job, and settled down. I had an awesome boss, one that knew I was *nat*, but was never prejudiced about it. I met Pate and his minions while working there. They liked to come in and harass me. When I didn't give in to his advances, he killed my boss and torched the place. From there, I was with the Dominion for two years or so. They experimented on me and turned me into… this." She motioned to herself for effect.

Selene couldn't help her clasped fists or fiery demeanor. She stared at the wall like she wanted to punch it, and really considered doing so until Rikkard spoke up.

"That makes sense."

"No shit."

Before she could make a move at the wall, Rikkard gently took her hand and unfolded her fingers. She glanced at him with wide eyes. She'd never seen him be gentle in her life, let alone kind. Heat boiled inside her chest and flushed her cheeks.

"Whether the plan calls for it or not—" His fingers clasped her chin gently, turning her to face him. Her eyes met his and his hand fell back to his side. "We'll kill him."

"We?"

"I'll be on that roof with you. There's no chance we won't kill him if we're both there."

Selene smiled. "Not a chance."

A loud banging on the door interrupted their moment.

"Hey!" Darius called. "What the hell are you two doing in there? Get out here! There's a party to be had!"

Selene grinned and opened the door.

"What if we were stark naked in here? The manners on you."

"I wouldn't mind seeing that." Flik flashed his teeth at her from behind Darius.

"I knew you were into guys. Only explanation for your overcompensation."

Flik balked and stared at her wide-eyed. Rikkard appeared at her shoulder. While Darius and Selene nearly collapsed in laughter, they ushered the other two back to the dining hall.

They must have been gone longer than she realized. The moment they entered the room, the lights were dimmed and music blared. Sarah and Kayl waltzed around the room, smiling at one another in a way Selene had always envied: it was the way she wanted to be looked at, like she was the only woman in the world.

"Selene?" Rikkard's fingers brushed her elbow.

Kayl dipped Sarah low, and her high voice rang in a laugh.

Selene shrugged, and joined the others. Darius flew across the room to a large cooler packed with ice and bottles of clear liquid. She knew all too well it was much more than water. Her large friend tossed her a bottle before handing one to Flik. Even Rikkard picked one up in passing.

"*Finally!*" Rem sighed dramatically from a nearby table. Or at least there had been a table under all that mess. "We've been waiting *forever!*"

"It's been like fifteen minutes. Simmer." Selene took a seat beside her young white haired friend before popping the cap off her liquor. "What do you have for me?"

Rem's grin spread fast. He launched into detailed technical explanations, pulling weapons and gadgets from the table. Selene let it all wash over her, drinking to numb the boring tech talk. She didn't understand it, and didn't need to. As long as they worked when it came time to use them, she didn't care what made them tick.

When Rem finally pulled out her modded laser rifle she leapt from her seat and snatched it so fast, she nearly pulled Rem off his feet.

"Yes!" She held it to her chest. "I've missed you." Selene grinned as she checked over the safety, trigger, cell cartridge and grip. Holding it to her shoulder, she could already feel the difference. The gun was lighter, black with blue lines zipping through it. When she charged it up, the blue glowed fiercely. A faint hum vibrated through the device. Selene could tell he'd increased the power output. "Beautiful."

"Thanks!" Rem smiled, and leapt up to show her the new adjustable sight, and extended barrel. Selene let him talk while she played with her rifle, happy to have its familiar metal back in her hands. "Oh, I also added this option." Digging through the pile, he pulled a small metal grappling hook from beneath a plethora of pulse grenades. "You can hook this onto the barrel and switch the power mode." Rem flicked a switch beside the trigger. "This way you can shoot the hook without incinerating it."

"Cool." She grinned.

Rem prattled for a while longer before she finished her bottle. The liquid went down harsh; its taste bitter against her tongue, but the warm buzz it filled her with was always worth it.

"Darius!" she called. Without looking up, he tossed another. She caught it midair. "Thanks!"

He raised a hand in recognition but was much too preoccupied telling Flik and Sav about the past exploits of the smugglers. All three of them huddled together, Darius making exaggerated gestures with his hands.

"The wall exploded, distracting the two Dominion soldiers behind me! They're so fucking stupid; I can't believe they decided to follow me in there. I tossed one of their bodies out the hole I blasted in the wall. I mean, we had to get the crowd out of there somehow." Darius recounted his version of when they'd saved the two Bengal tigers from Bakura. She couldn't help but grin at the memory. Warmth blossomed in her chest.

Standing with a slight wobble, she sat down beside Sav to join their conversation, laying her rifle on the table.

"That's nothing," she said. "You weren't even there for the best part!"

"Which part was what exactly? Did you *see* the damage that explosion caused?"

"Of course. But you weren't there for the shootout with Dominion soldiers, *or* the speeder chase."

Sav and Flik looked between them with wide eyes, while Darius scoffed.

"Just because you and Rikkard got to tangle with pirates, doesn't make it the most exciting part of the night."

"Pirates?" Sav blinked.

"They were practically harmless." Selene rolled her eyes.

"That's not what I heard from the boss!"

"Rik was only half conscious until they boosted him!"

"Still a fairly reliable source."

Back and forth they argued, about their exploits, missions and fights until Sav and Flik were staring at each other with wide-eyed wonderment. Selene had almost forgotten they'd just found out they were smugglers. What did they expect, military missions and night ops?

"The explosion in Bakura was nothing compared to the air chase through New Manhattan." On her other side sat Rikkard, with his *don't trifle with me* face on. "Selene used the Gatling gun on the Class Five to shoot out half the Dominion speeders in the city."

"I almost forgot about that." She smiled.

"How do you forget about that?" Flik waved in the air to punctuate his statement.

"It was a while ago." She shrugged.

"All right, you win." Darius sighed. "But we're not counting the Old Chicago mission in this debate, so don't you dare bring that up!"

"Oh! Now *that* one was fun."

"You nearly died," Rikkard said dryly.

"So? Still fun."

"You're all insane." Sav shook his head.

"Are not!"

Their banter continued into the night as more and more bottles emptied. More laughs rocked the room, food was had, and the Alliance members even shared some of their stories. Most of theirs didn't involve car chases and shootouts, but their skill was still impressive. Their last one seemed to be their most interesting, and even Rem joined them to hear about how Lanny rigged a desert speeder to blow the gate.

Hours later, it was well past midnight, and the boys were still comparing stories, as well as arm wrestling to see how many of them it took to beat Darius. After all four of them piled onto his arm, they nearly won. Nearly.

Selene wandered over to join Sarah, who sat alone with a smile firmly planted on her face. Kayl was nowhere to be seen.

"Whatchu doin' over here alone?" she slurred, her head fuzzy. Selene laughed with Sarah as she stumbled into the seat beside her. It had been a long while since she'd drank this much of Darius's special brew.

"You've had a few." Sarah smiled.

"Only a couple."

"It looks like everyone is having fun and getting along. I never thought I'd see the day when we had military on the ship."

"Me neither," she admitted. It was still a bit odd having the Alliance members aboard, but they fit in much better than expected. A few more nights like this and they may have to pilfer them from the rebellion. "Where's Kayl?"

Sarah shrugged. "He said he had something to do. I think he just can't handle his liquor." They both grinned. Kayl wasn't known for his drinking habits, in fact, last time they'd stayed in Bakura for a few nights, Kayl got wasted and got sick over half the ship.

"That sounds like Kayl."

"Rikkard is acting a bit different." Sarah shot her a sidelong look, a devious smile on her lips.

Selene couldn't hide the flush from her face. She squirmed under Sarah's knowing purple gaze. Whether it was from her comment or the booze at this point, she wasn't even sure. "Is he?"

"Yes." Sarah laughed, nudging her shoulder. "He finally told you didn't he?"

"Told me what?"

Sarah smiled and shook her head. "If you don't know what I'm talking about, then he hasn't. I won't ruin the surprise."

"Oh come on, Sarah! Now you *have* to tell me."

"Not a chance." She winked.

"You're terrible."

"That may be so." Sarah grinned. "But at least I've always got your back."

"True." She always had. Even during their most famed mission yet. Old Chicago had been a minefield, and only Sarah could save her life with one vile of adrenaline and hardly any medical supplies.

"In all seriousness, Rikkard has really changed since your return." Sarah reached over and took her hand, squeezing lightly. The warmth of her hand spread through her bones, and she leaned back into her chair.

"You're right." Selene squeezed back on the alien's slim fingers. "I don't know what you'd all do without me."

Sarah laughed again and Selene joined in. She had missed this more than words could properly say.

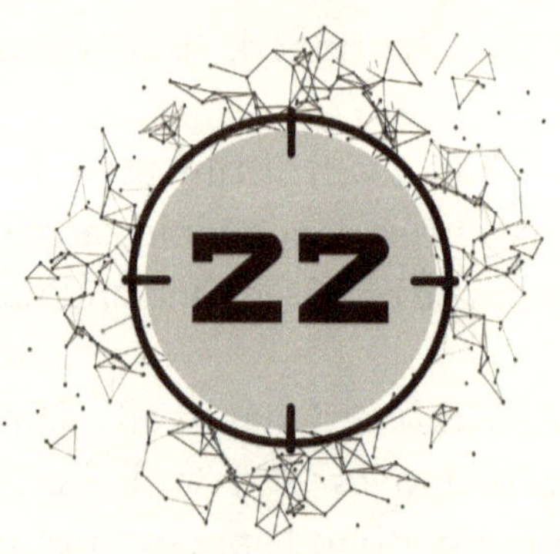

"I ASSUME YOU'VE ALL HAD a good night's sleep." The Director leveled her gaze at each of them.

Their party had gone long into the night, leaving them all tired and a bit hungover. It was the first time any of the Alliance boys had experienced this, and it was fairly amusing to see them sticking close by trash bins in case they threw up. Selene couldn't help but grin every time one of them shot her an accusing glare. She felt mostly fine, just a bit dehydrated. They'd all slept long past their meeting, and it wasn't until early in the afternoon that someone from the Alliance came to retrieve them. They'd all slept in the dining hall, Selene and Sarah cuddling with a sleepy Kong, while the others lay on chairs, tables or the floor. The soldier had been baffled at the sight of them.

Late in the afternoon, it was time to get down to business. The hard lines of the Director's face most certainly conveyed as much.

"Yes ma'am." Sav gave the Director a curt nod before he stepped up to join her.

The woman rose, bringing a small device with her. She pointed it at the large screen on the back wall. It lit, casting a blue glow on the entire room.

A detailed map of Election Square in downtown New

Manhattan was on the screen. The heights of each neighboring building were marked, as well as the location of the Dominion guards and rooftop security. But it was the main stage that the Director drew their focus to.

"This is where the final ballots will be cast by human citizens. The two candidates running for president will be shaking hands with civilians here, and here." She pointed to each location, before detailing the stage security measures, including metal and energy detectors, rigorous soldier presence and unfailing ID checks. "We won't risk anyone getting caught on that stage. We can't have any Alliance information getting back to the enemy." She paused. "More than has already been leaked that is."

"How can you be sure Governor Pate will be the victor?" Kayl stepped from the back of the room, his brow furrowed and arms crossed over his chest.

"We have spies of our own." Sav grinned. "The results have been rigged."

Kayl nodded and stepped back.

"Our soldiers will be dispersed through the crowd," the Director continued, using a small controller to point behind the crowd control barrier several feet from the stage. "You will all be in this crowd."

"I have teams set up already," Sav added. "We'll divide everyone on the fly just in case."

"We need you all ready in case things go wrong." The Director narrowed her eyes. "You *must* be ready to take the president without fail. Crowd control may also be needed once our plan goes off. Your job will be to take Governor Pate from the stage."

Selene tapped her fingers against the table. The Director had promised her the killing shot, but most of their plan banked on taking Pate alive. She exchanged a quick glance with Rikkard on the opposite side of the conference table. He held her gaze, his chin dipping in a barely noticeable nod. She was glad they were on the same page.

Even if the Alliance wanted Pate alive, they'd kill him.

"There will be a hovercraft waiting on top of the Arros Condo building here." Sav pointed at a blue spot illuminating on the roof of a silver skyscraper over half a dozen blocks away. A glowing orange circle appeared next, two blocks west of Election Square. "A van will be waiting here to take Pate and a small team from the city."

"While Pate is being extracted, Lan will hack the election broadcast and send our message to the world," Tine continued.

"Rem is going to help me with that," Lanny said.

The Director nodded. "Satisfactory, as long as the job gets done within two minutes of the election results. As for Selene, you'll be our backup. If we can't take Pate off that stage, you will shoot him from this building." She moved her pointer to the tallest of the surrounding skyscrapers. "You will only shoot if we fail to capture Pate. You'll have a direct shot if it comes down to it. There will be guards on the roof checking for snipers, so stay vigilant."

"Not a problem," Selene said. "Rikkard will be with me."

"Understood."

"When I give the signal, team A will move into position." Sav took his own pointer from the table. A red dot appeared at the crowd control barrier. "Team A will pass security with non-lethal force. Team B will enter through the gap Team A has created. Team B will head right for the stage where they will overtake security and extract the president. Team C will stay on standby to assist, here and here." Sav pointed to either side of the stage. "Team D will remain in the crowd as a last resort."

"Sarah, we hear you have medical training." The Director met Sarah's purple eyes across the room. Sarah shifted uncomfortably under the old woman's steely gaze.

"I do," Sarah said. Before Selene had joined the smugglers, Sarah had been their medic for nearly a decade. She had more than training, she was the best Selene knew.

"We'll have you on Team Delta as a medic."

Both of Sarah's brows rose into her hairline. "I can fight as well as anyone here."

Kayl twitched from his place on the back wall, putting himself into his wife's line of sight. Sarah glanced his way and sighed. Even though Kayl was bound to put himself in danger, he refused to let his wife move to the front lines. Selene understood. She didn't want Sarah hurt any more than Kayl.

"Fine."

"Excellent." The Director stood.

"If anything comes up, we'll all be on a comlink." Sav tapped the side of his head where a black cuff wrapped around his ear. "You'll be able to inform us of any suspicious activity."

Flik nodded. "Got it."

"That is all we have for you at the moment. If you have any further questions, Sav will be leading this mission." The Director nodded at the man, who straightened, his heels clicking together. "Best of luck. The Zahkx Alliance thanks you."

The Director fled the room, her long white lab coat snapping behind her. The door swooshed closed, leaving the others in silence.

"So you're in charge huh?" Flik leapt to his feet, grabbing Sav in a headlock and rubbing his hair aggressively with his fist. Sav grabbed Flik's arm, gritting his teeth and wincing.

"Yes! Stop that!" Sav said.

"If you're the boss, you'll have to command it comrade!" Flik grinned.

Sav grabbed Flik's elbow, slipping from his hold and catapulting Flik over his shoulder onto the conference table. The sheet of metal clanged and shook beneath his weight. Flik groaned as he slipped off it. Darius erupted in laughter alongside Lanny and Rem.

"Don't mess with the boss, got it." Flik gave him a sloppy salute before flopping back into his chair.

Selene stood and wacked Sav's shoulder. "Go easy on the invalid. He was nearly dead yesterday you know."

"Hey!" Flik barked.

Sav flashed a grin at them both. "You have a point! Then again, so were you."

"I'll have you know I could still kick your ass."

"Is that a challenge?" Sav cocked an eyebrow.

"Hell yes. I'll whip you into shape before tomorrow." Selene winked. "You do remember last time we fought, right? Maybe you'll learn something this time."

"You're on." Sav motioned for the door. Selene followed, the rest of their large group trailing behind.

A few hallways later, Sav led her inside a familiar gym—the one she'd walked into on her first day with the Alliance. Instead of veering to the rows and rows of occupied workout equipment, he steered to a joining room. The floor dipped beneath her feet, squishing as she walked. Several duos fought at the far end of the long room, their forms flying through the mirrors lining each wall. The front of the room was clear.

While their friends lined the wall, Selene stepped out onto the mat-like floor. She stripped off her belt and daggers, handing them to Sarah, who grinned. She knew as well as Selene that no man was a match for her.

Her limbs tingled with anticipation. Selene had no idea what would happen tomorrow, and didn't want to think about it. A fight would be the perfect distraction.

"Just so you know, I went easy on you the first time." Sav stepped out to face her across the mat. His holsters were missing. "I won't be so nice this time around."

"I'll hold you to that." Selene stretched her arms out, shaking the tension from her limbs.

"Ready?" Sav asked, bringing his fists up.

"Bring it."

Sav lunged, green eyes flashing with mischief. Selene grinned and jumped to the side, rolling over her shoulders. She leapt back to her feet and spun in a roundhouse kick. Sav blocked with his forearm, twisting into a sweep. Selene laughed as she grabbed his shoulders and leapfrogged over his head.

"You can't use my moves against me." She brushed wisps of brown and blonde from her eyes. Energy coursed through her limbs, fueled by pure adrenaline. Every worry over tomorrow disappeared.

"I can try." Sav shrugged and aimed a punch at her head.

Selene ducked low. His fist sailed overhead as she drove her elbow into his gut. Sav doubled over, air spilling from his lungs. She spun, sweeping his feet out from under him. His back hit the floor with a thud, muffled by the padding.

He sprung back to his feet surprisingly quick, snapping his foot out. Again, she ducked. Sav spun low, his ankle catching hers. Her eyes widened as she toppled to the floor.

A chorus of *ohs* sounded from their watching friends.

Selene narrowed her eyes. Sav lunged again, but before he landed she rolled out of the way, the wind from his fists a scarce few inches from her face.

"Nice!" Darius called.

Leaping up, Selene waited with her fists up for him to come at her again. Only he didn't this time. Instead he stalled, raising his own fists and dancing back and forth from foot to foot.

"What are you waiting for?" she snapped.

"I got you." Sav grinned.

"Lucky shot."

Selene dove to the side, faking a kick at his gut before spinning in the opposite direction. While he moved to block her kick, she snapped her elbow out, catching his lower back. He buckled, rolling from her reach when she lunged. On his way back up she caught him. Grabbing onto his shoulders, she leapt, spinning from his reaching hands, wrapping her legs tightly around his neck. She brought him down, her back hitting the mat hard. She held on, squeezing his head between her thighs while bending his arm back, gripping his wrist with determined fingers.

Sav let out a startled cry when he landed. He clawed at her legs, twisting in his panic, but she only bent his arm back further. He yelped in pain.

"Give up?" Selene asked through gritted teeth. She may be strong, but Sav was too.

"How the—"

"I told you, you couldn't win."

Sav struggled for a few more moments before he sighed. His

body went limp in her grasp. He tapped the mat. Unfurling her hold, Selene grinned deviously as she climbed to her feet. Wiping the sweat from her forehead, she stood with a hand on her hip.

"Just like last time." Selene offered her hand.

"Just like last time." Sav took her hand and pulled himself to his feet.

Their small crowd broke out in applause, some more enthusiastic than others. Kayl stared off in boredom. Sarah elbowed his side and he joined in the clapping.

"Thank you, thank you." Selene took a bow.

"Well now that you've kicked my ass, maybe we should get the equipment ready for tomorrow," Sav said.

"You're just trying to make everyone forget you lost, *again*." Selene smirked.

"I have no idea what you're talking about." Sav retreated to the sparring room doors, a grin on his face as he waved over his shoulder.

"Yeah, right!" Selene called, stomping after him. "I'm not letting you forget about it that easily!"

With her adrenaline gone and her short-lived fun behind her, reality caught up. Tomorrow Selene would face the man who ruined her life. She'd put a bullet or a laser through his head and be happy about it. But what if the mission didn't call for it? Would she really screw over the people who saved her from the Dominion?

Selene bit down on her lip, and ran a rag over her rifle. The black metal shined. She'd cleaned every piece of her gun at least three times already.

Would betraying the Alliance be worth it if she got to kill Pate? Could she justify his death? An image of his smirking face came to mind. Her fingers turned into claws around the ridged grip of her rifle. His lips quirked to one side, his amber gaze pierced through her. He smiled as she emerged from the vat, her own torture chamber. He fussed over her, touched her, and worst of all, *he* sent her to that place. Angry tears burned to the surface.

She had her answer.

"Selene?" Sarah touched her shoulder gently.

Selene started. Blinking back tears, she avoided her friend's gaze until her vision cleared. She coughed to break the silence and give herself an extra moment.

"Yeah?" Selene glanced up at Sarah. Her purple eyes glistened, and her forehead pulled together. Selene knew Sarah's look of concern all too well. "I'm fine." She smiled.

"Are you sure?" Sarah asked, taking a seat beside her.

No, she thought. She wasn't fine. She was angry, livid about things out of her control. But by dawn in two days' time, she'd be happy, and everything *would* be fine.

She nodded.

Kayl chose that moment to join them, waltzing into the loading bay of their cargo ship. She sat on a large crate near the center of the room, her various weapons spread around her. Kayl glanced at them both, offering Sarah a nod before continuing to a large storage rack on the right side of the room.

"I'm sure." Selene peeled her fingers away from her rifle. She set it across her lap and returned its cell cartridge to its chamber. It snapped in place, glowing faintly. "You don't have to worry about me."

"You're a crap liar." Sarah smiled.

"Sarah?"

They both looked up as Lanny boarded the cargo lift.

"There you are." He trotted over to join them. "I need you to look over our emergency kits and make sure we haven't missed anything."

Sarah nodded. "Of course." She slipped off the oversized crate and onto the floor.

They waved goodbye as they left.

Once their retreating forms disappeared into Alliance HQ, Selene went back to cleaning her rifle. She was glad the Director had stationed Sarah in Team Delta. They were the least likely to see any action, and were thus the safest. If there was one thing Selene and Kayl could agree on, it was Sarah's safety.

A clang across the metal floor drew her attention.

"Shit," Kayl muttered. He crouched to retrieve an empty power cell from the floor. When he stood, their gazes met across the room. His navy eyes darkened and he quickly turned away.

Selene cocked an eyebrow. "What's your problem?"

Kayl's shoulders went rigid, then slumped as he sighed. "You're my problem."

"Because I didn't die like you wanted?"

Selene still remembered what he'd told the rest of the crew. She was dead and he'd seen her body. Why would he tell them that? He'd always had it out for her, never liked her since the day Rikkard found her on his ship.

"I didn't want you to die." He rolled his eyes.

"Then why would you lie?"

He narrowed his eyes. He was quiet for several long moments. What lie would he tell her? He *had* seen her body and thought she was dead? He didn't want the others going after her? He hated her enough that he *hoped* she was dead?

"The crew has changed entirely since you arrived." Kayl held her gaze. "You bring too much risk. You're reckless, but charismatic. The others don't see that you're manipulating them into doing what you want. Even *Rikkard* loves you for Aldar's sake." Selene started. "I told them you were dead so they'd forget you. So they'd move on with their lives. You're a liability in our world. You're going to get us all killed with your crazy schemes." He paused. "I won't let you do that to my wife. She will not get hurt because of *you*."

Selene stared with wide eyes. She couldn't believe what she was hearing. He actually thought she was the reason for all of his problems.

"I would never hurt Sarah, or any of you for that matter—"

"Not on purpose. But I won't let it be an accident either."

Kayl's eyes narrowed again, his navy eyes almost black. His lips curled in a deep frown, wrinkling his green skin. He hated her. Selene could see that now. She'd always thought he disliked her because she changed the smugglers, which was true. They weren't the Smugglers Legion anymore. But it was more than that. He actually thought she was dangerous.

Maybe she was.

"If you're so worried about me, why haven't you done something sooner?" she asked.

"I'd be skinned if I lay a hand on you." Kayl rolled his eyes.

"Fine." Selene looked away. She wanted to prove him wrong. She would prove she wasn't a danger to him, his wife, or this crew. She'd keep them all safe, get everyone through tomorrow, and then go from there. "You should go with Delta group tomorrow."

"What?"

"You want to keep Sarah safe?" Selene snapped. She leapt from the crate, rifle in hand. "Then go with Team Delta. Keep her safe." She swung the rifle's strap over her shoulder. "At least we can agree on that." Selene collected the rest of her gear, returning it to her utility belt and dagger straps.

Stepping from the cargo bay, Selene left Kayl in silence.

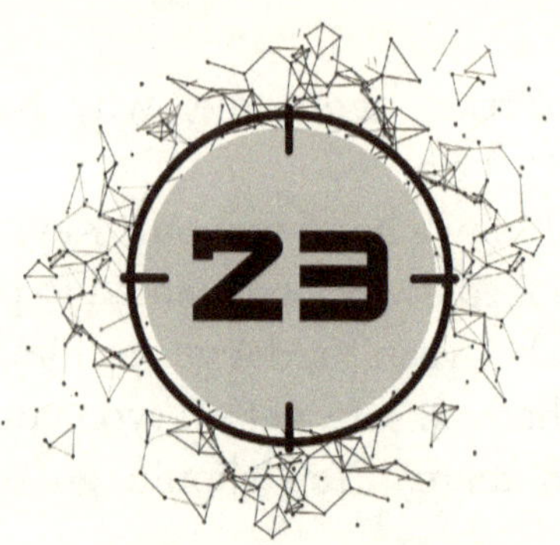

STANDING BACK IN THE CONFERENCE room, Selene and the smugglers faced Sav, who stood straight, arms crossed behind his back. He wore full Alliance gear, black body armor from head to toe. After the previous night's preparation, they were ready.

"Is everyone ready?" Sav inclined an eyebrow.

She nodded.

"Good," Sav said. "We're heading out in ten minutes."

Wide eyes met Sav's. They were told it'd be last minute when they headed out, but this was a bit extreme. Nerves ran down her arms to her fingertips.

"Get your things and get to the hangar," he continued. "Your sniper will be waiting for you." Selene nodded. "Get moving."

With only ten minutes to make it across Alliance headquarters, everyone sprinted from the room. Selene led the way to the cargo ship, where each of them gathered their weapons, strapped on their suits and flung anything they may need into packs. Selene even found a moment to pull on her signature half black, half green wig. She smiled at the sight of it. It had been a long time since she disguised herself. She missed the thick bangs and sleek colors. Joining the others, they all dashed for their ride.

Exactly ten minutes had passed when they all met at the

hangar.

Sav was already there, motioning them all into the back of a hovercraft. He did a double-take when Selene bounced up with her new do.

"Nice hair." He grinned.

Selene winked before boarding.

"Let's go!" Sav barked at the others, shouting over the humming of the propellers. "Everyone in!"

They all crowded inside, boots slamming up the metal walk. Once their eyes adjusted to the dim interior light, Selene could make out the shapes of other Alliance soldiers, all seated in rows along the walls. Her team joined them, strapping in for the short flight to New Manhattan.

Finally, election night was here.

New Manhattan city; with skyscrapers so high you could break your neck trying to see the tops of them, and streets so busy only the automated systems built in to each hovercraft kept them from colliding. She'd flown through the city many times, making her experience on the ground somewhat breathtaking.

Now that night had fallen, the white buildings of New Manhattan glowed like beacons: Titans of metal, glass and smooth white plastic. Colors and images danced over their smooth surfaces, advertising products of every kind, including the latest in cloning mods and upgrades. They were built to endure, to survive anything from earthquakes to hurricanes. This new alien civilization would outlive them all. When humans, clones, and aliens finally died out, would these architectural anomalies remain, or eventually decay like the rest of them?

Selene wrinkled her nose at the ads on the buildings and turned away.

"Selene." Rikkard touched her arm lightly as they walked. She looked from the startlingly beautiful world around her and zeroed in on the single most stunning pair of eyes she'd ever seen.

"Yes?" She arched a brow at him.

"Are you okay?"

Selene couldn't help the smile that pulled at her lips. She remembered a day when Rikkard would only ask her that on her deathbed.

"I'm fine. Just checking out the city. It's been a long time since I've seen these streets." She hadn't thought of it until now, but she did remember a time when she walked New Manhattan with innocent doe eyes. She'd been seventeen and naïve. She'd never seen the city before, nothing beyond the Outskirts.

Rikkard nodded, leaving her be. He kept close, and she silently thanked him for his small efforts. Sarah was right, he was changing, and she had a feeling he was doing it for her.

Together they walked with the rest of their friends. The smugglers melded seamlessly with the Alliance soldiers. As one, they walked the streets, blending into the crowd as they made their way to Election Square. The goal was to become one with the flow of people moving into the square. The Alliance had provided jackets to hide their weapons. They did a good job of hiding the large metal bulges.

"We're almost there." Sav shot her a look over his shoulder, making sure she'd heard him through their comsets.

She nodded in understanding. They'd spoken more in the hovercraft on the flight to New Manhattan. Selene and Rikkard would slip off once they reached the square and make their way around the Camros building. After they took out any guards in their path, they'd use the service elevator to get to the top floor, then use the stairs to reach the roof.

"Ready?" Rikkard leaned in, his warm breath brushing her neck.

"Ready," she said.

Rikkard led her away from their group as the stage came into view. She didn't have time to stop and take it in, but she had a decent picture in her mind from what the Director had shown them.

Selene jogged behind her captain as he weaved through the crowd. Her guns bounced against her back and side as she moved, reminding her to keep her jacket closed tight. Most of the civilians surrounding them stopped to let them go with a smile, their eyes flashing with amusement at seeing a young couple slip off somewhere quiet. On any other day she might have considered it, but today they had a mission.

Once they were clear of the crowd, Rikkard slowed his pace. She had the immediate urge to pull a pistol from its hiding place, but she squashed it quickly. She couldn't draw attention yet.

When they finally slipped around the back of the gray stone and steel building, Selene was surprised to find the alley clear of security.

"Here." Rikkard stopped at the service entrance Sav had mentioned. He pulled a laser pistol from his coat and shot the lock. It burst free.

She pulled out her own gun and stuck her back to the wall. Rikkard slammed his boot against the door, kicking it in. Together they leapt inside. Selene positioned her gun to the right, and Rikkard went left. The storage area the door opened into was devoid of life.

"This is way too easy." Selene lowered her pistol.

"They must only watch the main part of the building." Rikkard moved across the floor, working his way slowly through storage boxes as he canvassed the area.

"Could just be on break."

Rikkard paused in the hallway joining the room to the rest of the building. "I heard voices this way." He motioned to the right side of the hall.

"Must be guarding the elevators."

Selene joined him, taking in the left side of the hall before they made their way down the right. Voices floated down the corridor and the dim light turned bright, illuminating gray featureless walls.

"All this security for nothing." A man sighed.

"At least this is the slackest post possible." Selene thought she could distinguish the voices of at least three men joined in laughter.

Selene shot Rikkard a look and held up four fingers. Four men were up ahead, if not more. They all sounded fairly young, but she couldn't be sure how fit they were.

Rikkard checked a nearby archway. A kitchen waited beyond the open door. He held up a finger. She paused at his command and waited as he ducked inside. When a loud clang sounded, she stared wide-eyed between the open door and the end of the hall. Her heart leapt into her throat. What the hell was he doing in there? Was he trying to get them caught?

"What was that?" a man said.

"We should check it out," another added.

Before Selene could decide on a plan of action, Rikkard grabbed her arm and rushed a few paces forward before shoving her sideways through an open door. Selene nearly lost her balance, careening towards a nearby shelf, but Rik caught her wrist, pulling her back up.

"Sounded like it came from the service kitchen."

Rikkard pulled her behind a large shelf stacked with boxes, giving them a view of the door while staying hidden in shadow. He kneeled behind a large container, motioning for her to do the same.

"You two head into the kitchen. We'll check the other rooms."

"Got it."

Selene ducked low beside Rikkard, whose left hand rested against her back. She cursed herself for slinging her rifles across her back. She'd much rather feel his hand than metal pressing into her spine.

"This door is open too."

Selene glanced up. A shadow blocked the light filtering in from the hall.

"Just a storage room."

"Check it out." The man in charge nudged him inside. The short man who entered didn't turn on a light, only glanced around, raising a laser rifle to his shoulder while he moved through the rows of materials. "You too." Another man was pushed inside.

"Fine, fine," he growled. "Hands off." The second man spotted the first and proceeded to the left side of the room, directly toward where they were hiding.

Shit.

Holstering her pistol, a plan quickly formed in her mind. Selene held a hand out to Rikkard, motioning for him to move back. He complied without question. Pulling two blades from her left bicep strap, she waited, heart pounding in her ears. When several moments passed, the second soldier stepped into their row. Selene leapt faster than he could blink, pulling him down by his neck and cutting off his scream with her gloved hand. When he fell to the floor, she placed herself under him to muffle the sound. Her grip turned rigid. She pulled back her arm enough to drive a dagger into his throat.

Holding on tightly, she closed her eyes and waited as he thrashed. It only lasted a few seconds, his fingers clawing desperately at her arm, and then he went still. She let out a breath before rolling him off her and pushing his body deeper into the shadows. Selene hadn't realized it until after the deed was done how easy it had become to kill a man.

When had that happened?

Maybe around the same time the Dominion started killing little boys in front of her. Her fists clenched and she took a calming breath. Not now.

Rikkard rejoined her then, a look she couldn't quite decipher on his face. He opened his mouth to speak, but Selene held a finger to her lips. This wasn't over yet. He nodded and followed as she moved soundlessly to the back of the room. Selene stopped at the end of the stack, peeking out to see the other soldier glancing to and fro, peering down each aisle. When he turned his head towards them, she stepped back to the safety of her shelf. But the man paused.

He'd seen them.

His feet turned toward her with a soft squeak. How could he have seen her? Her mind raced. She froze. Not all aliens had it, but some did, which is why they made boosters for it.

Night vision.

Selene pushed Rikkard back gently until he got the point and retreated further down the aisle. Rikkard couldn't see in the dark, but she could. At least being an Icarus had some advantages.

Ducking low, she shimmied her way over a small crate and lay between the shelves, which were just wide enough to hide her body. Waiting as the man passed the aisle next to theirs, Selene slipped from her hiding spot, bracing herself with her fingertips and the toes of her boots. Once his shoulders disappeared around the stack, she stood, another two daggers in her grasp. She followed him quietly until he reached the other side.

A quick intake of breath told her he saw Rikkard. Her heart sank into her gut. She threw the knife. The man would only hear a quiet whisper of air before it lodged into his skull. The soldier fell with a *thunk*, her dagger protruding from the back of his head.

"What was that?"

Selene sighed. Now they'd alerted the other two men. At least now they'd taken down half their team, and as long as no one else was nearby, they wouldn't hear the final two. Withdrawing her pistol, she nodded at Rikkard. He raised his own and led the way to the door. They stood on either side, pinning themselves to the wall until footsteps stopped at the entrance. They waited.

The two men peered inside, their shadows blocking the harsh light of the hall.

"Archer, Garen, respond," the man in charge commanded. No answer.

They stepped inside. The whine of laser pistols sent them both turning, but not quick enough. Two flashes of red broke the darkness. Each fell to the floor with a thud, holes vaporized through the center of their skulls.

"Part of me wishes that was harder," Selene said. She felt nothing when she looked at their lifeless bodies. Her heart had hardened much more than she'd realized.

"Don't think about it." Rikkard headed for the door. "They're a means to an end."

Selene followed Rikkard out the door and down the hall. "Taking a life is really so easy for you, huh?"

"Since when has it given you trouble?" He paused and turned to her. She nearly collided with him. He had a point.

"Nevermind."

He was right about one thing. She didn't have time to think about it. Taking a life hadn't been easy for her, until now. Either way, she had to be on that roof and ready to kill the one man her conscience couldn't feel guilt over.

Pushing ahead, Selene reached the elevator first and hit the up button. It must have been close, it took hardly five seconds to ding open. Selene stepped inside and turned to face the exit. Rikkard stepped up, taking a moment longer than necessary to stare at her with some unknown question.

"Get in here already," she said.

Rikkard stepped inside. Selene closed the doors and hit the button for the hundredth floor.

"This won't take us to the top," Rikkard said.

"Nope. We'll have twenty flights to go. I think we should assume we'll have guns waiting for us outside this door. We should be ready." Selene shot him a look.

Rikkard only nodded and crouched at the opposite end of the small space. Selene mirrored him, but pulled her modded rifle from her back to her shoulder. She flicked the safety off and let her gun charge as high as it would go. As soon as those doors opened, she'd give them a shock.

Selene tapped her trigger finger impatiently against her rifle. The floors sailed by, the LED panel above the door flickering as each floor passed. When their ascent finally began to slow, her whole body froze. She took a deep breath and aimed. The movement around them stopped. They both waited for several long moments.

Finally, the doors slid open.

Gunfire pierced the back of the elevator. Selene gritted her teeth and let off a shot. It blazed outward, leaving an empty hole in the place of a man's hearts. Rikkard fired next, his shots fast and accurate. Together they took out everyone in sight. Ten dead bodies littered the seamless white floor, blood spreading around their fallen bodies.

Her breathing stilled with the quiet. Selene peeked right and Rikkard looked left. Only Dominion bodies were left in their wake. Selene tried not to let her gaze linger too long on their empty eyes, and young faces. She knew it was a trick; they were aliens or clones, all ageless in this century. They weren't kids, or even young adults—they could be hundreds of years old and she'd never know it. But the more their blood pooled against the linoleum, the more she regretted killing them. They had no idea who the Dominion was any more than she had.

"Hopefully no one comes to check on these guys." Selene stepped over a puddle of blood lingering between two lifeless bodies.

"If I know Rem he'll be jamming any Dominion transmissions so no contact will get out of this building. No one will be alerted to our presence."

"Great," she said. "I hope you're right."

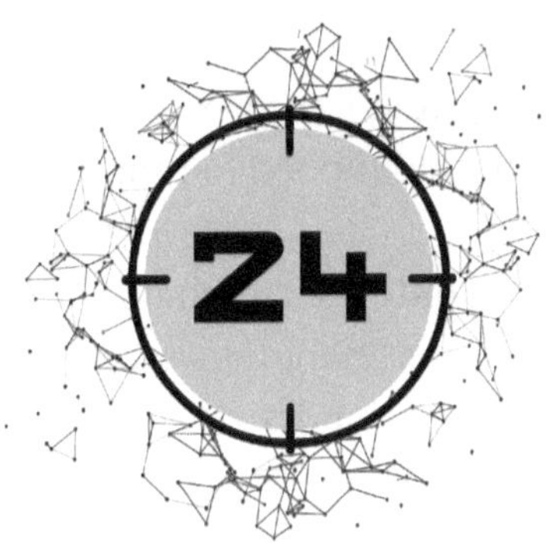

THEIR BOOTS SLAPPED AGAINST THE metal stairs, the sound reverberating through the tall stairwell. Selene leapt two steps at a time, rifle in hand, and sweat amassing on her forehead beneath her wig. She should pace herself, take these stairs slowly and check for enemies or traps. But her adrenaline pushed her up and up, higher and higher. She needed to get to that roof and get positioned. They'd spent far too much time already dispatching guards. If they weren't quick, they might very well miss the whole show and with it, her one chance at revenge.

Her desire to kill Pate drove her higher, even as her legs cramped and sweat dripped off her forehead. She needed to be there. She needed to kill that man, whether the Alliance sanctioned her shot or not.

When they'd run at least ten floors, Rikkard finally called for her to stop.

"Selene!" Rikkard leaned against the cement wall at one of the landings, panting. She stopped mid step and turned, her breath not coming quite as heavy. "We can't continue like this. We'll have no energy for another fight."

Selene clenched and unclenched her fists around the handholds of her rifle. "What if we're already too late?"

"We're not. They would have compensated for how much time we needed to get up here. You'll get your shot. Just don't kill us on the way there."

A wide smile broke across her face. "Was that a joke?"

"It might have been." He shooed her more slowly up the stairs. "Let's keep moving."

"You're just trying to hide the fact that you've acquired a sense of humor since you started hanging out with me." She grinned as she started back up the stairs one at a time. They still had several flights to go, and she had to admit he was right. If they didn't slow down, she was going to be a puddle of mush when they hit the roof.

Many flights of stairs later, they finally arrived. Selene had her breath back, and hadn't run out of energy—yet. Rikkard seemed to have recovered a bit, as well. Stopping at the roof access, Selene waited to the side while Rikkard pressed his ear against the door. She couldn't hear a thing and was fairly sure he wouldn't be able to either, but still he paused and listened. Selene busied herself checking her rifle. It was charged and ready when Rikkard looked back at her.

"There's at least two," he said.

"How can you hear through that thing?" She motioned to the thick steel door.

"Modded hearing." Rikkard tapped his ear with his index finger.

"Oh." She blinked at him in surprise. She never knew he had such a mod.

"On three."

Selene nodded in agreement, readying her rifle while Rikkard raised his pistol.

"One. Two. Three!"

The door swung outward, and Selene leapt out. Two men with rifles kneeled by the edge of the roof. Selene snapped the barrel of her gun in their direction and fired. One went down in a heap. The other had a single moment to whip his head in her direction before his expression was forever removed from his face.

Selene took a deep breath, her heart pounding erratically in her chest. She stepped further onto the open roof, moving the barrel of her gun left and right, checking for other targets. Rikkard moved in the opposite direction. Wind whipped at her body, hair and weapon, threatening to pull her over. Over one hundred and twenty stories in the air, they nearly reached the clouds. The Camros building had to be one of the highest in New Manhattan. As she looked out across the city, she didn't see many rooftops that reached their level.

A shot sounded, hollow with the heavy wind pressing against her ears. Selene spun. Rikkard ducked behind an air vent, while a rogue third guard took cover behind a fuse port large enough to take up a good quarter of the roof. Her heart plummeted for her boots. Blood sprayed the side of the air vent.

Damn it, Rikkard.

Steeling herself from calling out, Selene snuck around the opposite side of the fuse port to get a better line of sight. She held her rifle tight to her shoulder, cold metal pressing against her skin. She aimed down the sight. The black clad man appeared in her crosshair, his attention on Rikkard and the air vent. She shot. Blood splattered the back of the metal port. He collapsed to the cement roof. She hadn't realized her gun was set so low. She'd killed him, but the damage wasn't quite as fierce as she had been expecting.

"You okay?" she called. After patrolling the remainder of the roof, checking for other enemies, she stopped beside her captain.

"I'll live," he growled, limping from his position.

"Did you really go and get yourself shot?" Selene placed a hand on her hip, lowering her gun completely.

"Shut up." He glared as he sat beside the ledge facing Election Square. There was a neon sign below it, casting a blue glow on Rikkard's dark hair.

Shaking her head, Selene rifled through her pack until she pulled out a small white cylinder. Inside were the smallest of nanobots.

She tossed it to him. "Better hurry up."

He caught it and sighed.

With a smile on her face, she finally unclipped her black jacket and discarded it beside Rikkard where the wind wouldn't carry it away. Setting her rifle beside him, she pulled the large sniper rifle from her back, its sleek black metal cold even through her gloves. Its barrel was long, its body heavy. She grinned. Now this gun would pack a punch.

Stepping to the edge of the roof, she peered over the three-foot high cement barrier—the only thing keeping her from falling to her death. Below, the square was lit like Christmas. Brilliant images of the potential country leaders flashed across the large bulletins, the building faces, and the huge fifty-foot high screen behind the stage, which was nestled at the center back portion of the square. The stage was large in itself, with rows and rows of people waiting in line.

"We're not too late." She smiled. Relief flooded her chest.

Flipping the tripod from the base of her sniper, she dropped to one knee, bracing the butt of her gun against her shoulder. She flipped up the sight and flicked off the safety. The rifle whined, thick strips of red charging through its frame. She checked the ammo cartridge, grip and adjusted for the wind before settling in and peering down the sight. The zoom was substantial, switching at her will. Zooming from ten times to forty took mere seconds. The moment she focused, she found Pate. Tall, dark hair slicked back, mid-thirties, and his signature slanted smirk.

Her index finger inched toward the trigger.

How could he stand down there and smile like he didn't have a care in the world? Little did the people of New Manhattan know, he was one of the most corrupt people in the city, if not the country. He was the reason her life had been ruined. He was the reason she was an Icarus. He sentenced her to years of torture, and he just *stood there*. Again her finger twitched toward the trigger.

One shot. That's all it would take.

She could shoot him through the head and it'd all be over. The Dominion wouldn't have a guinea pig to use for their government and she'd have the satisfaction of ending the life of a leech.

"Selene," Rikkard said. He shuffled but the sound was muffled. She couldn't take her eye off her target. One shot and it would all be over. "*Selene.*"

Selene snapped back, ready to shoot an angry glare at Rikkard. Her knuckles were white around the rifle's grip. Her breathing was heavy. She froze, realizing almost too late that she could have ruined the Alliance's entire plan. She took a deep breath. She had to let them play the footage of Pate before she took him down. She owed them that.

"What?" she finally asked.

"Not yet," he said. Somehow he knew what she had been looking at. He knew she'd almost sealed Pate's fate.

Nodding, Selene leaned back. "Not yet."

Rikkard leaned forward, taking a pair of binoculars from his pack. He flicked the zoom switch to take in the finer details.

"The crowd is starting to thin around the stage," he said.

"The last ballots?" she asked. He nodded. As soon as the last ballots were cast, the plan would be in motion. The Alliance would storm the stage to capture Pate the moment the results played across the screen. She'd wait until their message was displayed to the world, then she'd end it.

Rikkard stood and jogged to the roof access door. He jammed it with a Dominion rifle in case of pursuit.

Selene turned back to her sniper. She gently placed it back against her shoulder and positioned herself. This time she kept her finger away from the trigger. She zoomed out to take in the whole stage. From here they could still hear the blare of the mic as an announcer called to the final voters. A young woman with blue hair waltzed across the stage with a wide smile. She spoke to Pate quickly and shook his hand before proceeding to the booth at his right.

Every muscle within her tensed in anticipation. Just a few more minutes. As soon as those voters were off the stage, everything would begin.

Selene and Rikkard sat in quiet anticipation until the last of the civilians fled the area and the screen behind the elected flashed bright white. The United American flag flashed across it in an impressive display of animation. Rikkard kept his face in his binoculars and his eyes on the game. Selene watched through her rifle sight.

Once the flag disappeared, the images of both Pate and his opposition appeared, with sparkles around the borders. The real Pate turned and winked at the camera. His opposition smiled and gave a thumbs up. A long drum roll boomed through the speakers, the images on the screen swirling in a circle. After several circuits, the image of Pate's opposition burst in an explosion of light, bringing the new President to the forefront. Fireworks lit the sky as well as the screen.

Cheers filled the square, echoing far up into the night sky. Her heart dropped. Selene cursed them and put her eye back to her sight, zeroing in on Pate. She had to be ready. Her moment was coming.

After a solid minute of cheering, the city lights flickered and went out. Darkness consumed the square. Rem had set the lights and their generators to fail as one. But one light remained—which was not part of the plan.

Pate smiled at the crowd. The stage remained lit, a soft yellow glow on the dark streets. Something was wrong. She could feel it. Suddenly members of the Alliance were taking down Dominion security and charging the stage in a wave. Screams of distress and confusion replaced the earlier cheers of excitement.

"This isn't right." Rikkard shifted beside her.

Selene aimed her sight below, zooming out to see the soldiers rush the stage. When they reached within ten feet of Pate and his damn smirk, they leapt back as if struck by something. Bodies pushed the first few forward before they could warn the others, pinning them against something unseen. Selene gasped, as the first wave was stuck frying alive against the invisible shield while others tried to file in behind them.

"Shit." Rikkard leapt to his feet. "Shoot! Shoot him!"

Selene didn't hesitate. With her aim back on Pate, she narrowed in; her finger finding the trigger it longed to pull. She shot. Waiting a heartbeat, she watched. Pate didn't drop to the floor. He didn't scream, or even budge. Selene shot again, and again and again. Sweat dripped down her forehead and her heart rammed against her ribs.

"Did you miss?" Rikkard asked.

"I *never* miss!" Dread burned inside her. Taking shot after shot, she waited for him to drop. But he never did. Cursing, she leapt to her feet, chucking the sniper back to the ground. "There's a fucking shield."

"What?"

"They have a shield!" Selene yanked her wig from her head in frustration and threw it to the ground. Her hair tumbled over her shoulders for only a few seconds before whipping into the wind, blinding her. She pushed it back. "A fucking shield. I can't believe this."

"They knew we were coming." Rikkard stared below, eyes wider than she had ever seen them. "They knew."

"Then someone we know and trust is a rat!" Selene grabbed her discarded energy rifle. She switched it over to low energy mode before rifling through her bag. "This isn't over Rik. I'm going to kill that bastard." Her fingers shook, slipping through weapons, medical gear and supplies.

"What are you going to do?" He glanced back.

"I'm going down there." She grabbed the bag with an angry grunt and dumped its contents. Pistols, knives, grenades and more skittered across the cement.

There it was.

She took the grappling hook Rem had given her and loaded it into the barrel. Though they'd both been drunk at the time, an important memory like that stuck around. Once it was safely inside, she yanked the power cartridge from its slot, shoving it into a pocket of her utility belt. She pulled a long metal cord from the ground and attached it to the fusion port inside the cartridge slot.

"You can't be serious."

"I've never been more fucking serious, Rik."

Once the cord was in and locked tight, she returned her gaze back to the chaos below. The Alliance members had backed off, dragging the injured with them. Dominion soldiers corralled them, pushing them further into the crowd. They couldn't get a ring around them with the huge size of the crowd. The most security could do was push everyone back. Gunshots went off left and right, both energy and old fashioned bullets piercing the air, echoing in the hollow square. It was nearly impossible to get energy weapons in that crowd unless they were Dominion, so they'd come well prepared with some old school rifles, shotguns and pistols.

"You'll get yourself killed," Rikkard snapped.

"I'm not going to jump *on* the shield. I have an idea."

A loud banging had both of them glancing across the roof. She froze. The roof access door shuddered. They had been found out.

"Explain before throwing yourself into danger!" Rikkard grabbed her arm and turned her to face him.

"We don't have time. I'll explain once we're down there."

"You'll explain *now*."

Selene barely resisted rolling her eyes. Rikkard shared her stubborn attitude. "There's a power box attached to the stage, just like the one in Bakura, the one we used to disable the cage and get those tigers out of there. This one will definitely be more complex, but we can blow it with the energy core in one of our pistols. Once the shield is down, the plan is back on."

"That sounds like suicide. We'd be completely out in the open."

"Once the others see what we're doing, they'll be our distraction. They're already doing a fine job. And besides, the stage is already clear, aside from the shield." Rikkard took a moment to check her findings. He reluctantly nodded in agreement.

"Fine. But if you get us killed, it's on you."

Selene grinned as another bang shook the door to the roof. She'd said nearly the exact same thing to him once. "Wouldn't dream of it."

SELENE STEPPED UP TO THE ledge and surveyed the buildings below. She needed to pick the building closest to her target, one she could still leap from without getting herself killed. She had a pulley to hold onto during her descent; one with brakes, but Rem already admitted it had yet to be tested. What better way to test it than in the field? Or at least that's the excuse she gave Rikkard. He'd glared when she'd said it, but so far he was going along with her insane plan.

"That one." She pointed to a tall silver building with neon signs all across it, now dark. It was close enough that they could leap over the guard fence and dive right onto the stage, but far enough from the Dominion soldiers that they shouldn't draw attention right away. "I guess it's up to you now Rem. Let's hope this thing works."

"I can't believe we're doing this." Rikkard glanced nervously at the roof's door.

"Believe it." Taking aim, Selene looked for the perfect spot. A thick plastic ledge wrapped above the first floor. Perfect. It was a fairly small drop from there.

She aimed and pressed the trigger. The grappling hook flung from the tip of her gun knocking her back, the recoil changing her aim. It was only by an inch or two, but with this amount of distance between it and her, that would be a significant change for their descent.

Once she had her feet under her, she checked to see where she had struck. The metal cord pulled right, ending just above the second floor. That was a much farther drop.

Her eyes widened. "Shit."

"What?"

"I didn't compensate for the recoil."

"Shit."

Shouts from the roof access door drew Rikkard's attention while Selene inspected the area with her sight. A large sign sat a few feet from her grappling hook, close enough to swing to and climb down to the first floor. She breathed a sigh of relief. The descent from there would be much shorter.

The door behind them shook.

"Perfect." She grinned. "We're good. I see a way down. When we get there, head to the east side of the stage. That's where you'll find the power box."

"Got it."

Selene pulled the end of the cord from her rifle and backtracked it to the air ventilation system, tying it tightly around one of its grates. She tugged on the cord. It stayed tight. Rejoining Rikkard by the edge of the roof, Selene handed him a pulley. He kept his pistol trained on the coming enemy, hardly glancing up to see what she handed him.

"Hook this onto the rope." She demonstrated the brake system. "Use these to stop yourself. Start braking half way down, and do so slowly or you'll lose your balance and splat into that wall over there."

"Cheery."

"Yep. So take my word for it. Start braking sooner rather than later." Next she handed him a harness buckle. Both of them wore utility belts that should save them if need be. "Hook this to the rope, in case you lose your grip." Rikkard nodded. "Okay. We're good to go."

"One last thing." Rikkard ripped his gaze from the door and

stepped closer, wrapping an arm around her waist. He kissed her, his lips eager to embrace hers. Selene leaned into his warm kiss, wrapping her free arm around his neck. When he pulled away a moment later he smiled, if only slightly. "We're good to go."

"I'll say." With a wide grin, Selene turned from Rikkard and picked up her rifle. She returned the power cartridge to its chamber and switched the power back to lethal.

Once she had it slung over her back, she hooked her belt and pulley to the rope. Rubbing her hands together to make sure she was ready to hold up all her body weight, she finally placed her fingers around the hand holds. Her heart raced, with excitement, adrenaline and anxiety. They didn't have much time to pull this off.

"See you down there." She shot another smile at Rik and dove off the ledge, letting herself be whisked away by the current. She cleared the roof. A crack sounded from the access door. Her heart leapt to her throat. Selene twisted to see if they'd gotten through, but she was falling too fast. Wind encompassed her, pulling at her body, clothes and hair. Her shadow passed over Election Square, disguised by the darkness engulfing the streets, keeping her safe as she flew. She looked back. Rikkard had better follow. She turned to the oncoming building.

The crowd was in chaos, bodies trampled by those fleeing onto side streets. Chaos was good. It gave them time. She flexed her fingers around the metal bar.

It seemed too soon when she reached the halfway point and had to start slowing her descent. Her fingers wrapped around the brakes and she pulled lightly at first, getting a feel for their strength. Relief coursed through her as her descent slowed. The brakes didn't squeal or shudder; they worked perfectly. Gradually she pressed harder.

The details of the building before her became clear. Her arms ached, and she dared not look back to see how Rikkard was fairing, or if he'd made it off the roof. Nausea rose into her abdomen. She shook her head. Rikkard would make it. Setting aside her sore muscles, she inched forward until she came to a full stop at the edge of the building. Cries rang out from the nearby crowd. Gunfire split the air.

Feet up against the smooth metal wall, she gauged the short distance to the platform beside her. Scrambling for the sign while unhooking herself, she somehow managed to swing to the top of the sign without killing herself—just in time for Rikkard to join her much more gracefully than she had managed.

Relief coursed through her and she had to resist throwing her arms around him.

"You're all right," she said.

"Of course," he said.

Selene scanned what she could see of him. No blood soaked his clothing aside from the minor leg injury he'd already acquired. *Thank Aldar.*

Working her way down the sign, Selene used the grooves as hand and footholds.

Rikkard climbed down after her. She flashed him a smile before dropping the last few feet to the ground below. She landed soundlessly, taking a quick glance at the rioting crowd before stepping deeper into the shadows and away from the glow of the stage. Rikkard landed with a soft thump.

Dominion soldiers continued to push the Alliance and the rest of the crowd back. Pate watched the chaos from behind his shield with a smirk. Her blood boiled at the sight of him.

"Get that shield down." Selene didn't dare take her eyes off her target. From behind the stage, the fifty-foot screen was still dark. Something had to be going wrong with Lanny and Rem. She couldn't wait any longer.

"Be careful." Rikkard gave her a long look. Selene nodded. After a short pause, he slipped from the shadows and moved carefully around the opposite side of the stage.

"You too," Selene whispered. She stepped from their hiding spot. She had to keep Pate's attention on her, or Rikkard wouldn't be able to get the job done.

Slipping through the empty security gate, Selene leapt onto

the stage. Pate's eyes immediately shot to her. He looked over her face, her hair and her body, his smirk pulling to one side. Anger flared to life inside her chest, fire licking at her throat. She gritted her teeth.

"Selene," he purred. "How good to see you."

"Wish I could say the same." Selene stepped in front of the shield, her shoulders square. She withdrew her pistol from its holster, and flicked the safety off. The whine of its charge filled the silence between them.

"Some time away from the Dominion has done you good. Your spunk is back." His smirk turned into a grin, a sick one that showed his teeth.

"My *spunk* never left." Selene raised her pistol and pointed it directly at his forehead.

Pate chuckled. "You know what this is right?" He gestured to the faint yellow glow of the shield around him.

"Obviously."

"Then how do you expect to shoot through it?"

"I don't." Pate shook his head. "I remember everything you've done to me now," she continued. "It's time we settle the score."

From the right side of the stage, the glow of the shield lit Rikkard's waving hand. The signal. The energy core was ready to go. All she needed to do was activate it. Eyes on Pate, she kept Rikkard's shadow in the corner of her eye, making sure he retreated to a safe distance.

"There's nothing to settle. I did you a favor getting you involved with the Dominion. Your body will do great things for mankind."

He was so full of it.

"You're insane." Selene couldn't help but roll her eyes.

"I'm completely sane."

Behind Pate, the screen finally flashed back on. Its glow lit the square. The roaring of the crowd quieted. Across the screen flew pictures of Pate with the Dominion. Secret meetings with well-known Dominion officials in dark rooms; maps and plans in the background for the bombing of Old Chicago two years ago. A video surfaced next, Pate standing over a vat in a lab, gazing down at Selene's naked form, a smirk on his face. The medical spider above shifted to life, the plastic of the vat's lid opening to allow knives and needles to enter.

Her screams silenced Election Square.

The Pate in the video laughed. Evidence of his involvement with the Dominion continued to pile up: more experiments, more Icarus and more illegal dealings. Security footage of Pate in Bakura popped up next. He handed credits over to a weapons smuggler she knew all too well. They shook hands and several Dominion soldiers moved dozens of cloning pods into the back of a hovercraft.

The pictures and videos painted not only him, but the entire alien government as terrorists. Pate was done. Each image would be his undoing.

They would be the final nail in his coffin.

Cries of outrage rose all around. The people of New Manhattan shouted obscenities at their new President. Selene smirked.

"You're the psycho that ruined everything I once had." Her eyes locked on his. She was ready. A few more seconds and she would have her revenge. "You ruined my life. Allow me to destroy yours."

Selene turned her pistol to the side. A startled look passed over Pate's face as she aimed and fired at the power box. As soon as she let her shot go she dove to the ground. Reactors were lethal, especially when set to explode.

She covered her head as the explosion rocked the stage, casting fire and shrapnel in every direction. The platform beneath her shook violently. Before it was over, the air went quiet and the blast pulled inward, imploding.

When she peeked from beneath her arms, the lights had gone out, aside from the bright glow of the screen—which continued to project all of Pate's misdeeds. With the ground steady beneath her, Selene rose, pistol recharging in her hand. She scanned the stage for the presidential candidates, but Dominion soldiers were rushing from behind.

"Pate!" Fire lit her gut and coursed through her veins. "You can't escape me." Selene jumped to her feet. Pate's amber gaze widened and he turned to run. This was it. Her moment.

She shot.

The blast of red carried through the air and straight through his back. He collapsed in a pool of his own blood, his heart vaporized. She lowered her pistol, her heart pounding in her ears.

His slick black hair disappeared between rows of Dominion guards coming to his aid. They picked him off the floor, protecting his lifeless head with riot shields. It was done. She had her revenge. Her heart clenched and her eyes burned.

Pate and his lackeys descended the back stairs of the stage, disappearing into the shadows. Selene stepped forward, ready to find Rikkard and get out of here.

She was hardly half way across the stage when a whoosh of air came from above. She looked up to see a boot flying down at her. Selene lunged forward into a roll, coming up on the other side and leaping to her feet several paces away. What the hell?

In her place stood a woman with ginger hair tied back in a tight ponytail. Her back to Selene, she knew who this girl was. She could never forget.

"Ivy," Selene hissed.

"I hoped I'd get to see you tonight, *Icarus*." Ivy turned, her blazing green eyes finding Selene's face. Clad in a sleek white suit with black and silver trim, she was the negative mirror image of Selene. Selene growled. *Perfect*.

Ivy stepped into her familiar battle stance, the same she'd used during their fights in the Dominion laboratory. Selene gritted her teeth, trying to fight back images of orange hair flying as Ivy beat her through the obstacle courses, a wicked grin as she stalked Selene through the maze of mirrors, Ivy's face when she threw that dagger into her abdomen.

"Today is your lucky day." Selene took a calming breath.

She'd dealt with Pate; she could deal with Ivy.

Selene had a pistol in her hand, and so did Ivy. Both had the safety off and were fully charged. There wouldn't be enough time to shoot her without being shot herself. She had to stay pragmatic, look at the now and worry about the past later.

"I wouldn't call it luck."

Selene smirked. "I suppose not. You're looking well after our last encounter. Do any digging?"

Ivy's anger flared so fast it was almost palpable. Fury danced in her eyes and her fists tightened at her sides. Selene had beat her twice now in combat.

She only hoped she could do it again.

"I don't know what you're talking about."

"Really?" Selene laughed. "Because you should." A thin collar wrapped Ivy's throat—the only difference in their attire. It blinked red. "So you did do some digging. Or is that not why you're suddenly a leashed mongrel?"

"You bitch!" A snarl ripped from between her teeth.

Ivy dove forward, gun out. But her footing was sloppy and Selene easily kicked her gun from her hand. It clattered across the stage a few feet away. Selene raised her own pistol to Ivy's forehead. Ivy dodged, kneeing Selene in the stomach and elbowing the side of her face.

Selene gasped, pain ripping through her skull like a knife. She stumbled, and in a flash Ivy knocked her gun away.

That's what she got for being cocky.

"I'm the bitch?" Selene snapped. "You nearly got me killed. All I did was tell you to look into why we are what we are. Whatever happened next is your own damn fault."

"Everything was fine before *you*!"

"Nothing is fine in this new world, Ivy. Nothing."

Ivy jumped at her again, as gunfire rose in the dark night sky. Ivy's hands flew for her throat. Selene stepped out of her reach and grabbed her shoulder, pushing her back over her heel and sweeping her legs from beneath her. But Ivy used Selene's own momentum against her, grabbing her by the suit and twisting. Selene flew forward, Ivy rolling over top of her.

Grunting at the impact, Selene slammed her fist into Ivy's

abdomen. Ivy gasped and doubled over. Selene took her chance to draw her legs back and rammed her heel into Ivy's chest. Ivy flew several feet, and Selene leapt up.

Rikkard waved at her from the side of the stage. She shook her head and motioned to the crowd. There were still members of their team that needed help. Rikkard hesitated.

Selene reached for the rifle at her back. But Ivy was back too quickly, gripping the rifle's strap and using it to whip Selene into the announcer's glass podium. The podium shattered. Selene threw her arms up to protect her head.

Shards sliced through her suit, and pain stabbed her limbs, igniting her rage. She had to keep a clear head, but the screaming and gunfire twenty feet away was distracting. Biting down on her anger, she tried again for her rifle. Ivy brought her foot back to kick her. It was her rifle or a block. Selene's heart leapt. She chose to block. Her forearm took the blow. She pushed Ivy backwards. Selene jumped to her feet, aiming a kick at Ivy's face. Ivy leaned out of reach, but Selene had anticipated that. Throwing her rifle from her back as a distraction, she used the momentum of her spin to turn her small leap into a roundhouse kick.

Her rifle clattered away, Ivy looked after it, long enough for her to land a powerful blow to the side of Ivy's head.

Ivy fell to the ground with a heavy thump.

Selene took a moment to glance to where she'd last seen Rikkard. A dozen paces away, he held off a small group of Dominion soldiers who'd broken from the pack. She smiled.

Glass cracked as Ivy turned onto her side. Eyes watering, Ivy glared up at Selene. Blood trickled from her nose and broken lip. Selene lunged for her rifle. Ivy stuck a foot out, tripping her mid lunge. She went down. Air exploded from her lungs. She fought for breath. Ivy crawled onto her back, nails digging into her suit. Selene took a deep breath and slammed her elbow into Ivy's gut, but Ivy already had what she wanted. A dagger sliced through her suit and across her upper back. Her eyes went wide.

Selene screamed and reached the last few inches for her rifle. She couldn't let Ivy win. She wouldn't. Her fingers wrapped around her rifle's grip. *Yes!* She twisted, grinding her teeth together as she kicked Ivy off. She couldn't risk another stab. Selene landed hard on her now blood soaked back. Shards of glass stabbed her bare flesh. She winced, and panted. But it was over. Selene pointed her rifle at her opponent.

Ivy's eyes widened. They stared one another down, Selene trying to battle her rage while Ivy slowly realized her mistake. She held her hands up in defeat, slowly sliding through the glass to sit up. Ivy had hardly slid an inch when Selene held the sight to her eye. She lined up a shot, Ivy's forehead between her crosshairs.

"Hey, wait a second!" Ivy blanched, her face paled.

"Every time I let you live is another chance you get to kill me." Selene flicked the safety off. Her rifle whined.

"I don't want to kill you, Selene." Ivy smiled a fearful little grin. "Why would I want to kill you? We're just sisters playing, right?"

"You are not my blood."

"No... But we were both created for the same purpose. We're Icarus. I found what you were talking about last time we ran into each other." Ivy gulped. She was trying to talk her way out of this execution. Part of Selene wanted to believe Ivy could change, but another screamed at her to finish this. "You were right. They created us to... to house themselves. They want us to take over the humans, and their government. They want to use us for Aldar knows what."

"I know."

"But I didn't. I didn't know before I... tried to kill you. I was jealous. You're so much more than I am, and they don't want me. I've always been the favorite and then... And then *you* came back."

"I didn't have a choice."

"I know," she growled, "and that was the worst part. You were better without even *trying*. Sure you didn't measure up at first, but I've been in that fucking lab half my life."

Selene arched a brow. Part of her felt sorry for Ivy, the part that knew what the Dominion could do, especially to someone so young. "Then why didn't you escape?"

"To where?" She laughed, a humorless flat sound. "The desert? I'd die. The city? I'd be found. They track us like prized prey, Selene. You can't be that naïve, can you?"

"I know what they can do. But I need to decide what to do about *you*."

Ivy gulped. "Let me go. I won't come after you again."

"How can I trust that when you're on their side?"

"I'm not. Not really. They have this thing on my neck." She motioned up at it. "They track my every move. If I don't do something they like, they punish me."

"The vat."

"The vat," Ivy agreed.

Selene leaned up, slowly climbing to her feet. Ivy came with her, the light from the fifty-foot video screen illuminating the small cuts on her pale face. Selene raised the barrel of her gun and leveled it at Ivy's chest. She didn't have much time. Rikkard could only hold off the Dominion soldiers for so long and this little dance would be over. Did she really want to kill Ivy? This girl had known nothing but the Dominion her entire life. Could she really blame her for turning out the way she had?

"Selene!" Rikkard called. Her captain popped up at the edge of the stage, no soldiers in sight. Blood soaked his shirt. He leapt onto the platform, jogging to meet her.

When Selene looked back at Ivy, she got a good look at her ponytail disappearing into the crowd. No. Her heart skipped.

"Ivy!" she called.

Cursing, Selene leapt to follow. Rikkard grabbed her arm.

"It's too late," he said.

"She's *right there*."

"We've got to *go*."

Looking over his shoulder, the rioting crowd rushed forward like a wave in search of their lying, thieving President.

"Shit. Let's go." Rikkard nodded and together they leapt from the stage, melding with the darkness and then the crowd.

Soldiers were quick on their tail. Selene wielded her rifle, red beams flying through the crowd, destroying the faces and chests of each Dominion agent who chose to pursue them. With Rikkard by her side they shot each of them until they were far enough that no one could be sure where they'd gone.

"We've got to meet up with the others," she whispered loudly. People pushed and pulled against her in a current of bodies. She held her weapons tightly, and let herself be led. Rikkard followed closely, hand gripping her elbow to keep from losing her.

"We'll find them," he assured her, leaning in next to her ear to be heard. If he had the enhanced hearing he said he did, she had a feeling this was a stressful crowd to be in. Yells rose up, and angry voices flashed left and right. She made a mental note to ask him later.

"Hey!" a shout caught her attention at the edge of the crowd. "Over here!"

Selene recognized Sarah's voice, even if she could hardly see her. Working diagonally through the crowd was a little harder, like wading through rapids, but eventually she made it. Sarah wrapped her arms around her shoulders.

"Thank Aldar you're all right!" Sarah said.

"Of course I'm fine!" Selene laughed and embraced her. Warmth surrounded her shoulders and pressed against her cheek. She silently thanked Aldar herself, glad her best friend was still alive. She stepped back. "A few cuts can't stop me." She paused. "Where is Kayl?" Her heart sank. She told him to protect Sarah for a reason, and here she was alone with Sav.

What was more important than protecting his wife?

"We lost him in the crowd." Sarah rubbed her palms on her shirt. Her forehead wrinkled with worry.

"We'll find him," Rikkard said.

Selene caught Sav's eye over Sarah's shoulder. "I got him."

Sav grinned, flashing his perfect white teeth. "You're amazing." He wrapped an arm around her shoulder, hugging her quickly. "Our message hit the air too, and now the people of the world can draw their own conclusions."

"The world will know what he was," Selene agreed.

"We should get going. We can celebrate later. The Dominion is still in control here."

Selene nodded. "Let's go."

Sav motioned for them to follow. They broke from the crowd and jogged into a side alley, slipping onto a less populated street. They kept their guns out and ready in case of trouble.

And did trouble ever come, in the form of a small squadron jogging across the street in military formation, headed to Election Square. The second they spotted Selene and her friends a block away, their leader brought them to a halt.

"Shit," Rikkard spat.

"*Of course,*" Selene said. "Take cover!"

The front row of the squadron dropped to one knee while the second stood at their backs. They took aim. Selene dove behind a parked Class Two speeder alongside Sarah, while Rikkard and Sav dove to the other side of the street behind a large cargo truck with a Dominion booster store insignia on its side.

Selene crouched low to the ground with Sarah at her back. Sarah made a small gasping sound at the sight of the long cut down her spine, but Selene silenced her with a wave of her hand. She pulled her rifle from her back and handed a fully charged laser pistol to Sarah. Being part of the Team Delta medical team, Sarah was armed with a twentieth-century bullet pistol, which wouldn't be enough to fight these guys. Her heart raced. She glanced at Sarah. She had to protect her.

Selene threw the safety off her rifle and charged her gun. Down the street she could make out the charge of a couple dozen energy rifles. She gulped. This was not going to end pretty.

"Terrorists to the nation, come out with your hands up and your weapons down. If you do not, we *will* fire."

Selene flashed a look across the narrow street at Rikkard, who nodded. There was no way in hell they were going down without a fight. Her knuckles went white around her handholds.

"If you think we're the terrorists, then clearly you need to take a better look at your own government!" Selene adjusted her rifle against her shoulder.

"You have ten seconds to comply, or we will use lethal force to bring you down!"

"You can fucking try."

Then a miracle happened. From the other side of the street, Sav motioned them all down, seconds before he threw a pulse grenade.

"Get down!" someone yelled. But it was too late for the soldiers.

Selene ducked low, turning to shield Sarah from the blast. The grenade went off precisely where it was meant to—right in front of the Dominion squadron. The explosion shook the surrounding buildings, sending body parts and gross bits all over the street.

The implosion followed, the grenade pulling all the sound from the air along with all the bits of crushed soldier before it smashed into the pavement. Selene peeked from behind her protective barrier.

She couldn't fight the smile from her face when she looked at Sav. "You're a bloody genius."

"Thanks." Sav grinned.

"Let's go." Rikkard urged them all from their hiding spots. He led them to the damage further down the street. It was a gruesome mess, with bodies littering the pavement. Selene grimaced. How many lives were they going to take in order to stop the Dominion?

"We need to get to the extraction point," Sav continued. "We only have another half hour at most."

"Right." Selene nodded her agreement.

They skirted the charred road and body parts, stepping carefully between the carnage.

A shot went off.

Selene whirled as a flash of red grazed the air. It flew behind her and hit her best friend square in the chest. Sarah's eyes widened. The woman who'd saved her ass far too many times to count, collapsed.

"Sarah," she gasped.

Everything became slow motion. She turned too slow, raised

her rifle too slow, and saw the soldier on the ground, still alive, too late. With his rifle held weakly in his hands, he turned on her next. Selene barely took in his shaved head and mangled body. She screamed and shot him in the face. His expression blasted away with one ray of fire. She shot him again and again until her hands slipped from her rifle and it clattered to the ground. Her heart stopped.

She turned to take in the damage.

Sarah lay unseeing, purple hair a halo against her pale skin. Her violet eyes took in the starlit sky. Blood poured from the hole in her chest. It hadn't gone directly through her heart, but it was close enough. Selene dropped to her knees at Sarah's side. Her hands shook as she reached for her.

"Sarah." Selene wrapped her hands around the front of her suit. She shook her. Felt her neck for a heartbeat.

Sarah's thick lashes fluttered. "Selene."

"Don't you dare die on me!" Her whole body trembled.

"I'm sorry…" Her voice trailed off and her eyes closed.

"You're sorry?" Her voice broke in a humorless laugh. "You have nothing to be sorry for." She smiled even though tears burned her eyes. "Sarah."

Sarah's lips parted, but her eyes didn't open. She didn't move. Didn't breathe.

"Sarah." Selene shook her shoulders, jostling her still form. "Wake up. I told you, you're not allowed to die on me." Her fingers shook as she pressed them against her throat. No heartbeat. "Sarah, wake up!"

Her voice broke. Her heart broke. Everything felt suddenly broken, her fragile world cracking like glass.

A grief stronger than any other pumped through every inch of her being. Her whole body quivered. Part of her knew there was no coming back from that chest wound. But the other half of her refused to believe it. She placed her hands over the gaping wound in Sarah's chest. She had to stop the bleeding.

Sarah's smile was gone, her face devoid of color. Her fingers twitched against the blood slipping between her fingers. Sarah's arms would never embrace Selene again after a long night, she'd never bring her back to her office to fix some injury she'd gotten or a problem she needed to talk through. She'd never watch her and Kayl dance, or envy their marriage. Selene would never laugh or sing or cry with her again. Sarah would never keep her sane or make sure she ate after days on a mission.

What the hell was she supposed to do without her?

"Sarah," she cried. Tears welled in her eyes. She didn't have the strength to fight them back. She pushed harder, but blood still gushed over her fingers. "Sarah, wake up. I need you to stay awake."

"Selene." Rikkard wrapped an arm around her shoulders but she shook him off.

"I-I need something to stop the bleeding!" Her lips quivered, and her hands shook. "Why didn't that grenade kill them all? Why didn't I see him lying there?"

"It's not your fault." Sav shifted nervously on the sidewalk. "None of us saw him. I was sure that would get them all."

"I should have seen him. I should have killed him." Her hands became fists. It was no use. Blood pooled below Sarah's lifeless body. Selene wrapped her hands around the front of Sarah's white suit. "Why didn't I see him?"

Gunshots pierced the quiet street.

Selene didn't move. She hardly registered the sound. Her whole mind tried desperately to grasp at Sarah's last moments, to see her more clearly, to jump in front of her and take that blow. She'd rather be the one dying on the sidewalk than see her best friend lying in her own blood.

"We've got to go." Rikkard gripped her shoulder and gently pulled. Again, she shook him off, but this time he was insistent. Wrapping an arm around her waist, he pulled her to her feet.

"No!" she gasped.

He turned her to look at him. "We can't stay here." Her eyes sought Sarah's lifeless body over his shoulder.

"Selene, if we don't get to the extraction point, we're never—"

"Fine," she snapped, interrupting Sav. Her fingers trembled

as she wiped Sarah's blood on her black suit. "Fine, whatever." She wanted to pick up Sarah's body and take her with them. She could carry her, hand off her gun to Rikkard or Sav. Her heart stilled, tight in her chest. But her weight would slow them down. She couldn't bare losing Rikkard too.

Why in Aldar's name hadn't she seen that soldier?

"I'm sorry, but—"

"Let's just go."

"All right." Sav turned to the far side of the empty street. He motioned them to follow and took the lead.

Rikkard held onto her shoulders gently, directing her to follow. Selene took a long last look at her best friend before she turned. She knew the image of Sarah's dead body would be permanently etched in her mind.

THERE WAS NO GETTING TO the extraction point. The further they went, the more they had to detour to the back streets, and they ended up going around in circles. Everywhere was littered with Dominion soldiers. The sky, the streets, the rooftops—everything was under city-wide Dominion lockdown.

Selene trudged along with her two comrades, keeping her eyes peeled for danger. She tried to force herself to push Sarah's death from her mind and focus on the task at hand and stop wiping tears away. She knew she had a job to do, and yet Sarah's final words, pale face and dead, vacant eyes stayed glued to her mind. She had to get Sav, Rikkard, and herself to safety. She had to keep anyone else from sharing Sarah's fate. She was ready to throw her body in front of the next gunshot, and keep anyone else from being taken down tonight.

This was her fault. Her hatred had brought down her best friend, and might get the rest of them killed. If she hadn't been so hell bent on destroying Pate, maybe Sarah would be alive. Maybe she would still be with the Dominion, and her friends would be safe from her toxic presence. Maybe she deserved to go back.

After wandering the streets for hours looking for a way to the extraction point, Sav stopped. They had yet to reach the end of town. The streets were utterly deserted.

"We're not going to make it," he said. "The comlinks are down and we have no way to request a new extraction point."

"What's plan B?" Rikkard looked at the rooftops, taking in each dark corner like it was a coiled snake ready to strike.

"There really isn't one."

"Do or die huh? Just like our last mission." She shook her head.

Rikkard shot her a sideways glance. He'd done a lot of that since they left Sarah on the sidewalk. Selene had a feeling he was waiting for her to fall apart. So was she.

"I do have an idea," Sav continued. "There are Alliance supporters in the city. Lanny and Flik would know them too. If they didn't make it either, they'd be waiting out the night with someone trustworthy."

"Where are these Alliance supporters?" Rikkard cocked an eyebrow.

"There are more than you think. I know a bar nearby. We can slip in the back. No one will see us."

"And you're sure this is the only option?"

"We can't exactly shoot our way out of here," Selene snapped. "Let's just go with the man. Unless you can come up with something better." She knew it wasn't fair, to take out her anger on him, but she had to feel something but despair. So she clung to her anger like a crutch. She kept it close. It might be the only thing to get her through the night.

"Fine." Rikkard held her gaze for several long moments, trying to figure her out. "Lead the way."

Sav nodded and led. They took a long detoured route, through side streets and alleys, sticking to the shadows, and constantly ducking to hide from patrol cars and squadrons like the one they'd already decimated.

Not long into their trek, a siren blared briefly and a voice came over the city speaker system: "Anyone without military authority, return to your homes and stay indoors until further notice." If that wasn't enough to scare the city folk, she didn't know what was.

They didn't see a single civilian after that. Selene had to assume it was because the Dominion had everyone under their thumb. City folk were so used to the pampered life of New Manhattan they didn't think twice about obeying their leaders. This thought is what made her doubt the Alliance and their work. How would some images and videos on a screen really convince these lemmings? Though they had rioted in Election Square, they were followers by nature, and would stick with the status quo as long as they could live forever in luxury.

Selene bristled and spat on the ground. She hated every last one of them. While they sat in their ivory towers, the people in the Outskirts were either starving, killing each other, or lighting up on drugs and boosters—shooting whatever they could into their veins to make themselves forget. These people would never understand that. Not while the Dominion was around.

After a few close calls with Dominion patrols, Sav stopped near the southern edge of the city. He motioned for silence, and they picked their way across the street and into a well-maintained alley with dim light emanating from a back door.

The door stood ajar with a chubby man standing inside it, cigarette in hand. The small flame lit his bulbous features and scruffy black hair. For a moment she thought he might be a *nat* like her. But the swirl of white tattoos curling beneath his skin was unmistakable. He was an alien, a strange looking one. Most were fairly attractive, with beautifully colored hair and skin. This one seemed out of place amongst their beauty.

"Zhao." Sav emerged from the shadows.

The man jumped, the cigarette startled from his mouth. It fell to the ground, its small red ember winking out.

"Sav!" He narrowed his eyes. "Damn it, child. I told you to stop sneaking up on me. You can use the damn front entrance you know."

Sav grinned. "But where's the fun in that?"

Selene and Rikkard stepped from the darkness against the wall, taking a step closer to their friend. Maybe their presence would tell Zhao why they couldn't use the front door.

"You brought company." Zhao arched a brow and stomped out the remainder of his cancer stick. "They don't look like your usual type."

"They're new."

"Ah." He smiled and waved them in. "Come on then. I'm Zhao, this is my bar."

Sav motioned for them to follow. Selene and Rikkard exchanged a look before entering. They were used to sketchy places—after all they'd been to Bakura dozens of times—but they'd never seen a place *this* sketchy.

"Are you sure this is an Alliance hideout?" Selene whispered to Sav once they stepped inside. Grime lined the hall. Sav gave her a grin over his shoulder. Clearly he'd been here before. At least that put her at ease.

Sav led them down a dingy hallway with fluorescent light and bleak gray walls. The building became increasingly uninviting as they passed the back of the bar through a short passageway— literally behind a glass shelf of bottles. Though liquor wasn't permitted under the new Dominion regime, underground bars still got away with it. Selene scanned the outside of the bar from her vantage point. Several aliens and clones milled throughout the dim room, creating a bit of a ruckus even over the loud electronic music.

Selene paused. A group with hoods drawn and cloaks wrapped tightly around their bodies stood out from the others. From what she could see, each had at least a dozen weapons on them. Not bad, but they wouldn't be the worst competition.

"Y'all should be safe back here," Zhao drawled from behind. She wasn't sure where he was referring to until Sav opened a door. More laughter filtered in, as well as a brighter light. She squinted and stepped inside.

Selene wasn't exactly sure how they were gambling, but she could find no other explanation for the shouting and little alien rodents inside a large box. Each of them had a different color painted on their back. They were hairless, with beady eyes and sharp teeth. They ran in circles seemingly at random, until one leapt into the air and landed on top of another. The little beast dug long incisors into its opponent's neck. Blood burst across the bottom of the box. It was dead before it knew what hit it.

"What the hell are those things?" Selene asked.

The cheering and booing hushed, and the six men crowded around the box shot glares in their direction. Brows creased and faces leered. Clearly they had no idea what the three of them were doing here. But no one questioned Zhao; they just left him alone as he motioned the three of them to the other end of the room.

Sav sat back on a long gray sofa, tattered and torn to bits. While he made himself comfortable, Selene kept her rifle charged at her chest. Sav might trust these guys, but she sure as hell didn't.

"Make yourselves comfortable." Zhao shot an expectant look at her and Rikkard, who continued to hover. Rikkard took to leaning against the back wall, the best vantage point in the room, while Selene tentatively sat on a slightly less damaged sofa.

"They don't bite." Sav laughed.

"It's not the upholstery I'm worried about." The sketchy men gambling in the corner had her on edge.

Sav nodded. He leaned back and rested both of his arms over the back of the couch.

"Anyone care for a drink?" Zhao asked.

"No," they said as one.

"I wouldn't mind one, Zhao!" a guy from the game shouted over.

"Not you, yah heretic!" the old man growled back. "I'm talking to the youngsters. Keep your ears to yourself."

"Grumpy ol' coot!"

"I'll show you grumpy!" Zhao charged over, and Selene lost interest in their conversation.

"What do we do from here?" She looked at Sav. "What's the next part of the plan?"

"Plan?"

"Yes." She resisted glaring at her fellow Icarus. She always had a plan, and didn't appreciate it when others didn't fall into her rhythm.

"Waiting mostly." He shrugged. Her eyes narrowed. Sav gave her a nervous smile. "Fine, fine. We can either wait here until daybreak, see what happens throughout the night, or we can make a break for it."

"You want us to stay in this," she lowered her voice, "dump, all night?"

"It's not so bad—"

"Bakura is cheerier than this place."

Sav sighed. "Fine, we can get out of here. I'm not sure where you expect us to go."

"Home. The ship, the Alliance, anywhere that isn't in this god forsaken city."

Rikkard joined her on the sofa.

"Where can we get speeders?" Rikkard glanced cautiously at the men as they shouted. Apparently another foe had fallen.

"There might be a sales yard nearby. We'll have to ask Zhao. I'm not familiar with the area."

"But you have been here before?" Selene arched a brow.

"Of course."

"Then ask. The longer we wait, the more likely we are to be found." Rikkard narrowed his eyes at Sav, his tone harsh. Rikkard was apparently as big a fan of Sav's cavalier attitude as Selene right now.

"All right, all right." Sav stood and made his way over to Zhao, clapping a hand on his shoulder and grinning as he led him away near the door.

Selene scooted closer to Rikkard.

"I don't like this place." She wasn't sure if it was just her overworked nerves, or the actual bar. A cold sweat built up on the back of her neck. Shivers ran up her bare spine, and the longer cut stung. She'd been to establishments like this many times, and never had a problem with them. Something about this place threw her off. She couldn't put her finger on what.

"I don't either."

"What should we do?"

"Get out as soon as we're able."

Selene agreed. Sav laughed with Zhao and Rikkard straightened. His gaze fell on the door to the room—their only exit. She watched his face, looking for some hint of what he was thinking. He simply stared, lips pressing together in a firm line.

When he didn't say anything for some time, she nudged him with her shoulder. "What is it?"

Rikkard tilted his head so his ear faced the door. He was listening to something outside. Selene sat back and waited patiently, watching Rikkard for hints. When seconds later he leapt to his feet, she nearly fell back in surprise.

"We need to get out of here. Now," he snapped.

"Don't have to tell me twice." Raising her rifle, Selene flicked it on to charge. The high pitch noise brought all eyes in the room on them. "We're out of here Sav. Something's up."

The door cracked as several men busted into the room, taking down the door and Zhao in the process. Sav leapt back, eyes wide with shock as he yanked a gun from its holster, just in time to get the butt of a rifle in his face. He fell back, blood spurting from a head wound.

"Sav!" Her first instinct was to rush forward, but the next person through the door charged in her direction. The clone had bright red hair and yellow eyes like the sun. He moved faster than anyone she'd ever seen. He leapt.

Rikkard stepped in front of her just in time, and the clone came down on him. Rikkard's fist slammed his cheek, but missed when the clone ducked to the side.

Before Selene could react, another alien leap-frogged over his comrade, knocking her to the floor. Her rifle was firmly sandwiched between their bodies. He grinned viciously, flashing razor sharp teeth.

"You're the one the coppers are out to get." He howled a laugh, bathing her in his foul breath. She shivered. "Good thing we're here to get yah first." The man reached for her neck with sharp black nails.

Selene squeezed one of her arms free. Pulling a dagger from

her bicep, she drove it into his left eye. The man yowled and fell back, blood spurting across her cheek. Selene pulled her leg from between his and kicked him in the groin.

The man collapsed, tears and blood mixing as they streamed down his face.

"Asshole," she spat.

Speedy lay sprawled on the floor several feet away in a pool of his own blood. Rikkard fought a man much larger than he, with arms so thick they rivaled those of Darius.

"Get down!" she shouted.

Rikkard dropped to the floor almost before she got the words out. Selene raised the tip of her rifle and fired. The man flew across the room, a hole scorched through his chest, and into the gamblers, toppling right across their mini-ring and releasing the rodents on their tormentors. The little beasts scrambled this way and that, climbing the pant legs of the gamblers and burrowing into their bodies.

The gamblers screams filled the room.

"You okay?" Rikkard gave her a concerned look, but it wasn't *her* blood splashed across her face.

"Yes. Get Sav."

Rikkard nodded and ran the length of the room, picking the unconscious Sav up by the arm and swinging him over his shoulder. Sav was a large man, so the display of strength definitely impressed her. Selene covered him while his hands were occupied with his burden, firing at the three other men who came running in. One of them fell to the floor, a hole in his chest, while the last two retreated.

Once they were gone, Selene slammed the door shut and yanked Zhao to his feet. She pushed him hard into the wall and held her rifle to his chin.

"How do we get out of here?" she snapped.

Zhao gulped audibly and nodded toward a back door. It was hidden behind an industrial shelf. "Two lefts and you'll see an exit sign."

Selene stepped back and lowered her gun before she

remembered—they still didn't have a way out of the city. "Where can we get speeders around here?"

He paused for a moment, his eyes distant. When he refocused, he pointed at the front side of the building. "Head that way. Two blocks over and you'll find a dealership. They won't be fast as can be, but they'll get you out of the city."

"Thanks." She turned to Rik and Sav. "Let's go!" Selene motioned for Rikkard to follow and pushed aside the shelf with ease. Whipping the door open, she led them down a dim corridor. They ran down two more halls before the glow of a neon exit sign signaled their salvation. "There we are." She sighed in relief. Selene threw the door open and stepped into the night air. Once Rikkard and Sav were through, she closed it behind them, jamming the doorknob with a discarded plank of wood leaning nearby.

"Well that was unexpected." Sav groaned as Rikkard leaned him against the building. They were back in an alley on the opposite side of the building from where they'd entered. This alley was not quite as well maintained.

"You think?" Selene stepped quietly through the few feet of space between buildings, taking in their surroundings. She wanted to make sure Sav was okay, but she left that to Rikkard. She was the only one with a rifle at this point. "We all good over there?"

"Yep." Sav sighed.

"You'll need nanos as soon as we're able," Rikkard said brusquely. "You might have a concussion."

"Well I can confirm that one. None on you?"

"We left our packs on the roof." Selene moved from one end of the alley to the other. Peeking into the street, she gave it a thorough once-over. No one in sight. She leaned back and gave the two men a look over her shoulder. "If you guys are done bonding, we should get out of here."

"Yeah, yeah." Sav waved her off. He didn't walk completely straight, but he didn't seem too off-balance. The concussion must not be severe.

"You're lucky you don't have any memories to bring up that way. Those are some nasty-ass dreams." With the adrenaline from their little run in, she was feeling a little like her old self. One look at Rikkard, however, and the whole night's events came rushing back. The depths of his blue eyes held anger and hurt, not at her, but at the world. She looked away, pushing Sarah far from her mind.

"I can imagine." Sav stopped beside her. "Let's go."

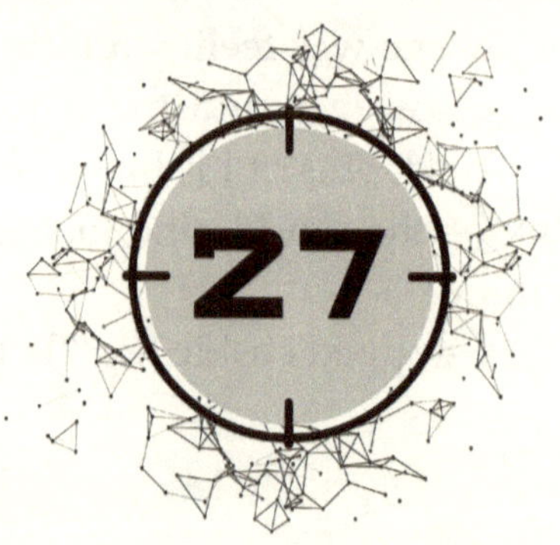

PARKED IN A SMALL LOT on the corner, the speeders were right where Zhao said they'd be. Rows and rows of different class speeders littered the lot, in varied size and level of tech—from Class Ones for regular New Manhattan residents, to Class Four cargo lifters. Like he had said, none were the fastest, but they were doable and all came with autopilot. At this point, that's what Sav needed, a nice smooth ride home, and maybe some rest.

"Think you can hack them?" Sav took a seat on the back of a top down model.

"Of course he can," she said. "You wouldn't believe the speeders he's been able to hack lately."

Rikkard shot her a look. She promptly shut up.

"I'll pick our ride this time."

Selene smiled at the small joke, glad he was trying to make light of the situation. She waited with Sav while Rik picked out two speeders. Both ended up being Class Two with slight military capabilities. She had a feeling they were refurbished illegally, but said nothing, letting Rikkard work his magic.

Keeping low and out of sight behind a Class Three, Selene surveyed the empty street, rifle at the ready. A few city guard crafts whizzed by, their white-and-black-striped siding standing out in the dark night. None stopped to pay them any mind. Still, they worried her. If so many were around, it would be hard to take to the sky and fly out of town. They could stick to the streets, but again, there were patrolmen riding by. Still, it was their only option. They'd stick together and do whatever they could.

A loud crackle startled Selene from her position. She leapt, turning with her rifle at the ready. Blue light lit her face as her weapon charged.

Rikkard raised an eyebrow. "Cool down."

Selene sighed. The crackle grew quieter, and a voice came over the speaker. It was faint, but it sounded like military banter.

"Wait, what is that?" She lowered her gun and stepped over to see what Rikkard had done.

"I tuned in to the Dominion's frequency. We'll hear their every move."

"We'll be able to avoid them and get out of here without being seen." She grinned. "Good news Sav!"

"I heard!" Sav got up from his spot on the ground. He'd moved there a few minutes ago when a patrol craft flew by. "We should get going."

"Agreed," she said.

Sav hit the release button on the side of his speeder. The top slid open, allowing him to climb in. "I'll follow you guys."

"Sounds good." With his head in bad condition, it would be best for him to follow their lead. Once he was safely inside, he gave her a thumbs up and allowed the hatch to shut. Selene gave him a small wave as Rikkard climbed in the front cubby. He sat at the helm, leaving the seat behind him free. She slid into the back, the faux-leather seat squeaking beneath her. The hatch shut with a soft click. The interior lit up.

Rikkard dimmed the soft blue lights, fingers flying around the cockpit as he pushed and pulled gauges, typing in instructions for their craft to fly. She was used to much simpler models, and hoped Sav could fly one of these things. It would certainly give her pause.

"Stay tuned in to their channel," she said. "I want to hear every word."

Rikkard turned up the volume. Voices flooded the small cockpit. She sat back, strapping herself in, rifle laid across her lap. Finally, they would get out of this city. Her stomach rolled. They might be heading home, but some of them didn't make it. She silently hoped that their friends had fared better and gotten free of the Dominion-infested crowd.

The next several hours trying to escape the city were spent in turmoil. Every time they heard of movement over the scanners, they stopped and hid to listen. Sav chugged along behind them. She had a feeling he'd be getting irritated with them by now. But still, it was their only way to freedom.

"How much longer?" She sighed.

"I don't know," Rikkard said.

It was at least the third time she'd asked the same question and gotten the same answer. So she sat back and gazed out the window. Her senses were still on high alert, and she couldn't help but jump at every shadow. How much longer until they were free of this city? She could only guess.

Rikkard pushed their speeder from their hiding spot in an alley. They moved quietly, the soft thrum of propellers the only alert to their position. Leading them across the street, they both froze when a patrol speeder rounded the corner a street away.

"Back, back back!" Selene said, but Rikkard already had their speeder moving. They bumped into Sav's before he saw what they were doing and quickly reversed. "Did he see us?" She tried to peer over Rik's shoulder to see, but they were back in the shadows.

"His movements aren't being documented," he said.

"Damn lazy alien."

So they waited in their alley for the car to pass. But after several minutes of silence, it didn't appear.

"Where the hell is it?" she snapped.

Rikkard didn't answer, only listened to the Dominion frequency.

After another long pause, she finally stood in her seat. Her head smacked the roof before she bent over. "Ow." She rubbed her head as she leaned across the low back of Rikkard's seat. Selene shimmied up to their scanners, fingers flying as she flicked them on. A three dimensional view of the area popped up. The range was short, only showing the surrounding block. There was nothing on this guy. She flicked it away, but kept her waist pressed against Rikkard's shoulder as she thought, finger poised on the command keyboard.

"He's just sitting there, and he's not on the scanners. That can only mean they pulled the GPS from the dash. But why would they bother?" Rikkard wondered in silence, while she sat back angrily. "We're only a few blocks away!" She groaned.

"I'm getting out to see what he's doing."

"What?" She sat up quickly. "No way. What if he's waiting for us out there?"

Rikkard gave her a level look. "If he is, I'll kill him." Rikkard brandished his pistol and let it charge to solidify his statement.

"Well I guess if you want to be rash, that works."

He scoffed as he disengaged the hatch over their heads. He knew as well as she that she was the reckless one. Nerves prickled across her arms.

"Be careful."

"I will." He nodded and disappeared into the dark alley, slipping around the corner at the end.

Her heart hammered in the silence. Selene stared at the place where his shadow had disappeared. She wished he'd come back. Sighing, she sat back, keeping her ears open. She waited. The longer she sat in silence wishing for Rikkard's enhanced hearing, the more uncomfortable and worried she became. Images of Sarah's dead body flashed before her eyes. Fear clawed at her insides. She took a few deep breaths. When those didn't help, she stood and leapt from the cockpit.

There was no way she was going to sit here and let him die.

She checked on Sav, who gave her a tired wave, before raising her rifle to her shoulder. She flicked off the safety and let it charge as she jogged the length of the alley. She peeked around the corner, just in time for Rikkard to run headlong into her.

They collided and nearly knocked each other over. Her rifle clattered to the ground while Rikkard tried to keep them both upright; grabbing her around the waist and bracing them both on the alley wall.

When their sudden movement came to a stop, they were both left breathless, staring at one another.

Once she got over her surprise, she grinned. "Nice to see you too."

A hint of a smile pulled at his lips. "We should go." Rikkard leaned away from her and picked up her rifle, handing it back to her.

She gave herself a moment to miss his warmth. "You sure know how to ruin all the fun."

"There will be plenty of fun once we're out of here."

"Is that a promise?"

"More like a threat."

This time Selene was sure he smiled. She couldn't help but laugh as she climbed back into the speeder. They were both quickly seated. Moments later, they crossed the street in silence, and Selene got a good look at a blood-spattered patrol ship parked halfway down the street. She was sorry she'd doubted him.

They finally cleared the remaining buildings, and the sandy wasteland came into view. They stayed tuned to the Dominion frequency, but nothing clear came through about anything suspicious in their area, so they quickly took off into the night. Across the desert they flew, Sav's speeder not far behind. They picked up speed now that they were in the open. Rikkard drove them behind dune after dune, staying clear of the Outskirts surrounding the city. They were sure Dominion soldiers would be on the lookout for them there.

As they flew further and further from the dark city and Titanous towers, the droning of soldiers faded to static. After they'd spent five full minutes in dead air, Rikkard shut it off. They lapsed into silence.

Selene stared out over the desert, watching the stars. The sky was clear, with no clouds to block her view. It was ironic that such a nice night could be so horrible. Thinking back on the last few hours, all she remembered was fear, nerves and running. She felt like cattle or some sort of deer, being herded and tossed around by the Dominion like a toy. Somehow they'd known about the Alliance's plan. Even though they couldn't stop her from killing Pate, the one death that wouldn't have gone unnoticed on tomorrow's news, her chest was hollow.

The only death that mattered was Sarah's. She was sure they'd lost dozens, but Sarah was her friend, her best friend. She'd been the one to welcome her to the fold and convince her to stay with Rikkard and his crew. Rikkard had urged her to stay and help out, but Sarah had been the one to make her feel like family. She'd made Selene want to stay with these people, to be one of them.

And now her reason was gone.

Selene sighed and leaned back in her seat. She couldn't have imagined their night going quite like this. The only thing worse than this day would be the following ones. She'd be confronted time and time again with questions and sympathies, from both the Alliance and her friends. She'd have to tell Kayl his wife died meaninglessly, because of her own reckless stupidity. She'd have to tell him he was right and the love of his life was gone. Now that was pain—a pain she couldn't begin to understand, and it was all because of her.

When the Alliance headquarters finally came into view sometime later, dread settled firmly in her gut. She feared not only Kayl, but the others. What were they going to do now? Their plan had worked, even if it cost them in the end. Would New Manhattan citizens rise up against their government, spurred by the documented terrorism of their own president, or would they falter and remain the helpless lemmings she'd always known them to be?

An image of the city riot following their video blast came to mind. Maybe there was hope for the citizens of New Manhattan yet.

With her never-ending dread, came frustration. She had joined the Alliance to make a difference, but all she'd done was get her best friend killed. How could she have been so naïve, to think that these rebels could make a difference? They weren't revolutionaries; they were a black spot in history.

Selene kicked the back of Rikkard's seat. He didn't say a word, only glanced back. He knew better than most not to interrupt her while in turmoil. He could end up at the wrong end of her gun if he wasn't careful.

Landing in the loading bay of their large cargo ship, they came to a smooth halt, followed quickly by Sav, who landed a little rougher at their right.

Rikkard disengaged the ship and let the hatch rise. The cockpit went dark. The hatch had hardly opened when she whipped off her seat belt and leapt out.

Sav climbed out next to them, his legs wobbling. He gave her a curious look. "You guys good?"

"Yep." Selene raced to the back of the loading bay to shut the doors. Once they were closed, she returned. Sav gave a quick and awkward goodbye before excusing himself. Rikkard shut the hatches and turned to face her. She opened her mouth to speak, but he cut her off.

"We're all right now." He raised both eyebrows at her. He was trying to tell her she was being irrational, that she needed to calm down and take a breath, or at least that's what he'd normally say. Instead he was treating her like a startled animal.

"*Nothing* is all right," she snapped.

"Selene—"

"That was such a mess. A fucking mess. Sarah is dead because of me, because I chose to get us involved with these people."

"You weren't the only one to—"

"I know, I know, you all agreed to it." She paused. "Maybe Kayl was right. Maybe this was a bad idea." She shook her head.

Rikkard stepped closer. She took a step back. Part of the torrent inside of her wanted to be soothed, but the more violent side of her just wanted to break things.

Choosing to keep her violent side in check, she sat on a large cargo box and placed her head in her hands. She gripped her hair tightly and blocked it all out, just for a second. But then Rikkard broke back through.

"You did it, Selene." Rikkard reached for her. She let him this time. He pulled her up and held her hands. "It's over now."

"But there are so many questions, so many unknowns. We have no idea where we're going from here. We have no idea if the Alliance or our crew will recover from this. For Aldar's sake, we don't even know if the rest of our crew is still alive. What if they're all dead?"

Before she realized it, she was crying. Rikkard pulled her into his arms. He held her against his chest. "We'll deal with it." His voice wasn't quite monotone, and it wasn't quite soothing.

"How?"

"We'll figure it out. You always come up with a plan."

Selene couldn't help the humorless laugh that bubbled from within. "Not this time. This time I can hardly think."

"You don't need to, not right now. Let's wait and see if everyone is all right first. Once we take stock of things, we'll decide on a game plan." Selene slowly nodded into his chest. He was right. He had to be. If he wasn't, she might very well lose her mind before the night was over.

Once the hurricane within her stilled, she took a deep breath and relaxed into his embrace. He held her tightly, a muscled god with a dangerously beautiful face. Her cheeks slowly flushed. The hard abs beneath his shirt pressed against her fingers and his warm breath brushed her ear. She wanted nothing more than to disappear into his arms and let herself melt away with him.

Tilting her head back, she inspected his piercing blue eyes. He looked back at her with the most warmth she'd ever seen in his icy gaze. Closing her eyes, she leaned up and kissed him. Rikkard loosened his embrace, moving his hand up to the side of her neck. His thumb gently massaged her jaw while his lips met hers time and time again. She held on to him, desperately hoping to disappear. She didn't want to fight anymore. She didn't want more of her friends to die. Most of all she didn't want to be the one making decisions. All they brought about was death.

So instead of thinking, Selene kissed him and let her body do the thinking. Rikkard didn't seem to mind, and held her close, even as she nudged him further into the cargo bay. Once his back was to a large crate, she pressed her body against his.

His breath escaped against her lips in a soft gasp. Selene let her hands do the talking, gently feeling their way down his side and beneath his shirt. Rikkard left one hand by her face, while the other slid down her back, over her curves and settled on her hip. He gently pulled her body closer.

They were both so lost in themselves that Selene hardly registered the high pitch charge of a laser gun nearby. Apparently neither did Rikkard, because it came as a shock to both of them when the blast pierced the air and found her right shoulder. Her eyes flashed open and her body froze. Everything went hot and then cold. Blood dripped down her skin, but she had yet to feel the pain of impact.

Stars swirled before her eyes and she lost her balance. Rikkard caught her before she slid to the floor, coming with her. He was on his knees with her cradled in his arms. He was saying something. Dimly she could hear words, but her senses were going dull. She blinked slowly, like cold molasses. Everything was slow, Rikkard's lips moving in words she didn't hear, his movements, so angry as he turned to whoever had shot her. He shouted something she didn't hear.

Once it was obvious she wasn't getting up again, Rikkard laid her gently on the floor. Her head lolled in his direction, as he stepped over her.

He didn't even draw his gun, only roared as he charged at Kayl.

Selene silently realized that Kayl was the one who shot her. He held his pistol pointed in her direction, his eyes wide, and his stance fierce. He knew Sarah was dead. This is why he'd shot her, he'd found out before they could tell him, and he blamed her. So he was taking her away, with one shot from his pistol.

He was taking her life as revenge against Rikkard, and her recklessness.

Blinking slowly, Selene watched them fall in a heap to the floor. They rolled over each other until Rikkard was on top. His fists pounded Kayl's face again and again. He continued until he'd had enough and withdrew his gun from its holster. Somehow she heard the whine of its charge. And then she waited for the shot.

"She did it for me." Kayl's voice broke. "Sarah worked with them to protect *me*."

The bay door quaked as it opened, retracting into the ceiling. Blinding light filled the room. Selene squinted into it, then closed her eyes. When she opened them again, Dominion soldiers poured in. They grabbed Rikkard, who struggled, kicked and screamed. He took out a few of them before they took him down, knocking him out with the butt of a gun.

Selene tried to reach out for him, tried to twitch her fingers in his direction, but she couldn't move—and she was so cold.

Another slow blink passed and Rikkard was dragged away unconscious. Someone helped Kayl to his feet, but he pushed them away, storming toward the brilliant light.

That light and those soldiers were the last thing she saw. After her next slow blink, the light didn't return. Her eyes stayed shut, and darkness took her.

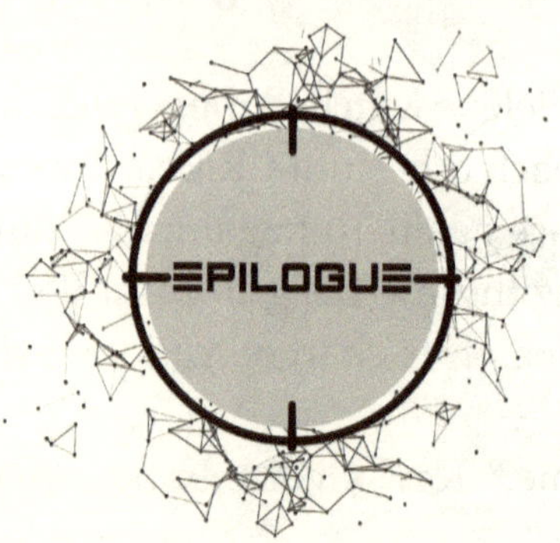

WHITE WINGS WERE THE FIRST thing she thought of when she came back to reality. Selene blinked slowly. Had she just been dreaming? Or was she finally dead? If there were white wings around her, maybe she was in Heaven? Maybe the aliens had been wrong and a god existed? If angels surrounded her, she would certainly believe it.

But when Selene blinked again, sheer curtains billowed in the breeze overhead. They moved gently, their folds whispering through the air—like wings. She sighed. So she wasn't in Heaven. She was alive. Why would she think she should be dead? Her eyebrows scrunched.

Where was she and what the hell happened last night?

Selene racked her brain for the memories, but her brain worked slowly. When she finally broke through the haze, tears flooded her eyes.

Last night had been a disaster. Sarah was dead. The Dominion had won. Even with Pate's death, she'd lost. What was worse, Rikkard had been taken. She had no idea where he'd been taken to.

Her racing heart stopped. What had Kayl told Rikkard before she blacked out?

She did it for me. Sarah worked with them to protect me.

It was impossible. Sarah would never work with the Dominion, even if it meant protecting Kayl. She'd never give in to their tyranny.

Her eyes burned, and her certainty wavered.

Sarah could have been the mole this entire time. Of all people, Sarah? She could have been feeding information about her, the Alliance, and all of their smuggling. But why? What did they have on Kayl that was so bad Sarah would risk all of them?

Selene bit back an angry snarl. She pushed her tears away and clenched her fists. In her mind's eye, she kissed Rikkard, only to fall at Kayl's gunshot. Then everything was slow motion, and the Dominion was taking her Rik away. But where?

"Rikkard," she whispered.

Lying here wouldn't do her any good. So she moved to get up.

Her wrists caught on something. She looked left and right, and tried to sit up. A long white strap snapped taught across her waist. Two bands tied her wrists down. Panic rose inside her faster than usual. Her breathing quickened and her heart raced. She pulled frantically at the straps, until someone chuckled.

Selene froze. The blood drained from her face, and goosebumps rose over her flesh. No. It couldn't be. Not *him*.

Slowly, Pate stepped into her line of sight, a tilted smirk on his face. "Good morning."

Her eyes widened. This was impossible. He was *dead*. Shocked into silence, Selene could only stare in horror at her captor. He still looked the same as always, perfectly coiffed with slick black hair shaved up the sides and dark amber eyes. He stepped up to her bedside.

"How are you feeling? Did you sleep well?" He stood with his hands clasped behind his back, and his chest out. White bandages peeked from under his black shirt. Whether he was trying to intimidate or impress her, she couldn't be sure.

Her heart sank for her stomach and her head spun.

She pulled at her straps. "This is impossible. You're dead."

His grin widened. "Not quite, my little spitfire."

Selene shook her head. Her blood ran cold. "I killed you

myself."

Pate simply laughed and leaned down. "In the age of clones, does one ever really die? He plucked one of the straps holding her wrists down.

Selene recoiled, a snarl at her lips. She narrowed her stinging eyes at him. "Where the hell am I? What happened to Rikkard?"

He shrugged.

"Why am I here?"

"You're here because I want you here." He smirked and sat on the bed beside her.

Selene yanked against her restraints. "You're a psychopath." She wanted to hit him, grab him, throttle him, whatever she could—but the straps on the bed held her down. Frustration boiled in her stomach.

"I get what I want."

"And why in Aldar's name do you want *me*?"

Pate smiled, less sly and more like he pitied her. She bristled. "You're special, Selene. You're a far bigger player in this game than you know—which is why I had to keep you. When the right time comes, you're going to be my weapon. You only have your Alliance friends to thank for that."

"Your weapon?" she scoffed. "Why the hell would I work for you?"

His smile dropped into a deep frown. The expression made him look much older than his clone's face would have her believe.

"Everyone thinks you're dead," he said, instead of answering her question. "Rikkard, your crew, the Alliance... the whole world thinks you're gone. I made sure of it. All you have is me now."

"I don't want you," she spat, fury lighting her veins.

Pate snapped forward. His fingers closed on her chin. Her jaw ached. She tried to yank her face away but he pulled it right back. He was much stronger than she remembered.

"You will."

"I won't," she said. "Not ever."

Pushing her face away, he stood and pulled the holds on the

straps from the bed. They all fell away. She leapt up, but he was faster, catching her arm and dragging her from the bed. Selene swung to make a break for it, but he yanked on her arm. She wasn't as strong as she was yesterday.

He must have done something to her.

That thought frightened her more than any. If she wasn't strong enough to get away from him, how could she take him down?

Pate stopped in front of a full-length mirror, holding her shoulders with his fingers like talons. Facing the mirror, Selene got a good look at her chocolate brown hair, no longer streaked with sun kissed highlights, and deep brown eyes.

"You are *mine* now. No one will come for you." He locked eyes with her in the mirror.

Selene started away from her reflection, elbowing Pate in gut. She stumbled and fell to the cold marble floor, her heart thumping against her ribcage.

"What the hell did you do to me?" She touched her hair, and then her face. Where were her green eyes? Where were her muscles? Why was she so weak and fragile?

Pate worked his jaw, his face twisting in anger. But after a moment his rage disappeared and he walked toward the door on the other side of the room. The exit was seamless and slid open as if from nowhere. He paused and looked back over his shoulder.

"Enjoy your new body." He turned and fled, leaving her alone in silence.

Selene stared after him, the gravity of his words sinking in.

Her new body?

She looked down at herself, a question on her lips she didn't dare ask.

If she wasn't a natural born human anymore, or an Icarus manufactured by the Aldar Dominion, then what was she? There was only one possibility.

Pate had taken her body and switched her mind, like he himself must have done a dozen times. She was a clone, one of the masses.

How the hell was she supposed to get herself out of this one?

END OF BOOK ONE

A NOTE FROM THE AUTHOR

Thank you so much for taking the time to read *The Aldar Dominion*! I hope you loved the adventures of Selene and Rikkard as much as I did. If you'd like to continue reading the *Dominion Rising* series, please consider joining my Mailing List to stay up to date!

Whether you enjoyed *The Aldar Dominion* or not, please consider leaving an honest review on your preferred retailer and Goodreads! It really helps gain exposure for the book and get it in the hands of new readers!

If you'd like to be a part of my Street Team and get early access to all short stories and novels, consider joining today!

I hope to see you again in the next book!

ACKNOWLEDGEMENTS

This book would never have been completed without the help of my favorite sci-fi fans, my parents, Bill and Peggy, whom this book is dedicated to. Growing up in a fantasy and sci-fi loving environment has given me story ideas for the ages, and I could not be more grateful!

I'd also like to thank my writing buddies, Kellie and Mickey, who constantly push me to be the best writer I can be. I couldn't do this without you, ladies!

Last of all, thank you so much, kind reader, for taking the time to read *The Aldar Dominion*.

ABOUT THE AUTHOR

KATHERINE BOGLE'S debut young adult novel, *Haven*, came second in the World's Best Story contest 2015. She currently resides in Saint John, New Brunswick with her partner in crime, and plethora of cats.

Find her online at:
https://katherinebogle.com

ALSO BY KATHERINE BOGLE

Princess Haven was never meant to be Queen.

Her immortality has saved her time and time again, but when the last of her royal family dies at her feet, she is next in line to rule a nation on the brink of war. With no formal training on how to be Queen, Haven must rise to the occasion with the help of her best friends, and personal guard, or risk losing everyone she has ever loved.

With war to the West, and no escape to the East, the evil tyrant Kadia sets her sights on the six kingdoms. Haven's neighbors are quick to fall under the swords of Kadia's shadow soldiers, leaving a sea of bodies and a clear path to Haven's only home. Haven must make a choice; take her people and flee to the foreign Republic across the sea or lead a last stand against a powerful dictator.

Daughter of Chief Ruin, Breen is one of the most fearsome
warriors in the Southern Delica Tribe, but nothing can stop the
Emperor from reaping the Savage Lands for soldiers.

When her village is attacked, Breen is taken from her home and
her family to the Seaburn Academy, where southern savages
are broken and chained into a life of service to the Empire.
Through the beatings and torture, Drakkone, one of the few
Seaburn-born soldiers, brings solace to her days and gives her
hope for the future.

Once freed of the Academy dungeons, Breen is sentenced to
daily training between her plots for escape. But one night of
unexpected passion turns into a problem bigger than either of
them could have imagined.

Breen and Drakkone must risk capture and flee the city or
death might be a blessing compared to eternal imprisonment.

Join Haven and her siblings on four unique adventures in a time when war ravaged the six kingdoms...

HAVEN has always hated royal gatherings, and jumps at the chance to sneak away for a race through town on horseback. But when the young princess is injured, her ancestry is brought into question.

Much is expected of the heir to the Rythern throne, but when **LUCIAN** is forced to leave the warfront by his father, his reluctant agreement comes at a price.

The battle for Helms Keep has disastrous consequences for **MARCEL**. Soon he finds himself fighting both enemy forces and his own memories.

ASTRID is sent to the family summer home in the Cinder Mountains for her own safety. Only she doesn't expect the knee-high snow and frigid temperatures. With only her guards to protect her, Astrid must dig deeper than she ever thought herself capable of in order to survive.

www.ingramcontent.com/pod-product-compliance
Lightning Source LLC
Chambersburg PA
CBHW051644180726
48284CB00006B/1863